# THE BLUE

# MOGHUL

*A fast-paced adventure story*

*set in the exotic Philippines*

By

# Giles Wilcox

MURILLO PUBLISHING
ISBN: 978-1-0685181-0-2

*To my beautiful daughters, Cayetana & Alexandra.*
*Try and make your dreams come true, especially when it comes to*
*adventure and travel. But remember,*
*people are more important than places and things.*

# CONTENTS

# ACKNOWLEDGMENTS

The British Museum's India Archives, London
The Maritime Museum, Greenwich, London
The Victoria and Albert Museum, London
Raymond Schwab of Horizon Sun Charters, Palawan, The Philippines
Jeremy Green, Head of Department of Maritime Archaeology,
Western Australian Museum
Michael Backmann - Asian, Islamic & Tribal Antiques, London
Raymond Schwab - Horizon Sun Charters
Image of Pedro Murillo Velarde's 1744 map of the Philippines kindly
supplied by Norman B. Leventhal Map & Education Center at the
Boston Public Library
David Pike, D2D - Cover design and annotated map of The Philippine
Archipelago
All those friends and family who encouraged and supported me
You know who you are!

MAPA DE LAS YSLAS PHILIPINAS HECHO Por el P.e Pedro Murillo Velarde

THE
PHILIPPINE
ARCHIPELAGO

LUZON

South China Sea

Manila

Pacific Ocean

BUSUANGA

Coron

El Nido    LINAPACAN

THE BACUIT
ARCHIPELAGO

PALAWAN    Puerto Princesa

Sulu Sea

# CHAPTER 1

## *The Kimberley, Australia*

The research vessel bobbed on the azure water, a small white speck in a huge expanse of blue, dwarfed by the immensity of its surroundings. Beyond the nearby red sandstone cliffs, the arid, gorged interior of the Kimberley stretched as far as the eye could see in this remote part of north-western Australia.

The crew busied themselves to handle marine samples from the second dive of the day; one more to go before heading along the coast to check out another ecosystem with a view to creating a marine reserve. Hopes were high they'd get what they had come for. As they readied themselves for the divers to surface, the distinctive noise of a helicopter cut through the stiff breeze, approaching quickly, skimming the iron-red cliffs like a large insect as it angled down towards them.

Peter trod water 20 metres from the ship. Although on a rest day to give his body a break, he found it hard to stay out of the water, so he had snorkelled out to see if he could spot the divers and give them a hand when they surfaced.

He watched the chopper zero in, expertly lowering itself onto the small circular landing pad, its blades whirring in rhythmic synchronisation, the bright blue and yellow insignia unmistakable. It was a company bird.

He finned briskly back to the vessel, wondering how they'd known where he was.

As he climbed the ladder onto the wide transom, he saw Mitch, the company pilot he'd known since childhood, coming from the deck above, and not looking his usual cheerful self. With a sinking feeling in the pit of his stomach, Peter shed his snorkelling gear and shimmied up two sets of steps to greet him.

'Hey, Mitch.'

'Hey, Pete.'

'You're a little off-piste.'

'You been diving the past twenty-four hours?' Mitch looked deadly serious.

'No. Surface duties. Haven't been down since yesterday.'

'Thank God, mate. He's in bad shape. There's not a second to lose. If you're lucky we might get there in time. Put some clothes on. Let's get going.'

Peter felt his gut wrench. He'd always dreaded this moment, pushing it to the back of his mind.

Five minutes later, the chopper was airborne again, buzzing low over some of Australia's most rugged terrain towards Broome, where Peter switched to a company Learjet, flight plan already filed, with priority clearance for take-off. On arrival in Perth, a chauffeur was waiting to drive him to St John of God Subiaco Hospital.

In the anteroom, family members were already gathered, sitting, standing, looking stressed, tired and anxious – the atmosphere said it all.

*So, this was it, then*, he thought.

Samantha, his younger half-sister, smiled wanly as she walked over and kissed him on the cheek, then guided him into the corridor, where she hugged him tightly.

'Thank God you're here,' she said, her eyes two pools of helplessness. 'He's fading fast and been asking for you since yesterday, mumbling incoherently, hanging on with everything he's got.'

'Is he conscious?' Peter asked, in a voice more controlled than he remotely felt.

'He's in and out, but looks like he could go any minute.' She gripped her brother's hand tightly. 'You'll need to see if he registers your presence. I pray he does.'

They returned to the anteroom, where Peter acknowledged his stepmother and his other half-sister, before turning the door handle and slowly entering.

The room was dimly lit, the curtains drawn. In the single bed against the far wall lay his father, frail and withered, on life support, tubes everywhere – a shadow of his former self. Peter gave a sharp intake of breath as the reality of what faced him hit home hard, filled with regret they hadn't seen each other for three years, not since the falling out. They'd both been pig-headed and wouldn't get the time back. He walked over and pulled up a wooden chair beside the bed, then gently reached for his father's white, heavily veined hand, a hand dotted with liver spots, that had seen a lifetime of adventure. His eyes filled with tears.

'We left it too long, Pa,' he said, finding it hard to get the words out, neither of them having been much good at emotional talk, though their love for one another was as strong as blood could make it; so alike, no one could ever doubt they were father and son. The old man's breathing was laboured and rasping for a good ten minutes before Peter felt the faintest pressure from his hand. Watching his father's dry cracked lips trying to move, he leant in, feeling his light breath on his face as his father tried, with everything he had left, to say something.

'It's okay, Pa. I know you love me,' whispered Peter. 'We're good now.'

For what seemed like an age, no words came out. His father's lips twitched, opening and closing sporadically, the rasping of his chest distressing to listen to, his eyes closed, before eventually vocalising some disjointed sounds. The pain and effort were clearly immense.

Peter leant closer, trying hard to make out what he was saying.

Painstakingly long and drawn out, it sounded like 'F … i… n …' – his father's breathing became suddenly rapid, then shallow and staccato, slowing again, with long pauses between breaths as he made incoherent noises, as though in a troubled dream. Again, there was faint pressure from his father's hand, his lips moving imperceptibly, with such effort, it hurt Peter to watch.

Barely audible, he made out something like 'M … o …' before the old man's hand fell away, his lips closing for the last time, his very lifeblood ebbing with his final words.

Looking at his father's gaunt face and emaciated body, Peter was enveloped by immense grief like nothing he'd experienced, and sat holding the lifeless hand, tears streaming down his face, until a doctor and nurse gently steered him away.

# CHAPTER 2

## *Perth, Australia*

They sat in a semicircle in the comfortable air-conditioned offices of Callister and MacLean for the reading of the will. The first time they'd all been together, minus his father, for a long time.

Angela Blake Hamilton, Peter's stepmother, sat with Tiffany, his elder half-sister, on her left, next to Henry Jones, the company lawyer, who knew more secrets about the family than anyone else and a long-time friend and confidant of Harry Blake, the deceased.

Beside Henry sat Samantha, Peter's younger half-sister, the only member of his extended family to whom he was close. Peter sat to her left. Expectation and uncertainty lay heavy in the air, given they represented one of Australia's wealthiest families: Blake Hamilton Industries, a holding company spanning everything from mining, cattle-ranching and pearl farming to vineyards. There was a lot at stake.

When Harry's last will and testament was read out, there were fortunately few surprises for those present: the bulk of his estate went to Angela, his wife of thirty-two years, with substantial trusts for Tiffany and Samantha and financial provision for Peter, the conditions to be administered by Henry, formulated on Harry's instructions.

Harry had also left his only son the entire contents of his private study: to include all furniture, books, antiques, artefacts, rugs, documents and photographs – the whole nine yards, with many valuable collectors' pieces.

In relation to this bequeathal, Harry's instructions were crystal clear: no one but his son should be allowed into the room unless authorised by him; it was up to him alone to decide what to do with the contents and he should be given reasonable time to do so.

The study had been Harry's sanctuary, the repository of his life's adventures, containing the inspiration for his dreams, some fulfilled, others unfortunately not. After all, Harry Blake had been one of the country's most colourful adventurers before becoming a business tycoon and marrying Angela Hamilton, the wealthy socialite heiress to a mining empire, in the 1980s.

Relieved there were no hidden surprises – 'Harry specials', as she called them – his widow didn't give a monkey's about the contents of the study. They could go to his bastard son.

The sooner he cleared it out, the sooner she'd be rid of him.

# CHAPTER 3

## *Perth, Australia*

S hortly after Harry Blake's passing, a private funeral service had taken place, after which, in line with his wishes, his ashes had been scattered in the sea off the coast near Broome in the Kimberley, where he'd set up his first pearling operation.

Three weeks later, a high-profile memorial service, attended by anybody considered anybody in Australia's business, political and social circles, was followed by a large reception hosted by Angela Blake Hamilton at the sprawling family estate on the outskirts of Perth. True to form, she gave an Oscar-winning performance as the grieving widow, closely aided by Tiffany, her protégée.

Given Harry Blake had been one of Australia's wealthiest men, reporters from the world's TV stations had massed outside the front gates, looking to make headlines, speculating about what would happen with the various businesses and who would run what, given he'd been a hands-on tycoon who'd maintained tight control of his empire. Although naturally wary, he'd always entertained the media, giving them soundbites to thrill and titillate, keeping them guessing as to what his next merger or acquisition might be. Unlike his wife, he'd been a warm-hearted man of the people, loved by his employees. Like Kipling's famous poem, he'd walked with kings while maintaining the common touch.

It was from this jamboree that Peter had sneaked off to his father's study. Sitting in the office chair behind the leather-topped antique partner's desk, he used his feet to slowly circle the room, enjoying the tranquillity as he took in the contents that reflected the very essence of his father.

There was a large antique globe on a stand. Various wooden chests. Antique jewellery and writing boxes, hundreds of years old. Ethnic tribal rugs covered the floor. On the walls were bejewelled Indian daggers; photographs of adventures and treasure hunts his father had been involved in; prints of galleons and Indiamen, a real passion of his; and bookshelves crammed with historical volumes, reference books, atlases and maps. Collectively, an eclectic panoply of the favourite items collected by a man with a lust for life and adventure.

As he looked at it all, Peter felt more connected to his father than for the past three years, since their falling out. Memories swamped his head from when he was a young boy, taken on trips to remote and exotic parts of the world, to his teenage years and the holidays they'd spent together. All the time his father's final mutterings were reverberating in his head.

Peter knew that although his father had been one of the richest men in Australia, it wasn't money that'd motivated him, but rather his passion for adventure and his lust for life, with a fascination for how the past shaped the present and the future. Especially those periods of history when exploration and trade had been key drivers for the Old World discovering and exploring the New, connecting them, bringing together vastly differing cultures, religions and ways of life.

His father had managed to bring his romantic view of the past to life with his passion for maritime treasure hunting, which began as a young man, always reading about or researching ships that had sunk with valuable cargoes, trying to find opportunities overlooked by other treasure hunters.

Most treasure hunting, if it didn't involve the recovery of a known wreck, was detective work, unless a serendipitous find by a local fisherman or diver triggered a search from physical evidence. You either looked for something or reacted to something, both hopefully ending with the same conclusion, notwithstanding currents, tides, shifting weather patterns and storms over centuries. The attraction for many was that it wasn't an exact science. One had first to piece together historical facts, rumours, scientific evidence and local knowledge and then, the most valuable thing of all in this eclectic jigsaw puzzle to see the ultimate picture that would deliver the prize: intuition. The ability to jump seemingly unbridgeable gaps – where missing pieces threatened to negate the dream – and land successfully the other side, picking up the trail, making sense of the whole. In essence, a treasure hunt, if approached correctly, was a combination of adventure, excitement, passion and luck. What could be more exciting than that? According to Harry Blake, not much.

He'd been fortunate enough to possess the rare ability of a great nose for the truth. As a result, he'd backed many expeditions to search for and recover lost treasure, some of which Peter had been involved in. His true passion: locating missing Manila galleons and East Indiamen that had ploughed the oceans during colonial times.

As Peter pondered this, a knock on the door brought him back to reality.

'Mind if I come in? I thought I might find you here.'

It was Henry, company lawyer and long-time confidant and friend of his father.

Peter gestured with his hand. 'Please, be my guest.'

'Thanks,' said Henry walking in and standing opposite Peter. He'd looked the same for as long as Peter could remember, with something of the quintessential English butler about his demeanour that was comforting.

'It's peaceful here, compared to the chaos outside.' Henry gave a thin smile, his eyes roving. 'Feels strange, doesn't it? I always thought this room the very essence of what Harry was. I feel his presence strongly, as though he might just walk in and tell a joke.'

Peter could see how much Henry missed his old friend, knowing they'd been close through the good and bad times.

With a puzzled expression, he asked, 'Why did he leave all this to me, Henry?'

The lawyer smiled. 'Because everything that was important to him is represented here. The people he loved most. The passions he followed single-mindedly. The successes he had. And the dreams he hoped to fulfil. He thought you were worthy of all that.'

'I walked out on him and didn't see or speak to him once in three years,' Peter said, with a mixture of guilt and remorse.

'That didn't mean he didn't love and think about you,' Henry said gently. 'He understood why you took off after that blazing row. Your stepmother put him in an impossible position. There was a lot going on you weren't aware of. But he kept close tabs on you and knew exactly what you were up to. Your well-being was of the utmost importance to him. How do you think Mitch found you so quickly? He was proud of your achievements and liked what you're doing. It's what he did in his youth and would still like to have been doing himself ... I know, because he told me, often.'

'I wish it hadn't ended like this,' Peter said with a look of regret. 'There were things I never managed to tell him. She changed him and poisoned our relationship.'

Henry shook his head. 'That's what you think. But underneath he never really changed ... though sadly he wasn't happy. We'd sit in here, drinking his finest Scotch, and he'd tell me how he wanted to set up a treasure-hunting and marine preservation division that you could head up and which the two of you could jointly work on. He knew he'd pushed you hard, but he was under a lot of stress. Your stepmother never forgave him for having an affair with your mother before they got married. She made him pay more than you realise.'

'Was he sick then, Henry? Did he know at the time we fell out?'

'Yes. He'd just found out, though still hoped it was treatable.'

'Fuck.' A brief silence. Then, 'Who else knew?'

'Just me.'

More silence. Then, 'Thanks for being a good friend to him, Henry. I know he valued your friendship greatly. You were the only one he trusted.'

'He was a good friend to me and I owe him a great deal,' said Henry, his voice cracking slightly. 'We brought different things to the table, but we helped each other. After all, that's what friends are for, isn't it?' Looking at Peter as if for confirmation, he shuffled a little. 'Before you go, we need to discuss the details of the financial provision he made.'

'Can we do it in a couple of days? I need to sort out a few things while I'm on leave.'

'Of course, but let me know. It's important.' Henry gave a wry grin. 'I'd better head back into the fray to stop the media spreading malicious gossip. You know how it is.' Reaching the door, he turned and said, 'Don't spend too much time alone. It's not healthy. And remember, I'm always here if you need help or advice.'

Peter nodded. 'Thanks, Henry.'

'It's the least I can do.' With that, Henry closed the door behind him, ever the faithful retainer.

Peter sat in silence for what seemed like an age, staring at a framed photograph of himself and his father on a liveaboard dive boat in the Caribbean when he was a teenager. Taken some twenty years earlier, when he'd first learnt to scuba dive, it was one of those happy milestone memories, and must have been for his father, too, because it held pride of place.

All the while his father's dying mutterings circled Peter's mind. He felt sure whatever the old man had been trying to tell him was connected to what was in this room, as he played the words over and over: 'Find' and 'Mo', whatever that meant. Where to start was the question.

He opened the centre drawer of the desk in front of him and as he poked around the contents, he noticed the bottom was loose. Lifting it, he saw a solitary white manila envelope with his name on it, written in his father's distinctive, flamboyant handwriting.

He slit it open with a letter opener, sat back and starting reading:

*Dear Peter,*

*If you're reading this I'm no longer alive, and it's my biggest regret we didn't get the opportunity to put things right between us as I know, without any doubt, we both wanted to. There are many things left unsaid and I've very much missed not seeing you these past three years. But you must know I don't blame you in any way. I've kept my distance but followed your exploits with love and pride. You are my one and only son and I love you more than I could ever tell you.*

*The relationship between a father and son is a fragile one, especially if they are alike in temperament and emotions. Clashes are inevitable, as the constraints and concerns of the older generation impact on the freedoms and dreams of the younger.*

*In my case, I became swamped by my business empire and thwarted in my real ambitions, and in being who I really was, by Angela. I loved her wholeheartedly when we met and married, but she tried to change and control me, which inevitably impacted on you. She became a woman who wasn't the one I thought I'd married and I hope you understand and can forgive me.*

*I loved Rosanna, your mother, more than you'll ever know and was close to going back to her and leaving Angela and the high life behind, but with two young daughters and thousands of employees, whose livelihoods depended on me, I chose to stay, even though I wasn't happy. That's perhaps my biggest regret. Life always gives one impossible choices and you suffered as a result of mine.*

*You're similar to me in many ways, Peter, but you must pursue and find your own way in life, hopefully seeking adventure and following your passions, and in the process finding a good woman to love and start a family with. A true, close family, with a man and a woman who truly love and care for one other, and have children born from that love, is God's gift.*

*We all need money because without it life's impossible; that's the reality, but too much doesn't make you happier, believe me. That's the perception, not the reality.*

*I've had an uncanny knack for making lots of it, setting up and investing in profitable organisations, but it was never making money that drove me, it was always my passion for adventure that made me successful. And I know I've passed that on to you – it's part of your DNA. Whether or not you make a lot is unimportant; it's the by-*

*product, not the destination.*

*For this reason I've instructed Henry, my oldest and dearest friend, to make specific financial provision for you, in line with certain conditions I've set out, which I hope will be to your benefit, and consistent with this ethos. He'll explain the details. I want you to be financially secure, ideally through your own efforts, which will give you a sense of pride and respect that no amount of money can. You need to have some hunger and ambition, channelled through real passion. It helps make you who you truly are; believe me, I know. From what I've seen you're on the right track.*

*In this regard, I've left the bulk of my estate to Angela and the girls, protecting the employees of the company as far as is possible for a man now deceased and no longer in control. Sadly, Tiffany has taken after her mother as a master manipulator, and they will continue to do what they do best. Leave them to it, they'll secure their own fate, but look after Samantha. She loves you dearly. You have much in common and she's loyal and trustworthy. She'll find her own way and I'm optimistic it will be a good one.*

*If you've found this letter, you'll be sitting in my study, the contents of which I have bequeathed to you – lock, stock and barrel. This room has always been my sanctuary, refuge and inspiration, filled with artefacts, objects, books, documents and photographs I hold dear. Things that remind me of what makes me tick; my passions, the adventures in life I've enjoyed and, above all, my dreams. One must always dream. These things will be of no importance to your stepmother or Tiffany, but some will have sentimental value to Samantha. Let her choose some things that she would like to remember me by.*

*Although I've been sick these past three years, a secret which I kept to myself and Henry until only recently, I've not wasted them. In my darkest moments, when I could see little light at the end of the tunnel, I retreated here, focusing on one of my true passions: the search for a specific treasure that lies, without any doubt in my mind, in the Philippine archipelago. One I believe only you are capable of finding. Henry is broadly aware of a project I've sanctioned for you to pursue,* with funding allocated, but not the details.

I first got wind of this treasure when I was a young man doing much what you're doing, contracted to various marine organisations engaged in search and recovery. I had a real lust for life, above all for the oceans and what lay beneath. One summer, in my late twenties, I spent several months in the Western Philippines working for a yacht charter company based out of Puerto Princesa, in the province of Palawan, taking rich clients scuba diving around the islands to earn some extra cash. The owner had three forty-foot sloops, each luxuriously fitted with top-of-the-range navigational equipment and compressors, and we confined our trips to the outlying islands around the northern tip of Palawan. It was one of the happiest times of my life. A true paradise and one of the most beautiful places I've ever been, both above and below the water, so it's no surprise it's been designated a UNESCO world heritage site.

During this time, I came across a book on one of the yachts about the British East India Company, which I devoured, reading all I could about the subject. It became something of an obsession, and I could recite, practically verbatim, all the British East Indiamen recorded as having gone missing in a storm or by poor navigation, or destroyed by enemy warships. Most importantly, I could list the names of those wrecks that had subsequently been located and those that hadn't, the latter naturally interesting me the most.

And it's with one of these that the treasure I want you to find is inextricably linked. However, it's not simply a case of a ship having sunk and locating it; it's more complicated and interesting than that.

I first heard this story way back, when I worked on that yacht charter. Bad weather had prevented us from sailing and we managed to find safe anchorage and hole up for two days to ride out a typhoon off a small island in the Bacuit archipelago, off El Nido, in north-western Palawan. The three of us were drinking Mai Tais and copious amounts of San Miguel on one of the sloops as the wind howled and the full fury of the typhoon was unleashed. There was myself; Karl Johansson, a Swedish financier, who'd chartered one of the yachts for *two weeks, and whose fiancée had flown back to Manila a few days earlier; and Declan O'Connor, the owner of the charter company.*

*Declan was a real old-school, good old-fashioned Irish adventurer, a loveable rogue, who also traded ethnic artefacts from around the Philippines internationally. He had his finger in a lot of pies, was adept at sailing the grey area, and you couldn't help but fall under his spell; he was a good man at heart.*

*Above all, he had the gift of the gab and an easy manner that engaged you immediately; his charisma was magnetic. He could make a stranger feel like he'd known him for years and was one hell of storyteller, seamlessly blending fact with fiction – and that night we covered a lot of ground. But what has stuck in my mind all these years later was the tale he told of a legendary treasure of such immeasurable value and beauty ...*

Peter read the remainder of the letter slowly, increasingly spellbound by the story his father set out and the proposition he was offering. He had a captivating way of writing that brought the pages to life, as if he was recounting things personally from the armchair opposite.

When he finished reading, he realised that what his father had bequeathed him was his final adventure, a quest which he himself could no longer be part of, but which, if they'd been reconciled before his death, he would have wanted them to jointly embark upon.

Scanning the bookshelves, Peter selected two volumes: one about the British East India Company, the other the Manila galleon trade. He put Miles Davis and Stanley Turrentine on a loop, to mellow things out a little, poured a large tumbler of Havana Club Especial, then settled into his father's comfortable leather armchair, put his feet up and began reading.

He read until the early hours, until his burning eyes and saturated mind could take no more, eventually falling asleep in the chair, the books scattered on the floor, his arms and legs splayed, exhausted.

The following morning, he woke to the sound of a vacuum cleaner and it all came back to him.

Realising he was at a critical juncture, he knew without a shadow of a doubt what he must do, and arranged to meet Henry later that morning.

# CHAPTER 4

## *Perth, Australia*

Peter sat in Henry's office, high up in a modern skyscraper overlooking the spectacular vista of Perth harbour, the surrounding buildings a shining example of a modern metropolis in the "Lucky Country", built from mineral wealth and phenomenal natural resources.

'So, let me get this straight, Henry,' Peter said, looking across the desk. 'I'm supposed to fly to Palawan in the Philippines to try and find this Declan O'Connor guy, who told a story a long time ago about a sunken treasure my father believed exists somewhere in the thousands of square kilometres of ocean that comprise the Philippine archipelago?'

'That's pretty much it. Were you expecting more?' said Henry, his voice deadpan, but with a hint of a smile.

Peter frowned. 'I guess not. And I'm funded, right?'

'That's right. But after you've located and met Mr O'Connor, if that necessitates embarking on a venture that will cost, you'll have to report back for authorisation.'

'And what will trigger that?' Peter was looking for a catch.

'I've unambiguous instructions from Harry, which are pretty generous if things pan out as he predicted.'

Peter stood up and said with a wry smile, 'Of course you do, Henry. Why didn't I anticipate that?' The answer was predictably annoying but simultaneously captivating. He clearly had no choice but to fly to the Philippines. Nothing ventured, nothing gained was a dictum his father had loved to repeat. How many times had he said that?

He wasn't paying, so what the hell did he have to lose? A break would do him good. He needed time by himself, without the obligations of work.

'Do you have an address?' he asked.

'Just so happens I do.' Henry's smile seemed to be saying this was another of Harry's entertaining escapades that may or may not be worthwhile, but would probably be great fun … *I don't know. You don't know.*

It was the thrill of the chase: something a Blake could never resist.

He handed Peter a slip of paper that read:

*Deep Blue Divers – El Nido – Palawan*

*Great*, thought Peter.

\*

After some wrangling with the boss of the marine survey company, Peter managed to extricate himself from the second phase of the Kimberley project, assured he'd be welcomed back. Economical with the truth, he'd spun a yarn about the intricacies of what needed sorting in his father's estate.

Telling them even part of the truth wasn't an option. The last thing he wanted was the door to be closed on future projects, because he was passionate about protecting the ocean. He also had yet to meet anyone who could keep a secret – no matter what they swore.

*I've one more thing to do*, he thought, hitting a speed dial on his mobile.

'Where the hell have you been?' came Samantha's anxious voice. 'I've been really worried. You just disappeared from the reception. Are you okay?'

'I'm fine, Sam. But I miss him big time. Look, something's come up, something he put in motion before he died. I'm going to be busy for the next few weeks, taking time out from the Kimberley project. I need some space and a change of scene; time to think properly. Can you slip away and I'll elaborate?'

'Let's meet at the point,' she said, 'where we used to go as kids. Say around eight?'

'I'll be there. Perhaps we'll be lucky enough to get one of those amazing sunsets the old man loved so much.'

# CHAPTER 5

## *Manila, The Philippines*

Peter flew into Manila early the following evening, after an uneventful seven-and-a-half-hour flight. Upon arrival, he was greeted by a hotel representative with his name on a signboard, and a hotel Mercedes then drove him through the bedlam of traffic to the Sofitel.

It was hot and humid, unlike the drier heat of Australia, and felt close, as if a storm was brewing. Nevertheless, he was pleased to be somewhere different, with the opportunity to engage his mind on something new and potentially exciting. The past few weeks had been strange. The loss of his father hung heavy on his psyche. He'd never felt he belonged at the estate. His stepmother had never made him welcome and there was little left for him there now, except Samantha.

Although he had sole rights to his father's study, he would have to decide what to do with the contents. He knew his stepmother wouldn't tolerate him coming and going at will. At least he'd squared that with Henry before he left. If he wasn't there, she wouldn't fret too much.

He tried to put her out of his mind, helped by the cheerful calypso music playing on the loudspeaker system. As he looked through the atrium towards the pool complex, he saw people chilling, enjoying themselves, drinking cold beer and cocktails among the palms, as waiters set up buffet tables for dinner and the sun set into the spectacular blood-red and orange visual feast for which Manila Bay was renowned.

*

Upon arrival at Ninoy Aquino Airport, Peter had been oblivious of the small, wiry Filipino who had ID'd him, then followed the hotel Merc in a jeepney, blending in among hundreds of others in the busy traffic. At the hotel, the man – Dakila – sat in the vehicle on the other side of the drop-off, and made a call as he watched Peter enter the lobby.

'He's checking into the Sofitel, alone,' he said matter-of-factly.

'Don't let him out of your sight,' replied a distinctive South African accent with a menacing undertone. 'Shadow him. I want to know where he goes and who he meets. I'm betting he'll fly out early to one of the islands. You need to ensure he's met at the other end and tailed, unless you can get on the same flight.' A pause. 'If you lose him, believe me, you'll pay.' The man was all stick and no carrot.

'Yes, Boss,' said Dakila, unruffled. As a gang member with a comprehensive network of associates on most of the islands, he was used to doing this sort of job. It wouldn't be challenging and meant easy money. The man would be hard to lose given his appearance, and if it did happen, momentarily, they'd quickly re-engage if word was put out.

*

Peter dumped his bag in his room and freshened up. He contemplated going into the city, but couldn't be bothered by himself. Deciding to eat by the pool, he watched a tribal dance show and live music from a talented, attractive young singer doing a medley of old favourites. Sipping a cold San Mig, he speculated about how his trip would pan out and what he needed to do. He had a rough plan, but it would be an evolving agenda. There were a couple of places and people he needed to visit in Manila as part of his search, but he decided to do those on the way back, keen to track O'Connor down without delay.

He reckoned that once he met the man face to face, he'd know if this was a wild goose chase or had legs. It wasn't that he didn't trust his father's judgement, but it was important to have eye contact and read body language personally on things like this. It was possible that his father, in his weakened physical state, reminiscing about a story he'd heard so long ago, had unintentionally mixed fact with fiction. He'd said himself O'Connor was a master storyteller.

However, given the tale had clearly motivated his father through the darkest hours of his terminal illness, Peter felt duty bound to check out what he'd been given. He would take it as far as he could within a reasonable time frame while his other commitments were on hold. It would be cathartic. But he would draw a line in the sand if it became intangible.

Although he copped an early night, his sleep was troubled, hot and sweaty, despite the air conditioning. He tossed and turned as faces from the past came in and out of his dreams, like demons tormenting him, relieved when the early morning call woke him. After a light breakfast by the pool, he was driven to the domestic airport in good time for his flight.

It was a clear, hot, steamy tropical day.

Ninoy Aquino Airport was a hive of activity, as the epicentre of a spider's web of air routes covering 7,100 islands spread over 300,000 square kilometres. Scheduled flights operated to cities like Cebu and Davao, with myriad small charter planes operating between smaller tourist destinations.

However, many of the more remote resorts could only be accessed by small prop planes, flying to remote jungle landing strips, where guests would be transported by four-wheel drive across wild territory, often over large distances, to meet up with an outrigger and then island-hop to their final destination. The spirit of adventure was ever present in these islands, in contrast with a world where almost everywhere and everything is seamlessly connected and super-easy to get to.

# CHAPTER 6

## *El Nido, Palawan*

The fifty-seat ATR aircraft left on time, bumping down an hour and twenty minutes later at Lio Airport, serving the small town of El Nido – "The Nest" – in Palawan, some 400 kilometres south-west of Manila, and so-named because of the swifts found locally, whose nests were highly prized in Chinese cuisine.

From its origins as a fishing village, the town had become the gateway to the Bacuit archipelago: a mecca for scuba divers, travel junkies and adventure-seekers keen to explore its jaw-dropping natural beauty and prolific marine life – the main draw being the dramatically beautiful islands dotting the archipelago, with towering limestone cliffs dripping in jungled vegetation, powder-white beaches fronting turquoise, crystal-clear waters, and pristine coral reefs teaming with exotic fish.

Not surprisingly, the area had become a showcase for bio and geological diversity, frequently cited as having some of the clearest waters and most beautiful beaches in the world, and featuring in Condé Nast's top ten.

Peter clocked a multitude of nationalities on the flight over, the majority being young adventurers who'd come to kayak, sail, climb, dive and chill out in the stunning surroundings. This was his kind of place. He was excited at the anticipation of meeting Declan O'Connor and where that might lead, as well as the opportunity to explore such a pristine marine ecosystem. There was a buzz of adventure in the air. For a fleeting moment, he wished he could share it with someone, but quickly dismissed the thought.

Outside the no-frills airport, a row of drivers stood by an array of motorised tricycles, vying to take people on the short ride into town. Peter walked over to one who looked keen for business. 'I'm looking for Deep Blue Divers,' he said to the small, barefoot man in a dirty, sweat-ridden vest and brown shorts, his face seemingly locked in a perma-grin. 'Do you know them?'

'I know, I know,' the man said unconvincingly, shaking his head up and down, only two teeth visible.

Wondering how hard it could be, Peter said, 'Okay, let's go,' and climbed aboard as the man secured his bag precariously to the back of the rickety apparatus. Fifteen minutes later he extricated himself outside a shop that appeared to sell everything. Among an array of signs outside was one that read:

*Deep Blue Divers – Gateway to Paradise!*

Paying the man handsomely, Peter walked inside. Some young couples were checking out face masks and snorkels on a carousel, being ably advised by a diminutive Chinese–Filipina woman; her age, hard to guess, but her sales pitch, evidently well-practised.

The crammed shop was on the ground floor of a two-storey wooden colonial structure. The outside had seen better days, but the inside had a pleasantly eclectic, frontier feel, obviously catering for the visitor who'd forgotten something. A kind of last-chance saloon before heading to the island resorts, where similar things would cost three times the price.

The shop assistant re-directed her attention to Peter as the couples pontificated about quality, branding and price. 'You look like diver,' she said as if clairvoyant, looking up at him.

He smiled engagingly. 'How did you guess?' *What was the probability of that in a place like this?* he wondered.

'What you want? Good place to stay?'

'I'm interested in diving with Deep Blue. I saw the sign outside. How can I contact them?'

'One of best.' She grabbed him by the arm, guiding him to the back of the shop, disappearing through a cubbyhole and reappearing behind the counter where she flipped through a dog-eared notebook.

Peter looked up at a faded map of the Bacuit on the wall. 'Where are they located?'

'One of islands,' she pointed vaguely at the map, 'about hour from here. Come to town two, three time a week. Pick up, drop off client. Stock up provision. You lucky. Divemaster here tomorrow, 10am. Come back then. Agree package, okay?'

'So, they have availability?'

'Think so.' She beamed up at him from behind the counter. 'Last-minute cancellation. Somebody sick. I make sure know interested.'

'Sounds good,' Peter said. 'I'll come back in the morning, bright and early. And a nice place to stay?'

Coming back through the cubbyhole, she led him by the arm to the entrance of the store. 'My cousin, Vincent. I call him. He come take you and luggage hotel. Very comfortable. Air con, mini bar,' she said whirring her hands joyfully, as though it was the Ritz.

'Great,' said Peter. He'd been through this routine many times the world over. He'd check it out. If it was clean and half decent, he'd take it, preferring to stay local. It was the best way to pick up gossip and find out the lie of the land, more often than not over a few cold ones and not being tight on the cash; after all, most things were cheap here compared to Australia, and tongues wagged after a few drinks.

He knew nothing went unnoticed in a place like this. The trick was to tap into the knowledge pool and extract what you were looking for; to give you a head start or perhaps an edge at a later date.

*

What Peter didn't know was that he'd been spotted at the airport by a contact of Dakila's who would keep tabs on him while Dakila tried to get on the next available flight. Dakila knew he couldn't risk not handling this personally. Jan Bekker wasn't a man to piss off. He'd recently killed another gang member just for losing a package.

Bekker had acquired a nasty reputation in a short space of time, which wasn't easy given the competition in these parts. Dakila guessed he was now under the protection of one of the gangs, as there was no way he could operate like this without being sanctioned by some pretty powerful people. After all, there was a strict criminal hierarchy. You couldn't just come and shit on someone else's territory. If you didn't follow the protocol, you wouldn't last long.

Dakila's contact agreed to watch Peter like a hawk until he could take over. After gauging the sensitivity of his baby-sitting assignment, and squeezing on price, he would earn a few much-needed pesos.

*

The hotel was barely a step up from a youth hostel, but was clean enough, so Peter paid upfront for a night, dumped his bag and explored the town for a while before returning to lie on his bed, checking emails and reading about the Bacuit.

Early that evening, he asked Vincent if there was a good place for fresh fish, cold beer and a nice atmosphere. Sure enough, Vincent knew just the place. Another cousin owned a bar downtown. He'd introduce him personally to ensure he got the best service.

They walked down to the bar-cum-restaurant, called Davilo's, which was situated on a wide veranda extension on stilts protruding from the back of a wooden village house with uninterrupted views of El Nido bay.

The bar was packed with young adventure-seekers from all over the world, drinking, chatting and laughing noisily as ceiling fans circled lazily to the steady beat of chilled music.

Vincent introduced Peter to his cousin, Davilo, who gave him the 'the best table in the house': a two-seater next to the balustrade with a cracking view of the bay.

Vincent headed off while Davilo went to man the small bamboo bar. Peter scanned the menu, ordered grilled fish, then walked over there.

'Great place you've got,' he said, after ordering a cold San Mig.

'It's the hottest ticket in town, man,' Davilo said in an American–Filipino accent, as he served cocktails to a couple of female backpackers.

*Right,* thought Peter. 'I'm here for the diving,' he said.

'Well, you picked the right place, my friend.' Davilo glanced up as he poured Peter's beer. 'Nowhere better. I don't care where you've dived, or what you've seen, this place will blow your mind. Who you diving with?'

'Deep Blue, hopefully.'

'Good outfit, man.' He nodded his approval.

'What makes them so good?'

'One of the longest established. Know these waters like the back of their hand.'

'Who owns them?' Zeroing in.

'Old Irish hand – Declan O'Connor. Real colourful character. Came here in the eighties and never left. Bit of a legend round here.'

'Does he still run things?'

'Far as I know, but he's getting on. Must be quite old now. Haven't seen him for a long time.' Davilo's eyes narrowed with the realisation. 'It's a slick boutique operation. Well-experienced dive instructors, two with him for many years. The rest usually work a season or two before moving on.' Davilo's hands worked the pumps for more thirsty backpackers.

'I guess he married a local?'

'What makes you say that, man?' Davilo looked up at Peter while emptying two Coke bottles into ice-filled glasses with the expertise of the consummate barman.

'To stay so long.' Peter took an appreciative sip of beer. 'In my experience, only a woman can make a man stay the other side of the world so far from where he was born.'

Davilo's face cracked into a broad grin. 'You're right, man. Chicks have that power. To tie a man down. But not me. I've seen what it does to friends and family. Destroys them. Chicks always change, man.' He gave a knowing look, as if sharing a unique insight. 'They metamorphose into something the polar opposite to what you signed up for. Like a butterfly in reverse. It's a trap. Like a black widow wanting to mate, before eating you.' Davilo gave a shrug of his shoulders, as he looked at Peter and wiped his hands on his apron. 'I like my freedom, man. And I like women. And I mean *women*. You hear me, bro'?'

Peter gave a broad smile. 'Loud and clear. I dig your philosophy ... so, this Declan guy married a Filipina?' Keen to extract information while on a roll.

Davilo shook his head. 'His wife died in a diving accident a few years back. Real tragedy. But she weren't no local. Swedish, I think, or maybe half-Swedish. Don't rightly remember.' His eyes became distant, as if trying to conjure an image. 'But she was one hot chick, man, I tell you. Tall, tanned, blue eyes, blonde hair ...' For someone who couldn't remember, he was making a big effort.

'What happened?'

'No one knows for sure, but there were rumours. One, that she ran out of air on a deep wreck dive and her pony malfunctioned. Another, that she got fatally hit by an oceanic whitetip. In fact, now I think of it, it's pretty much since then that Declan hasn't been seen. He don't come into town no more to socialise like he used to.' Davilo paused briefly for reflection before sorting another round of drinks for some Spaniards.

Walking back to face Peter, wiping his hands again, he said, 'He was the real life and soul, you know, even though an old guy.' A look of admiration, a slight shake of the head. 'Like a magnet that old and young gravitated to, with a real gift for storytelling. If he told one in front of a large group, you could hear a pin drop, that's how good he was. Guess it's the grief, man. That's what the loss of a loved one does.' Davilo had transformed within minutes from a virtual mute into a chat show host.

A waiter appeared loaded with plates, signalling Peter's food was ready.

Peter smiled at Davilo. 'Look, I'm gonna eat, then beat it. It's been a long day. Thanks for your hospitality. I'll look in on the way back. You've a great place.'

'The pleasure's mine, man. Enjoy the diving and stay safe. Believe me, you won't want to leave once you've tasted the fruits. You'll see,' he said, grinning from ear to ear, as though his prophecies always came true.

The place had filled up, the music now louder and more energetic than before, the space morfing into a nightclub as people crowded the bar and the dance floor pulsated. Across the street, in the shadows, but with a clear view of everything, the hood kept close tabs on his target, chain smoking, periodically spitting onto the tarmac, constantly checking his smartphone.

Peter headed to his table, ate a surprisingly delicious grilled red grouper with salad and fries, then headed to his hotel for an early night. It was hot and humid, the air con physically but not operationally present during another night when the demons of his past came to visit. Most, one by one, sometimes in unison, some faces as clear as a crystal 3D model, others distorted and warped, but all somehow very real, each signifying the mental baggage he carried and needed to exorcise.

The following morning, he rose early. As he walked down to the seafront, past Davilo's, he recognised a man he'd seen the night before, loitering, squatting, smoking, and following him with his gaze. There was an air of danger about him, Peter thought, and although not currently a threat, his image was retained

The picture-perfect bay looked beautiful in the early morning light, with colourful bancas anchored on the azure water and islands dotting the horizon. Peter loved this time of morning, always peaceful and cool, before the heat began its slow, steady ascent once the sun got up.

After a short stroll along the waterfront, he walked back and checked out of his hotel, then headed to the general store, holdall over one shoulder. It was 9.20am. Plenty of time to meet the dive representative. When the Chinese–Filipina saw him approaching, she made a beeline, all love.

'Good to see you, Señor Rodriguez,' she said taking him by the arm.

Peter always used his mother's surname when travelling. It helped protect him from the trials and tribulations of being a Blake.

29

He hadn't told her, which meant her cousin must have.

She looked up at him, grinning quizzically. 'Hotel good, no? Nice food and music at Davilo's, eh?' She made a surprisingly agile twirl. 'Nice girls, too, eh?' A knowing wink, from someone who clearly liked to keep abreast of things.

'All great, thanks.' Peter winked back. 'Excellent recommendations.'

'Deep Blue here soon. You wait.' She gestured towards a white plastic chair outside the entrance. 'Sit in shade.'

'I tell you what. I'm gonna head down the street for a coffee. I'll be back by ten. Make sure they don't leave without me.'

Peter walked to a café further up the street, found an empty table outside and ordered coffee and juice. It had Wi-Fi, so he checked his emails. No dramas. Henry was looking forward to hearing from him and wished him luck, confirming he was keeping Angela at bay and had bought more time in respect of the study and its contents. He sent a WhatsApp to Samantha, telling her he was okay and hoping she was coping with everything in connection with sorting out the estate, his stepmother and Tiffany.

Looking at his watch he saw it was almost 10am, so he briskly headed back to the general store, keen to hook up with Deep Blue.

As he walked into the shop, at the far end a tall blond woman with long feline legs, with her back to him, was leaning casually on the counter, talking to the Chinese-Filipina woman. She wore a white cotton armhole vest, cut-off denim shorts, Reef flip-flops and her right ankle sported an array of colourful friendship bracelets.

'What's this guy's name, Angel?' Clear English, slight trace of an accent. 'I can't hang about; we've got a busy schedule. The boat's loaded with supplies and refuelled. I need a quick turnaround. I'm sorry but he'll just have to go with another operator.'

'He's called Rodriguez,' Peter said, approaching with a broad grin. 'Peter Rodriguez. And you don't have to hang about, assuming we can agree terms. I'm all set.'

The woman turned and instantly took his breath away. She was a knockout. As her cool blue eyes assessed him methodically, like a doctor looking objectively at a patient, he guessed she was in her early thirties. Her demeanour was cool, in that she wasn't rude, but neither was she overly friendly. Perhaps 'confident' was the word, but he wasn't sure of that either.

'You're just in time, Mr Rodriguez,' she said, hands on hips. 'I'm Sophie, one of the dive masters at Deep Blue. I understand you want to dive with us?'

'That's right. I want to do some sport diving around the islands. You guys come highly recommended. I would've booked, but didn't know I was going to be here till the last minute, so thought I'd chance it. Can you accommodate me?' he asked, his manner projecting charm with a little vulnerability thrown in for good measure

'Well,' she said, matter-of-factly, 'you're lucky. We had a cancellation yesterday, which is unusual as we're otherwise fully booked. We take bookings for either three days, full board and lodging, or a week. The cost of diving depends on the number and type of dives you make, with additional rates for equipment you may need to hire, which, in your case' – looking him up and down, eyes settling on his bag – 'is going to be pretty much everything, unless you're hiding something.'

She gave a wry smile. 'It's your choice. The prices are fixed and non-negotiable. Our accommodation's comfortable, with air conditioning and all the mod cons. We have a nice pool with a fully stocked bar area, as well as a good restaurant that uses quality local produce. The accommodation's not basic, nor is it super luxurious, but somewhere in the middle, because it's diving we specialise in and where we excel.

'Oh, and the scenery and views are world class,' she added with a stunning smile, the gauntlet succinctly thrown down.

'I'm all in,' said Peter. And he meant it on every conceivable level. She could have said virtually anything looking as she did, and he'd have been in.

'Then please follow me. Is that all you've got?'

'Yup.'

'Fair enough.'

She had a charmingly no-nonsense manner about her as she led the way out of the store and walked towards the waterfront, like a gazelle, her long, athletic legs locking in Peter's gaze without effort.

As they approached the jetty, he spotted a large rib at the far end watched over by a diligent local. 'Deep Blue Divers' was stencilled along its side in large blue letters, with the circular logo of a shark and dolphin juxtaposed, in blue, turquoise and green, separated by thick curving white lines, like a yin and yang symbol.

Sophie said something to the old man, handed him some notes, then turned to Peter.

'Well, this is ours,' she said, sounding a little more conciliatory. 'Hop in and let's head out. I hope you'll like our set-up.'

'Me too,' he said, jumping in with a practised ease, which clearly didn't go unnoticed, and stashing his bag securely. 'I like your logo. It's eye-catching.'

'Thanks. I designed it.'

'Are you an artist?'

'No, but I was passionate about getting it right and knew what would look good.'

'Well, you nailed it. What's the island called?'

'Bambam.'

'Great name.'

She fired up the twin Evinrudes, then deftly manoeuvred the boat around, taxiing towards deeper water, before pushing hard on the throttle, accelerating rapidly, pointing the bow south-west as it rose high out of the water.

As she stood tall, upright and beautiful behind the wheel in designer tortoise-shell sunglasses, her blonde hair trailing in the wind, Peter thought her profile suggested a strong, determined woman in control. He also thought she had an unbelievable body.

It was hard to talk above the wind as the rib smacked the waves, so he went and stood beside her. She turned and flashed him another killer smile, then looked back in the direction they were heading.

Sophie had clocked from the outset that he was handsome and in good shape, unlike many of their clients, and that his hazel-green eyes missed nothing. And although he was sure of himself, he wasn't arrogant, which she found attractive.

She prized herself on sizing up their clients from the moment they got in the rib, to watching them on their first dive. She had no doubt he'd be a good diver, but somehow sensed he was here for more. There was something enigmatic about him she couldn't pinpoint, which piqued her interest.

Peter stood next to her, a few inches taller, and they maintained silence as the rib navigated the breath-taking landscape before he shouted above the engine noise and wind: 'Don't you ever get sick of all this natural beauty?'

'Never!' she shouted back with a grin. 'But it's good to get off the islands once in a while and head to the city for a fix of chaos before coming back out and remembering why it's so damn good.'

Watching her expertly drive the rib, Peter felt his loins sending signals he hadn't felt for a long time as they powered past dramatic limestone islands, with colours that dazzled in a landscape like the best cinematography, screaming to every bone in his body to get into the water.

Peter felt his spirits lift for the first time since his father had died when a pod of spinner dolphins suddenly appeared, racing either side of the rib, flipping, weaving and arching high out of the water. The tiredness and weight of the past few weeks fell away as he pictured his father out here all those years ago, feeling the same awe and elation, and realised that it was among these islands that he'd met and fallen in love with his mother.

Peter felt somehow connected to both of them out here, which he hadn't expected, like a real family unit, united through time and space, and wished the trip to the island could last longer.

It was like being in suspended animation, in the perfect environment, with the perfect woman, sea spraying in his face, sun blazing and speed: now, that was adventure.

*

Dakila arrived on an early flight, met up with his low-life contact and watched from a safe distance as Peter got into the rib with the blonde woman and headed out towards the archipelago. Through his powerful binoculars, the writing and distinctive logo on its side were clear. He headed into town to get the lowdown on Deep Blue Divers, before updating Bekker. Now in Manila, the South African wasn't the least bit surprised; as if he'd expected to be told that was where Peter was heading.

He instructed Dakila, in no uncertain terms, he had to get himself or someone else onto the island to find out what Blake was up to. It wouldn't be easy. It wasn't like hanging out in El Nido. Bambam was a small boutique dive resort, necessitating a bona fide reason for being there. He would have to find a way.

# CHAPTER 7

## *Bambam, the Bacuit*

After passing Miniloc Island's celebrated big and small lagoons, Sophie and Peter tracked its north-western coastline, past deep, enticing inlets, glistening white beaches lined with palm trees, and unreal azure water. Every time they passed an exotic-looking lagoon or beach, another came into view that was even more spectacular.

After navigating the elongated southern extremity of Matinloc Island, Sophie angled the rib north-west, and powered it up between the Guntao Islands and Matinloc.

Fifteen minutes later, as a staggeringly beautiful island came into view, Sophie shouted, 'There she is!' and Peter caught his first glimpse of Bambam: a towering mass of limestone, covered in tropical vegetation and surrounded by azure water.

As they got closer, he realised it was in fact two islands, with a gorge-like channel running between them: the island to the left, a pitted skyscraper of sharp limestone turrets; the island to its right, equally rugged, but more open and elongated, where the dive resort blended into jungled undergrowth above a gleaming white beach, fringed by palms, with several bancas beached above the waterline.

Sophie eased the throttle, angling the rib towards a wooden jetty protruding into the turquoise shallows where resort staff carrying scuba tanks on their shoulders made their way down to a large banca moored alongside while crew helped divers secure their gear on board.

Peter thought it was a dive scene that could be witnessed the world over, in countless tropical locations. However, what differentiated each and every one was their cocktail of variables: the configuration of islands, ocean topography, water clarity, geology, elevation, vegetation and climate. Layered on top of which was cultural identity – that distinctive feeling of place, emanating from the ethnicity of the locals, their demeanour, philosophy and overall approach to life that permeated a micro location, making it unique in a way that couldn't be replicated.

'What an island!' he exclaimed as Sophie eased the rib behind another and threw a line to a boat boy.

Peter climbed onto the jetty. 'Who found this place?' he asked, giving Sophie a hand up.

'Some adventurous expats forty years ago, who ran yacht charters from Puerto Princesa for wealthy clients who wanted to dive remote locations. One time they sailed around the northern tip of Palawan down to this archipelago, known only to local tribes, and were amazed at what they found.'

She smiled, acknowledging staff and residents as they walked up the jetty.

'They came across this island on a subsequent trip when they had to hole up from a typhoon and were blown away by its beauty above and below the water. They put the Bacuit on the map, which is why it's so popular today.

Thinking it one of the most beautiful islands he had ever seen, Peter said, 'How long's it been a dive resort?'

'Since the early 90s. It started basic but it's evolved into the eco resort you see today.'

Feigning ignorance, he asked, 'Who owns it?'

'One of the original adventurers.'

'American?'

'No, Irish.'

'Does he live here?'

Sophie's eyes softened. 'Some of the time. But he moves around a lot and has several business ventures including some liveaboards operating Tubbataha and Apo Reefs, as well as around the Sulu islands.'

'Those are serious pirate waters.'

Sophie nodded. 'They are, but you have to be vigilant everywhere these days.'

'He sounds like an interesting man.'

'He is', she said gently, 'and he knows more about these islands than anyone I know ... He tends to keep himself to himself, but if you're lucky, you'll meet him.'

They walked up the boardwalk bridging the hot sand to a large thatched clubhouse that appeared to be the heart of the place. It was open to the elements on both elongated sides, with ping-pong and pool tables, and comfortable-looking rattan furniture on which books, magazines and board games were spread about.

 Some maps of the local area hung on the back wall, with notable landmarks clearly marked, together with photographs of boats, people and places, obviously taken over many years. In one corner, a whiteboard detailed the day's dives. Off to the right of the club house was a swimming pool, with a bar and restaurant area, set amidst exotic palms and banana trees.

Sophie approached the bamboo reception desk with Peter in tow. 'Gabe, can you check Mr Rodriguez into Swift View if it's ready?'

The man smiled broadly. 'No problem, Ms Sophie.'

The short, stocky, dark-faced man with a friendly smile asked Peter for his passport and credit card. 'Welcome to Deep Blue, sir. I hope you enjoy your stay. We'll do our best to ensure it's a good one. Diving conditions are excellent at the moment.'

Peter put money on it he'd be an experienced diver; people in these places always multi-tasked. He thought the staff were well-presented in white T-shirts with the dive logo on them, and dark blue shorts, and that the place had an air of laid-back efficiency.

Sophie said, 'I have to assist with a dive party now. So, I'd suggest exploring the island and doing some snorkelling, or Gabe can fix you up with a dive on Home Reef. We can discuss which dives might suit you tomorrow when I get back.'

'Sounds good. Thanks for the ride over. But do me a favour, please. Call me Peter.'

She flashed a smile. 'All right, Peter. Enjoy your day.'

She then headed back towards the jetty whilst Gabe escorted Peter to his accommodation. A short walk through jungled undergrowth along a boulder-lined track brought them to a small clearing on the west of the island, where a few scattered palms surrounded a solitary cabin perched on stilts, with a spectacular view across the gorge-like channel towards a precipitous tower of limestone on the other side.

It was constructed of tropical hardwoods in a traditional ethnic style, with steps leading up to a small veranda where there were two rattan armchairs and a hammock strung out. Rattan blinds were neatly rolled up on the open windows. Although it looked simple, the inside was comfortable and well thought-out with a fusion of stylish Scandinavian minimalism and Filipino tribal art and textiles, prompting Peter to think he might actually get some relaxation in such pleasant surroundings.

He dumped his stuff and freshened up, then walked back to the pool area for a bite to eat. The first thing he usually did whenever he arrived somewhere new was head for the water and explore his surroundings. And he couldn't wait to do that here given it was nearly a month since he'd been extracted from the Kimberley. He also wanted to soak up the environment, so that when he met Declan O'Connor he'd have a mental image of the place he'd operated from for so long, which might somehow help him understand the man.

As he walked through the clubhouse to access the poolside restaurant, a faded photo in a black frame with a white mount caught his eye. It was of a sloop, similar to a picture in his father's study. Three men in swim shorts stood on the foredeck with a striking-looking woman sitting cross-legged in front of them. All looked tanned. The man on the left was easily recognisable as his young father, even though it was so long ago. The one in the middle, he thought, was most probably Declan O'Connor, a handsome man of average height, with thick dark wavy hair, broad shoulders and a broad smile, his arms crossed. And to his left, the tallest of the three, a Scandinavian-looking man, clean cut, with short-cropped blond hair, who Peter thought might well be Karl Johansson. The woman at his feet looked like a young Ingrid Bergman and must be Johansson's girlfriend, fiancée or wife, Peter speculated. They looked happy, seemingly enjoying one another's company. However, Peter knew as well as anyone that the camera could lie.

It was surely a photo of the yacht charter his father had referred to in his letter, Peter thought, when they'd had to quickly find somewhere safe to hole up as a typhoon approached. He was certain that this photograph, of a frozen moment in time nearly forty years earlier, and the circumstances surrounding it, marked the beginning of this particular adventure, the sole reason for his standing there now. He shuddered as his intuition told him the story that would unravel might not be the one he was expecting.

*

In Metro Manila, Jan Bekker sat on a leather sofa in the lobby of the Hilton, talking on his mobile. Already on his third San Miguel and sweating profusely, despite the air conditioning, his belly protruded from his Hawaiian shirt like a late pregnancy as he stuffed peanuts into his mouth. His red-blotched, pockmarked face, set in a permanent grimace, made him look as if he'd been unhappy since the day he'd popped out of his mama's womb. Having made his way up the ranks by stabbing in the back those who'd trusted him most, he was feared by many, but was a good henchman for someone who could control him. He got things done.

'He's gone to find O'Connor,' he said in his thick South African accent, 'which means one thing: Harry Blake found something.'

He listened carefully to the person on the other end, whose instructions were irritatingly clear.

'Okay. I'll do what you say,' he said reluctantly. 'I'll be in touch.'

He waved the waiter over, ordered another beer, then booked in for a "massage" – liking to make the most of all available facilities when he travelled.

*

Peter decided not to scuba dive, but to snorkel to check out the marine environment and then scope out the island. His first impressions on the ride over had been good. The whole area looked like a rich marine ecosystem, which he hoped extended around the whole Bacuit.

He ate a club sandwich by the pool, then returned to his cabin and grabbed his snorkelling kit. He walked along the ridge and found a steep but just about navigable path which wound down to a small inlet nestled on the edge of the channel between the two islands. At water level, the cathedral-like scale of his surroundings was magnified, with jagged peaks either side dripping in tropical vegetation.

Standing on a small strip of bone-white sand, he surveyed the channel and towering mass of limestone opposite, then walked to the water's edge, sat down and slipped on his fins. He spat into his face mask and rubbed saliva around the glass, then rinsed it with seawater before easing himself into the water, keeping his UV protective top on.

He walked slowly backwards into the warm, yet refreshing, shallow water, and delighted at being back in his favourite medium. A few feet in, he sank down and propelled himself into the channel, to the chatter of swifts darting high above.

He trod water with his mask and snorkel pushed up onto his forehead, turning slowly around to take in the magnificence of his surroundings, noting it was a perfectly protected anchorage for any medium-sized yacht capable of slipping through the narrow entrance to his left. There was no one else around and apart from the swifts high above, it was quiet and secluded. He rinsed his mask, secured it to his face, then put his head below the surface, expelling water from his snorkel, and finned into the channel, surveying the exotic marine world beneath him.

Crystal-clear water stretched 25 metres in all directions, with a proliferation of hard and soft corals, and shoals of tropical fish of

40

every colour and hue. Peter recognised butterfly and angelfish, moorish idols and brightly-coloured clownfish nestled among sea anemones, gaudily patterned nudibranchs, and a large parrotfish destructively crunching algae off coral. In the deeper water, edging the middle of the channel, fan, brain and elkhorn corals sifted the current. Eyeing a couple of whitetips that lay motionless in a crevice, Peter thought it a pristine marine system.

Swimming lazily over this colourful feast, he approached deeper water in the middle of the channel, unable to make out the bottom. Just dark blue, the shallower edge abruptly stopping at a drop-off where large fan corals fed off nutrients gliding in the current.

Clocking movement, Peter turned, spotting a reef shark moving stealthily near the channel entrance, patrolling its patch, its menacing outline sufficiently far away not to trouble him.

He thrust himself vertical into the hot, humid air, and then breast-stroked slowly through glinting undulating water back to shore, reminding himself he was here for a specific purpose and mustn't get side-tracked, tempting as it was.

*

High up on a rocky outcrop, further up and along from the path Peter had taken down to the water's edge, an old man looked down through powerful binoculars. *So, the time has come,* he thought. He'd known it would. After all, he was his father's son.

*

Peter took his fins off and sat looking across the channel with his arms wrapped around his legs as his body dried quickly in the afternoon heat. Although revitalised, he was preoccupied about how best to approach things, not wanting to wait long to meet O'Connor and determine if there was something worth pursuing.

He returned to his cabin, had a quick shower, put on clean cargo shorts and a T-shirt, then headed back up the path to explore the island, aiming for high ground to get his bearings.

He followed the track which trailed above the channel in places, but wound its way inland much of the time, making it hard to look directly into the gorge below unless he fought his way over undergrowth and jagged rock, which he did periodically. The channel was longer than it had appeared where he'd swum, snaking around a bend and opening into a broad lagoon. At the opposite end from the entrance, it culminated in a narrow cleft leading to open ocean beyond.

After fifteen minutes, he reached what was undoubtedly the highest point on the island, with a small wooden viewing platform where another path led in the direction of the clubhouse. The vantage point had almost uninterrupted views in almost every direction, only the towering smaller island prohibiting a complete 360.

He speculated what might have come to pass in the old days, sure that early Spanish explorers would have sailed these waters, protecting their power base in Manila from Moros and Chinese pirates; and he thought it possible an East Indiaman might have strayed into them, either by design or by accident.

*

That afternoon, Dakila came up with a solution to his problem. He made a visit to Puerto Princesa to call in on the family of one of the dive instructors working on Bambam, explaining the dilemma he had and how only they could help him. Given the options so vividly set out, they willingly agreed to his suggested course of action.

*

Peter returned to his cabin where he lazed in his hammock, read and snoozed, swaying peacefully in the gentle breeze. Looking forward to seeing Sophie again, knowing she was his way in to O'Connor, he unintentionally fell into a deep sleep, waking as the sun set.

He walked to the clubhouse, where the atmosphere was chilled. Brazilian music drifted over the open space as guests milled around. After ordering a beer from the bar, he went and sat by the pool, watching young couples chat, eat and drink. A group of Italians were flaunting the latest, most fashionable diving gear to some other guests, whilst one or two people on their own read, swam or just people-watched.

Gabe brought Peter's beer over with a broad smile. 'How was your afternoon, sir?'

Peter took a slug which hit the sweet spot. 'Enjoyable thanks, Gabe. That's short for Gabriel, I assume?'

Gabe nodded cheerfully. 'Yes, sir, after the angel.'

'Tell me, how many people can you accommodate on the island?'

'Around forty. But more if you include guests sleeping on board their yachts.'

Peter looked out to sea. 'I haven't seen any.'

'There's a couple due in tomorrow. And during bad weather a few often come in to ride out a storm in the channel if they can't make it to El Nido.'

Peter smiled. 'Are you from around here?'

'No, sir, Manila,' Gabe said cheerfully. 'I came to visit my cousin in Puerto Princesa six years ago, heard they were looking for staff, applied for a job and have been here ever since.'

'What a great place to work.'

'I'm very lucky. Much nicer than Manila. Too much poverty there.'

'You're a diver, right?'

Gabe grinned broadly. 'Everyone dives here. It's what we live for.'

'I hear there's some good wreck diving.'

Gabe looked around to check he wasn't needed. 'Not bad, sir There's quite a few. We dive on pretty much all of them.'

Peter cocked an eyebrow. 'What level of difficulty?'

'There's something for everyone,' Gabe replied enthusiastically. 'Most are okay for novices and intermediates, but a few are deep and dangerous – only for experienced divers.'

'What period?'

'A mixture, sir. Tramp steamers, cargo vessels, a ferry, a World War Two Japanese ammunition ship, and some *galleones*,' he said, using the Spanish pronunciation, which always sounded more exotic. Peter wondered what his classification of a galleon was, given it was used liberally to describe any ship from the Spanish colonial era, and doubting a true galleon would have navigated these islands.

43

'Do *you* dive on them?' he asked.

'Yes, sir. I'm experienced on all wreck dives,' Gabe said proudly. 'But the best wreck diving's further north, around Coron and Busuanga, where a fleet of Japanese cargo ships were ambushed by American Hellcats and sank in shallow water.'

Gabe clocked some people waiting for drinks at the small bamboo bar. 'I have to go now, sir. Let me know if you need anything else.' He went back to make a round of Mai Tais for the Italians.

Looking beyond them, Peter spotted Sophie in the clubhouse, conferring with a group of dive instructors, huddled in conversation by the whiteboard, most likely planning the following day's dives.

He wandered over, and she looked up as he approached, while the fit-looking Filipino instructors, wetsuits peeled around their waists, carried on talking.

'Which would you recommend for me?' asked Peter.

'Did you dive today?'

'No. I snorkelled the channel and explored the island as you suggested. I have to say, it's one hell of an ecosystem. The marine life's extensive and the coral formations are really healthy. The number of species I saw, only metres from the shore, was exceptional.'

Sophie's expression showed she'd clocked that he was a professional diver, although in what capacity remained to be seen.

'I think you should join the group I'm taking with Marko and Jovy. We're diving a World War Two Japanese cargo vessel about an hour from here. It's in excellent condition with 30 metres visibility on a good day, and there are tanks and jeeps still strapped in the hold. But it's got its risks,' she added. 'There's live ordnance on board, and it's near a serious drop-off into deep ocean, so it gets some serious shark activity.'

Peter smiled broadly. 'That sounds great. What time's kick-off?'

'Eight am sharp. So, I'll need to verify your logbook tonight.'

'Not a problem.'

If he'd had to stump up a logbook with every dive he'd ever undertaken, recorded and signed off on, he'd have needed to carry a telephone directory, so his dives were logged on a divemaster website for those with full security clearance. But that was professional, not personal. So, he kept a sport log he could use in these situations, which was still impressive but didn't give much away regarding his line of work.

'I'll pop up to the cabin and get it, then perhaps you could join me for a drink when you're done? I can show it to you and there's something else I'd like to discuss.'

'Sure,' she said without hesitation. 'We'll be through in about twenty. See you by the pool.' She re-joined the divers' discussion, clearly in control and commanding the respect of the other instructors.

Peter went to retrieve his log from his cabin as darkness fell, thinking about his best approach, deciding he'd come straight out with it, not wanting to play games. It wasted valuable time. He was pretty sure Declan O'Connor would be aware of his presence, if he weren't in Manila or out of the country. A man of his reputation, with his background, wouldn't let anyone put a foot on his island without knowing who they were and what they wanted.

As he made his way back to the clubhouse, he saw torchlight flickering on the hillside, moving steadily through dense undergrowth. Then it was gone. He assumed it was a guest from one of the other cabins scattered around the island. It was bloody dark and could be more than a little spooky, if you spooked easily. Pirates weren't pipe dreams in these parts. Every resort had a good security detail or staff proficient with firearms. He'd seen a notice in the clubhouse about being vigilant and reporting anything that looked suspicious, however trivial it might seem. From experience he knew the threat was real.

However, poolside, things were chilled. The lighting cleverly created the perfect ambience: strong enough to see your food in the dining area, more subtle and romantic further away. On the beach, torches on poles driven into the sand flickered invitingly in the darkness, where a smattering of people sat with their thoughts.

Peter couldn't see Sophie, so he headed off to find a table by the pool.

He scanned the dinner menu, chalked on a blackboard by the bar, offering fish of the day, chargrilled kebabs and an abundance of salad and fresh fruit, and opted for grilled sea bream and a salad. He ordered a San Mig.

'Good choice,' Sophie said, startling him from behind. She sat down across from him. Lithe and tall, she stretched out her tanned, feline legs, her trademark ethnic friendship bracelets prominent around her right ankle.

Peter raised his glass. 'Care to join me?'

'I don't eat with guests, but I'll have a beer.' She gave Gabe a knowing look, and he brought one over in a bottle cooler straight away.

She took an appreciative slug, eyeing the small blue hardback book on the table. 'May I?'

'Be my guest.'

As she flicked through his log book, Peter admired her appearance. She was sporting a ponytail, tight-fitting jeans, a low-cut red cotton top and white pumps. However, Peter's eyes were drawn to the exquisite yellow gold cross with a rectangular emerald around her neck on a leather thong. The gold looked antique, its design and appearance similar to pieces he'd often seen recovered from Spanish wrecks. He made a mental note to ask her about it.

It took Sophie some time to go through the book; he was more experienced than most of the divers they hosted. The log was a litany of exotic locations: the Great Barrier Reef in Australia; the Red Sea off Egypt and the Sudan; various islands in the Ionian and Aegean seas in Greece; the Sea of Cortez, Mexico; the Blue Hole, Belize; cave diving in the Bahamas; shark diving in the Cocos Islands, Costa Rica; wreck diving on Second World War planes off Guam, in Micronesia and Papua New Guinea. And finally, Sipadan, south-west Borneo – all destinations people would kill to visit.

She closed the log and put it back on the table. 'You're quite the traveller, Mr Rodriguez,' she said, looking into his hazel-green eyes.

'It's Peter. And yes, I like to travel,' he said, grinning broadly, eyes playful, 'so am I good to go?'

'Seems the only place you haven't been is here,' she said, with a hint of sarcasm and a wry grin. 'Yes, you've full clearance for take-off.'

She made to get up. 'What did you want to ask me?'

'I'd like to show you something,' he replied, just as his food was placed in front of him.

Sophie sat back down and gestured with her hand: 'Please, go ahead and eat.'

'Thanks.' Between mouthfuls, as he tucked in, he said, 'You're Scandinavian, aren't you?'

'Part of me is.' Her eyes flickered, as if she was wondering if it was just a lucky guess.

'Great fish,' he said, knowing even if she felt hungry watching him eat it was obvious she wouldn't capitulate and send the wrong signal. However, she remained seated, clearly intrigued by what he had to say.

Peter cleared his plate in record time. 'Sorry. I was famished. I hope you don't think me rude.'

'I'm glad you enjoyed it.' Sophie pushed her chair back, and stood up. 'What was it you wanted to show me?'

'It's in the clubhouse,' he said standing up and pushing his chair in.

She followed him over. It was empty apart from a member of staff manning reception. Peter walked over to the collage of photos and maps on the back wall and pointed to the picture he'd studied earlier.

'What do you know about this?'

'It's a photo from the old days.'

'Do you know who the people are?'

'Just some old-time adventurers and divers.'

'Like the ones you told me about earlier?' He looked at her quizzically. 'The ones who discovered this place all those years ago?'

'Maybe, I don't know' Her eyes avoided the photo.

'Are you sure?'

'What are you getting at?' she said with a puzzled expression.

He paused, then said, 'My father's in this photo … and I think yours is too.'

He let the statement hang. 'Right here,' he said pointing to the figure on the left, the resemblance to himself, inescapable.

'And I'm betting the guy in the middle's Declan O'Connor, your father,' he continued.

Speechless, Sophie processed the implications of what he said.

'You look just like he did then,' came a strong Irish brogue from the shadows beyond the clubhouse entrance.

Looking round, Peter saw an old man, leaning on a cane for support, walking towards them, with fire in his bright blue eyes. 'Your father was a good man. One I am proud to have known.'

He paused, sizing Peter up. 'I knew you'd come here one day. It was inevitable.'

'Declan O'Connor.' Peter articulated the words almost mystically. Easily discernible from the old photo: the set of his shoulders and thick wavy hair, although grey now, was unmistakable.

'Guilty as charged, Mr Rodriguez, or should I say, Blake,' O'Connor said, walking into the light, leaning on his cane, a twinkle in his eye and a winning smile. 'I see you're acquainted with my daughter?'

Sophie watched, dumbfounded at the revelations.

'I'm guessing the other man in the photo is Karl Johansson and the woman's his girlfriend or wife?' said Peter.

'You're a good guesser,' said the broad-shouldered old man now standing beside him.

'It's a gift,' said Peter. 'Tell me, Mr O'Connor, is this the island where nearly forty years ago, shortly after that picture was taken, the three of you holed up and rode out a typhoon, and you enlightened the others about a lost treasure, one so incredible it barely seemed believable? The very reason I'm standing here now.'

'One and the same,' said the old Irishman, leaning on his cane. 'I told many stories in those days, and was somewhat of a raconteur, known for spinning a good yarn. I can tell you on many an occasion I mixed fact with fiction, which is always more compelling than pure fiction. The ability to check a few random facts adds credibility to the most far-fetched stories. We certainly drank the bar dry that night, talked about many old rumours and theories and about what happened to the sunken galleons and East Indiamen that were known to have carried their precious cargoes through the treacherous waters of this fascinating archipelago.'

'But there was one story in particular, I understand,' Peter said, 'involving a legendary treasure ...'

Declan O'Connor, always used to taking the lead, felt old and tired, having lived with this story and its repercussions for so long. It was time to put this thing to bed, one way or another, and seeing his old friend Harry Blake in the young man before him, he made a decision. After all, it takes but a moment for most people to judge a person, with the consequences that follow often lasting a lifetime.

'There was, or perhaps I should say, is, a story, one could even say more of a legend, about a romance and an associated treasure,' he said wistfully, 'but it's probably only a story.' The way he spoke about it and the tone of his voice suggested it was a story he believed in, one still very much alive in his old but active imagination. Peter could see how his father and this man had connected all those years ago, both adventurous romantics with similar passions.

'Then I think you owe it to me, and Sophie, if you haven't already told her, to recount it in full. I'm here because my father believed in it. And he believed in you.'

Peter also made an assessment from the short exchange, from the words and body language of Declan O'Connor, and his gut told him, without any shadow of a doubt, that this was a story based on fact, not fiction, and the treasure, whether gold, silver, jewels or precious stones, was out there somewhere, waiting to be recovered – if someone hadn't already got there first.

Declan smiled at the son of his old friend. 'I suggest you get an early night, Mr Blake, then go on your dive with my daughter tomorrow. When you return, come with her to *La Señora*, my yacht, and I'll tell you all I know. I promise.'

He walked over, kissed Sophie lovingly on the cheek, then turned and disappeared into the night.

Sophie took the photo down from the wall and, scrutinising it closely, said, 'He could be your brother.'

'And you bear a striking resemblance to your mother. She was a beautiful woman, judging by that photo.'

A tear streaked Sophie's face.

'I didn't mean to upset you,' Peter said, not knowing what to say as he looked into her piercing blue eyes. However, what he did know, was how strongly he was attracted to this woman he'd known for less than a day.

'We'll talk about this in the morning. I'll see you at the jetty at 7.30,' Sophie said, quickly regaining her composure.

'Okay,' he said gently. 'I'll see you then.'

'Goodnight,' she said heading into the darkness in the same direction as her father, clearly needing time to digest these revelations.

Peter headed to the bar, where Gabe poured him a generous measure of Don Papa on the rocks, which he took down to the beach. He sat for a long time thinking about everything, the music faint, as torchlight flickered on the gently lapping water.

He felt sure his father had been right to send him here, but how things would pan out was anybody's guess. It had been a long day and he felt tired. After a while, he made his way back to his cabin for an early night.

# CHAPTER 8

## *The Dive*

After an unusually good sleep, Peter got up early and walked down to the channel for a swim. It was part of his daily routine wherever he was in the world, and set him up for the day. Afterwards, he showered, then headed to the clubhouse for breakfast, carrying his facemask, snorkel and fins, the only diving equipment he'd brought with him. He'd decided for once he wouldn't lug everything around, despite his preference to use his own familiar kit, wanting to appear as low key as possible. Travelling light gave him greater flexibility.

He saw others he assumed were going on the dive, including the Italians and a couple in their early twenties. After a good breakfast, he went to locate a wetsuit and a Buoyancy Control Device (BCD), passing one of the dive instructors pointing at a map of the islands on the clubhouse wall with some guests, as boat boys marched refilled scuba tanks and refreshments down to the outrigger.

Peter could see the equipment was top quality and in good condition, which bode well. After locating what he needed, he walked down to the jetty, where he spotted Sophie on a banca.

'Morning,' he shouted. 'Permission to come aboard?'

'Sure,' she replied, looking up.

'I didn't mean to upset you last night,' he said, climbing in.

Sophie continued securing equipment 'You've nothing to apologise for. Let's concentrate on the dive and talk about other things when we get back.'

No mention of Declan or his suggestion to meet on his yacht.

'Sounds good,' Peter said, making his way to the back of the outrigger.

The others came down the jetty and boarded with the excitement and expectation that always accompanied trips like this. The Italians, true to form, were super-animated, talking non-stop about the possibility of some shark action, while the young couple couldn't keep their hands off one another.

It was another fine day: the sea flat and calm, the colours of everything nicely saturated at this early hour. As resort staff brought the last of the scuba tanks and stashed food and drink into cool boxes, another couple legged it across the beach just in time.

In total, there were nine guest divers and three dive instructors, including Sophie. Santo, the skipper, would stay topside, keeping an eye on safety below and above water, especially in relation to other boats, changing weather conditions and spare air, and maintain a radio link with the island: not responsibilities to be taken lightly.

'A quick word before we set off,' Sophie said in a confident, clear voice. 'Can you please carry out a thorough equipment check? It's too far to pop back if you forget something.'

Everyone methodically checked their kit, confirming they were good to go.

'Conditions are good,' Sophie said, 'so fingers crossed we'll have a great time. It's a thirty-minute ride out, so enjoy the scenery.'

Santo deftly manoeuvred the banca out through Home Reef, then accelerated to fifteen knots in a north-easterly direction.

Peter thought Sophie did sexy without effort, her white one-piece bathing costume showing beneath her peeled-down wetsuit as she went to the bow to chat with fellow dive instructors, Jovy and Marko.

Feeling a bit of a lemon as he sat between the couples, he politely extricated himself and went and stood next to Santo where, under the cool of the canopy, he reviewed with interest a chart of the archipelago.

As they powered across open water, past idyllic small islands,

Peter thought this place was extra special, even though he'd been to some of the best dive locations on the planet. The sheer drama of the islands with their towering limestone peaks swathed in tropical vegetation, powder-white sand and crystal-clear waters set it apart.

Boutique resorts dotted the islands in various configurations. Some had huts jutting out on stilts, others curved around lagoons, whilst others still blended into jungled undergrowth behind white beaches below towering limestone cliffs.

They passed bancas of all sizes and colours zigzagging the archipelago; most were filled with tourists island-hopping to spend several chilled hours in remote coves: swimming, snorkelling, kayaking and exploring.

Peter clocked a number of dive operators, and wondered how strictly they were regulated, knowing places like this always attracted cowboys who sullied the waters for professional outfits.

He recognised sloops, ketches, cutters, and catamarans – his personal favourite – as they powered through the Bacuit, until a stylish 1950s-looking motor yacht came into view. He wondered which billionaire it belonged to, as there wasn't a corner of the ocean they couldn't get to if the water was deep enough.

He decided that if there was any mileage in what O'Connor might reveal later, he would charter a catamaran, which would be therapeutic and practical.

After a visual feast of jungle-clad islands and water comprised of every kind of blue imaginable, Santo cut the engines in an open stretch of water west of Cadlao, with no other boats in sight.

Sophie made her way to the back of the banca and asked everyone to gather round. 'Well, this is the dive site. Before kitting up, I'll run through the dive plan. So, listen carefully.'

Marko held up a plastic A3 schematic of the wreck, detailing its dimensions, depths and position relative to the substantial drop-off it was angled towards. The divers huddled closer to get a better view as a welcome breeze tempered the heat.

Pointing, Sophie said, 'As you can see, it's a long vessel. The stern lies at 15 metres, with the bow angled down edging the drop-off at around 30 metres. It's become a reef in its own right and a refuge for all kinds of marine life. As mentioned to some of you already, this is a shark hangout: they really like it here. So, you need to be vigilant at all times. There are requiem and pelagic sharks because beyond the drop-off it's open ocean. It's a rare spot in that regard.'

Looking at the faces around her, she said in a more serious tone, 'The shark you want to be most wary of is the oceanic whitetip. They're inquisitive, bold and on occasion downright aggressive, though they generally stick to deeper water. The same goes for tiger sharks and great hammerheads. If myself, Marko or Jovy think there's a serious threat from anything we see, we'll terminate the dive and head topside. Understood?' She made eye contact with everyone, her face serious. This wasn't a joke. Everyone nodded. However, the Italians, unable to contain their excitement about the prospect of shark encounters, continued jabbering among themselves. Peter had a premonition they'd be reckless and need watching.

'In relation to entering the wreck, as with any wreck, there are serious hazards,' Sophie continued. 'For the most part, this one's easy to navigate. Of particular interest is what's in the hold – there are jeeps and lorries still secured to the floor. But remember, there's also live ordnance, so don't go touching anything.'

She started buddying everyone up: 'You four Italians will split into two. Each couple will buddy up with their partners. I'll buddy with Peter. Marko and Jovy will take four of you each.'

She was authoritative, conveying professionalism and trust. 'Follow their lead and adhere to any instructions they give you,' she continued. 'They're experienced and know the wreck well. If you blatantly ignore their instructions, you won't be diving any more with Deep Blue. I don't mean to put a dampener on things, but we take safety seriously. A diver died down here last year, from another dive operator I hasten to add, because he ventured off on his own and ran out of air. He was experienced with many hours logged. Above all, do your best to be economical with your movements and control buoyancy. Believe me, you don't want to be yo-yoing around the hold. That way you'll maximise dive time.'

She scanned their expectant faces. 'Any problems, you know the drill. If your buddy can't help, signal an instructor and we'll do our best to keep things safe. Lastly, we're big on safety stops. The bow of the ship is close to the maximum non-decompression dive limit. Don't be tempted to head over and down the drop-off, as that's when things can go badly wrong. There's a strong current, which as well as sweeping you along will take you down and we won't be able to come and get you if that happens.'

The outrigger undulated gently in the current as the divers started zipping wetsuits and kitting up as Sophie wound up.

She picked up her pink fins and mask. 'Dive time's twenty minutes, calculated from maximum depth. We'll take a three-minute safety stop on the way back up at 5 metres. There'll be spare tanks suspended in case anyone needs more air.'

It seemed a lot to take in. Peter knew there was a tendency to treat pre-dive briefings as if an air stewardess was running through the safety drill on an aeroplane before take-off – bad karma to entertain the prospect that something serious might happen.

Sophie looked around a final time. 'Any questions?'

A universal shake of heads.

'Okay, let's go then. Buddy up and enjoy the dive.' She zipped up her wetsuit and bent over to adjust her BCD. 'I look forward to comparing notes later.'

*

Back on Bambam, one of the dive instructors, Chook Santos, was on administrative duties, which included manning reception, checking stocks and inventory, and dealing with bookings. As he flicked through the arrivals book, he took a phone call informing him his mother was critically ill and he should return home immediately. Visibly shaken, he cleared things with management and within the hour was taken by rib to El Nido, where he caught a bus for the bone-shaking six-hour journey back to Puerto Princesa, his home city.

This was problematic for Deep Blue, who were now a dive instructor short, with a group of Spanish divers and a couple of yacht charters due in the following day. They'd need to find a replacement quickly, given strict protocols on guest-to-instructor dive ratios in relation to the validity of various insurance policies.

Serendipitously, Chook called in before leaving El Nido, telling them he'd bumped into a cousin, a qualified dive instructor, who was looking for a temporary position before taking up a permanent role in the Visayas. He was happy to fill in for Chook, who could vouch for him.

Deep Blue was delighted to have him on board. Problem solved.

That same evening, Chook's replacement arrived and introduced himself as Ramón Rivera. Stocky and swarthy, he had a slit of a scar running in a curve from the left corner of his mouth halfway up his cheek, an ear stud, and prominent tattoos which he tried to hide under the sleeves of his T-shirt.

He was introduced to the other dive instructors, and shown where to bunk, then quickly brought up to speed given that the following day would be hectic, with an early start. He proved to be a fast learner, this being by no means the first time he'd been brought in at such short notice for a job like this. He relished the prospect of what he'd been briefed to do. It was what made him tick. Raised in a pearl-diving community in the Sulu islands before being drafted into a Manila gang, he was an exceptional free diver, someone who could hold his breath for a seriously long time.

\*

The divers kitted up, zipping up wetsuits, stretching fins on, hefting and tightening weight belts around waists, adjusting BCDs and scuba tanks. Each buddy made last-minute safety checks on his counterpart. Regulators were purged, air and pressure gauges double-checked.

Sophie, who was always last to get in the water, watched the two groups back-roll into the blue, which was now more royal than navy, constantly changing in the light as the high sun beat down mercilessly.

With her hands on her hips, she turned to face Peter. 'You know we're connected by our past, don't you?'

'Yes. But we're not bound by it,' he replied.

Securing her face mask as she headed for the side, she said, 'Stick close to me. I know this wreck well.'

'You need to keep an eye on the Italians,' Peter said as he sat next to her on the gunwale.

'Agreed,' Sophie said, then back-rolled into the blue.

Peter quickly followed her, admiring her figure as they slowly descended into the clear rich waters of the Bacuit.

Diving never failed to excite him. Wherever he was in the world. Whatever the conditions. Whatever he was diving on. It was the anticipation and excitement of not knowing what he'd encounter and how the dive would pan out. This time he was just grateful to be buddying such a gorgeous woman who floated his boat on every level. He checked his gauges then turned the blue dial on his Tudor Submariner Snowflake to zero, which was always his benchmark of dive time even though his digital Suunto was more accurate. Given to him by his father for his twenty-first, he was never without it. It had literally accompanied him on every dive he'd ever been on. Battered and scratched, it was his single most precious possession. His father had owned an identical one.

They continued their slow descent and before long the top of the wreck came gradually into view. It was impressive. Peter had dived on many wrecks, some fully intact, others almost impossible to visualise as they would have been in their original condition. However, he was always conscious that most were underwater graveyards, where people had lost lives and unexpectedly come to rest, never to be reunited with family, friends or loved ones.

The type of ship and the circumstances under which it went down, if known, dictated the aura surrounding it, the visibility and clarity of the water, critical to how a ship appeared. In this case, the *Asahi Maru*, a cargo vessel, had been ferrying supplies between islands to strengthen a Japanese position during World War Two when

American Hellcats returning from a mission had opportunistically opened fire. A sitting duck, the ship had sunk quickly after taking direct hits below the waterline, with all hands lost.

At the depth it lay, many of the bright low-energy colours of the spectrum – the reds, yellows and oranges – were expunged, so blues and darker colours prevailed, the ship appearing a dark, ethereal grey. However, colourful coral formations had taken hold in every available nook and cranny, transforming the ship into a gargantuan artificial reef structure, lit by shafts of sunlight.

The divers explored the wreck in three distinct groups: Jovy and the four Italians entered the bowels of the vessel in the huge hold; Marko and the couples hovered at the stern, where there was an abundance of marine life; while Peter and Sophie finned down the entire length of the ship towards the drop-off, appearing as silhouettes against the open water and limitless blue ocean beyond.

Sophie hadn't exaggerated about it being a shark hangout; it was teeming with different species. Grey reef sharks patrolled the divide, while silvertips weaved in and out of the hold and various openings along the ship.

Sophie signalled to Peter not to go beyond the drop-off, and they maintained neutral buoyancy as a group of manta rays appeared ethereally out of the blue, majestically gliding by before disappearing into the gloom.

Peter clocked the vertical drop off into deep water: pelagic shark territory. Staring into the open water he was able to just make out, at the limit of his vision, the ghost-like outline of a school of scalloped hammerheads, most likely congregating at a wrasse cleaning station, he thought.

Sophie signalled for him to follow her back up towards the hold and he okayed her. They swam in smooth synchronisation, well-matched as buddies, each in total control, using minimum effort with maximum efficiency, relaxed and at ease in their element. Peter thought Sophie looked great in her blue and pink Scuba Pro wetsuit. He periodically checked his air and depth gauges with a practised eye, monitoring how long they'd been down, and noting they were almost a third of the way through the dive, at 25 metres, with one hundred and fifty bar of air left in his tank. He knew the less experienced divers would use their air less sparingly than the others, and hoped the instructors would keep an eye on that potential danger.

They reached the rectangular opening of the hold as a silvertip catapulted out from the black, bottomless void below, startling them as it swam up the hull and entered another opening.

As Jovy and the Italians finned up from the darkness, Jovy made the okay signal, indicating everything was cool, which they reciprocated. Peter noticed two of the Italians trailing the others and thought they should be closer together.

Jovy led the Italians down towards the bow while Peter followed Sophie into the hold. Faint shafts of sunlight penetrated openings above the inky blackness as they activated flashlights and inflated their BCDs to prevent themselves descending too quickly into the cavernous void. They could have been wearing space suits, floating in deep space – the visual effect was similar as their torch beams eerily lit up lorries and jeeps that had been secured to the deck for seventy-five years, like a frozen moment in history. The only sound was their echoed breathing as bubbles from their regulators trickled steadily upwards.

Half a dozen sharks weaved in and out of the vehicles and the corroded sections of hull and bulkhead as they floated beside one another. Peter glanced at Sophie's piercing blue eyes through her pink Tusa mask as she indicated for him to follow her, which he okayed.

They swam low over the corroded military vehicles, then finned slowly back up, making their way out of the hold and up along the hull, where they entered the heavily decayed bridge through vacant window frames. A large shoal of goatfish flashed this way and that in perfect synchronisation, while a school of sliver trevally hovered skilfully in the rich current outside the empty windows, like guardians of the deep. In the distance, various shark species massed further along the divide.

Exiting the bridge, Peter scanned the length of the wreck to locate the others, spotting Marko with the couples still at the shallower depth of the stern, enjoying the marine life and views without having to go deeper, take more risk and use more air.

Looking in the other direction, he spotted Jovy but only two of the Italians, which meant the other two had peeled off. The only place they could be was the wrong side of the drop-off. Catching Sophie's attention, he pointed his middle and index fingers towards his eyes, then towards Jovy and the Italians. She immediately clocked the gravity of the situation and they swam rapidly down towards them, all the time scanning the length of the drop-off, searching for the others before spotting them 5 metres along and more or less the same distance below.

One gripped the arm of the other, desperately trying to help him, but abandoned further attempts when his companion ripped the mask and regulator from his face. Peter suspected nitrogen narcosis was the cause of the diver's irrational behaviour, the man now in danger of running out of air, drowning or getting the bends and putting other lives at risk. He saw a group of grey reef sharks massing for a closer look, pectoral fins angled down, attracted by the commotion: a serious situation.

Processing all this in seconds, Peter finned quickly down to the struggling divers, signalling to Jovy, who focused on the Italian who'd had his regulator ripped from his face, grabbing him and inserting it back in his mouth; the diver greedily gulped air, severely panicked.

Peter grabbed the problem diver, who clearly had no idea which way was up or down, using his considerable strength to right him and drag him back up above the drop-off to a shallower depth, in the hope the narcosis would wear off. By now, Jovy had stabilised the other Italian, who was wearing his facemask again and seemed calmer. However, the panic and exertion had cost him serious air, which was their next problem.

Meanwhile, Marko, realising the seriousness of the situation from the stern of the wreck, had reacted instantly, escorting the couples to the surface, carrying out the requisite safety stops and clearing the way for the others.

Topside in the banca, they cleared the decks, ready for an emergency situation. With Santo's help, Marko secured a couple more tanks at the five-metre safety stop and they made ready to assist the divers as they resurfaced.

Deep Blue had never lost a client and didn't intend to now, as all safety drills were put into action.

# CHAPTER 9

## *La Señora*

Later that afternoon, Peter and Sophie secured the small rib to the back of the beautiful classic fifties sloop. Peter admired her flowing lines as they boarded, bending low as they entered the well-proportioned saloon, which was significantly larger inside than it appeared from out; its width was especially deceptive, the floor polished teak, and the quality and precision of the woodwork throughout was of the highest order.

Peter thought it the equivalent of his father's study, with books, charts, maps, photographs and ethnic tribal artefacts scattered about, giving a real flavour of the wildness and cultural diversity of the islands O'Connor had inhabited most of his lifetime and made his home. Peter thought the guy was a maritime nomad, the emerald green fields and rolling lush countryside of his native Southern Ireland a distant memory, yet somehow still alive in his very essence, having shaped him from an early age into what he now was.

Sitting in a comfortable-looking swivel chair beside a small teak table, Declan gestured for them to sit down opposite.

'Welcome to my floating sanctuary, where it seems appropriate to convene to discuss this matter,' he said, his eyes locking onto Peter's. 'Sophie told me you saved a man's life this morning and that you're one hell of a diver. I'm impressed. But then your father was one hell of a diver too, so perhaps I shouldn't be surprised.'

'I know what I'm doing – most of the time,' Peter said, modestly.

'I understand you're a marine biologist?'

'That's correct.'

'Where did you study?'

'The University of Queensland. Then I did a master's in marine archaeology at Cadiz University, in Spain.'

'So, you work full time?'

'I think you probably know what I work on, Mr O'Connor.'

'Well, humour me, please.'

'I'm currently contracted to a research vessel in the Kimberley, looking at creating marine reserves,' Peter said patiently.

'But that's not all you do, is it?' Declan gave a wry smile, glancing at Sophie.

'No. I also contract out to some big salvage operators, helping locate and recover lost ships.'

Declan leant on the table, clasping his hands together. 'But not just any ships, right? These are treasure ships, with cargoes rumoured to be virtually priceless in today's money.' He gave a broad grin. 'And from what I understand, not just any salvage company, but more often than not for Treasure Seekers International.'

'You've obviously done your homework.'

Declan sat back. 'I like to know who I'm confiding in.'

'So, are you going to enlighten me with the story that so impressed my father, or have I come on a wild goose chase?' Peter challenged.

Declan looked at him appraisingly. 'I intend to recount what I told him all those years ago. I owe him that much. Then you can make up your own mind.'

Through the portholes, the sun blazed without mercy on the royal blue water as the yacht undulated gently.

Sophie remained silent, watching her father and Peter interact. He was in the dark as to whether she knew the story but she gave nothing away.

'You've heard fragments of this, Sophie, but never the whole story,' Declan said with a hint of regret.

'Then I need to hear everything,' she said.

Peter sensed an undercurrent between them on the subject, one affecting their relationship. He suspected it involved her mother and there were some ghosts to be laid to rest.

'In that case I'll tell you all I know,' Declan said. 'It's a long story, but an interesting one, from a unique period in British and Spanish history. And what the hell else have I got to do?' He paused for effect, then began in his compelling brogue, in a manner that made them want to huddle round and listen attentively.

Declan leant forward, his eyes almost the colour of the water outside. 'The story begins in 1762, almost 250 years after Ferdinand Magellan staked his claim on behalf of Spain to the islands among which we now sit. The islands from which the legendary Manila galleon trade emerged and flourished.

'The Seven Years War was in full flow, pitting the British against the French in their fight for control of the colonies and trading rights in North America and India, particularly Bengal, the richest province of the subcontinent. France was allied with Spain and, surprisingly, Austria, who'd switched sides in what became known as the "Reversal of Alliances". Britain, in turn, was allied with Portugal, Prussia and Hanover because King George, who was German, was on the throne. It was the first global war between the superpowers fighting for geopolitical superiority.

'In January 1762 the British formally declared war on Spain and planned an attack on Havana, Cuba, which gave a certain Colonel William Draper, the commanding officer of the British East India Company's 79th Regiment of the Foot, based in Madras, the idea of capturing Manila, the Spanish trading jewel and its Asian stronghold.'

Grinning, Declan said, 'What made his plan so attractive was his proposal for a joint army and naval operation spearheaded by the East India Company to be launched from India, which would be much quicker than sending a force from England, enabling a huge element of surprise.

'If the British could capture Manila, they would, they thought, in one fell swoop, secure the riches and wealth they assumed proliferated because of the galleon trade, simultaneously enhancing their strategic position in Asia, and complementing their trade with the Chinese Qing dynasty.

'So, in October 1762, ten ships of the line and two East Indiamen, with a combined force of 2,000 men, sailed into Manila Bay, led by Rear Admiral Samuel Cornish and Brigadier-General William Draper, whose rank had been elevated for the occasion, in an unprecedented collaboration between the British military and navy, for once working in perfect synchronisation.

'Now, fortuitously for them, Manila was under the temporary governorship of Mexican-born Archbishop Manuel Rojo del Rio y Vieyra who, as a man of the cloth, believed in the wrath of God, but was no military tactician. And it was this, more than any other factor, that played perfectly into British hands.

'The Spanish rallied as best they could, harnessing a significant local force to defend Manila and the nearby port of Cavite, where they constructed and launched their infamous galleons. However, after fierce fighting, the British successfully captured Manila, a remarkable achievement, in the same year capturing Havana, Martinique, St Lucia and Grenada.'

Peter said, 'I had no idea about this episode.'

Declan smiled and shook his head. 'Not many people do. It's a part of history usually skipped over, but a fascinating one nonetheless. Anyway, leaving nothing to chance,' he continued, 'the East India Company sent a man called Dawson Drake on an Indiaman called the *Essex*, who was installed as governor with a full complement of civil servants.

'Now, there are two important things to understand.' Declan looked at Peter and Sophie in turn. 'Firstly, the treasury was depleted: the cupboard was bare. The rumours of riches in Manila were a fallacy, although the galleon trade itself was lucrative for those who invested in it, which I'll come to.

'Secondly, because of the time it took for news to travel by ship, the British occupied Manila for eighteen months, until April 1764, even though the Seven Years War had formally ended with the Treaty of Paris in February 1763.' He grinned. 'Back in Europe they were unaware the British had captured the city.

'As there were no riches in Manila, the British focused on tracking down galleons, and how the galleon trade operated is important to the story. It comprised of two legs: an outward trip from Acapulco, in New Spain – present-day Mexico – across the Pacific to Manila of galleons laden with silver from mines in Potosí, Peru, which was used to pay for exotic goods and help ensure the colony functioned effectively.

'And the return leg, when Manila galleons sailed back from Manila to Acapulco, laden with Oriental treasures, silks, porcelain, spices, and a plethora of valuables, some on the official manifest and a substantial portion not, smuggled by corrupt officials and passengers.'

Sophie smiled. 'So, our treasure was on a galleon?'

Declan held up his forefinger. 'Bear with me, girl, I'll get to that.'

Sophie nodded and kept silent.

Declan continued. 'At the same time as all this, the Honourable British East India Company, or "John Company" as it was known, was operating autonomously from its strongholds in Calcutta, Madras and Bombay, its senior management, the eighteenth-century equivalent of the PLC board of a modern-day multinational.

'Since its formation by royal charter in 1601, it had accumulated huge wealth for its shareholders and senior officials, with its own army and navy, and its fleets of East Indiamen ships that ploughed the seas laden with silks, cotton, tea, spices and bullion.'

Swivelling his chair, Declan pointed at an antique map on the cabin wall. 'These magnificent ships sailed two primary routes: one between England and India, around the Cape of Good Hope; the other from India up to China, via the Strait of Malacca, up through the Dutch East Indies and past the Philippines to various Chinese entrepôts.

'Now of direct relevance to our story was Robert Clive's, aka Clive of India's, victory at the Battle of Plassey in 1757, when he beat the French and overthrew the Nawab.'

'Who was the Nawab?' asked Peter, fascinated by the story.

'The Moghul's representative,' said Declan. 'A very important, powerful, rich and influential man, whose defeat was significant because it enabled the British to gain control of Bengal, India's richest province, and its phenomenally wealthy treasury.

'As a result, senior officials of the so-called "Honourable Company", amassed vast personal fortunes through bribery, theft and extortion that took place on an unprecedented scale. Priceless treasures were plundered from the Nawab, wealthy merchants and Indian middle men, and most of this treasure found its way back to England, funding the purchase of country estates, political favour and titles to enable a life of luxury upon retirement. And no one did this more flamboyantly than the infamous Clive.'

As if trying to gauge their attentiveness, Declan said, 'I hope I'm not boring you, but all this is directly relevant to understanding the story.'

Peter shook his head. 'Not at all. It's fascinating'. And he meant it; he knew little about this period in history that had brought the infamous British East India Company into direct contact with the Spanish Philippines. He could only speculate where the story was heading, given the colourful cast of characters and historical backdrop, and now understood why his father had been so captivated by it, as he pictured Declan recounting the tale all those years ago, in his compelling Irish brogue, while the typhoon had battered them in the channel.

Declan looked at Sophie. 'What about you, girl?'

Sophie smiled. 'I'm listening. So far it's an interesting history lesson. Rest assured, I'll interrupt you if I want to,' she added.

Peter thought she must be used to Declan's stories, how he constructed them carefully, as if painting a large canvas so that as the picture emerged there was a real understanding of the full context.

'I'll keep going then,' he said. 'It's many years since I recounted it, so bear with me if I have to backtrack slightly.'

They nodded, keen for him to continue.

'Now on the *Essex*,' Declan said, 'which was the Indiaman carrying Dawson Drake and his small civil service, was a young naval officer, one Lieutenant Robert James Sinclair. Having only recently arrived in India, he'd been drafted into this enterprise at the eleventh hour to act as liaison with the local Spanish population because he spoke Spanish.

'He quickly established himself as a unique asset, interacting, placating and befriending the small group of wealthy Spanish families, who had effectively become prisoners in their homes, cut off from the outside world.'

'What was the population back then?' asked Sophie.

'Around two thousand,' said Declan. 'The majority a supporting cast of Chinese merchants and middlemen, some Japanese, and of course the locals.

'Now, going back to Sinclair – in addition to his liaison duties, he was secretly charged by Rear Admiral Cornish to find out through networking with these wealthy families any intelligence he could about galleons that might have sailed from Manila or be expected in from Acapulco, as well as secret locations where valuable cargoes might have been cached, in light of the fighting.

'In this capacity, and with his ear to the ground, Sinclair picked up rumours about the Vásquez family and decided to see what he could find out.'

Shifting to get more comfortable, and clearly in the groove, Declan said, 'And so it came to pass that Lieutenant Robert James Sinclair, of the Honourable British East India Company, met Condesa Isabella Martínez de la Cruz, a beautiful Spanish countess, recently arrived in Manila to consummate her betrothal to one Pedro Romero Vásquez, a wealthy merchant. A marriage of convenience, if you will, between two wealthy families to unite them in Las Islas Filipinas and New and Old Spain, and to cement a lucrative partnership for further mutual enrichment.'

Declan smiled conspiratorially. 'Señors Vásquez, senior and junior, were instrumental in forming consortiums to fund the galleon trade. Their investors included wealthy merchants, government officials and members of the Catholic Church, who loved a gamble and had their finger in every pie imaginable where profit and vice were concerned.

'Now, as you might imagine, there were rigid guidelines laid down by the Casa de Contratación – the House of Trade – set up by Queen Isabella of Spain in 1503, which governed the maximum load that could be transported on a galleon as part of the official manifest, specifying individual allowances for passengers. Supposedly fully transparent, and overseen by the Governor himself and his appointed captain and senior officers, therein lay both the problem – and opportunity.

'When a fully-laden galleon arrived in Acapulco after its long voyage from Manila, effectively two things happened: the sale of the official cargo on behalf of investors, after payment of customs duties and the King's Fifth, a 20 per cent tax levied by the King of Spain; and most pertinently, the sale on the black market of the unofficial smuggled cargo.

'Now, what made the Señors Vásquez unique was that as well as being masters of working the system they had a USP, specialising in the construction of bespoke travelling pieces of all sizes, shapes and designs, encompassing chests, writing boxes, bureaus and cabinets, each with an infinite variety of secret compartments used to smuggle precious, high-value commodities into New Spain.

'Their clients comprised wealthy noblemen, members of the Church, military officers, government officials, up to and including the Governor, with demand consistently high. Everyone was at it. If you think a galleon could accommodate hundreds of people, the scale of the enterprise is more easily visualised.'

Intrigued, Peter and Sophie remained quiet, seeing no reason to interrupt Declan as he recounted the fascinating story.

Declan said, 'The key to the Vásquez's success was twofold: firstly, their close relationship with a Chinese family of skilled master craftsmen who constructed these bespoke items from a wide variety of exotic Philippine hardwoods; and secondly, the Condesa's family in New Spain, who fenced the smuggled valuables through their network of wealthy aristocrats in Acapulco, Mexico City, Veracruz and Lima, selling at maximum profit, and splitting the proceeds.'

Caught up in the telling of the story, Declan appeared transported back in time, his eyes taking on a faraway look.

'When Robert Sinclair met Isabella Martínez de la Cruz, it was love at first sight. She was dark-skinned with jet-black hair and almond eyes, belying her Andalucian heritage. He was tall, athletic and blond, with blue eyes and a winning smile.'

Thinking that Declan was really embellishing now, Peter interjected, 'Excuse me for interrupting, Mr O'Connor, but there's an obvious question: How do you know all this?'

Grinning, Sophie looked quizzically at her father.

'Please, call me Declan. And I'll call you Peter, if that's all right?'

'It's fine.'

'Through a diary I discovered about a year before I told your father the story.'

'Where?' asked Sophie.

Declan held up his forefinger. 'I'm coming to that.' He looked at Peter. 'As you may or may not know, I run a successful antiques business, trading ethnic, tribal and colonial artefacts sourced around the Philippines, many of which are sold internationally to collectors and aficionados. Although my focus is these islands, I also trade items from further afield, especially Mexico, Spain and South East Asia, from a reliable network of contacts I've developed over the years.

'As well as placing pieces through dealers and intermediaries in Hong Kong, Mumbai, London, Paris and New York, I deal directly with certain individuals.' He smiled proudly. 'In this regard I have wealthy clients searching for specific artefacts or historical pieces, who have, if you will, a wish list. And it was while sourcing for one of these that this whole story came to light.'

Declan had clearly lost none of his story-telling skills, knowing when to pause for maximum effect, emphasise a word or sentence, or switch tack to retain interest. Peter didn't think he'd been lying when he said he used to blend fact with fiction; the skill, from a listener's perspective, was to distinguish one from the other. But he felt confident what Declan had recounted so far was true, albeit told in a romantic, flamboyant manner. The scene had been set, the actors skilfully introduced, with the nub of the story still tantalisingly out of sight, leading the listener to second-guess where this was heading; the possibilities were enticing.

Continuing with no change in enthusiasm, Declan said, 'There's always good demand from dealers and collectors for quality bespoke wooden pieces – preferably with some romantic provenance – and if there's a mere suggestion of a secret that comes with them, that's nirvana. To this effect I had scouts looking for pieces that would fit the bill.

'As you might expect, they often turned up in unusual places – around the islands, as well as further afield. Some passed down from one generation to another, some were looted; others stashed in an attic or cellar or used as a seat or storage container by some local tribesman in the back of beyond, or gathering dust in some outhouse, shat on by chickens and bats.'

He paused. 'However, this whole story emanates from a particular piece a contact of mine came across in a convent outside Mexico City. Many antique items from the colonial period found their way back to New and Old Spain, and I'm always on the lookout for fine pieces I can place easily or that fit a client's wish list, convents and monasteries being fruitful hunting grounds.

'The piece in question was an exquisitely made eighteenth-century writing box of unique design. Constructed from two rare tropical hardwoods, native to the Philippines, it had an original silver plate lock and intricate silver mounts. When I saw photographs, I knew I had to have it. It was a rare find, which I was confident I could turn for a healthy profit, despite having to pay a hefty price.

'It was delivered to my restoration workshop and retail store, which I'd set up a few years earlier in the old city of Intramuros.' Looking somewhat embarrassed, Declan said, 'It's become a popular tourist destination since, selling tribal art and figurines, which suits my purpose.

'When I first set eyes on the box I was very excited. It was in good condition, exceptionally well designed and constructed with the best materials of the day. However, it needed some minor restoration before it could be sold. I identified it as being mid to late eighteenth century, undoubtedly made by Chinese master craftsmen in Manila, who were renowned in those days for this style of writing box. It was a sought-after collector's piece, one I could perhaps jazz up some interesting provenance around to increase the price. But, as it happened, I didn't need to. The provenance lay within, found by accident. And it was from this the story first came to light.'

Declan leant back in his seat, massaging his legs to keep the circulation going. 'We knew a lot about these types of boxes. How they'd been cleverly designed with secret compartments to confound even the most knowledgeable back in the day. Whilst it was being restored, we found a false bottom containing a diary in remarkably good condition, beautifully handwritten in Spanish, in brown ink on old parchment. Fortuitously I'd studied Spanish as a young man in Salamanca, and as I sat down and started reading it, I quickly realised I'd inadvertently stumbled across one hell of a story – if it was true. The kind dreams are made of.'

He looked at Sophie and Peter, who were captivated by the story and his contagious enthusiasm. 'It was a story that got my heart pumping as I digested what was written within those pages, the excitement of which I can feel even now as I talk about it all these years later.'

Declan had come to life, as if visualising his younger self reading the words written centuries earlier.

He said, 'It was the diary of Condesa Isabella Martínez de la Cruz setting out the whole story from start to finish in a compelling, emotional, first-hand account.'

Sophie said, 'You mean from when she first met Robert Sinclair?'

'That's right. It's a comprehensive account of everything that happened from then on.'

The sun had begun its slow descent and darkness wasn't far off. Declan had covered a lot of ground but by no means got to the heart of the matter.

'Where's the diary now?' asked Sophie.

'In the writing box, hidden safely in the shop,' Declan said wearily, evidently tiring.

This wasn't a story to be rushed, despite his enthusiasm. 'I think we should take a break,' Sophie said gently.

Silhouetted in the half-light, Declan said with a hint of frustration, 'I need to finish the story. So you understand it in its full context.'

Sophie gently placed a hand on his shoulder. 'Let's take a break and freshen up and you can continue on the island. We're tired, too. It's been one hell of a day.'

After a short silence, Declan said, 'Perhaps that's a good idea. A rest would do me good and benefit the telling of the remainder of the story. It's a long one and I want to tell it properly. I'm sorry, I know you've both had a difficult day.'

Sophie gave Peter a look, which he immediately understood.

They stood up and headed up to the stern, climbing into the small rib and motoring the short distance to the island, where they headed to the clubhouse.

Ramón, the substitute diver, was in a group with the resident dive instructors, planning the following day's itinerary as they approached. He recognised the tall European man and the attractive blonde he'd seen earlier when the injured man had been stretchered off a banca for medical attention. He'd seen them take the rib over to the sloop, wondering who they'd been to meet, and whether it was the man whose photograph he'd been shown. He had to get on that yacht. Something important was in play.

# CHAPTER 10

## *Bambam*

Sophie went to check on the Italian, who was being carefully monitored. The details of the diving accident had been kept under wraps, to avoid any panic. He'd be transported to the mainland the following morning. She then went to confer with the instructors over the dive agenda to ensure the various abilities of guests had been properly taken into account, before checking over arrivals, departures and various administrative tasks with Gabe.

Meanwhile, Peter went to his cabin and relaxed in the hammock, reading and reflecting on the story so far, trying to second-guess the conclusion. After freshening up, he headed to the pool around 7.30pm, where he saw Sophie chatting to some guests, so he sat at Declan's private table on the far side of the pool.

Gabe appeared shortly with a cold San Mig, which Peter sipped appreciatively as he soaked up the chilled atmosphere.

Before long, Sophie joined him, looking visibly refreshed. Her hair was down, and she wore a light-blue Indian cotton dress, projecting boho chic without effort.

Gabe brought her a beer and Peter raised his glass. 'Cheers.'

'Cheers,' she replied and they clinked bottles. 'These are well deserved. You did an amazing job this morning. If it wasn't for you, that man would be dead.'

'It was a team effort,' Peter said modestly, then cocking an eyebrow: 'You said you'd never heard the whole story before, which means you've heard part of it?'

'Just snippets over the years. Dad's always been interested in treasure ships, like your father, and successfully located the remains of two galleons, one in the Bernardino straits, the other up near Micronesia.' She paused, as though choosing her words carefully. 'But this story's been with him a long time, both as an obsession and somewhat of a curse.'

'Can you elaborate?'

'I think he should tell you himself.'

Peter changed tack. 'That's a beautiful emerald cross. Is it from one of the galleons?'

'Yes. Dad gave it to Mum,' Sophie said, twirling it between thumb and forefinger. Peter was about to ask what happened to her when Declan made his way over to join them.

Peter gave a wry smile. 'You know what the treasure is, don't you?'

Sophie just smiled as Declan took a seat. Gabe arrived with a bottle of Don Papa, three tumblers and an ice bucket, and poured a large measure on the rocks for Declan, then left them to it.

Looking refreshed and alert, Declan took an appreciative slug. 'Well, I've covered a lot of ground, but it's time to come to the heart of the matter.' He looked at Peter. 'Do you have any idea what the treasure is?'

'Before Dad died, he uttered a word that sounded like "Mo". I'm guessing it's Moghul treasure stolen by the East India Company.'

'Well, you're on the money, son.' Declan grinned, slamming his fist on the table. 'If the Condesa's story is true, our treasure's a priceless Indian diamond. Allow me to elaborate.'

Leaning in, he lowered his voice as if to gain their confidence, conscious of the guests sitting along the poolside. 'There are a number of famous Indian diamonds which are priceless, not just because of their size and beauty, but because of the legends surrounding them on their convoluted journeys over hundreds of years.

'Like Greek myths, these legends have multiple contradictory versions, with holes that can be picked apart, and much speculation relating to long periods when they went missing, their whereabouts unknown, until mysteriously resurfacing decades later in another location, under different ownership.'

Swirling rum and ice in his tumbler, Declan said, 'The highest quality rough diamonds came from the Kollur Mine, in the Guntur district of Andhra Pradesh in south-east India.

'Many of the most famous diamonds in the world, including the Koh-i-Noor, the Orloff and the Daria-i-Noor, were cut from large rough diamonds, which were forensically assessed for flaws, inclusions, brilliance and how they caught and reflected light, so each could be cut to maximise colour, clarity and other attributes. Indian and Italian diamond cutters would then often cut multiple diamonds from the same larger rough stone, the Rose and Moghul cuts being most favoured back then.

'Their colour, in particular, made them highly sought after. For instance, the Koh-i-Noor in the British crown jewels is a large colourless white diamond, with a faint blue tinge, whilst the Daria-i-Noor in the Iranian crown jewels is a rare pale pink. The Orloff, in the imperial sceptre of the Russian crown jewels, has a greenish-blue hue, whilst the Hope Diamond, in the Smithsonian Museum, is a deep ocean blue.'

Sophie and Peter listened attentively as Declan continued. 'Some of these diamonds were passed down the line of Moghul emperors, but many fell into enemy hands, gifted and plundered in equal measure. Those that resurfaced, like the ones I've mentioned, now either sit in bank vaults or imperial jewellery collections, rarely seeing the light of day, or, conversely, are on show in museums with thousands of visitors filing past, captivated by the legends and myths that surround them.'

'What determines a diamond's colour?' asked Sophie.

'It's down to chemical composition and how it absorbs light,' replied Declan. 'Certain colours are much rarer and more coveted than others, blue diamonds being the most sought after of all, and accounting for less than 0.1 per cent of all diamonds. It's because they contain trace elements of boron, which absorbs red, orange and yellow light, that they have their unique colour.

'Now, although many of these legendary diamonds had unique attributes, because they disappeared for long periods, and, more often than not, were re-cut so their size and shape became different, their provenance is often questionable.'

Declan sat back and took another sip of rum. 'A good number of these stones were documented by a celebrated French nobleman in the seventeenth century, a man called Jean-Baptiste Tavernier, whose patron was Louis XIV. As a renowned buyer of diamonds, he travelled widely around India and was entertained at court by Moghul emperors, where he was shown some of the most talked about valuable diamonds of the day. And, luckily for us, he wrote about some of them and made detailed drawings, which he published in his renowned book, *Six Voyages*, in 1676.'

Declan lent in again, looking conspiratorial. 'Now Tavernier's directly relevant to our diamond because he's the first to mention its existence. In 1666, he purchased an exquisitely coloured 112-carat semi-cut blue diamond in Golconda, originating from the infamous Kollur Mine. It became known as the Tavernier Blue, and it's from this diamond that the Hope Diamond, now in the possession of the Smithsonian Museum, is supposed to have originated.'

Rumbling the ice bucket, Declan added several cubes to his tumbler and poured more Don Papa. 'When Tavernier was first shown what became known as the Tavernier Blue – *un beau violet* as he later referred to it – he was also shown a much larger semi-cut blue diamond, which he wanted more. However, despite countless generous offers, the Moghul emperor wouldn't part with it, so Tavernier had to settle for the smaller but nevertheless still magnificent diamond.'

'And so our diamond came from the semi-cut diamond he couldn't buy?' surmised Peter.

'That's right, son.'

Aware of the need to establish provenance, Peter said, 'I assume it was described by Tavernier in his *Six Voyages*?'

Declan nodded. 'Yes it was. I've a copy that makes fascinating reading. No wonder it was a bestseller back in the day. There's a brief description of the first time Tavernier saw the semi-cut stone, cross-referenced to a later trip to India where he was shown a rose-cut diamond, referred to as the Blue Moghul, which he estimated at two hundred carats. He wrote that he was sure from its colour and appearance it had been cut from the large semi-cut stone he'd been shown several years earlier.

'I quote: *A stone of such mythical beauty, encompassing the myriad blues of the ocean, its hues constantly changing in the light, like the ocean itself, with a magical quality, being of a size and purity unlikely to ever be seen again.'*

'Did he draw it?' asked Sophie.

Declan nodded. 'Yes, there are several drawings.'

'So what happened to it?' Sophie was clearly keen to get to the heart of the story.

'Its journey's not documented. There was speculation that, like the Great Table, Great Mogul, and Shah diamonds, it could have been stolen by the Persian ruler, Nadir Shah, in 1739, when he plundered the fabled Peacock Throne.

'It's believed the Koh-i-Noor, Daria-i-Noor and Orloff came from these larger famous diamonds when they reappeared years later, re-cut and smaller than their predecessors, though still magnificent. There's only Tavernier's descriptions to refer to. All we know from the Condesa's diary is that the Blue Moghul somehow came into the possession of the Nawab of Bengal, but she doesn't mention how.'

'What's the Hope worth?' asked Sophie.

'Conservatively, $350 million,' said Declan, poker-faced.

Sophie's eyes gleamed in the muted light. 'How many carats is it?'

'A mere forty-five, now.' Declan grinned as he sat back to let the impact of the statement sink in.

'So, the Blue Moghul's priceless,' said Peter, leaning back in his chair with his hands behind his head.

Declan nodded smugly. 'By far and away the largest blue diamond ever recorded. Without doubt one of the most valuable diamonds in the world.'

'Presumably it was stolen from the Nawab?' said Sophie.

Declan nodded. 'By a senior official of the East India Company no less, who colluded with the captain of an East Indiaman to smuggle it to England.'

Sophie looked perplexed. 'How the hell did the Condesa know all this?'

Declan grinned. 'This is where is gets interesting. After the first six months of British occupation in Manila, they found no more galleons or hidden cargoes after their initial capture of the *Filippina* and *Santísima Trinidad*. Sinclair was posted back to India and secured passage on an Indiaman that had stopped off at Manila on its way back from China to Madras.'

Sophie said, 'What was the ship's name?'.

'She doesn't mention one.'

Peter said, 'And the Blue Moghul was on this Indiaman?'

Declan nodded. 'Smuggled by the captain, no less.'

Sophie said, 'Which was shipwrecked?'

'That's right, girl. Hit a reef during a typhoon somewhere in the Western Philippines.'

'And Sinclair survived?' surmised Peter.

'According to the Condesa's diary there were four survivors: the captain, Sinclair and two crew members, who against the odds made their way ashore to a small island. The two crewmen drowned trying to leave the island a day later. However, Sinclair and the captain were rescued on the fourth day by local fishermen, and were taken to an island many leagues away where there was a Catholic mission and so they were looked after by a priest.

'It was there, as the captain lay dying in a delirious fever, that he told Sinclair about how the Blue Moghul had come into his possession and was being smuggled on his ship. Some time later, the priest helped Sinclair secure a passage on a Dutch trading vessel and he made the tortuous journey back to India, via Dutch Batavia.

'There he wrote to the Condesa, detailing what had happened, recounting the captain's story, with a rough map he hoped would enable him to find the location again, promising to return so they could try and locate the diamond and then elope.'

Declan clocked Sophie and Peter's expressions. 'I know what you're thinking, but bear with me, please. Being a Latin romantic, and wanting to commemorate their love, the Condesa commissioned the Chinese craftsmen who worked for the Vásquez family to construct two identical writing boxes that between them would reveal the location of the wrecked Indiaman. One she kept. The other she sent by ship to Sinclair with a reply to his letter.'

Declan threw his hands up in mock horror. 'But she never heard from him again. Pablo Vásquez broke off the engagement when he found out about her affair and she was exiled to New Spain. Ostracised by her family and condemned to live out the rest of her days in solitude, she wrote a full account of what had happened in her diary, which she hid in her writing box.'

'What happened to Sinclair's original letter and drawings?' asked Sophie.

'Vásquez burned everything in a rage when he found out about her affair.'

Declan leant in conspiratorially. 'This famous diamond, the Blue Moghul, is quite simply the one that got away. One of the largest, most valuable diamonds of all time, with a provenance, an illustrious history and a captivating name. And it's sitting somewhere on the ocean floor in the Philippine archipelago waiting to be located and returned to its former glory.'

He paused for breath as he looked at them. Silence. Peter remembered what Davilo had told him back in El Nido: that when Declan recounted one of his stories, you could hear a pin drop. Well, if one had dropped now you'd hear it all right. He wasn't sure if it was Declan's superb storytelling, the subject matter or the dramatic conclusion. It was one hell of a story. Could it be true? It seemed plausible. He wanted to believe it, and could see Sophie was equally captivated.

Peter said, 'So if this Blue Moghul actually exists, then its provenance could be verified by comparing it to the Hope?'

'That's right, son.' Declan gave a broad grin. 'The Hope's the largest deep blue diamond in the world: type IIb, rated VS1, which means it's slightly included with faint white graining. If it's subjected to UV light and allowed to rest, it emits red phosphorescence. If the story's true, then the Blue Moghul would have the same composition. Plus, there are Tavernier's drawings in his *Six Voyages* to refer to,' he added.

Sophie said, 'Where's the Condesa's diary now?'

'Securely hidden in my Manila store.'

Peter said, 'Who else knows about the story and the diary?'

'The three of us: me, Harry – God rest his soul – and Karl Johansson.'

'What happened to Johansson?' Peter clocked from the eye contact between Declan and Sophie that it wasn't a subject they liked to talk about, as he remembered the old photograph hanging in the clubhouse, with Johansson and the beautiful blonde at his feet.

'He went back to his native Sweden and took over the family timber business,' said Declan.

'And never expressed any interest in pursuing the story?'

'You need to tell him, Dad, it's important,' Sophie said.

'Was Sophie's mother Johansson's girlfriend or wife back then?' Peter asked perceptively.

'Ingrid was his fiancée,' Declan said sombrely.

'And you had an affair?'

'I fell in love the moment I set eyes on her. And she with me. We couldn't help ourselves,' he said, his eyes welling up. 'Karl didn't find out till he got back to Sweden and she called the whole thing off. Shortly afterwards, she came out here to live with me. A few years later, Sophie was born.'

Sophie put her hand on her father's shoulder. 'She was the love of my life,' Declan said, the pain of her memory etched on his face as he put his hand on Sophie's, suddenly looking much older than moments earlier when he'd been talking about diamonds and a historical romance.

'I'm guessing that wasn't the last time you heard from him?' Peter said, putting the pieces together quickly.

'No,' Declan said quietly. 'He vowed he'd get revenge. He never married and, like your father, went on to make a fortune, diversifying into shipping, logistics, fish farming and hydroelectricity.'

Sophie gave him a look. 'Tell him everything, Dad. Then it's all on the table.'

Declan nodded. 'Like Harry, Karl was captivated by the story I recounted that fateful night; after all, he too was an adventurer. We were birds of a feather. The following day, when the storm abated and the hangovers were wearing off, I tried to brush it off as a fanciful yarn, but neither would buy it. I could see it in their eyes. They were hooked. There was a suggestion we should work together and do something about it, but given what happened afterwards, we went our separate ways.

'I never spoke to Karl again after he returned to Sweden. But he sent me a letter, after Ingrid broke off the engagement, saying he could never forgive us for what we'd done; that we would always need to be looking over our shoulders, watching our backs, because one day revenge would be delivered.'

Peter said, 'Have you come across him since?'

Declan gave an imperceptible nod. 'I'm pretty sure he's made it his mission to try and locate the Indiaman. I know through my contacts he's been scouring auction rooms and dealers, like myself and Harry, to try and locate Sinclair's writing box. And one more thing,' Declan said, pausing briefly, 'he's the main shareholder of Global Salvage Inc.'

So that was it, thought Peter. Three men drunk on Bambam nearly forty years ago, during a raging typhoon, and a story of a treasure so compelling it would impact on all their lives and progeny. If Johansson was the primary backer of Global Salvage Inc., that spoke for itself. They were cut-throat, aggressive, and not a company you wanted on your back if there was the slightest whiff of finding anything of remote historical or financial value. Peter had come across them many times and none of his encounters had been pleasant, especially after he'd made it clear on numerous occasions he didn't want to work for them.

'Did my father know Johansson was looking for it all this time?'

'He knew Karl was captivated by the story, like him, and bound to pursue it. He was also aware of what happened between Karl and me and the threats Karl made. I don't know if he knew he was behind Global Salvage, though. We communicated for a short while afterwards but eventually lost contact.' He smiled fondly. 'Clearly Harry had the Midas touch when it came to business and before long was running an empire on a scale I don't think he could ever have foreseen.'

Peter reflected they'd each been successful in their own right. 'And what about you, Declan? Have you been looking for it all these years?'

'We've all been looking for the missing part of the jigsaw puzzle in the hope the Condesa's story, as set out in her diary, is true. If Sinclair's writing box could be found, then in conjunction with the Condesa's box it should reveal the location of the sunken Indiaman, enabling a search to be initiated.' He shrugged. 'But the likelihood is, it never will be.'

'Did my father and Johansson see the writing box and diary?'

'After what happened with Karl, I didn't share anything with him,' Declan said adamantly. 'He never saw what the box looked like, or the diary, though of course he knew about both from the story I told.' He paused reflectively. 'I've had several break-ins over the years at my Manila store and I'd bet my bottom dollar it's Karl and his henchmen. Your father knew more as I confided in him about the actual written content of the diary and the detail of the Condesa's writing box. And he knew what it looked like because I sent him a photograph.'

Peter said, 'Could I see the writing box and diary?'

Declan shrugged. 'I'd be happy to show them to you. They're in Manila. But they won't tell you where the wreck is. Sinclair's box is the key to that.'

'I'd still like to see them. When Dad died, he bequeathed me the contents of his study, which is where I found a letter from him that led me here. He must have had good reason to do that. I don't think he wanted me to come here just to hear you tell the story again. Knowing him, I think he wanted me to meet you face to face, hear the story first hand, make my own mind up, and put the pieces together.'

Looking at the son of his old friend, Declan slapped his knee decisively. 'Manila it is, then. We'll leave early on a rib. I was going to fly up tomorrow anyway as I've business to attend to.' He stood up and leant on his cane, looking at Sophie. 'Can you join us?'

She shook her head. 'I need to hold the fort. We're short-staffed. Two yachts and a dive group from Puerto Princesa are due in tomorrow. Chook had to leave suddenly because his mother's sick, but he found a replacement who I need to bring up to speed. You know the routine.'

Declan nodded. 'Okay. I'll go with Peter. We'll fly out first thing and be back the day after tomorrow. When we return, we can talk some more. But without Sinclair's box and its secret, I'm afraid there's not much we can do to locate the Indiaman.'

He looked at Peter. 'I'll arrange things with my pilot so we're all set for the morning.'

*

Henry answered the phone. 'How's it going down there?' His voice sounded unusually detached.

'It's a beautiful part of the world, Henry. A good change of scene from my normal routine. But I haven't come across anything to warrant asking you for more funding.'

'So, Mr O'Connor hasn't enlightened you on the potential whereabouts of any treasure, then?'

'He told me the same story he told Dad many years ago. It's a great story, but I'm not sure there's any mileage in it. What's the latest on the estate?' Peter asked, changing the subject.

'Your stepmother's champing at the bit. So, the sooner you can sort it the better.'

True to form, the bitch was on his case, thought Peter.

'I'll know within the next few days if there's anything worth pursuing. Either way, I'll fly back, deal with the study and wrap up whatever else needs sorting. I'll be in touch, Henry. Let me know if anything changes your end.'

'I will. Good luck then.' Henry's voice sounded unusually strained, as though Peter would need it. He made a mental note to check if Henry was all right when he returned. He was getting old. Perhaps the strain of Harry's passing and the legal spider's web he had to untangle, with his stepmother on his back, were getting to him.

# CHAPTER 11

## *Manila*

Declan and Peter flew into Manila airport in Declan's small Cessna, early Monday morning. They were greeted by his driver in a blue Toyota Land Cruiser, who drove them towards Intramuros, the oldest part of the city, where Declan's tribal arts and crafts and colonial antiques store was located.

It was a slow, tortuous drive through heavy traffic as garishly painted jeepney taxis crammed with people scurried here, there and everywhere – everything colourful and chaotic.

The abject poverty of Metro Manila, with over fourteen million people, hit you like the heat when you drove through it. Street kids worked the traffic, begging and selling worthless items, in stark contrast to the beauty and tranquillity of Bambam and the visual delights of the Bacuit.

Declan had been quiet during the flight and Peter had respected his privacy, admiring the magnificent landscape below them of tropical islands, azure waters and expanses of bone-white sand, emphasising the size of the archipelago and the distance of Bambam from the capital.

'How often do you fly here?' said Peter, breaking the silence.

Declan turned to face him. 'Depends on business. Usually a couple of times a month. Sometimes a client wants to discuss a wish list; other times I want to hand over a piece being collected by a wealthy customer. It's important I'm present as I get a lot of repeat business because I understand what my clients like and they know I'll deliver.'

He smiled. 'Sometimes my staff tell me of a rare piece that's made its way to the shop that piques my interest, and I just have to see it.'

'Do you have a house in Manila?'

'I used to. But it's easier to stay in a hotel now. I spend a lot of time on my yacht these days, which is where I feel most at home since my wife died.'

Peter wondered when he'd find out what had happened to her, but didn't know Declan well enough to ask.

As the four-wheel-drive stopped at traffic lights, two scruffy, half-naked kids, with lank black hair and pleading brown eyes pressed faces and hands to the car window, their hands cupped together, begging for money, mouthing inaudible words to the hushed silence within the jeep.

Declan hit the window button and thrust a wad of pesos into their hands, saying something in Tagalog, before sliding the window up again.

'Do you always do that?' asked Peter.

Declan shook his head. 'Hardly ever. The gangs work most of these kids and take the bulk of their pickings. Sadly, it's a way of life. That's the depressing side of these islands.'

Before long, the driver was weaving through the narrow streets of Intramuros, eventually arriving at a small section of renovated two-storey Spanish colonial townhouses. Stylish iron balconies protruded from long symmetrical windows, two per floor, testament to how well people had lived here back in the day.

On the furthest one there was a large carved wooden sign that read "Tribal Arts and Crafts" set over a broad rectangular entrance. Wide stone blocks ran halfway down each side, and a set of Spanish colonial-style, heavy brass-studded dark wooden doors were pinned back. Stone steps led up into the shop where two life-size wooden Ifugao tribal warriors stood sentinel either side of the entrance: one, a man with a spear and shield, the other, a woman holding a rice bowl.

The Land Cruiser stopped outside and Peter followed Declan inside. He surveyed the huge space with interest. It was a feast for the eyes, looking like a mix of an anthropological exhibition, a colonial antiques store, map shop and tribal arts and crafts centre. Buzzing with tourists, it was essentially a large split-level ground floor of several hundred square feet with a gallery running around the first floor.

Ethnic rugs covered polished hardwood floors amongst an array of chests, cabinets and boxes, and wooden tribal figurines from around the islands and ethnic knick-knacks filled every nook and cranny. It was the sort of place one could browse for hours, learning about the ethnic diversity of the 300,000 square-kilometre Philippine archipelago. Tribal masks, spears, axes, knives and colourful textiles covered the walls, one of which was dedicated to old photographs and antique maps of the archipelago and various island groups, with the Bacuit, Sulu islands and Visayas featuring prominently.

Peter thought that as well as being an Aladdin's cave of treasures at the hub of Declan's international colonial antiques business, it was clearly also a tourist magnet.

Leaning heavily on his cane for support, Declan greeted staff with a nod and a smile as he walked through the shop, stopping at the far end where he spoke briefly to an old Filipino, then unhooked a thick red cordon at the bottom of a well-worn wooden staircase and slowly made his way up the shallow steps. Peter followed him up to the gallery and into a large, comfortably furnished room off to one side.

Once upon a time, the spacious colonial room, which was in immaculate condition, would have been a drawing room, with its high ceilings and generous windows enabling natural daylight to flood in. Now, with its shutters pinned back and windows shut, an efficient air conditioning system maintained a comfortable temperature. Across the street, Peter could see identical buildings from the same period in various states of repair, collectively bringing back to life the story Declan had recounted.

He envisaged the Condesa in these lavish surroundings: servants buzzing around, the sound of horses' hooves and carriage wheels on the cobbles outside, the windows wide open to capture any hint of a breeze. It would have been in a room just like this that she and Robert Sinclair had first met. The perfect place for Declan's colonial antiques business. Peter had to admit the man had style.

There was a brief knock on the door as the elderly Filipino brought in coffee and biscuits. Declan thanked the man, and he left quietly after being instructed they shouldn't be disturbed. Declan then bolted the door and beckoned Peter to sit as he walked over to a large antique globe and, reaching beneath it, pressed a button which made the top half, the northern hemisphere, peel up and over until it was flush with the equator, like the soft top of a sports car, revealing a box about fourteen inches long, ten inches wide and eight inches high. He took the box and placed it on the table next to Peter, then sat down with a look of smugness, as if to say: *Now it's your turn, young Blake.*

Peter examined the exquisitely designed box with its intricate marquetry, constructed in a striking two-tone wood combination, one light, the other dark, with silver mounts, an elaborate silver lock and clasp on the front, inlaid with the initials I.M.C. clearly discernible on the top. His heart raced as he placed it in his lap, and carefully raised the lid to look inside. Unsurprisingly, it was empty.

Declan chuckled. 'What did you expect? The diary would just be sitting there?'

Peter shot him a look.

'I'm just testing you, son,' said Declan, grinning. 'You need to remember what I told you when I recounted the story.'

Recalling that the Vásquez family specialised in making bespoke items, Peter said, 'Well, obviously there's a trigger for the hidden compartment.'

Declan didn't proffer any assistance as Peter scrutinised the box from all angles, pressing various spots to see if there were any pressure points. However, try as he might, he couldn't find any and placed it back on the table.

'Okay, so it's hard to open,' he said. 'I'm impressed. But if someone knew the diary was in here, or suspected there might be something of interest, all they'd need to do is get a sledgehammer and smash it to pieces.'

'In theory you're right,' Declan conceded. 'Which is why I keep it well hidden.'

The ring of Declan's iPhone punctured the atmosphere; he fumbled in his pocket and extracted it. 'Hi, Sophie,' he said, clearly pleased to hear from her. However, within seconds his eyes turned hard blue steel, narrowing, as he listened intently. 'Don't do anything for now. Leave everything as it is. I know everything I have and where it should be. Get one of the boat boys to sleep on board till I get back. And don't involve the police. They're the first to get paid off.' He sounded stressed. 'We'll try and get back tonight. Otherwise, it'll be first thing in the morning. Put me onto Gabe now and take good care of yourself, you hear me, girl. I'll call you when I know when we can get back.' There was a pause then he gave Gabe various instructions, ending with: 'Guard Sophie with your life, Gabe, you hear me? We'll come back as soon as we can.'

Declan slammed the phone on the table. 'Son of a bitch!'

'Your yacht's been broken into?'

'That's right, which means one thing: you're being followed.'

'Only two people know I'm here, and I trust both of them,' Peter said in disbelief, thinking of Henry and Samantha.

Declan walked over to the window and looked out. 'That's what you think. I'm betting you've been tailed from the minute you arrived.'

'I haven't told anyone where I'm going or what I'm doing.'

'Someone thinks Harry found something and passed it to you after he died. That's the only explanation.' Declan's face was knotted in frustration. But what he said made sense.

'Well, if I was followed to the island we've probably been followed here, too.'

'Let's get the hell out of here and get this properly hidden.' As Declan walked over and picked up the box, there was a knock at the door. 'I said don't disturb us, Pablo!' he shouted.

'It's important, sir,' said the old Filipino.

Declan hastily walked to the globe, shoved the box inside, shut it, then went to unlock the door. As he slid the bolt, the door was violently pushed in, and suddenly Pablo was standing in the centre of the room with a sawn-off shot gun pressed to his head by one of two scrawny thugs covered in tattoos.

His partner-in-crime snap-kicked Declan in the stomach, so he sprawled across the floor, his cane flying towards Peter. The intruder then aimed his semi-automatic at Peter's head, smiling cruelly, like a nervous kid on crystal meth – or shabu as it was known locally.

'You give us box. One like this,' said the youth, holding up a photo.

'Let me look.' Declan tried to sit up, painfully clutching his stomach and gasping for breath. 'This is my shop, not his.'

The man with the shotgun pushed Pablo towards Peter, keeping it trained on both of them, while the other guy showed Declan the photo.

It was a close-up of the writing box he'd just shown Peter.

'It's not here,' Declan snarled. Peter could see he was gambling they'd have been told not to kill him unless they got what they wanted. He'd doubtless experienced equally distasteful situations over the years, especially when he was younger. However, there was no doubt in Peter's mind these guys were killers who would take someone out without a second thought if they felt the urge.

The man with the photo bent down and pistol-whipped Declan in the face.

'You fuck me, I kill you! No care!'

'I'm not fucking with you,' shouted Declan, wiping blood from his face with the back of his hand. 'I can't give you something I don't have. It's not here.'

Peter tensed every bone in his body, racking his brains for what he could do. But having a sawn-off shotgun pointed at him by a lunatic didn't give him many options. Although he was strong and quick, he wasn't a trained fighter. He would see if an opportunity presented itself.

Police sirens could now be heard in the distance, together with a serious commotion downstairs. The smaller, meaner-looking thug, with a crazed look in his eyes, aimed his pistol at Declan, then at Peter, grinning through crooked teeth, then back at Declan, before turning to Pablo whom he double-tapped in the head. The old Filipino crumpled to the wooden floor like a collapsed puppet.

'No box, no daughter,' said the youth, alternately pointing the handgun at Peter and Declan as he and his partner retreated backwards towards the door.

They exited quickly, firing off several rounds as they ran downstairs and made their way across the floor of the shop, sweeping the space with their semis, randomly shooting things up as they went. As they reached the stone steps to the road outside, one of the staff members, who'd taken cover behind a tea chest, hurled a bronze statue at the back of one of their heads. The man's legs folded as he dropped on the steps face down, while his accomplice catapulted himself into a blacked-out 4x4, hotfooting it away, wheels screeching, closely followed by a large SUV. The shop staff immobilised the fallen thug, tying his hands behind his back, dragging him inside the store where they trained his own gun on him until the police arrived.

Upstairs, Peter helped Declan prop himself against the desk and clean the blood off his face.

'I'm okay,' Declan insisted. 'I need to make sure Sophie's safe. They'll go after her and she's alone on that damn island.'

As they listened to the increasing noise of police sirens, Declan grabbed Peter, pulling him down to eye level, with a fierce determined look. 'We tell 'em nothing other than we got held up at gunpoint and they wanted money and merchandise, ya hear me?'

Peter nodded. 'Okay.'

'The police are in the pay of the criminal gangs and we don't know who our enemy is for sure. So, we'll sort this ourselves, right?'

'Sure,' confirmed Peter.

It was two hours later before they finished making statements at the central police station. Because Declan was well known, they let him go without endless questions. He'd told them he had no idea what this was about, except the store contained a lot of valuable merchandise. Crimes like this weren't unusual in this part of the world, so it wasn't viewed as anything out of the ordinary. The police confirmed the thug would be questioned at police headquarters, charged with murder and held in the notorious Bilibid Prison until trial. They promised they'd relay any relevant information they got out of him as to the motive behind the attack. Declan knew that the chances of the youth, who was undoubtedly a gang member, getting out of that prison alive were non-existent given he'd failed in his objective.

Declan's driver drove them to the airport as fast as he could in slow, tortuous traffic. Declan had phoned ahead so his plane was cleared for take-off, but when they arrived at the airport there was more bad news. A tropical cyclone with the potential to become a super typhoon had unexpectedly changed course and was now tracking west towards the Philippines from Micronesia, with a direct hit predicted on the archipelago in the next twenty-four hours.

Declan called Sophie's mobile.

No answer.

He tried the main line on the island.

Nothing.

It didn't bode well.

# CHAPTER 12

## *The Bacuit*

The sky overcast, the flight back to El Nido was tense, with significant turbulence, the sunshine and exotic vistas now history. Seriously concerned for Sophie, Peter hoped for all their sakes they'd get back to Bambam in time, given events were heading on a course that couldn't be prevented unless they had some luck on their side. Remembering the replacement diver Sophie had mentioned, his heart sank as he realised they'd been expertly played. They had to get to Bambam, whatever it took.

When they landed in El Nido, the weather had taken a turn for the worse. Their priority was to find someone willing to take them to the island as there was no resort rib to greet them. Boats of every description bobbed in the choppy water out in the bay and halyards rattled; if the typhoon was even half as bad as was being predicted, Peter knew many of these could be trashed in a couple of days.

As usual, money talked. They persuaded another cousin of Angel, the Filipina shop owner who knew Declan well, to take them out to the island. He had a medium-sized banca, with a decent engine and a rudimentary cabin to protect them from the elements.

They set off without delay, through choppy seas and heavy swells; the usual exotic blues, azures and greens were absent, the water now Baltic, with a grey hue. The outrigger was slower than a rib, but its age-old design made it sturdy and it sliced through the waves, making steady progress, passing islands and remote resorts hunkering down for the onslaught.

On the beaches, palm trees swayed heavily and the drop in air pressure was palpable; they knew this was going to be one hell of a storm. Peter thought Declan had no doubt witnessed many typhoons. He'd seen a good number himself, but never a direct hit. He shivered as he thought of the potential devastation it might inflict on the fragile resorts in the area and the shanty villages scattered throughout the islands.

Driving rain slanted relentlessly from the heavens, making visibility difficult as they ploughed through the rough seas. Fortunately, the boat owner and Declan knew these waters and their hidden hazards, enabling them to expertly navigate the archipelago when others would've had to turn back. They knew they were pushing it to be out in such conditions but had no choice. Making reasonable time, they came across little traffic other than some yachts heading for safety wherever they could find it, which might include Bambam if they knew about the hidden anchorage.

After what seemed like several hours, but in fact was only a fraction of that time, the faint outline of Bambam appeared on the horizon. They strained their eyes to get a better view, but it was impossible to make anything out clearly through driving rain.

Peter thought Declan must surely have felt as though he'd been transported back in time to when he'd been with Harry and Karl on the yacht charter all those years ago, looking for a safe place to ride out the storm, remembering how they'd found sanctuary in the channel just in time, when the story he'd told had started this whole thing.

Peter, too, thought about how it was that typhoon that was responsible for bringing them to the island and for Declan telling that fateful story, the reason he himself was here now under similar circumstances.

As they neared Bambam, Declan guided them through Home Reef, and the skipper dropped them on the beach as rain sheeted down and the sea churned with white horses. He then reversed the boat back out and headed for the protection of the channel, which Declan had pointed out on approach.

'Go and find Sophie!' Declan yelled at Peter. 'I'm okay.'

Peter legged it to the clubhouse where he found Gabe securing things, helping to batten down the hatches for the onslaught.

'Where's Sophie?' Peter shouted. 'We couldn't get through on the mobile or landline.'

Looking anxious, Gabe shouted back, 'She hasn't come back from the dive group that went out this morning, sir. Telephone not working. No mobile signal. Two-way radio not working, either.'

'Where are the others?'

'Securing everything, helping guests bring things here. It's the safest place when the storm hits.'

'Anyone got a short-wave radio?'

'The boss, I think.'

'You need to fetch it so we can find out what this typhoon's up to.'

'Yes, sir.'

Declan appeared in the doorway, looking bedraggled and every bit his age. His face was heavily cut, one eye black and puffy. Gabe rushed over, helping him to the rattan sofa, onto which he slumped, the strain of the past few hours showing.

'You hurt, sir. I get some help.'

'I'm okay. But a shot of rum wouldn't go amiss.'

Peter recounted what Gabe had told him.

Declan looked anxiously at Gabe. 'Who was in the dive group? Where did they go?'

A young couple, a single guest and Ramón, the dive instructor filling in for Chook. Miss Sophie wanted to check him out, sir.'

'No other instructors?' Near panic in Declan's voice.

'No, sir.'

'Where did they go?' Peter asked, looking at the dive board, knowing Declan had asked Gabe to guard Sophie with his life, but knowing how headstrong Sophie was.

'Manta Reef drop-off.' Gabe hesitated, then added, 'But maybe, because of the weather, somewhere different last minute.'

'Wouldn't they let you know if that was the case?'

'Usually, but the comms are down.'

'Did you move my yacht?' asked Declan.

Gabe nodded. 'Yes, sir. It's in the channel. One of the boat boys on board. Miss Sophie very strict about that.'

'Well, that's something.'

'I need your most powerful rib and a couple of strong divers,' said Peter.

Declan frowned. 'You think it's sensible to go out in this?'

'You got a better idea?'

Declan looked at Gabe. 'Get Marko and Jovy, fast as you can.' Then at Peter. 'You need to get going. This is going to be one hell of a hooley. We're in for a battering.'

Gabe ran to find the divers.

Warnings on the short-wave radio reported Typhoon Carolina heading on a south-westerly track across Luzon, the main island where Manila was located, towards the centre of the archipelago. They knew that even if they weren't in its direct path, it could wreak havoc.

Out at sea, they saw a yacht approaching, its lights shining dimly on the bow.

As Gabe came running back, Declan shouted, 'Any yachts in the channel, apart from mine?'

Gabe nodded, out of breath. 'Two that came in this morning, sir.'

'Help this yacht in there then,' Declan shouted.

Peter, who had changed into a wetsuit, joined Marko and Jovy as they came running down the boardwalk with their gear, heading to the end of the jetty where one of the boat boys had brought a rib alongside.

Declan stood drenched in the driving rain, his face contorted in anguish as he beckoned Peter over so he could hear him through the howling wind and rain, pulling him close.

'Sophie's a very special woman, Peter. She means the world to me. And she meant the world to her mother, God rest her soul. Do whatever you have to, you hear me. Whatever it takes!' he shouted.

Peter nodded, looking the old adventurer in the eyes, giving him the appropriate reassurance, gripping him firmly on the shoulder. He then turned and jumped into the rib. Marko steered the boat through Home Reef before powering full throttle towards Manta Reef. Peter noticed Jovy had stashed a couple of semi-automatics under the console and a couple of spear-fishing guns had been strapped to the side of the boat, out of harm's way.

'How far's this place?' he shouted.

'Twenty-five minutes at this speed,' shouted Marko as the rib smacked repeatedly on the choppy water.

Despite the exhilaration of being out in rough weather, they wore serious expressions.

Peter shouted, 'Did you talk with this Ramón guy?'

'We didn't get much chance,' shouted back Jovy. 'He only arrived yesterday. We saw him at the briefing last night. Then again first thing this morning.'

'He look like gang member,' shouted Marko, shaking his head grimly. 'Lots of tattoos he trying to hide.'

*Not too reassuring*, thought Peter. 'Have you heard anything from Chook?'

'Nothing since yesterday. Guess his mama's very sick.'

Peter shouted above the wind. 'Look, fellas, we don't know if this Ramón guy has done anything or not. So, if we get there and everything looks normal, we *act* like everything's normal and wait until we get back to rumble him. It may be there's a simple explanation for everything. But if that's not the case, and things are bad, then we'll need to immobilise him. Our priority's to keep Miss Sophie and the guests safe, even if he gets away, right?'

'Yes, boss,' they said in unison, willingly accepting Peter as leader and showing him total respect, having seen how he'd handled himself on the wreck dive and saved a man's life.

The rain eased a little, and visibility improved slightly, but the wind steadily increased in intensity. Everything was grey, not the paradise it usually looked in bright sunshine. Peter was now in professional mode, and having been in numerous life-and-death situations, above and below the ocean, was used to thinking clearly under pressure. He felt confident he had two good men with him from what he'd witnessed on the wreck dive.

The rain resumed in a steady driving sheet as they scanned the horizon, looking for a clue as to where the small outrigger might be.

'We're nearly there,' shouted Jovy as Marko angled the rib out from an island and headed into open water. Several minutes later, he eased the throttle, and slowed to a virtual stop.

'This is where we normally come,' Marko said, yet the sea was devoid of boats as far as they could see, other than their own rib rocking violently in the large swell.

'Well, if they were here, they're long gone,' said Peter. He looked at the two men intently. 'Where would you go, if the weather was turning and you wanted to do an enjoyable, quick, easy dive before heading home?'

They conferred in animated discussion, given there were countless dive sites they visited depending on weather conditions.

Jovy acted as spokesman: 'We think Mis Sophie would have taken them closer to home. To either Barracuda Bommie or Seahorse Reef. She always like those two best,' he said with a faithful smile.

'Let's go then,' said Peter, 'the closest first.'

Marko throttled up the engines and they headed back the way they'd come. About halfway back to Bambam, they veered westwards up towards Inambuyod Island. It looked sinister and menacing in the poor light and rain, in stark contrast to its exotic allure when the sun was shining and the weather was calm. Marko expertly navigated the rib through narrow channels, past coves and between reefs and shoals. The wind howled as palm trees fringing beaches flexed like rubber, whipping around at ninety degrees. If the weather deteriorated, they'd be in serious trouble. Jovy and Peter sat either side of the rib, hanging on tightly as it pounded the water, all of them aware of how much was at stake.

Fifteen minutes later they arrived at Barracuda Bommie, a

seamount rising from the depths, stopping about 7 metres short of the surface and a magnet for every part of the marine food chain because of the rich nutrients welling up around it from the deep. Again, there was nothing in sight except a couple of yachts on the horizon, presumably heading for safe anchorage. Peter feared the worst as they headed to Seahorse Reef.

Seahorse Reef was about 30 metres from the north-western shore of a small island near Matinloc, which had a long tropical beach backed by rows of neat palms bordering dense vegetation. As they approached the reef, Jovy yelled, pointing into the distance, way down the beach.

Marko grabbed his binoculars and got a quick fix. 'There are two people. A man and a woman,' he shouted.

'Okay, take us in, quick as you can!' yelled Peter.

As they got closer he made out two people waving frantically. Once in the shallows, he catapulted himself into the water and sprinted up the beach as a man and a women ran towards him, looking cold and in poor shape.

'Thank God you've come!' screamed the young woman, who looked in her early thirties. 'We were nearly killed! The man's a lunatic!' she screamed, tears streaming down her face, her body shaking.

'Where are the others?' asked Peter.

'They're gone!' she said, crumpling to the sand. The man, now standing next to her, had been badly beaten and had a huge gash on his left arm.

Peter looked at him. 'Was it the diving instructor, Ramón?'

He nodded.

'I need you to be calm and tell me exactly what happened so we can try and find them.'

'Dead!' screamed the woman, hysterically. 'Tom's dead. He'll kill her too ...'

Peter tried to calm her as Jovy came up to join them. 'Is Tom your partner?'

'He's my husband,' she blurted. 'But he's gone. Our ... honeymoon

... nightmare ...' She sobbed uncontrollably as she collapsed at Peter's feet.

Peter gave Jovy a look, and the instructor knelt to help her.

The man he'd mistakenly thought was her partner was shaking with cold, bedraggled, but still in control. As Jovy led the woman up the beach to find some shelter, Peter asked the man, 'Is that a knife wound?'

'Yeah, the guy slashed me when I went for him.'

'Looks nasty. We'll get you patched up. Can you give me the real short version of what happened, so we can go look for Sophie?'

The man got the message and didn't pad it out: 'We were preparing for our second dive, when Annabel's' husband, Tom, caught this Ramón guy, real nasty-looking character, messing with the equipment. He challenged him and the guy lost his temper. Sophie intervened. Ramón took Tom by the throat, stabbed him several times, then pushed him overboard. I tried to grab him. That's when he slashed me and produced a semi-automatic, firing shots into the air, telling us to back off, then made us jump overboard. The outrigger then headed out to sea. It all happened so quickly.'

'Where and when did it happen?' Peter shouted, his voice trailing into the howling wind.

'About half a kilometre further down,' the man shouted back, pointing with his good arm, 'about 60 metres out on Seahorse Reef. Annabel and I just swam for it. I was pretty concerned. I was bleeding heavily and there'd been a lot of shark activity earlier. I've lost track of time. Probably about four hours ago. We knew the comms were down but thought under the circumstances you'd guess where we'd gone.'

'Which direction did they head off in?'

The man pointed towards Barracuda Bommie.

'Anything else I should know?'

'Once we made shore, I saw them disappear around that far island. The only thing I saw, not long afterwards, was a big 1950s-looking motor yacht coming in the opposite direction.'

They helped the man and woman into the rib and within thirty minutes they disembarked at Bambam, where staff tended to the injured guests as best they could. Everyone was now holed up on the island until the typhoon passed, and the murder would be reported as soon as the phones started working again.

Declan looked despondent and withdrawn as Gabe handed Peter a tumbler of rum, which he downed in one go, its warmth flowing through him.

'I'm sure they won't harm Sophie,' Peter said, trying to remain upbeat. 'Otherwise, there's no chance of them getting the box.'

Declan just stared ahead, looking daggers.

They heard on the short-wave radio that the typhoon was now on track for a direct hit on Luzon and the Visayas, upgraded to a Category 5 super-typhoon, a real monster, with a scheduled arrival of the early hours of the following day.

They had no option but to hunker down and ride it out.

Peter described the yacht that he and the other man had seen, sure it was connected to Sophie's disappearance.

'It's got to be Karl,' Declan snarled. 'He's on a mission to take everything precious from me. I'll kill him if he so much as lays a finger on her.'

'Can you tap your contacts for a list of motor yachts cruising the islands? There must be some record of who's in these waters,' said Peter, doing his best to calm Declan and stay rational.

'I can try,' Declan said in a monotone, his Irish charm unusually absent.

'If they've taken Sophie, it's logical they'll make contact and want to trade her for the box,' said Peter. 'After the typhoon passes and the weather improves, we can use your plane to locate the yacht.'

Declan looked at him blankly, clearly not giving a fuck about the diamond, only Sophie. She was the only thing that mattered, and Peter knew he'd do everything in his power to get her back, by whatever means.

As night fell and the storm unleased its full fury, staff and guests hunkered down in the communal area and prepared for a long haul until the full force of the typhoon passed. For the majority it was a bonding experience despite the severity of the onslaught, with bonhomie and laughter, joke telling, and card and board games, helped by a makeshift, but well-stocked bar. Adverse situations always brought people together.

However, for Declan and Peter it was an interminable night, with only their imaginations to fuel their anguish.

As predicted, Typhoon Carolina swept its destructive path through Luzon, skirting Metro Manila before rampaging devastatingly across the Visayas islands, in the centre of the archipelago, and tracking southwards towards the Sulu islands.

It was a long, wild night and following morning, until late the following afternoon the wind dropped, the rain petered out and an eerie calm descended on the island. The communal area had taken a severe battering but it had held its own, a tribute to its design to be able to withstand such an onslaught, although luckily they hadn't been directly hit.

Much of the guest accommodation on the island had been severely damaged and would need substantial repair or rebuilding. Amazingly, the yachts holed up in the channel were largely unscathed, the towering cliffs either side having enveloped them in their protective embrace.

Typhoon Carolina went down as one of the most destructive in the country's history, with wind speeds up to 220 kilometres per hour, making landfall multiple times as it swept through the archipelago before heading up the South China Sea to Vietnam, where it was downgraded to a severe tropical storm. Hardest hit was the Visayas archipelago, in the Central Philippines, with hundreds of people killed or rendered homeless.

But the Filipinos were a resilient race, used to picking themselves up and starting over, as their forefathers had done for millennia: after all, not many countries in the world experienced volcanic eruptions, earthquakes and typhoons on such a regular basis as these disparate islanders because of their unique geographical location.

*

Sophie was sinking. Down a vertical drop-off, into the dark depths below. Feet first. The other divers were now far above, silhouetted against the faint light from the ocean's surface. Drifting slowly down. Arms and legs spread out like a star. When she inhaled from her regulator nothing came out – she'd run out of air. It would be a horrible death. A giant squid lunged out of the darkness to grab her. She tried to scream. Nothing came out. It missed her the first time, sank back down, then propelled itself up towards her again, tentacles open wide, sharp beak angling in like a surgeon's scalpel. She felt excruciating pain as it grabbed her leg, slicing it open, shaking her violently, as hundreds of other squid appeared from below, rising towards her. As it dragged her down, Sophie jolted awake, realising it was a nightmare. Her blurred vision fought for control as a large, ugly, pockmarked face grinned down at her: the face of a giant turtle. At first she couldn't hear anything, but gradually she made out some words:

'... nice rest ... darling ...'

The huge man effortlessly pulled her upright into a sitting position on the narrow bed. Although her vision was swimming, Sophie instinctively knew she was on the lower deck of a yacht, in crew quarters.

'There's food and water in the corner,' said the man with a strong South African accent. 'I'm going to untie you. I suggest you eat and drink. We'll come and see you later. We've a lot to talk about, you and I.' There was real menace in his voice and demeanour.

Not having the energy to speak, Sophie nodded. Turtle Face untied her hands then left the cabin, smirking, locking the door behind him. She swung her feet onto the floor and rubbed her eyes; all she could see through the porthole was blue ocean.

Slowly, what had happened at Seahorse Reef came back to her as she remembered the typhoon tracking in. But she had no idea how long she'd been there. Her head hurt. She must have been drugged.

The typhoon had clearly passed, if it hadn't changed course at the last minute, and the yacht was moving at a steady pace. She drank some water and ate some watermelon. The water alone made her feel better. As her mind cleared, she remembered the whole sequence of events over the past few days, and realised she must have been kidnapped because of the diamond.

She cursed herself for taking the young divers out alone with Ramón. She hadn't liked the bastard from the outset and should have trusted her instincts. Because they'd been short staffed, she'd made an error of judgement which had cost a man his life.

But she was her father's daughter: tough, resourceful and determined, and she wouldn't be held without a fight. As she wondered who the yacht belonged to, various scenarios played out in her imagination, all of them dominated by the image of her mother's agonised face, sinking into the depths.

# CHAPTER 13

## *Bambam*

S taff helped guests to make contact with family and friends. There wouldn't be any diving for the foreseeable future, so they made plans to return home, which was a challenge in itself.

Declan had tapped his contacts in the marine world – including the Philippine Navy – to try and locate any large motor yachts cruising the islands that fit the description of the one they'd seen, and was awaiting a response, now the internet and phones were working again.

While he was talking to Peter, Gabe walked over, handing him a phone.

'Hello,' said Declan, looking anxious.

'O'Connor?' – a strong South African accent.

'That's me.'

'It'd be a shame to lose your daughter as well as your wife, don't you think?'

A drawn-out pause.

Peter could see from Declan's face it was the call they'd been both dreading and hoping for.

Clenching the phone, Declan's eyes narrowed. 'Tell me what you want and I'll get it to you. On the condition my daughter's unharmed and released.'

'She's a very pretty woman,' said the taunting voice. 'Not my usual type, but I'm prepared to make an exception. Those blue eyes, blonde hair, and long, long legs –'

'Tell me what you want,' Declan said through clenched teeth, working hard to retain control, otherwise he'd play into the bastard's hands. Peter stood next to him speculating how this was going to work out, wondering where Sophie was being held and what sort of state she'd be in. From what he'd seen, she was mentally strong, but these sorts of experiences affected people differently.

Declan listened carefully to the tiresome voice. 'You've two items a colleague of mine believes are rightfully his,' he said. 'All you have to do is give them to us. It's really that simple.'

'I want proof of life before negotiating anything. Let me speak to my daughter.'

'This isn't a negotiation, Mr O'Connor.'

'I've told you what I want.' Declan's voice was steely.

'A piece of free advice, Mr O'Connor. I wouldn't gamble your daughter's life if I were you. I suggest you get both boxes ready to hand over. We'll be in touch with instructions regarding how and where.'

The line went dead.

Declan turned to Peter. 'They think Harry found the other box and you brought it here.'

'Well, you know, I think he might have done,' Peter said, to Declan's obvious astonishment. 'I mean, why else would he have left me the contents of his study and a letter that sent me out here?'

'You think he found Sinclair's box and it's in his study?'

'It's possible,' said Peter. 'It's full of antiques and there are lots of boxes, some similar to the one you showed me.'

Declan seemed to have found a new lease of life, his mission to get Sophie back as quickly as possible. 'Well, if Harry did find it, they don't know that,' he said. 'They're just speculating because you're here. Someone in Perth must have put them onto you.'

Peter had thought the same thing, but had no idea who it could be. He would have to fly back to Perth and try to find the box. But first they had to formulate a plan, given Declan only had the Condesa's box and the clock was ticking.

'Any feedback on yachts cruising the islands?' Peter asked.

Declan checked the laptop on the reception desk, then turned it to face Peter. 'Something's just come through, but it's a long list,' he said.

Peter pulled up a stool, sat and starting scrolling through. It was a lot more comprehensive than he'd anticipated. Declan must have some well-placed contacts, given the quick response and how he'd dealt with the police in Manila after the assault.

'We can whittle these down pretty quickly,' Peter said encouragingly, 'by eliminating those too far away at the time Sophie was taken, looking at their last known positions and the type of vessels. Some are too small, others too big or modern. The yacht I saw was very distinctive, a real throwback to the fifties.'

After looking through the list and googling various images, they were left with a handful that potentially fit the bill, eventually settling on one called the *Griffin*, registered in Hong Kong.

Studying the image Peter was sure it was the same vessel he'd seen going out to the wreck dive, so he went to locate the diver they'd rescued from the beach, who confirmed it certainly looked like the one he'd seen, but in his state of panic couldn't be sure.

The ship in question was a British Navy World War Two minesweeper, similar in design to Jacques Cousteau's legendary *Calypso* that had been converted into a luxury yacht by a French tycoon. It was 40 metres long and could accommodate twelve guests in style, plus crew. With its white hull and bridge, and teak deck, it had the stylish appearance of a 1950's motor yacht befitting the likes of Grace Kelly.

Peter said, 'Have you seen it before?'

Declan nodded. 'Yes, but never paid much attention to it, other than admiring its style.'

'Once the weather settles we can take your plane up ...'

The phone rang. Declan swiped it. 'Dad, it's Sophie, I—'

A pause, then, 'She's alive and well, O'Connor, so listen carefully.' The tiresome South African again.

'I've only got one writing box,' Declan said, 'and it's in Manila. I've no idea where the other one is. That's what we've been searching for all these years. To my knowledge it hasn't been found.'

'Oh, I think you do, Mr O'Connor. I think your old friend Harry Blake found it and his son brought it with him or has shown you what was in it.'

'I can only give you the box I have. It's in Manila, so I need time to get there and retrieve it. The typhoon's caused a lot of damage. I've no idea if the airport's operational or whether that's even possible.'

'It's 5pm. You've got twenty-four hours. Make sure your mobile phone's charged and you have a full signal when you get to Manila. It would be a shame to miss our call. And don't do anything stupid, like call the police. The clock's ticking.'

The line went dead. Declan's expression suggested he'd just made a mental note to rip the man's head off given half a chance. He told Peter about the ultimatum, who queried whether there was anyone senior in the police he trusted and could approach.

'Not an option,' said Declan. 'If I go to the police, the kidnappers will know within minutes and they'll ...' Pulling himself together, he said, 'Gabe, get hold of José and see when it's possible to fly to Manila. I think conditions are good enough to get a rib to El Nido. Peter, can you come with me? I want to check what was taken from my yacht.'

They headed to the jetty and took one of the ribs through Home Reef over to the channel, in no time arriving at Declan's sloop. It'd taken some minor knocks, not that he was bothered given current circumstances. A wide, friendly smile from a brown face with white teeth greeted them: the boat boy who'd been charged with guarding it. It wasn't clear if he'd ridden out the storm on board or taken refuge and returned afterwards; either way, he'd done a good job.

Declan handed the boy a wad of pesos in gratitude. He stuck them into his shorts, dived off the boat and swam to shore, disappearing up a steep path into the undergrowth.

When they entered the cabin, it was pretty much what they'd expected. Precious items were strewn everywhere, many broken, photos with glass and frames smashed. The break-in hadn't been executed with kid gloves on the sly but done in a hurry. Peter felt sorry for the old man, and guilty, thinking that none of this would have happened if he hadn't come out here. Declan bent down and picked up a coffee-table-size book, then flicked through it, carefully checking every page.

'What are you looking for?'

'A photograph.'

'Of what?'

'Like the one that thug showed me of the box in Manila. I stupidly forgot when I recounted the story to you and Sophie that I had one here.' Looking up, he said pointedly, 'The only other one belonged to Harry.'

Peter saw the book was entitled *Spanish Colonial Woodwork and Furniture of the Eighteenth Century.*

Declan stood up, looking despondent. 'They obviously got the photo from here.'

'You think it's Johansson?'

'Not a doubt in my mind. The question is, what do I do now?' Peter was in no doubt the old man was feeling Sophie's absence strongly, like an ache in his chest, having become so used to consulting her on things of importance. Normally one step ahead, he clearly couldn't fathom how things had come to this so quickly.

Peter thought the best thing he could do, given the time it would take to fly to Perth and back and the urgency of the situation, was to speak to Samantha. She could go to his father's study to look for Sinclair's box.

Declan cocked an eyebrow when he heard Peter's plan. 'You trust her?'

'Completely. She's the only one I trust, apart from Henry. She's got Harry's genes.'

'Well, let's see if she can find it then.'

They drove the rib back to the resort, passing the other yachts that had taken refuge in the channel, most fortunately unscathed.

When they approached the beach, the extent of the typhoon's

damage became more apparent. It would be an expensive, time-consuming operation to get things back to normal at the resort. Nevertheless, the staff were doing a sterling job of clearing wreckage, cleaning up communal areas and helping guests, whom they'd soon start shuttling to El Nido.

Peter went into the office behind reception and tried to contact Samantha. It was a poor connection, but when he eventually heard her voice, his spirits rose immediately.

'Thank God you're all right, I've been worried sick!' Samantha said anxiously. 'The devastation's all over the news.'

Peter spoke calmly. 'Don't worry; I'm fine, Sam. We rode the typhoon out on an island and weren't directly hit.'

'You're bloody lucky. Lots of people have been killed. When are you coming home?'

'I'm not sure. Things are unravelling quickly. Look, Sam, I need you to do something really important.'

'Okay,' she said, sounding nervous.

'I need you to use the key I gave you and go into Dad's study.'

He described in detail the appearance of Sinclair's antique writing box, asking her to try to locate it and, if she could, to hide it somewhere safe. He also asked her to take photos of everything before removing anything. Sam was good with a camera. He knew she'd do it properly.

'Don't tell anyone about this,' he said. 'Not even Henry. Promise?'

'I promise,' she said, still sounding nervous. 'I'm working at head office but can go this afternoon. What's this all about, Peter? It's all very cloak and dagger.'

'All I can say is that Dad put me onto one of his treasure hunts and things have become complex and dangerous. The box contains critical information. Bad people are after it, who'll stop at nothing to get it. So, make sure no one, and I mean *no one*, knows if you find it. Just remove it and put it somewhere safe. Someone's life depends on this, Sam.' The tone of his voice was unambiguous; he'd never been more serious.

'You're scaring m—'

The call disconnected and Peter couldn't make it work again. He cursed, but was confident she'd do it, just hoping he wasn't putting her in danger.

He went to update Declan. 'Let's hope she finds it,' the old man said, sounding more in control. 'We need to be holding the cards, otherwise we won't have sufficient leverage to get Sophie back. I need to get to Manila as soon as possible.'

'I'm coming with you,' said Peter.

'Grab your things then, and let's get going. My plane was damaged but José's located a small turboprop that can fly us over.'

Jovy powered them over to El Nido in a rib. Three hours later, they were once again in Manila traffic, inching painfully slowly towards Intramuros. Because of the devastation caused by the typhoon, it took even longer than before. Jeepnies lay trashed by the side of the road, pylons had crashed down, and palm trees blocked multiple sections of road, with substantial flooding.

A multitude of diversions took them through numerous *barangays* – shanty slums – where the impact of the typhoon was devastating, with hundreds rendered homeless, their fragile homes ripped apart as water and rubbish cascaded everywhere. It was a national emergency.

# CHAPTER 14

## *Perth, Australia*

The electric gates opened slowly and Samantha turned her blue convertible VW Beetle into the driveway of the estate only to see her mother's red Mercedes SL500 driving towards her. She slowed and they stopped parallel to one another.

Looking through large dark glasses, her mother said neutrally, 'I didn't think you were coming until the weekend?'

Samantha smiled. 'I forgot some things.'

In the passenger seat, Tiffany didn't bother to greet her sister, just watched the exchange, expressionless, keen to get going.

'We'll see you at the weekend, then,' her mother said without warmth. 'Don't be late. There are important people coming.' The Mercedes continued down the driveway which bisected manicured lawns, turned left out of the gates, and was gone.

Samantha parked in the wide forecourt, then entered the house, which was pleasantly quiet, pretty sure she had it to herself. The servants would be in their quarters at this time of day. She walked through two ground-floor reception rooms, then along a wide corridor lined with spotlighted recesses containing priceless porcelain antiques with valuable paintings of various parts of Australia filling the wall spaces in-between.

At the end of the corridor, she came to a small reception room with more paintings, a sofa and comfortable armchairs. On the wall, in pride of place, was a large portrait of her father, Harry Blake, which she thought captured his very essence. Dressed in bush kit, with chinos, R.M. Williams leather ankle boots, a blue denim shirt and his favourite Akubra, his tanned, lined face was full of character, with that slightly crooked smile she'd loved so much. With piercing blue mischievous eyes, he bore a striking resemblance to Paul Newman, which they'd often teased him about, as he stood against a backdrop of red sandstone gorges, the blue ocean beyond in the Kimberley, which had been his favourite place on earth. As she looked at the painting, Sophie felt her breath constrict, wishing with all her heart he was still with them.

Since his death, her mother and Tiffany had distanced themselves, making her feel isolated and alone. She wished she could see more of Peter, whom she had a real connection with, but in her heart she knew she'd have to find her own way.

With the key Peter had given her, she opened the study door and entered. After a moment's hesitation she locked it from the inside, leaving the key in the lock.

Surveying the contents of the room, much as Peter had during the wake, she felt her father's presence in everything she could see and touch. There was even the faint smell of him, as though he'd been there earlier and would return later, as was his routine. She knew he'd spent a lot of time alone here when his illness had taken hold, which they'd all respected.

She took her Nikon from her backpack and began photographing everything as Peter had requested. Periodically, she checked the images on the LCD, ensuring they were in focus and properly exposed. As she did so, she looked carefully at the multitude of boxes, small chests and wooden items Harry had collected, but saw nothing matching Peter's description. Her eyes searched the staggered shelves lining one wall, packed with books and an eclectic variety of antiques, until her gaze settled on a light brown cardboard box on top of a stack of old *National Geographics*. As she walked over to it, she heard the sound of a key being put into the lock, striking the one she'd left inside. Her heart skipped a beat.

The key rattled again, followed by a man's voice. 'Is anyone in there?'

*Henry.*

'Yes, it's Samantha, hang on a minute.'

She unlocked the door, her heart pounding. If Henry was surprised to see her, he hid it well. It seemed they both had an explanation to give, although she knew Henry had been charged by Peter to look after the room in his absence.

She gave a friendly smile.

Henry smiled back. 'I didn't expect to find you here.'

'Peter asked me to choose something I would like to remember Dad by,' she said, trying to sound casual, her voice slightly defensive. 'He said that's what Dad had wanted and gave me a key.'

Henry scanned the room over her shoulder. 'Well, have you seen anything you like?'

Sophie shrugged, holding the door half open, blocking his entry. 'I've only just walked in and need to have a proper look.'

Henry nodded. 'I just thought I'd check in as Peter asked me to keep an eye on things. And your mother's naturally keen to get things sorted ... I hadn't realised anyone else had a key.'

Samantha smiled. 'That's good of you, Henry. But if you don't mind I'd like to sit here by myself for a while? I feel close to Dad here.'

'I understand.' Henry glanced furtively towards the shelves. 'I'll leave you to it, but let me know if I can be of any help. I miss him too, you know.'

With that, he left.

Samantha realised she was trembling. Something wasn't right. The fact that Peter had told her not to mention anything to Henry worried her. She locked the door again and listened for a while, but heard nothing more.

She walked over and lifted the cardboard box from the stack of magazines and took it to the desk. It was an unopened and well-wrapped DHL parcel with some weight to it. Her heart pounded as she took a pair of scissors to open it.

# CHAPTER 15

## *Manila*

After a tortuous journey from the airport, Peter and Declan arrived at the Manila Hotel, a classic colonial hotel, like Raffles in Singapore or the Peninsula in Hong Kong, an oasis of comfort and charm in a bustling metropolis.

Declan was clearly well known, as staff fussed around him and he greeted several by name.

Approaching the reception desk, Peter asked, 'Are we going to pick up the Condesa's box from your store?'

Declan shook his head. 'No. I had it removed. They'll be expecting us to go back.'

'So, where is it?'

'With someone I trust.' No explanation was forthcoming.

Once they'd checked in, they went up to their rooms. Peter decided to call Samantha and used his mobile rather than the hotel landline. He was about to hang up when she finally answered.

'Sorry, it was on vibrate.' Sophie sounded nervous and slightly out of breath.

'What's wrong?'

'I'm sending you a photo.'

There was a beep on Peter's phone. He opened WhatsApp and double-clicked into a photo. Zooming in, he gave a sharp intake of breath. It was an identical box to the Condesa's: same two-tone wood, same design and intricate marquetry.

'Holy shit, Sam, you bloody found it! Where was it?'

'In a DHL box couriered from England. From the stamp it looks like it arrived some time ago, but was probably only put there recently by one of the housekeepers given everything's been so chaotic.' Peter remembered one of them also had a key.

Sam told him about Henry; Peter didn't know what to think. After all, he'd been charged to look after the study in his absence. However, a seed was sown which would only grow and niggle.

'Where are you now?' he asked.

Sounding frightened, Sophie said, 'Still in Dad's study. I don't know where to hide it.'

'Take a deep breath and relax, Sam, nothing's going to happen. Take it to the bank and put it in a safety deposit box. I think that's the safest place for now,' Peter said, reassuringly.

'Then what?'

'I'll come back as soon as I can and deal with it.'

'Okay,' she said, sounding calmer.

'You've done really well, Sam. I'm proud of you. And Dad would be too. Text me when you've done it. And please, look after yourself. You can reach me on this number if my mobile won't work.' He read out the hotel number. 'I'll be in touch shortly, I promise. I love you.'

He rang off, and headed down to the hotel lobby, where he spotted Declan sitting on a sofa off to one side, talking agitatedly on his mobile. Thinking it was probably the kidnappers, Peter waited nearby. Shortly, Declan came over, leaning on his cane, the bruises on his face the full spectrum of autumn.

'I'd like you to meet some friends of mine,' he said.

The way he said 'friends' implied they weren't the dinner party type.

Declan cocked an eyebrow. 'What are you grinning about?'

'I think you might want to sit down.' Peter handed him his iPhone.

Declan scrutinised the image. 'Mother of God ...' He looked at Peter with a shocked expression. 'It's identical ... so the son of a bitch actually found it ... this changes everything.'

Ten minutes later, a blacked-out Range Rover picked them up outside the hotel entrance and headed into the heart of downtown

Manila. It took more than an hour to navigate the grid-locked traffic before it pulled up in front of a nightclub with a garish neon sign proudly declaring: "Banana Club".

They were led through the empty club, around a dancefloor with poles where a couple of girls were getting in some practice for that night's punters. They filed past a closed bar through a large empty seating area, then out behind another bar, through a back corridor lined with beer and Coke crates where they were ushered into a silver BMW 7-series saloon, again with blacked-out windows. It sped off, weaving expertly through the traffic. The car that had tailed them from the hotel waited outside the entrance until the driver realised he'd been duped. Jan Bekker wasn't going to be a happy man.

Fifteen minutes later, the BMW arrived at an exclusive upmarket compound of large, well-spaced-apart villas in Dasmariñas. The main entrance was heavily protected by security guards with dogs, however, they were ushered through without fuss. Shortly, they arrived at the entrance to a large villa enclosed by a high white wall, topped with curled barbed wire, with strategically placed CCTV cameras along its length. The electric gates opened automatically and the Beemer slid in and parked in the driveway, which was encircled by lush tropical gardens. A Ferrari, Maserati and two Range Rovers were parked in front of a large garage. Pink bougainvillea sprawled over the façade of the Spanish-style villa.

A muscular and expressionless man escorted Peter and Declan through the large split-level, open-plan and luxuriously furnished house to a pool area at the rear where two scantily clad young women reclined on sun loungers as samba music pulsated in the background.

At a table some distance to their right, three men were playing cards, each chomping on a large cigar. Rum and coke bottles lay scattered about. As Declan and Peter approached, the man in the middle, a tough-looking thickset individual wearing a *barong* – a traditional embroidered white shirt – with black trousers and open sandals stood up, a wide grin on his face. Peter thought he looked like a toad, with a jet-black toupée.

'Declan, my old friend, it's been far too long!' he said theatrically. 'You never come and see me these days. I've missed you.'

'It's been a while, Rocky,' said Declan as they embraced like long-lost brothers, though Peter thought it looked more like politeness on Declan's part.

Declan introduced him. 'This is my friend, Peter.'

'Any friend of Declan's is a friend of mine. Please, come and join me,' said Rocky effusively, shooing away the two men who made themselves scarce.

'So, you have a problem you think I can help you with?' he said, leaning back, taking a chug at his burner, clearly adept at talking with it clenched between his teeth, and templing his hands. The way he said "problem" suggested he was used to dealing with other people's problems, and it was obvious from everything Peter had seen that the man was on the wrong side of the law. He remembered what his father had written in his letter, about Declan having business dealings in the grey area, and wondered how the two men interconnected, suspecting it must be in relation to Declan's colonial antiques business.

Declan was economical with the truth, telling Rocky that some thugs had broken into his Manila store, threatening them at gunpoint, while Sophie had been kidnapped from Bambam to extort money. They had come to Manila to make an exchange, and were awaiting instructions about where and how that would take place.

'So, you need some moral support from your old friend, Rocky, is that it?' Rocky sat back, still templing his fingers, clearly enjoying the role of Godfather.

'I need some serious fucking back-up,' replied Declan, his face conveying the gravity of the situation.

Rocky didn't look the sort who did anything for free, but he listened attentively, and appeared willing to help. Declan asked Peter to let them speak privately for a minute. As Peter walked over to the pool, he heard Declan ask Rocky about South Africans connected with local gangs.

He viewed his surroundings with interest; everything reeked of ill-gotten gains. The girls looked like bar girls; Rocky looked like a boxer, with a flattened, broken nose; the two guys who'd been playing cards were packing semis in shoulder holsters. He wondered what Declan would offer Rocky in return for his help. Or perhaps the guy owed him. Yes, that was probably it, he thought.

Peter sauntered over to where the girls were lying by the pool and stood with his hands in his pockets, looking at them stretched out catching non-existent rays, one in a bright pink bikini, the other sporting nothing but a black thong.

'Nice place to chill,' he said.

'You American?' asked one of them, staring up through oversized dark glasses.

'Australian.'

'Wanna swim?'

'Perhaps another time.'

'Maybe drink some Fosters?' She looked at her friend, sniggering.

He grinned. 'I need to stay sober, so I can ride my kangaroo.'

They fell into fits of laughter. Then the one who'd asked the question got up, took off her bikini, dropping it to the grass, and dived into the pool. The other girl stood up, small firm breasts on full display, and went and sat on the edge of the pool, dangling her feet in the water.

Declan waved Peter back over, his discussion with Rocky apparently concluded.

'If we can resolve Declan's problem,' said Rocky, putting an arm around Peter and talking to him like a confidant, 'and I hope that we can, it would be a pleasure to show you some nightlife, Mr, er?'

'Rodriguez,' Peter replied, shaking the man's outstretched hand. He had one hell of a grip. 'That's kind. I'd like that,' he said, thinking the opposite.

'You Spanish?'

'Half Spanish. Half Australian.'

'Interesting combination.'

'Works for me.' Peter maintained a confident smile and rock steady gaze.

Rocky escorted them out to the front of the house, and gave Declan a look before he got into the car which said, *'Trust me. I'll give you what you want.'*

They were then driven back to the hotel in the blacked-out Beemer.

'What's his real line of business?' Peter asked.

'Ex-gang head,' Declan said matter-of-factly, as if he'd said "accountant". 'Has his finger in many pies.'

'And your relationship?'

'Fragile. But I helped him once. He owes me. I don't do anything illegal, Peter, but you have to learn how to navigate certain people and things in these islands, which necessitates dealing with all types; otherwise, you get nowhere, especially in the colonial antiques business.

'As I've told you, the police are effectively the same thing, or worse. These days Rocky's cleaned up his act and tries to be respectable, though, as you'll have seen from the company he keeps, he finds that difficult. But given current circumstances, there's no one else who can help me the way he can, and certainly not at such short notice. We need to hope we get the call soon.'

It came sooner than expected. Declan held his mobile firmly to his ear as the South African voice he now detested grated down the line:

'You've made good time, Mr O'Connor. I hope the Manila Hotel's comfortable. I assume you have both boxes?'

'As I've already told you, I only have one box, which is in a secure location.'

'Then you have a problem, Mr O'Connor; or, more accurately, your daughter does.'

'Blake's son didn't bring anything with him because he doesn't have anything. You've got my daughter. I'd have to be a pretty cold bastard to lie under those circumstances, don't you think? I suggest you talk to your boss. If he's got an ounce of intelligence, he'll realise I can't give you something I don't have.' Declan presented a good case for the defence, thought Peter, and undoubtedly had balls.

Declan heard the man talking faintly to someone in the background while he held his hand over the mouthpiece, obviously checking further up the food chain.

'We'll start with the box that you say you do have, then,' came the reluctant reply.

Declan remained firm. 'You only get the box if you release my daughter, unharmed.'

'We'll see what we can do,' said the voice, making no promises but proceeding to give Declan specific instructions as to where and when to meet.

*

As soon as Declan and Peter left Rocky's house, Rocky put the word out and his men quickly tracked down Jan Bekker to the Hilton, where he was ID'd in the lift lobby. The South African's association with a rival gang was well known, and he'd been cropping up with far too much frequency to ignore, interfering with some of Rocky's primary business lines. This was an ideal opportunity to kill two birds with one stone.

Bekker left the hotel in a blacked-out Mercedes E Class, which one of Rocky's men tailed to the port of Manila where the typhoon had wreaked havoc. Containers lay strewn over the tarmac like multi-coloured blocks of Lego, their spilled contents being cleared by an army of specialist vehicles and cranes.

Bekker's Merc skirted the secure areas, entering a complex of export warehouses, where items waited to be shipped around the world in an army of super-sized container ships. Rocky's man, in a battered, unremarkable Toyota compact, kept his distance, as he watched the Merc stop outside an old warehouse with a corrugated roof which Bekker entered.

A large sign along the roofline pronounced, in faded red letters, "Best Tropical Fruit Exports Ltd – Godown A", with Chinese characters in green underneath. Rocky's guy reported that Bekker went in alone and that there was another, almost identical warehouse adjacent: "Godown B".

Declan's instructions from the South African were to arrive at Godown A at 8pm, alone. The port area was near to both the Manila Hotel and Intramuros, which meant the hotel, warehouse and Declan's tribal arts and crafts store were all in reasonably close proximity. However, given current circumstances it was too dangerous to walk, so they'd agreed that one of Rocky's men, posing as a taxi driver, would pick him up.

At 7.45pm, Peter accompanied Declan down to the main lobby.

'Well, wish me luck,' Declan said, sounding like he could really do with some.

'I'm coming with you,' Peter said, unable to get Sophie out of his mind.

'These people are dangerous, which is why I've engaged Rocky and his friends,' Declan said, looking tired but determined. 'It's better you stay here. If I don't come back or things go pear-shaped, I know you'll do whatever you can to get Sophie back. I can see you're a good man, like your father.'

'If I hadn't come out here, she wouldn't have been kidnapped,' Peter countered.

'This isn't your fault, son, this is fate,' Declan said philosophically. 'It's what happens with something of the magnitude of this treasure and the make-up of the people searching for it. This treasure hunt was put into play over 250 years ago, when the boxes were constructed and the seeds of the chase were sown. You're here because of your father, who I involved with Karl by telling them the story all those years ago.'

Declan shrugged. 'The Condesa's legacy was destined to find its way to me. But unfortunately, as long as they've got Sophie, they're holding the cards. So, for her sake, I have to arrive alone. Rocky's people will be nearby. I'm going to give the bastard the box I have and use the other for leverage. I'm sure they have no idea whether Harry found Sinclair's or not.'

'I think they're surer than you think.'

'Okay, you can go with Rocky,' Declan conceded as he walked towards the entrance. I'll get him to pick you up.' He looked at his watch. It was 7.50pm. 'I have to go now.'

Outside, at the taxi drop-off, Declan recognised the taxi number he'd been told to look out for on the roof of a yellow Mazda. Making it seem a random fare, he let the one in front go to someone else while he bent to tie his shoelace, then got in the Mazda as it pulled alongside. The driver gave a knowing smile in the rear-view mirror and opened his glove compartment, proudly displaying a couple of locally made Armscor 1911 semi-automatics.

Like many such places, the outskirts of the port took on a whole new atmosphere at night, where extreme poverty mingled with the sleazier side of criminal activity as pimps touted for business and hookers paraded. The Mazda cruised slowly through the warehouse complex, where small groups huddled in the shadows, taking and dealing drugs, the glow of cigarettes flashing like fireflies.

The broken neon sign on Godown A was poorly lit, with only half the flickering light bulbs functioning. The Mazda stopped outside the narrow entrance, its headlights illuminating rubbish skips crawling with rats. Unable to spot any of Rocky's men, Declan prayed they were close.

He waited for the best part of five minutes, in line with the instructions he'd been given, until a large, overweight man with short-cropped ginger hair appeared in the doorway. Declan instinctively knew he was the South African he'd been talking with on the phone. His ugly, pockmarked, smug-looking face which looked like a turtle's, and his fat belly and leering sneer somehow matched his voice perfectly. Dressed in badly fitting white slacks and a loud Hawaiian shirt that hung tent-like over his abundant midriff, the man probed the shadows with a practised eye, then signalled with his pistol for Declan to get out.

'You bitter be alone, Mr O'Connor,' he said with the accent Declan found nauseating.

'I'm by myself, as you can see,' said Declan, his voice not betraying the sick feeling he felt in the pit of his stomach, not knowing if Sophie was alive or dead, here or somewhere else. He instinctively crossed himself as he got out of the vehicle, clutching a brown leather satchel tightly under his left arm. His face looked as if he'd had a good workover, which he had, and he was tired. The past few days had taken their toll. But he was a fighter and would do whatever it took to get Sophie back safely.

'I want to see my daughter. Where is she?' he demanded, looking up into the man's cold, dead eyes; not ones you could easily negotiate with, thought Declan. Nevertheless, he held the man's gaze steadily, conveying his resolve. He hoped whoever Turtle Face was working for kept him on a tight leash and had given him clear, sensible instructions. Declan had come across his type many times before: unpredictable and not good at following orders, the sort that usually left a trail of destruction.

'She's alive and well, Mr O'Connor,' the South African chuckled, 'you bitter come and see for yourself.' He waved Declan ahead with an Israeli-made Jericho semi-automatic that looked like a toy in his oversized hands, and they walked down a long corridor through an admin office, into a large warehouse, brightly lit by strip lights.

The space was crammed with crates of bananas, pineapples, mangoes and papayas, and a powerful smell of tropical fruit permeated the air.

Declan felt his heart pumping, knowing things could play out in a number of ways, the majority not good for him or Sophie. High above, on the other side of the vast space, he registered a mezzanine level with a glass-fronted office with people inside, and a gantry running alongside. He presumed the place was owned by an import-export business, used as a front by one of the gangs to launder money and smuggle goods in and out of the Philippines. Judging by the number of boxes with Chinese characters, it was probably Chinese owned. Although it seemed a clichéd meeting place for the exchange, he thought it was better than being asked to simply dead-drop the box and pray afterwards that Sophie would be released.

'Sit down,' the South African said, waving the Jericho. Declan obeyed and they sat on opposite sides of a small table in the centre of the warehouse, the sort where security guards or stevedores would while away their time playing cards, drinking and gambling. Declan felt like a sitting duck in the middle of the vast expanse, vulnerable and exposed. 'Show me the little box then,' the South African said, patronisingly. 'I hope for your sake it's a nice one.'

Declan opened the satchel and carefully extracted the antique writing box from its velvet cover, placing it on the table.

'There it is. Now give me my daughter. That was the deal. Where is she?' he snarled, seeing nothing but crates around them.

'Patience, Mr O'Connor,' said the ugly South African, turning the box to face him, stroking its surface as though he was a connoisseur or a blind man reading braille. It was obvious from his expression that he knew what the box should look like and clearly it met his expectation. After all, they had the photo from the yacht.

The South African opened the lid with his big stubby fingers, lifted out the worn black leather diary and was about to flick through it when Declan said, 'You better be damn careful or you'll damage it. And I'm betting your boss won't be too pleased, given it's over 250 years old and the reason he wants it.'

Surprisingly, the man heeded Declan's advice, putting it gently back, closing the lid, engaging the clasp and sliding the writing box back into its protective cover. That told Declan something important.

The South African leant back. 'Well, you've only given us half of what we want, so the question is, what do we do now?'

'My advice would be to release my daughter, Mr Bekker, or you won't get out of here alive.' A flicker of surprise in Bekker's eyes that Declan knew his name.

'Did you really think we'd bring her here for only half of what we asked for?'

'I hoped very much, for your sake, you would.'

'You know, I like you, O'Connor,' said Bekker, having well and truly lost the "Mr". 'You've got guts. But that's all that'll be left of you shortly.'

A gunshot crackled in the open space, and a bullet ricocheted off the concrete by Bekker's feet. He moved surprisingly fast for a man his size, grabbing the box, upending the table and diving behind a stack of crates, his other hand gripping the Jericho which he fired blindly in the direction the shot had come from. Declan moved almost as quickly, taking cover down an adjacent aisle of fruit crates, clocking the men in the office running down the staircase at lightning speed, weapons drawn as they fired towards him with startling accuracy, splinters flying from wooden crates and bullets ricocheting off the floor like it was a 1940's gangster movie.

'You've made a big mistake, O'Connor!' shouted Turtle Face. 'You'll never see your daughter again now!'

Declan knew the men from above were loose on the warehouse floor. As one appeared around the corner of the crates and raised his gun, a volley of bullets hit the man in the head and chest. He maintained his momentum towards Declan momentarily before falling face down on the concrete in front of him. Blood oozed from his damaged skull as gunfire erupted around the warehouse. There was a scream as another of Bekker's stooges was hit. Then silence.

Rocky appeared from nowhere, accompanied by several wiry, tough-looking men covered in tattoos. He helped Declan sit upright, putting his finger to his lips and indicating he should stay where he was. The other hood from upstairs had also been gunned down, which just left Bekker.

Rocky's men had encircled the warehouse and it wasn't long before Bekker was dragged out and made to sit in the chair he'd hastily vacated minutes earlier. The writing box lay on the floor next to where he'd taken cover, miraculously undamaged. Declan retrieved it, putting it back in his satchel, while Rocky's men tied Bekker securely to the chair.

Declan, Rocky and two of his men stood in a semicircle in front of Bekker, with multiple guns aimed at him.

'Where's my daughter?' Declan said, his eyes hard and unforgiving.

'Safe, but not here,' answered Bekker, showing no fear, his eyes cold and dead. 'You kill me, you'll not be seeing her again; and I'm not saying that to save my skin,' he added.

The way he said it made Declan believe it. He thought there was a good chance that even if they kept Bekker alive as a bargaining chip, he was expendable. His death would conveniently cut the link to Karl, whom Declan was adamant was behind this.

Peter entered the warehouse, taking in the carnage around him. He'd heard the shootout from outside, but had no idea if Declan was all right or if Sophie was inside. Damaged crates lay scattered everywhere, fruit of all sizes and colours splattered on the floor and walls. Rocky was definitely in his element, far more at home surrounded by tattooed thugs with a gun in his hand than by a swimming pool playing cards. He was champing at the bit to hurt Bekker, but Declan indicated he'd do the talking, wanting him unharmed for now. It was the only way to get Sophie back.

Declan said, 'If you want to live, Mr Bekker, I suggest you do some fast thinking about how you can broker my daughter's release.'

Bekker looked back at him with lifeless eyes. 'If I don't hand over this box, I was instructed to tell you that you won't see her again.' A pause. 'Oh, and he wants both boxes for her release. This one's simply a stay of execution. Let's say a token of good faith on your part.'

'Who?' snarled Declan.

Rocky walked up and stuck his beloved Glock into Turtle Face's temple, his trigger finger tightening. Declan shook his head. Rocky eased his finger but kept the semi pressed into the man's forehead.

'I don't know his name,' Bekker said adamantly.

'Karl Johansson,' spat Declan.

'As I just told you, I don't know his name and I haven't met him. I'm just doing a job.'

It was plausible. There was no way of knowing if he told the truth or not, but Peter's gut told him he wasn't and he sensed Declan thought the same.

'Where's the handover?' demanded Declan.

'I'm to confirm when I've got the box by texting a number. Then wait for instructions,' Bekker said matter-of-factly.

Peter briefly wondered if Johansson had brought the *Griffin* to Manila, but quickly dismissed the thought.

'In that case, you'll confirm you've got it,' said Declan, 'and when you receive your instructions, make the handover as planned. My friends here will take good care of you in the meantime.'

Rocky nodded with obvious relish.

*

Sophie had cabin fever. It was dark outside, she felt claustrophobic and had a residual headache that refused to go. With plenty of time to think, she'd reached the conclusion she was on Karl Johansson's yacht, kidnapped because he thought Harry Blake had found Sinclair's writing box and that Peter had brought it out here. Either that or it was pure revenge for her mother having left him all those years ago.

The yacht had been moving steadily for the past few hours. There'd been no further sign of the South African, thank God. She hadn't liked him at all; he gave her the creeps. The sound of the door unlocking interrupted her thoughts, and a Chinese man with an inscrutable expression, dressed in a smart, well-pressed white uniform, entered, placing a tray of food and a jug of fresh water on the bedside table, while a second Chinese crewmember with a handgun stood guard at the entrance, equally inexpressive.

'When's the big boss going to see me?' Sophie said jovially, trying to lift her spirits.

The man ignored her, left the cabin and locked the door.

Silence.

Looking at the appetising meal, she knew there was no point in not eating. She would need all the strength she could get, so she filled her plate and ate hungrily.

Her mind wandered around the Condesa's story and theory about the boxes. None of them knew if Harry Blake had located the second box. But just supposing he had, she speculated. Would that actually enable whoever was in possession of both boxes to determine the location of the sunken Indiaman and initiate a search for the Blue

Moghul? The secrets of the second box would need to reveal themselves before they could safely assume there was anything in the story. Was it fact or fiction? After all, it might just be the fanciful yarn of a heartbroken Condesa. By the same token, Sophie was sure Peter would not have come all the way out here without good reason.

However, one thing she was sure of was that if Karl Johansson was prepared to kidnap her and let one of his henchmen kill an innocent diver, he'd also be prepared to kill her. After all, it would be the ultimate revenge for her father winning the heart of his fiancée, her mother, all those years ago. Probably just the sight of Sophie would be a stab in the heart for him. She thought about how cruel love could be, as one person won someone's heart and another lost it in the process. Almost feeling sorry for Johansson, she wondered what drove him the most: the chance to get revenge on her father and mother, or the opportunity to locate the treasure and beat everyone to it. She suspected it was both.

*

Rocky took Bekker to a safe house for the night, while Declan and Peter returned to the Manila Hotel to clean up, discuss tactics and try and grab a few hours' sleep. Declan was worried that if Rocky harmed Bekker, the link to Johansson would be severed. Although Rocky had promised he wouldn't hurt him, given his close links to one of their rival gangs it presented a real temptation to settle a few scores and send a clear message.

Declan and Peter sat by the pool, talking strategy over cold beer in peaceful contrast to the firefight in the warehouse earlier, the businessmen and tourists around them oblivious to what they were going through.

Looking at Declan, Peter said, 'So, what's the plan?'

Declan leant in. 'Well, I never thought Bekker would bring Sophie. That would be too easy with only one half of the key; one box without the other leaves them none the wiser.'

'But gives Johansson a chance to validate the box and its contents,' countered Peter.

'It does, but on its own it's useless. So tomorrow we let Bekker hand over my box and we follow it.'

'How?'

Declan gave a wry smile. 'There's a transmitter in it. Oh, and it's not the real box. It's a replica I had made years ago in case of just such an eventuality. I have to say, a really good one, also made by a Chinese craftsman here in Manila. And the diary's forged, but with some minor, but shall we say, fairly critical, variations.'

For a minute his eyes sparkled like they had when he'd been telling the story on his yacht, a hint of his former self, and Peter grinned in admiration at his ingenuity.

Neither of them slept that night, rising early the following morning to meet Rocky, who was accompanied by several of his men and Bekker. The South African had received confirmation by text that the handover would take place at the Cultural Centre Harbour dock at 7.30am. Judging from his face, Peter thought he'd taken some punches during the night. However, undoubtedly tough, he just stared ahead, expressionless, during the short journey.

When they arrived at their destination, it was deserted. It was only two days since the typhoon had slammed into the capital, and business for the majority hadn't got back to normal. Not a tourist or businessman in sight. However, the sun was up with the promise of a hot day ahead. If they hadn't seen evidence of the typhoon's passing, they wouldn't have known it had ripped through a couple of days earlier.

'What happens now?' asked Declan.

'We wait,' Bekker replied.

They heard it first. Then made out the unmistakable silhouette of an incoming floatplane. It lost altitude, gently kissing the relatively calm water into wind, and taxied to the end of the jetty.

'I'm to give it to the pilot,' Bekker said.

'Well, I'm coming with you.' Rocky pushed him out of the Range Rover, his semi pointing through his jacket pocket at Bekker's back. 'I'll take you out at the drop of a hat if you fuck about. So, no sudden moves,' he said, sounding like he hoped he would.

Declan handed the box to Bekker who walked slowly down to the end of the jetty, with Rocky close behind him. A man got out of the plane, took the box from Bekker and reboarded. A silent exchange. Within minutes, the plane was airborne again, heading south-west.

'So can we have a proper chat with him now?' Rocky asked, barely able to contain himself.

'Be my guest,' said Declan, 'but keep him alive. We need him.'

Bekker was firmly escorted by two of Rocky's tough-looking henchmen and taken back to a safe house to receive some local hospitality.

Declan looked anxiously at Rocky. 'Are you sure we can trace the signal?'

'Relax,' said Rocky. 'We use these devices all the time to track merchandise around the islands. If a high-value package goes missing, we need to find it quickly. This is the latest technology.'

Peter had no reason to doubt him and could only guess at the sort of merchandise he was referring to. They drove to Rocky's house where they tracked the signal over the archipelago for two hours. Eventually it stopped south of Busuanga Island, near Coron, in northern Palawan province, having stopped once briefly on the way down, which they assumed was to refuel. They hoped the final destination was Johansson's yacht, but knew the box could easily have been delivered elsewhere. Not long after the signal stopped moving, Bekker's mobile rang.

Declan answered.

'I've got O'Connor's box,' said the immediately distinctive Swedish accent. 'That's good work, Bekker. Now all you have to do is get the other one and you'll get full payment, plus the bonus we agreed.'

Declan felt his heart pumping. He hadn't heard the voice in forty years, just the sound of it transporting him back in time, like a piece of music or a smell. He thought about the letter Karl had written to him after Ingrid had left him, and the fear he'd periodically felt all these years, thinking the worst might happen.

'Mr Bekker's indisposed,' Declan said, presuming the man on the other end would have the same sentiment on hearing his distinctive Irish brogue.

If Johansson was surprised, he didn't show it. 'Well, if it isn't Declan O'Connor, master storyteller, treasure hunter and traitor,' said the voice in its clipped economical tone.

'We had a deal, Karl. I want my daughter back. I've kept my side of the bargain. You have my box.'

'She's alive and well, for now. But, as you well know, without the other box it's useless. Just an object of beauty. I know Harry found it, otherwise his son wouldn't have come out here after his death to find you. So don't play games, Declan. I promised you all those years ago that you'd pay for what you did and I intend to keep my promise.'

He sounded cold and detached. Not the Karl he remembered before that fateful night. 'And give my regards to Mr Bekker; he's of no use to me anymore. You'll save me money.'

So Karl really believed the other box had been located, thought Declan. Which was a problem for all of them. He decided to play his next hand, which was all he could do under the circumstances.

'Blake didn't bring anything with him, but he thinks it's possible Harry could have located the other box. He collected many colonial boxes, which are being sorted with his estate in Perth.'

'Then I suggest he locates it quickly and brings it to Manila. You've got forty-eight hours,' said the clinical voice. 'You'll be contacted about when and where to hand it over.'

The line went dead.

Declan turned to Peter, who guessed the situation, filling him in on the specifics.

'We have a dilemma,' Declan said. 'We think we know where the *Griffin* is and we assume that's where Sophie's being held and that Karl won't release her until we bring him the other box from Perth, which we *think* is the right box, but don't know for sure.'

That was about the sum of it, thought Peter. Rocky was currently elsewhere, which suited them perfectly as he could be pretty intense and they needed to think things through properly.

'It's quicker for Samantha to fly the box here than for me to fly to Perth and back,' Peter said. 'Once we have it and Johannson makes contact, we can decide how best to get Sophie back, using it as leverage in conjunction with following the tracker on the box he's already got.'

Declan nodded, looking anxious. 'That makes sense. But what worries me is I don't know how stable Karl is and whether he just wants to find the diamond, so he's beaten Harry and me to it, or whether hurting Sophie and getting the diamond would be his ultimate revenge.'

Peter didn't know the answer, but the worst-case scenario didn't bear thinking about. He could see the prospect was eating away at Declan.

'Let's get Sinclair's box here and locate Karl's yacht; that way we'll be fully prepped when he makes contact,' Peter said.

Declan nodded in silent agreement. He liked young Blake. He was logical and uncomplicated, and reminded him of Harry. He knew he'd taken a shine to Sophie and could tell she liked him too. If he'd had a son, he would have wanted one like him.

'Let's go back to the hotel,' he said decisively. 'You can sort things with Samantha, while I get a plane organised.'

Rocky walked into the room, wondering what was happening. Declan explained the big picture, but not the detail. He needed Rocky's help to get Sophie back, but didn't want him locking onto the real reason for all of this. Otherwise, it could end up as just one more outfit to compete with, and he could do without Rocky on his back later. It had been a risk involving him from the outset, but circumstances had given him no choice.

Back at the hotel, Peter called Samantha. This time she answered straight away.

'I was worried, Sam. Did you find a safe place to put the box?'

'Yes, it's safely stashed in a Westpac vault. I sent you a WhatsApp.'

He checked. Sure enough, it was there. Must have got held up in cyberspace.

He cut to the chase: 'Look, Sam, I need you to do something really important. It's a big ask, but a woman's life depends on it.'

Sam listened.

At first she was reluctant, but eventually agreed to do what Peter asked. She knew he wasn't someone who exaggerated. This was serious. She also knew what their late father had been like and the incredible things he'd been involved in over the years, especially when he'd had a sniff of treasure, and knew that Peter was doing this because of him.

'You need to make up a plausible excuse and not tell anyone where you're going,' Peter stressed.

'Like what?'

'Say a girlfriend's got engaged and you're going to Sydney for a few days to celebrate. You've enough rich friends to make up something believable. And, for God's sake, don't be too specific with Tiffany and Angela.'

'I'm frightened, Peter. If someone's life's at stake, surely it's dangerous to travel with the box?'

'No one knows you've got it, Sam. All you have to do is take it from the safety deposit box and bring it with you on the flight. I'll be here to meet you when you arrive,' he said reassuringly.

But he knew she was right.

'Okay, I'll do it,' she said. 'But only because it's for you, and Dad got you into all this.'

Peter exhaled with relief. 'I'll book you a room in the Manila Hotel. You can chill out for a couple of days. It'll do you good to get away from the others and have a change of scene.'

*

Sophie awoke from a deep, troubled sleep. The yacht was stationary. The sea calm. Out of her porthole, blue ocean stretched as far as the eye could see. She had no idea of its location. If they were near land, it was on their port side, out of sight. She remembered hearing a seaplane land and take off late the previous afternoon, and was wondering how long she'd be kept like this when the door was unlocked and the two Chinese crewmembers entered.

'Come,' the slightly taller one said monosyllabically, beckoning with a handgun. He ushered her into the teak-lined corridor and frog-marched her, sandwiched between him and his colleague, up a spiral staircase, through the main saloon and out onto the stern deck. Thankful to be in the fresh air, Sophie took in her surroundings. An island lay about 50 metres off their port side, but she had no idea which. The sun blazed, the heat was intense. There was no sign of the typhoon's passage. There were no boats in sight. They were isolated and alone.

At the far end of the teak deck, which was lined with sun loungers, a rectangular table was formally set with a white linen tablecloth, silverware and bowls of fruit. The taller Chinese man indicated she should sit on one of the chairs.

If she hadn't been captive for the past twenty-four hours, she'd have thought it civilised; but under the circumstances it felt awkward and uncomfortable.

'Good morning, Ms O'Connor. I hope you've been treated well?' said an urbane, cultivated voice.

Sophie turned to see a tall handsome man with thinning blond hair approach. Casually dressed in white chinos and a dark blue Ralph Lauren polo shirt, he looked fit for his age, which she thought must be similar to her father's. She knew without a shadow of a doubt it was Karl Johansson, still recognisable from the photo on the clubhouse wall on Bambam, even though, like the others, he'd aged. Tall and athletic, he bore a distinguished, wealthy air.

He walked around the table and sat down opposite Sophie. 'Sorry to have kept you locked up for so long,' he said apologetically. 'I've been negotiating with your father, who hasn't given me what I want yet.'

He spoke in that slightly clipped, almost perfect English Swedes do so well, with economic efficiency but a trace of an accent betraying their native homeland.

'Kidnapping's a serious crime,' Sophie said with a serious expression.

'You look just like her,' Johannson mused as one of the crew poured coffee for him. 'She was a beautiful woman,' he went on as if in a trance, clearly picturing her mother's image from all those years ago, comparing the memory with the beautiful young woman before him.

'And you've never forgiven my father for marrying her.'

Johansson remained expressionless. After a prolonged silence, he said matter-of-factly, 'No, I haven't,' his eyes a mixture of sadness and bitterness.

Sophie realised her father was right: this man had been driven by jealousy and hatred all these years, despite his business success, and, one would have thought, countless opportunities to fall in love with someone else.

'So, are you just going to keep me prisoner until he gives you what you want?'

'He leaves me little choice.'

Sipping his coffee, Johansson beckoned one of the Chinese crewmembers over. 'Bring me the writing box, please, Chan.'

The man disappeared into the saloon and returned with an antique wooden box with a distinctive appearance and intricate design that Sophie thought looked like one her father had shown her once, when she was very young. She realised that if he'd felt there was no other option but to give up his most prized possession, then he must have felt cornered, which only served to reinforce their predicament.

Looking at the box, Sophie guessed Johansson needed her help as to how it linked with Sinclair's box to reveal the location of the shipwrecked Indiaman.

Chan had placed it carefully in front of Johansson, who sat admiring it, without touching it, like an aficionado. It was obvious from the way he looked at it that, like Harry Blake and her father, he was still obsessed by the story Declan had told them on Bambam all those years ago. The story that had motivated each of them, in different ways, in their lifelong search for the second box and the secret they believed it held.

As if reading her thoughts, Johansson said, 'The three of us have been searching for Sinclair's writing box all these years. If Harry found it – and I believe that he did, otherwise why would his son come here to seek out your father after his death – then the location of the Indiaman is closer than it's ever been.'

He shifted his gaze to Sophie. 'You know, I liked Harry. He was charismatic and lucky. Above all, he always seemed lucky.' Johansson smiled weakly. 'You know, I offered him an olive branch to see if we could find the treasure together, but he refused out of some misplaced loyalty to your father. Even though we couldn't locate the missing box, there was a chance of locating the Indiaman by other means. I know they both searched and searched for Sinclair's box for many years. But I'm not surprised it was Harry who found it,' he said, looking past Sophie out to sea, as if his mind was fusing the past and present through all the intervening years, like a spinning umbilical cord in a black hole.

'Have you seen it?' he asked her with an unsettling intensity in his eyes.

She shook her head. 'I didn't know it'd been found. I mean, what are the chances of finding one box from so long ago? Peter Blake was just following up on a story his father told him before he died, that's all. He didn't bring any box.'

'I know Harry found it,' Johansson said, with a certainty that made her think he really had done.

'What ultimatum have you given my father?'

'He's got until tomorrow to hand it over.'

'And if he can't, because Harry didn't find it?'

'I'm optimistic he will.' Johansson smiled thinly.

It sounded like work in progress, thought Sophie. She wondered if this man, who'd lived his whole live seeking revenge on her father and mother, really was unhinged or just an ice-cold killer? Only time would tell.

'Why did you bring me up here?' she challenged.

'Because you learn a lot from body language, if you know what to look for.'

Johansson suddenly stood up. 'I'm sorry, but I've business to attend to. If you'll excuse me.'

Chan came over, and together with his mute colleague, escorted Sophie back down to her prison cell. She hadn't wasted the brief exchange, taking in her surroundings and the layout of the motor yacht. She'd also made an assessment: Johansson was clearly clever and determined to see the whole thing through to its conclusion. If this was a poker game, he was all in.

# CHAPTER 16

## *Manila*

S amantha entered the arrivals hall at Ninoy Aquino Airport among a sea of tourists and businessmen, and Filipinos waiting for family members. Several planes had arrived simultaneously and it was chaos. She looked anxiously for Peter, conscious she was carrying an object that could potentially save someone's life, with all the risk that involved. When she saw him, a massive smile erupted on her face. She ran over and flung her arms around him. He'd always felt protective of his little sister and was equally delighted to see her. They had a special bond that was stronger than ever now Harry was gone.

'Well, I made it,' she shouted above the cacophony.

Peter took her case. 'You've no idea how important this is, Sam. I can't thank you enough. You've got it, right?'

'It's in there.' She pointed at the case. 'I didn't think it would get through as hand luggage. At least I hope to God it is.'

'Me too,' he said, putting one arm around her shoulders and pulling the wheeled case with the other. 'Let's get out of here.'

Declan's driver spotted them when they exited the terminal and drove them to the Manila Hotel. After Samantha had checked in, they went up to her room where she took the box from her case and placed it carefully on the writing desk. As he scrutinised it, Peter thought it looked identical to the Condesa's. Meanwhile, Sam took a Coke from the mini bar, feeling the heat and humidity. He then rang Declan, who knocked on the door a few minutes later.

Declan kissed Sam on both cheeks. 'I'm very sorry for your loss, Samantha; your father was a good man. I liked him immensely. I can't tell you how grateful I am you've flown all this way to bring this box.'

'You're very welcome,' said Sam. 'I really hope it helps to get Sophie back safely. I'd love to get to know her.'

Declan's mobile rang and he answered, holding it tightly to his ear.

'We understand our package has arrived,' said a voice he didn't recognise.

'Who's this?'

'Listen carefully,' said the voice.

Declan listened intently, then the call was cut.

He turned to face Sophie and Peter. 'I'm to go the Hilton lobby, where I'll be contacted.

'When?' asked Peter.

'Now.'

'Have they said when they'll release Sophie?'

'They said that once the box is verified, she'll be released. That's all. Just their word on it. No guarantees.' Looking distraught, he added, 'I don't see what else I can do.'

'Well, we've got a fix on the fake box through the radio transmitter,' Peter said. 'Give them this one, then we'll locate the *Griffin* from the air. Rocky's men can follow whoever collects it from the Hilton. If Johansson doesn't release Sophie, we'll rescue her with Rocky's help.'

Declan shrugged. 'I guess that's all we can do.' He walked over to the desk and studied the box with the delicately engraved initials *R.J.S.* on the top.

There was a knock at the door.

'Housekeeping,' said a female voice.

As Sam turned the key, a maid with a gun held to her head was roughly pushed into the room by two men wearing sackcloth balaclavas.

'Move!' shouted one of them, waving an Uzi.

Declan and Peter complied, moving away from the desk where

Sinclair's box lay in full view. Sophie and the maid were bundled over to join them while the man kept his weapon trained on them. Meanwhile, the other gunman, holding a semi-automatic, walked over, snatched the box and placed it in a motorbike courier's satchel.

They left the room as quickly as they'd entered. It was all over in seconds.

*

Rocky paced up and down the hotel room like a caged tiger, obviously feeling he'd let his old friend down. They'd been outsmarted and someone would have to pay.

Peter looked at Declan. 'I assume the weather's good enough to fly?'

Declan nodded; he'd been busy making calls after the box had been snatched. 'We'll fly to El Nido, drop off the Condesa's box and then head up to Busuanga.' He looked at Rocky. 'I presume there's still a signal from the transmitter?'

'It hasn't moved. It's east of Coron.'

'What've you done with Bekker?'

'He's been enjoying our hospitality, but he's one tough motherfucker,' Rocky said with admiration, rolling his 'r's rhythmically as he savoured his favourite word in a way that sounded poetic. 'Can I deal with him properly now?' he asked like an impatient kid who'd done everything he'd been told and wanted his reward.

Declan shook his head. 'You know I don't condone killing, Rocky. That's not my game. Keep him safe until we see how this pans out. Right now I need your help to get Sophie back. That's our priority. He's still useful.'

Peter said, 'I think Sam should fly back to Perth. It's too dangerous here.'

Declan nodded. 'I agree. That's sensible.'

'I'll get her sorted then and meet you at the airport.'

# CHAPTER 17

## *The Griffin, Coron*

The *Griffin* lay anchored off Coron Island, 120 kilometres north of El Nido.

The second writing box had been delivered by floatplane without incident. Karl Johansson now sat in the comfort of his luxurious saloon, with both boxes before him on a low coffee table, listening to "Spring" from Vivaldi's *Four Seasons* reverberate from the powerful Bose speakers. He thought the boxes were identical in every way and savoured the expectation of uncovering their secrets. He just had to figure out how.

He couldn't help but feel a cunning sense of achievement at having outfoxed O'Connor and Blake, and a hint of smugness passed over his normally emotionless face.

He had to now decide what to do with Sophie, knowing if he kept her captive, she'd be a magnet for trouble. It wouldn't be long before Declan figured out about the *Griffin*, if he hadn't already, and she'd served her purpose in enabling him to obtain both boxes. His beef was with Declan, not her, though he knew hurting her was the most effective way to cause maximum pain to his life-sworn enemy: an appealing proposition. But to hurt or kill her wouldn't help his immediate objective, which was to locate the Indiaman and search for the diamond.

Johansson was curious to see how she'd react at seeing the boxes reunited, and thought perhaps she knew something that might help him unlock their secret – it would surely take patience and some expertise. He knew how clever the craftsmen were back in the day when they'd designed these bespoke pieces with their secret compartments, always looking for new ways to conceal the contents. He was also aware that it could be booby-trapped if opened incorrectly, and its secret destroyed for ever.

He skimmed repeatedly through the Condesa's diary, but with his limited Spanish, frustratingly, he couldn't understand much. And the fact that Sinclair's box didn't have a key complicated things.

He looked up as Sophie appeared from the stairwell, escorted by Chan and his colleague. They walked over and Sophie was pushed into a black leather armchair opposite Johansson, who sat reclined with his legs crossed and his arms extended along the spine of the sofa.

'Matching boxes?' Sophie said with heavy sarcasm. 'I'm impressed. The question is, what are you going to do with them?' She gave him a taunting grin. 'I don't think it's simply a case of X marks the spot.'

'I think you might have some idea how they work together,' Johansson said calmly. 'I may not like your father much, but he was never stupid.'

Without showing any sign of recognition, Sophie observed that the boxes looked identical. 'He's never seen this other box, which I'm assuming has been brought from Australia. And nor have I. But given it's come into your possession so quickly, I'm pretty sure neither he, nor anyone else, has had a chance to unravel whatever secret it's supposed to hold.'

She was smart like her father, thought Johansson. And fiery for a Swede. Must be the Irish genes.

Looking defiant, Sophie said, 'Did it ever cross your mind this could all be bullshit? I think you need to wake up to the possibility that this might just be a romantic story from a dreamy Spanish Condesa with a really big imagination who liked a bit of theatre.'

Johansson prided himself on reading people and could tell from her posture, words and mannerisms that she didn't know anything that would help him. What she said made some sense, but he had no idea what Declan did or didn't know in relation to the boxes. Only what he could remember from when Declan had told them the story all those years ago on that fateful night, the words etched in his memory. That he'd come across a writing box through his colonial antiques business, in which he'd found a secret compartment containing the Condesa's diary, detailing the story of her love affair with Robert Sinclair, an Englishman from the British East India Company with a second-hand account of a sunken East Indiaman on which a reputedly priceless diamond was being smuggled. He'd understood from Declan that the key to locating the ship depended on finding a second, matching, writing box that should have been in Sinclair's possession. However, until recently, he hadn't known what the boxes looked like and if the key to locating the Indiaman was by using both boxes in conjunction with one another or whether the second box alone held the key.

'So, are you going to release me?' Sophie challenged, mentally strong despite her ordeal. 'My father's done what you asked.'

'I haven't decided yet,' said Johansson, once again detached and distant like the day before.

Sophie realised he wasn't bluffing. He really hadn't made up his mind and was making it up as he went along.

Johansson nodded at Chan who came over and took Sophie back down to the cabin. As she bent forward to get up, she deftly secreted a letter opener which had been lying on the table, shoving it up her sleeve.

# CHAPTER 18

## *Manila to Coron*

Samantha was clearly relieved to be flying back to the safety of Perth, having seen enough to know how dangerous things were, and never having been a risk taker.

She looked up at her brother lovingly. 'Look after yourself, Peter. This isn't worth getting killed for, whatever Dad put you onto. He wouldn't have wanted that. Get Sophie back safely and come home soon.'

She hugged him tightly and he reciprocated, pleased she was heading home but grateful she'd come with the box. It would be one less thing to worry about.

'You mustn't breathe a word of this to anyone, Sam. Not even Henry. Promise me.'

'You think he's in on this, don't you?'

'I don't want to, but it's a possibility, otherwise how could I have been followed? He was the only one apart from you who knew where I was going.'

It was the first time he'd articulated these doubts.

Sam looked incredulous. 'But he was Dad's best friend. He told him everything.

'Yes, he was, but perhaps Dad didn't tell him *everything*. I'm hoping he's innocent, but we can't afford to take chances.'

Peter looked up at the departures board. 'You'd better go; the plane's boarding.'

Sam made to leave, then turned and gave Peter one last tight hug before heading off, and with a wave of her passport, disappeared around a corner.

Peter made his way to the domestic side of the airport where Declan's charter plane was waiting. Fifteen minutes later they were airborne and en route to El Nido.

Sitting next to Declan, Peter said, 'Where's Rocky?'

'Putting together a small group on the basis that we're going to have to rescue Sophie from Karl's yacht,' Declan replied matter-of-factly.

'Do you really think Sinclair's box will reveal the wreck's location?'

'Who knows? All I care about is Sophie,' Declan said in a monotone, looking out of the window with a blank expression. 'But if it doesn't, then all this is for nothing.'

'Where's the Condesa's box?'

'Here.' Declan tapped a leather case next to his seat. 'Safe and sound.'

The journey was uneventful. When they landed at El Nido, things were gradually getting back to normal after the severe damage caused by the typhoon.

Gabe was waiting by the small airport terminal building, parked at the side of the runway in a 1970s red FJ40 Toyota Land Cruiser. Declan walked over from the small plane and handed him the Condesa's box in its brown leather case, asking him to swear on his grandmother's grave to keep it safe. He then walked slowly back to the plane, boarded and within minutes they were airborne again, as José, Declan's pilot, set a northward heading towards the location emitted by the radio transmitter.

The sun had pushed through. It was hot and humid again. The iridescent blues and greens of the sea, with periodic white gashes of bone-white sand, glinted on islands and parts of the coastal mainland as they flew towards the southern shores of Busuanga, east of Coron town, to their target location. Declan had told Rocky he'd try to locate the *Griffin* from the air while Rocky sorted a boat and crew for a rescue attempt.

'This is where American Hellcats sank a supply fleet of the Japanese Imperial Navy in 1944,' Declan shouted above the engine noise as they looked down at the huge seascape. 'It's one of the best places to dive on Japanese wrecks. At least twelve lie between 10 and 40 metres. Most in excellent condition.'

'Sounds like you know the area well?' Peter shouted back.

Declan nodded. 'I sailed through here with your father and Karl. We dived on practically every one of them.'

Looking through the small window, Peter could see how the Japanese naval fleet, trying to escape an attack in Manila Bay, had thought were safe hiding among the multitude of islands, until they'd been torpedoed to watery graves. He knew the area had become a mecca for wreck divers, using Coron town as their base, and thought the map of the archipelago spread out on his knees was helpful, but didn't do justice to the scale of what lay below.

As the homing signal grew stronger, Declan pointed to the island of Coron. 'Karl's yacht has to be somewhere around here.'

The plane flew low, at 3,000 feet, as they scanned for the *Griffin*, and it wasn't long before they spotted it nestled in the lee of a small island, anchored on the border between azure and deeper blue water. There was no other shipping in the vicinity, just the beautiful 1950's-looking retro yacht that couldn't be confused with any other.

'I wonder why he's come here?' Declan shouted over the noise of the engine, looking puzzled.

'Probably just kept moving,' Peter replied. 'After all, he has to hole up somewhere.' Looking down at the yacht, he wondered if Johansson had managed to open Sinclair's box, and was already one step closer to the location of the sunken Indiaman.

'Don't hang about!' Declan shouted to José. 'We don't want to look suspicious. Head to Coron and drop us off.'

José banked steeply, following instructions. Before long, they bumped down at Francisco B. Reyes Airport and from there they took a taxi for the twenty-five minute journey to Coron town where they'd agreed to meet Rocky and his men.

Upon arrival, they were dropped off at the waterfront. Peter wondered what Rocky had organised. However, sure enough, he was there to greet them, looking calm and relaxed, and certainly proving to be reliable.

Declan clapped Rocky on the back. 'It's exactly where you said it would be.'

'I told you the transmitter always finds what's lost,' Rocky said, grinning. 'I've everything we need. We'll head out at sunset. Come and see the boat and let's discuss tactics.'

He was clearly loving this.

They followed him down to a jetty where a sizeable, powerful-looking motor launch with five outboards was moored, looking every inch like it belonged to a Columbian drug cartel. On board, five swarthy-looking gang members busied themselves, causing Peter concern about executing a rescue attempt without compromising Sophie's safety.

Although she was their number one priority, he knew the ideal scenario would be to rescue her safely *and* retrieve Sinclair's box, otherwise, as Declan had articulated on the flight over, everything would be for nothing. They had no idea what crew complement Johansson had or what precautions he'd taken to protect himself. But given he'd kidnapped Sophie, engaged Bekker, a career criminal, sent the two thugs who'd killed Pablo at Declan's store, and had a diver executed, it was odds-on he'd be well prepared.

Declan took Peter to one side. 'I think it's better to leave Rocky and his men to do what they do best.'

'I'm going with them,' Peter said adamantly.

'You ever used a gun?' Declan clearly wondered what combat experience Peter had had, given he was a marine biologist, not a Navy Seal.

'Don't worry, I can handle myself. I've been on projects in pirate waters and had small arms training.'

Declan cocked an eyebrow. 'But never actually shot anyone, right?'

Peter said calmly, 'I've never killed anyone, if that's what you're asking. But that doesn't mean I don't know how to, if push comes to shove. You need someone to go with those guys.' He wouldn't budge.

'Okay,' relented Declan; what Peter said made sense. 'But focus on locating Sophie and getting her safely off that ship, whatever happens. Rocky's men will neutralise the guards and try to isolate Karl who I'm pretty sure will go to any lengths to protect himself and keep both boxes. If he gets to Sophie first, then he's calling the shots, like he's been doing all along, and it's game over.'

Peter knew Declan was right. They were taking a risk that depended on Johansson's state of mind, and neither of them knew how far he was prepared to go.

'I'll make sure you get Sophie back safely,' Peter said reassuringly. 'But if there's an opportunity to get Sinclair's box without jeopardising her safety, I'll take it.'

Declan nodded brusquely without saying more.

They talked through the plan with Rocky. Rocky and Declan would stay in the powerboat with the skipper. Peter and five gang members would board the yacht from a small tender, with the primary objective of locating Sophie as quickly as possible and immobilising any resistance they met, keeping her safe their number one priority.

The signal from the radio transmitter hadn't shifted, so they set out in the streamlined cigarette launch at dusk. Forty minutes later, darkness fell swiftly, and the skipper cut the engines and maintained position in the calm water. An early phase of the moon meant they weren't bathed in moonlight and they made out the twinkling lights of the *Griffin* in the distance, looking as enticingly beautiful at night as during the day. Through binoculars, they saw two armed crewmembers patrolling the upper deck, which meant more below decks. Various parts of the ship were illuminated; the stern deck, clearly visible, but empty. Lights from the saloon and some cabins below decks reflected on the dark water.

After fifteen minutes of watching patiently, a tall man wandered out from the saloon onto the stern deck. Declan scrutinised him through binoculars and felt his heart pound. Even after all this time, Karl Johansson was unmistakable. To have heard him on the phone after all these years was one thing, but to see him in person quite another. The fact he was holding Sophie prisoner somewhere on the yacht made Declan seethe with anger, and he gripped his binoculars tightly, spellbound, his face in a tight grimace.

Johansson was holding a glass of something, smoking a cigar; no doubt reflecting on his success at obtaining both boxes and outfoxing his old rival, thought Declan. Declan was sure Sophie would be below decks, but *where*? was the question. He started having second thoughts about what they were about to do. If Sophie ended up as collateral damage, his world would collapse, and there would be nothing left for him. She was the sole reason for his existence since Ingrid had died; a part of them both.

However, somewhere deep down, he drew on his inner strength, which he knew Sophie also had, and resolved they had to do this. He didn't trust Karl to release her of his own accord, and had heard nothing further since Sinclair's box had been snatched. That was assuming, of course, that the men who'd taken the box at the Manila Hotel were working for Karl and not a third party. If that were the case, things would become a lot more complicated.

Looking through his own binoculars, Peter said, 'I assume that's Johansson?'

'It's him all right,' Declan hissed. 'If that son of a bitch has so much as lifted a finger against Sophie, I'll kill him.' Peter didn't for one minute doubt him.

'We should go then.' Rocky came up behind them, his voice casual as if they were going to the cinema. His men were fully prepped. They'd discussed the plan and tactics. The time had arrived to put their plan into action, while they had a chance to get to Johansson. If they could reach him first, they stood a better chance of bringing Sophie back safely. To be as silent as possible, they'd row a small tender for the final approach. The speedboat would provide a quick exit at the appropriate time.

Dressed in black, wearing balaclavas, Peter and Rocky's men checked their weapons. Rocky's men had Uzis slung round their chests and carried an assortment of 9mm pistols and other weaponry. Peter carried a SIG P226, courtesy of Rocky, with spare magazines in his waistband, fortuitously the same model he'd used six months earlier on a dive boat off the coast of Yemen in the Red Sea where Somali pirates had been the threat. Peter and his colleagues had successfully thwarted various boarding attempts after a few hairy hours during which he'd fired multiple rounds and hit at least one of them.

Declan looked nervous and was frustrated, clearly wishing he was young and fit enough to be going with them, realising old age had finally caught up with him: this was a young man's game.

He grabbed Peter's arm before he got in the rib, and said gruffly, his voice cracking, 'Take care of yourself, son, and make sure you get Sophie back. She's all that matters, not the box, ya hear me?'

Peter smiled reassuringly. 'We're on the same page, Declan.'

He felt unusually calm given the circumstances, pleased they were about to act. All the talking and second-guessing had become tiring. Action meant results and a definitive outcome, whether good or bad. He got into the rib, and one of the gang members rowed them quietly towards the *Griffin*. It was almost 11pm. A hot sultry tropical evening. A couple of lights had gone out below decks, but the saloon light was still on. Johansson had gone back inside.

They'd studied plans of the yacht they'd found online and assumed the layout should be pretty much the same, bar some minor changes Johansson could have made after purchasing it from the previous owner, a French luxury-goods tycoon who'd chartered it out. The sea was calm as they approached the *Griffin's* starboard side. Given it was impossible to see from the waterline who was above, they knew they had to be silent in their assault.

One of the five men deftly threw up a rope with a silicon hook, which caught on the edge of the deck first time, and effortlessly hauled himself up until he was able to peer over, check it was clear, and then flip himself onto the deck. Two more of Rocky's men shimmied up, hot on his heels.

Peter and the two remaining gangsters cautiously made their way around the stern to the port side of the yacht, using the ship's hull to keep out of sight. Halfway along, the two men shimmied up without fuss. Then it was Peter's turn. So far no noise or suggestion they'd been detected, which made him think the other gangsters had taken out the guards they'd seen. One of Rocky's men beckoned him up, so Peter climbed the rope, not as effortlessly as his companions, but without much fuss.

Upon reaching the deck, he saw a white-uniformed crewmember lying prostrate along the wall of the vessel and wondered if he was dead, knowing Rocky's men wouldn't mess around. The three of them crept stealthily along the side of the yacht towards the stern, ducking underneath the dining room porthole towards the rear saloon.

Tentatively peeking through the saloon porthole, Peter saw a distinguished-looking, blond-haired man, who had to be Johannson, sitting on a sofa, smoking a cigar and looking relaxed as he studied the two writing boxes side by side on the glass table in front of him: one a fake, the other the real McCoy.

Peter felt his heart pumping at the risk they were taking.

Bending low, closely followed by Rocky's men, he crept stealthily beneath the first porthole, past a second, until he was at the corner of the main structure where it met the stern. Light flooded from the open saloon onto the wide teak deck as the surreal sound of Mozart's Piano Concerto 21 in C major drifted over the sultry night air: the calm before the storm.

As Peter made eye contact with one of Rocky's men who appeared on the other side of the vessel, the man dropped to the deck with the sound of gunshot as another of Rocky's men was chased onto the stern deck, instantaneously bathed in light in full view of the saloon.

With lightning reflexes for a man of his age, Johansson leapt from the sofa, quick to realise what was going on and reacting fast. Peter saw he had a handgun as he ran for the staircase in the corner of the saloon which led to the lower deck cabins, where presumably Sophie was being held.

Peter ran in hot pursuit, to bursts of machine-gun fire as Rocky's men engaged in a firefight along the starboard side. More crew members appeared from below decks. As suspected, the yacht was well protected. Peter quickly reached the spiral staircase, hot on Johansson's heals, shots splintering off the surrounding teak as he flung himself down the stairs into the lower deck corridor.

He ducked back for cover and knew he'd have to use his SIG if this was how Johansson was going to play things. It wasn't a prospect he relished, but he would do whatever it took to get Sophie back safely. Checking his semi was racked, with one in the chamber, he cautiously stuck his head around the corner.

Johansson had disappeared from view. Another gunshot rang out. Peter heard a significant commotion as he raced down the corridor, only to bump into one of Rocky's men, whose gun was held to Johansson's head, with one of the Swede's arms locked behind his back.

Rocky's guy frogmarched Johansson towards Peter, who ripped off his balaclava and demanded, 'Where's Sophie?'

'Alive and well, like I promised,' said Johansson, his voice smooth, calm and confident, despite the circumstances. He gave a thin smile. 'I must say, Mr Blake, you've rather taken me by surprise.'

'Take him upstairs and keep him in the saloon,' Peter instructed Rocky's man. 'Don't kill him, but don't take your eyes off him.'

Peter ran down the corridor, shouting Sophie's name.

'I'm in here!' he heard her shout as he came across two Chinese men out cold, lying in front of a cabin door. Peter rumbled their pockets and found a set of keys.

Turning the key in the lock, he shouted, 'It's Peter! You're safe now!' The door opened and Sophie stood before him, looking tired but in good shape, clearly having handled her ordeal with mental strength.

'God, am I glad to see you!' she said. 'Let's get the fuck out of here!'

'Sounds good to me.' Peter led her by the arm.

'Is Dad okay?'

'Don't worry, he's been worried sick, but he's fine, waiting close by.'

'What happens now?'

'I think a little reunion's in order.'

'I'm not big on reunions with murderers intent on killing my family.'

'I can understand that.' Peter was keen to crack on. 'Let's go upstairs. I'll call in Declan and Rocky.'

In the saloon, Johansson sat on the sofa with a gun pointed at him by one of Rocky's men. Despite being roughed up and blood trickling from his mouth, he remained defiant. Ignoring him, Peter led Sophie onto the stern deck, calling Declan on a walkie-talkie to confirm she was safe, then handed it to Sophie, whose eyes welled up when she spoke to him. Minutes later the speedboat was skilfully brought alongside, like a car doing a handbrake turn. In no time, Declan and Rocky stood beside them. Declan's relief at seeing Sophie safe was palpable. They hugged tightly, then he stood back, looking her up and down, checking she was unharmed, which she assured him she was.

'Wait for me here,' Declan said, then walked slowly into the saloon to where Johansson sat.

'This is unexpected,' said Johansson. 'I didn't anticipate the pleasure of your company quite so soon.'

'You can fuck with me, Karl, but if you fuck with my daughter that's a completely different matter.'

'As you can see, she's safe and well. I was going to release her, but you never gave me a chance.' Johansson's voice remained calm and reasonable, as though discussing a mundane business transaction. 'It seems you've friends in low places, but then you always did have, Declan.'

Declan leant on his cane and they locked eyes, each holding the other's stare, neither one backing down. Both tough, determined men, their looks saying more than words ever could.

'The dilemma I now have is what to do with you,' said Declan.

Johansson frowned. 'I hardly think you're going to kill me.

Powerful people know I'm here and that you've been causing me trouble. They've clear instructions if anything happens to me. I think you can trust me on this.'

Rocky entered the saloon, clearly not liking what he saw, racking the slide on his Glock. 'You want him taken care of?' If Declan said yes, it would be over in seconds. But he wasn't a cold-blooded killer, either first-hand or getting someone else to do his dirty work.

Sophie was safe and both boxes were in full view on the table.

'No. Take the boxes and leave us for a minute. I want to speak to him alone.'

Rocky took the boxes outside while Sophie and Peter watched from the doorway, standing next to two of Rocky's men who had guns trained on Johansson.

Declan pointed his pistol at Johannson. 'We're going to leave in a minute. And these men are going to escort you from these islands on the condition you never come back.'

'That's magnanimous. You always did like the grand gesture.'

'Sarcasm doesn't suit you, Karl. You should focus on your business empire in Sweden. If you come back and cause more trouble, my friends will have pleasure in taking care of you the way they know best and I won't be able to stop them.'

'Tell me, Declan. Do you miss your wife?' Johansson's eyes taunted his old friend. 'I heard she met a dreadful end.'

Declan moved at lightning speed, abandoning his cane as he made to smash the pistol across Johansson's face. 'You fucking bastard!' he screamed.

Johansson raised an arm to defend himself as the men collided, sprawling on the sofa and rolling onto the glass coffee table, which subsequently shattered.

Peter rushed in with Rocky, who hauled Johansson off Declan by the neck, while Peter restrained Declan, who, shaking with rage, aimed his pistol at Johansson's head. 'I should fucking kill you, you Swedish piece of shit!' he seethed.

Johansson said nothing, his stare locked into Declan's, the hatred of the past forty years unleashed.

Peter took Declan's arm, pulling him away. 'He's not worth it. Let's get out of here,' he said, registering the deep rage in the Irishman and the pleasure in Johansson's eyes at being able to hurt him so deeply with just a few words.

Declan's Irish brogue sounded like an IRA threat as he turned back. 'If you cross my daughter or me again, I swear to God I'll fucking kill you!'

He turned again and limped out into the fresh air, shaking off offers of assistance, while one of Rocky's stooges tied Johansson up securely. Three of Rocky's men stayed on board the *Griffin* to escort him and his yacht from the islands.

Sophie helped her father board the speedboat, followed by Peter and Rocky. The driver then powered back to Coron at breakneck speed, everyone thankful to put as much distance between them and Johansson as possible.

Thirty minutes later, they disembarked and walked up the quayside. Declan had calmed down. As they stood in a small group, about to disperse, he said, 'I owe you big time, Rocky and really appreciate what you've done for me and Sophie.'

Rocky cocked his head to one side. 'Friends must look out for one another, no?'

Declan nodded. 'In a perfect world.'

'We don't live in no perfect world, Dec. But we must try and make it better, huh?' Rocky clearly felt good at having helped his old friend. 'But I tell you one thing. If that motherfucker does anything else, then he dead, man. I mean, *really* dead.' He shook his head from side to side, his eyes, cold. 'I hope for his sake he don't cross you, Sophie, or Pedro here, because if he does, he cross Rocky, too. You hear me?'

Declan gave a wan smile. 'Loud and clear, my friend.'

Try as he might, Peter found it impossible not to smile.

'You know, I'm curious.' Rocky cocked an eyebrow.

Peter could see that Declan knew what was coming.

'What's with these boxes that's so important a man would want to take your daughter and try and kill you?'

Declan smiled. 'They're priceless antiques, Rocky, worth a fortune to a collector like Karl Johansson. They just don't make them like that anymore. Maybe it's hard to understand.'

'But why you need two boxes that look the same?'

'Because it's very rare to have two such exquisite, identical writing boxes made by the best colonial craftsmen from so long ago, during the Spanish occupation. As a pair, they're priceless. They represent a love story from eighteenth-century Manila. One belonged to a gentleman and the other to a countess.' As Declan had told Peter, a little bit of truth always went a long way.

Rocky squinted. 'So, how much they worth?'

'One million dollars.' Declan plucked a figure out of the air.

'I don't understand, man. All that hassle for one million dollars. For marijuana, yes. For cocaine, yes. But for two old boxes. That crazy, man.'

Peter wondered what the ex-gangster really thought. He excelled at playing the joker but was no fool. Only time would tell.

'I'm gonna split,' Rocky said. 'I got people to see. Stay safe, Declan. We're even now, but just say the word if you need something.'

He gave Declan a bear hug, then melted into the night, just the glow of his cigar visible in the distance. The speedboat was left tied to the jetty whilst Rocky's men escorted Johansson and the *Griffin* away from Philippine waters.

'There's a basic hotel in town where I made reservations, just in case,' Declan told Peter and Sophie. 'I think we could all do with some sleep. We'll fly to El Nido in the morning.'

Although he looked exhausted, his relief at having Sophie safely back was tangible. She in turn appeared to have handled her ordeal with genuine tenacity, clearly delighting in her freedom as they walked the short distance to the hotel.

In the lobby, Declan and Sophie hugged tightly, whispering to one another, their love and tight bond unmistakable. She kissed him goodnight and he wearily went up to bed with both boxes safely under his arms.

'You must be beat?' Peter said.

She shook her head. 'Not really. I just slept and speculated in my prison cell. You two had the toughest time ...' adding, '... it seems to have taken its toll on him.'

'It's the culmination of a lifetime's search and fears. Believe me, if it wasn't for his determination, you wouldn't be here now. He's a very resourceful man.'

She nodded. 'Yes, he is. But I know he couldn't have done it without you.'

Liking the way she looked at him, Peter said, 'I can't help feeling that if I hadn't come out here, none of this would have happened.'

'Your father gave you no choice.'

He shrugged. 'I guess you're right ... Fancy a drink before hitting the sack?'

She smiled softly. 'My mind's racing. I'd like that.'

They walked down the hill and found a bar on a street corner with a panoramic view over the bay, where boat lights twinkled. A mixture of locals and tourists chatted away as they sat around a rickety table and ordered beer and bar snacks.

Sophie said, 'You look exhausted.'

'I'll be fine with some sleep.'

'Tell me everything that's happened since I was kidnapped.'

'Okay,' Peter said, proceeding to recount all the events since she'd called Declan during their first trip to Manila, when his sloop had been broken into. It was a roller coaster of a story, but filling in the missing pieces put everything into perspective.

When he'd finished he said, 'What's your impression of Johansson?'

'He's a psychopath, hell-bent on finding the diamond.'

'So you think he'll be back?'

'There's not a doubt in my mind. It's just a temporary reprieve. I can't understand why Dad let him go. There's no way he'll give up now we've got both boxes and he thinks we may know how to unlock their secret ... which remains to be seen,' she added.

'Did he manage to open Sinclair's box?'

She shook her head. 'I'm pretty sure he didn't. He was too busy gloating and it's still locked.'

She recounted her conversations with Johansson, and how he'd behaved. In turn, Peter explained about the fake box and transmitter.

Sophie sat back and chuckled. 'The crafty bugger! I wondered how you'd found me.'

Changing tack, Peter said, 'I'm curious. Do you really believe this story? I mean, I know it captures the imagination, but do you honestly think there's a legendary diamond just waiting to be found on some ship-wrecked Indiaman?'

Sophie smiled. 'I really want to believe it. I mean, just look at all the trouble it's caused. Finding it would vindicate everything that's happened. Given it's a documented diamond – with a provenance – that went missing, it's factually compelling, and knowing the extent of what members of the East India Company pillaged, it's certainly plausible it was stolen from the Nawab and smuggled on an East Indiaman. Then having two identical writing boxes with Sinclair's and the Condesa's initials on them, given what was written in her diary, seems to reinforce the credibility of the story, don't you think? I mean, why would she make it up?'

She took a slug of beer. 'Now, *I'm* curious. How the hell did your father locate Sinclair's writing box?'

'Samantha found a Sotheby's catalogue in his study for a country house auction in Suffolk, England, with a photograph and description. The estate and its contents were being liquidated by a descendant of one of Sinclair's distant cousins. Sotheby's must have alerted him.'

Pausing briefly, Peter said poignantly, 'It was apparently delivered the day after Dad was rushed to hospital, and wasn't put in his study until the day before Samantha found it.'

Sophie could see the pain in his eyes as he talked about his father. 'Do *you* believe the story?' she asked gently, her eyes two piercing sapphires.

Peter leant back. 'You know. It's such an incredible story, I think it just might be true.'

'Knowing our luck, it's probably cursed. Let's face it, it hasn't brought a whole lot of joy, has it? We all know money doesn't bring happiness. Maybe that's why it's been hidden for so long. Some things just aren't meant to be found.' She paused then said, 'How were the Koh-i-noor and Hope diamonds cursed?'

'The Koh-i-Noor's supposed to put a death curse on any man who wears it, which is why as part of the British ceremonial crown it's only been worn by Queen Victoria, the Queen Mother and Queen Elizabeth. And a significant number of people who came into contact with the Hope died under mysterious circumstances.'

'Well, let's suppose for one fanciful moment we manage to locate this elusive Indiaman and against all the odds find this glitzy lump of blue rock.' She smiled mischievously. 'That would mean I'm the only one who can wear it!'

'I'll drink to that.' Peter raised his beer bottle and they clinked bottles.

From the sparkle in her eye, Peter thought Sophie seemed to have put her ordeal behind her and sensed she was warming to him with a connection on more than one level. He needed to find out what had happened to her mother, but the right time never seemed to present itself. However, one thing he was *sure* about was that he wanted to get to know her a whole lot better.

# CHAPTER 19

## *La Señora, Bambam*

The following day, after returning to Bambam, the three of them sat on *La Señora*, anchored 50 metres from shore. They'd decided to wait until they got back to the island to examine Sinclair's box, rather than try to figure things out in Coron; after all, they had waited this long so what difference would another day make?

The inside of the sloop had been returned to its former glory, looking as splendid as it had on the day Declan first recounted the story to Peter and Sophie.

They sat around the small teak table where the two writing boxes sat side by side. It felt special to see them reunited after so many years, lending credence to the incredible story within the Condesa's diary.

'How can we open Sinclair's box without a key?' asked Peter, looking at Declan.

Declan smiled. 'Well, fortunately Karl didn't force it.'

'Which means we're going to have to, unless we take it to your workshop and pick it,' said Sophie.

'It would be a pity to break such a beautiful piece, don't you think?' Declan had a sparkle in his eye.

'What do you suggest then?' said Sophie.

'Well, luckily for us, the Condesa was a cautious woman, and, knowing what her man might be like with keys, she kept a spare.' With a broad grin Declan held up a small brass key.

Sophie smiled. 'I really like this woman.'

Expectation lay heavy in the air. Even with the boxes reunited, their 250-year-old secret could remain elusive, or it could all be a hoax.

'Ready?' said Declan with a look of anticipation.

Sophie and Peter nodded.

Declan gently inserted the key into Sinclair's box. It was a perfect fit. Turning it slowly, the lock clicked. He lifted the lid, the hinges squeaking slightly, only to see empty space.

Undeterred, he said, 'The Condesa was a crafty woman. We know she would have contrived something special.'

There was still the unspoken concern that whatever it might have contained could have been removed at some point on its journey to its final resting place in a Suffolk manor house in England. Perhaps there had been letters or a map which were now in someone else's possession, the box re-locked and the key thrown away. Various scenarios played out in their minds. The best case being that the box had made the long journey from Manila, via India, back to England, and was repatriated with the rest of Sinclair's belongings after his untimely death, ending up in a distant relative's country estate all those years later, with no one any the wiser as to its potential secrets.

Declan picked the box up, studying it carefully, turning it this way and that, assessing it from every angle, and unable to find any pressure points like he'd found in the Condesa's box; his frustration was evident as he placed it back on the table.

'Let me try,' said Sophie, picking it up gently, examining it in much the same way. Scanning the inside of the lid she had an idea. 'Either of you got a knife?'

Peter obliged, handing her a Swiss army knife.

She carefully inserted the blade into the top left corner of the box, gently prying open a minute gap. With a simple twist, the inside of the lid sprang out, landing the other way up on the floor.

The three of them stared down in amazement at the intricately carved piece of wood with a distinctive religious cross in bas-relief that faced them.

A line, like the shadow from a sundial, extended from its centre towards its middle left-hand side.

'Sweet Jesus.' Declan picked up the beautiful piece and placed it on the table, his excitement contagious as they looked at one another, all thinking the same thing: perhaps there was something similar in the Condesa's box.

'I swear I've looked at her box a thousand times,' Declan said, shaking his head in awe, 'always thinking Sinclair's box was the key.' He picked up the Condesa's box and scrutinised the inside of the lid. Although it seemed a secure fit, on closer inspection it looked as though there may be room to insert a thin blade. Using the penknife, in no time they had the other piece of the jigsaw puzzle: a second piece of wood with a beautiful butterfly carved in the same bas relief style as the cross. When Sophie placed it to the left of the first piece, the shadow line from the first piece extended to the tip of the butterfly's lower right wing.

'Mother of God, it's true.' Declan sat down, and the colour drained from his face, which was a mixture of relief, amazement, vindication and excitement. Now, with these cryptic clues, they were one step closer to finally being able to search for the wreck of the Indiaman.

Studying the pieces, side by side, Peter said, 'I think the cross and the butterfly represent islands.'

Declan was in a state of shock, as if he couldn't quite believe after so many years they were now zeroing in on the potential location of a sunken Indiaman and a priceless diamond supposedly smuggled on it.

He said, 'The cross must be one of the Catholic orders. But the butterfly? I can't recall having seen an island shaped like a butterfly, can you?' he asked, looking at Sophie.

Sophie shook her head. 'No. But with over 7,000 islands covering 300,000 kilometres, and thousands of reefs of all shapes and sizes ...' She left the statement hanging.

Declan shrugged. Put like that, one could argue it was either a formidable task or one full of possibility, given that only 2,000 islands were inhabited and 5,000 named.

Declan's mobile rang and he answered. Seeing who it was, he put it on speaker.

'Bekker's escaped and killed two of my men,' yelled Rocky, fuming. 'You need to watch your back.'

'Thanks for the heads-up,' Declan said. 'You dealt with Johansson, right?'

'We made it crystal clear to the motherfucker what will happen if he returns.'

Declan rolled his eyes at Sophie and Peter, who knew the Swede would have some physical souvenirs from that "explanation".

Declan said, 'If they show up, we'll need your help.'

'Just say the word, Dec. Bekker's a walking dead motherfucker.'

The line was cut.

Sophie looked concerned. 'What do you think he'll he do?'

Declan said, 'He's unpredictable, but will want revenge and won't know if Karl's jettisoned him, but he will assume Karl has both boxes, which means he'll be after us when he finds Karl no longer has them. I'm betting, though, that Karl will re-engage his services.'

Peter said, 'There's no way Johansson's kept Bekker fully in the picture.'

'I agree with you,' said Declan. 'He won't know what's at stake. Either way, it doesn't bode well. We have to pray he doesn't involve the Ba-Gong – they're seriously bad news. Even Rocky looks like a valuable member of the community next to them.'

Sophie said, 'I think we should photograph these carvings and put them with the boxes in your Manila safe.'

'That makes sense,' agreed Declan, reaching over and selecting a map from a shelf and spreading it out on the table. It was a 1:50,000 topographical map of northern Palawan produced by the National Mapping and Resource Information Agency of the Philippines, providing excellent detail on island groups, individual islands, and surrounding water depths, shoals and reefs.

'Do you think there's a historical record of Catholic missions around the islands?' said Peter.

Declan nodded. 'There must be. The Jesuits, Franciscans, Augustans and Dominicans all competed to spread the word of God back in the day and it was only because of them that the Spanish retained any semblance of control of the islands outside of Manila. I'm sure all the denominations keep historical records, but *where* is the question. They're most likely scattered across archives in Manila, Spain and Mexico.'

After Googling on her iPad, Sophie turned it to face them, saying confidently, 'It's a Dominican cross.'

On the screen was the same design of cross as that carved on Sinclair's box.

'So, we've got two pretty good clues,' said Declan. 'A butterfly-shaped island and another which had a Dominican mission on it.'

Sophie said, 'We need to divide and separate. Why don't you go to Manila, Dad, and check for any record of Dominican missions, while Peter and I try to find any islands resembling a butterfly. I also need to ensure the building repair work's on schedule as several dive parties are booked in.'

'That's a sensible division of labour,' agreed Declan with renewed enthusiasm. 'I'll ask José to charter a floatplane so we can initiate an aerial search. It'll give us flexibility to land anywhere if the weather's half decent.'

'I'd like to underwrite the cost,' Peter said. 'After all, this is a joint effort instigated by Dad, who made provision for this sort of thing.'

Declan placed his hand on Peter's shoulder and smiled warmly. 'That's a generous offer, son, but thanks to Harry we're closer than we've ever been to locating the Indiaman. It's the least I can do.'

Declan seemed to have a new lease of life; his enthusiasm was contagious.

'Okay, but if we identify a probable wreck location, I'll charter a cat as we'll need a base to dive and explore from.'

'That's a good idea. And it's a deal,' said Declan. 'I know a good charter outfit.'

He placed his index finger north of Busuanga on the map. 'I think we should initially focus on this area. I think it's unlikely, though not impossible, that an Indiaman would have come south of Coron.'

A hunch from a man who knew these waters like the back of his hand.

'If our assumption that the butterfly represents an island is correct,' Sophie said, 'we should pray it looks the same as it did back then.'

'And hope it was properly drawn or described by Sinclair in his letter to the Condesa, which was the basis for the carvings,' said Peter. 'There's real scope for Chinese whispers here. If the butterfly represents an island, then they'd have needed a sufficiently high vantage point for the comparison to be made.'

'Well, we have to start somewhere,' said Declan, 'and hope by the process of elimination we'll find what we're looking for. If I can find out the location of any Dominican missions on the islands back then, at least we'll have a starting point.'

*

They were about to leave the sloop and head back to the island when Peter said, 'There's one important thing we haven't discussed.'

Declan and Sophie looked at him quizzically.

'The identity of the East Indiaman Sinclair took passage on.'

'There was no mention in the Condesa's diary, so it's a process of deduction,' said Declan. 'I've carried out a lot of research and some years ago I flew to London to visit the British Library, which holds the records of the entire history of the East India Company, from 1601 to 1874. It's a world-class archive of well-preserved material.'

'Presumably,' Peter said, 'there was an official record of all the East Indiamen that sailed each season?'

Declan nodded. 'There was. I've got the official lists of all Indiamen that sailed between 1760 and 1765, from England to India, as well as from India up to China. And a good number called into Manila on their way back to India.

'In addition, I researched all naval-rated ships of the line that were part of Admiral Cornish's invasion fleet for the Battle of Manila, as well as the Indiamen carrying supplies and the new governor.

'During the eighteen-month British occupation of the city, several Indiamen, laden with tea and porcelain after trading them for cotton in Whampoa, stopped at Manila on their way back from China.'

Sophie said, 'Any potential candidates you thought could be our ship?'

Declan nodded. 'Several. I studied every ship's journal I could lay my hands on. Incidentally, they make fascinating reading; you get a real insight into a captain's personality from handwritten entries, as well as life at sea with all its risks, adventures and hardships. Transports you right back in time,' he said wistfully.

'Now, at the outset of every voyage,' he continued, 'the captain was given his ship's official journal in which he would make daily entries about the weather, sea conditions, their general progress and heading, in addition to detailing longitude and latitude, the distance and bearing of the closest land, and anything else of note. It was a mixture of navigational log, notes of incidents and observations, as well as commercial trading entries. Reading an Indiaman's journal enables you to trace the route taken on both the outward and homeward journey, as well as glean from anecdotal entries which other Indiaman it came across and where.' Declan raised an eyebrow to reinforce the last point.

'What records were kept of missing ships?' asked Peter.

'That's a good question. There are various ways of tracking missing vessels. The most obvious being if there's a missing journal for an Indiaman recorded as sailing that season. On completion of a successful journey, after returning to London, all ships' journals had to be handed over to the Secretary of Staff at East India House. Only then would the captain and crew be paid. So I naturally cross-checked these. I then checked imprest and absence books for voyages at East India House, together with Court of Directors minutes and company correspondence during the period in question.'

'Wouldn't there be insurance records for missing Indiaman?'

Sophie asked.

Declan smiled. 'Yes. Most were privately owned by investment consortiums and insured with Lloyd's of London.'

'And?'

'I researched all possible sources and by deduction narrowed it down to an Indiaman called the *Earl of Suffolk*, listed as sailing in 1762, with no surviving journal. I found several references of her calling into Manila on her way back from China in the journals of two other Indiamen: the *Havana* and *Admiral Pocock*, which sailed the same season. There's no mention of her after that apart from a brief reference in a set of Court of Directors minutes, stating her as several weeks overdue in London.'

'Where would the captain keep the ship's journal?' asked Sophie.

'In his cabin. So, unless it was rescued by him or a crew member, it went down with the ship. Without it, unless there were survivors who knew the position of the wreck site and could use landmarks to remember it, it would be lost for ever, with an area the size of Europe to second-guess and search.

'One thing you need to understand,' Declan continued, 'is that commanders of East Indiamen carried out business on the side; it went with the territory as an acknowledged perk of the job. If there was an opportunity to profit from doing a little personal trading, they jumped at it, always looking for faster routes, which meant they often went off-piste, putting themselves at greater risk in uncharted waters with unknown reefs and shoals, and the ever-present risk of bad weather, especially in the typhoon belt.'

'How accurately could they calculate their position?' Sophie asked.

'You've hit the nail on the head, girl!' Declan grinned. 'Not very, is the answer. They could calculate latitude accurately, but not longitude, so were dependent on dead reckoning with a sextant, guided by night-time constellations. John Harrison's game-changing H4 chronometer didn't come into official use until a decade later, which means at the time our ship went down there was significant margin for error in calculating their location.

'They depended on waypoints and landmarks to cross-check position to ensure they were on the right course, which were updated after every voyage on company maps, pilots and almanacs. They also pillaged maps from enemy ships, especially from the Dutch and Spanish, who were excellent cartographers and comprehensively mapped the East Indies and Philippines.

'The most famous cartographer of all was a Jesuit priest called Pedro Murillo Velarde, whose revered 1734 map of the Philippines ironically shows the Spratly islands as undisputed Philippine territory. The point I'm making,' Declan said, 'is that if you take into account all these variables, it's impossible to know exactly where an Indiaman sank unless a journal was rescued with up-to-date entries or unless there were survivors whose accounts were reliable and the ship's position at the time it went down was accurately known.'

Sophie said, 'So you think Sinclair took passage on the *Earl of Suffolk?*'

Declan nodded. 'Yes, I do because I couldn't find another Indiaman that wasn't accounted for that season.'

'Well, let's hope you're right,' said Sophie. 'At least thanks to the Condesa we now have two clues for a rudimentary map.'

'Manila it is then,' said Declan, slapping his thigh and standing up. He gave a wry smile. 'The simplest ways are always the best.'

# CHAPTER 20

## *Manila*

Declan flew to Manila, heading directly to his shop in Intramuros where he locked both writing boxes securely in a new safe he'd had installed in the basement of his workshop, having substantially beefed up security.

After making some calls, he ascertained the best place to find out about the Dominican presence in the eighteenth century was Santo Domingo Church in Quezon City, the most populous city located in northern Metro Manila. As one of the largest churches in South East Asia, it was the Dominicans' regional headquarters and, given it had a museum attached, it seemed the logical place to start making enquiries.

Instead of using his driver, Declan hailed a taxi, telling no one where he was going. In less than an hour, it pulled up in front of a large concrete Spanish-style building, not looking at all like he'd expected.

The inner tranquillity inside the huge space was a startling contrast to the hustle and bustle outside, with light streaming through large stained-glass windows onto murals of Domingo de Guzmán, the founder of the Dominican Order of Preachers. *A true sanctuary for believers*, thought Declan.

Although not a practising Catholic, he'd been raised in the faith and was always respectful in a house of God, or in the presence of men of the cloth. His mother had been a devout Catholic and he had fond memories of her and fellow churchgoers, especially the parish priest. The church had been at the centre of their small rural community in Connemara, where Declan had had a simple but happy upbringing which he remembered fondly.

Scattered throughout the pews, people knelt in prayer or sat in quiet contemplation as shafts of light streamed through tall windows. Declan made his way over to a priest lighting candles at the altar, who informed him that Father Roberto García was the man he needed to talk to. He'd been associated with the church longer than anyone else and was responsible for keeping historical records, which was a personal hobby. He was due in anytime.

While Declan sat waiting in the first row of pews, his life flashed before him. He thought of his mother and father in Ireland; his first trip to the Philippines as a young man; and his adventures with Harry and Karl. But more than anything, he thought about Ingrid and Sophie. He'd been devastated after Ingrid's death, searching for answers, Sophie, the only reason he'd kept going. As he looked around the cavernous church, he felt peaceful, as though he was meant to have come here. Although no saint, he knew he was fundamentally a good person who believed in right and wrong. Why else had he let Karl go free after what he'd done? While he tried to rationalise things, an elderly priest walked past him towards the front of the church. Declan got up and went to introduce himself.

Father García was a small, sprightly man with a wizened face and benign countenance, without an ounce of spare flesh. His piercing light brown eyes looked straight into Declan's as he firmly shook his hand. A good judge of character, Declan intuitively knew the man would be knowledgeable but wouldn't pull any punches. He looked the real deal, not a superficial church politician, with a spiritual simplicity about him that would strip anyone with pretensions to the bone.

Declan had read that Santo Domingo had an archbishop and housed the national shrine of the Holy Rosary of La Naval de Manila as well as priceless icons, and how every year heaving religious festivals filled the streets with pomp and ceremony in its honour. He thought that Father García, however, projected the very antithesis of all that.

The priest ushered Declan out through a side door to a small room off a cloistered corridor, which was packed with books and manuscripts. To one side was a leather-covered antique writing desk where a nineteenth-century green reading light dimly lit piles of documents next to a large magnifying glass, an old-fashioned inkwell and several fountain pens.

Framed prints of various Dominican symbols adopted by the order over the years dotted the walls, one the same as the carving found within Sinclair's box: a circular seal with the Dominican cross in the middle, and fleurs-de-lis at its four extremities.

Underneath it was a map of the Philippine archipelago highlighting the Dominican presence around the islands, which was far more extensive than Declan had realised, and beside it another map detailed Dominican locations around Asia, again, surprisingly extensive.

Father García looked at Declan enquiringly. 'How can I help you, Mr O'Connor?'

'I'm researching the Spanish colonial period to gain a better understanding of what presence the various Catholic orders had around the archipelago, aware as I am that they all competed with one another back then.'

'Are you a historian?'

'No, I'm not.' Declan tried to sound sincere. 'But I've lived in these islands all my life and their history's a passion of mine. Given the Spanish were here for so long and the Church was so instrumental in maintaining the status quo through evangelising the various island tribes, I'm seeking a clearer understanding of how that happened.'

'You're searching for something,' said Father García perceptively.

Declan gave a wry smile. 'Aren't we all?'

An almost imperceptible frown crossed the priest's face.

'Are you religious, Mr O'Connor?'

'I was raised a Catholic.'

The priest smiled kindly. 'It's never too late, you know. Some people find God when they least expect to.'

Declan gave a weak smile. 'Do you have records going back that far, Father?'

'We have pretty extensive records,' the priest replied, his English clear and without a heavy Filipino accent. 'You know, this is the sixth time Santo Domingo Church has been reconstructed. The other five times were in Intramuros. The British ransacked our church after the Battle of Manila in 1762 and stole priceless treasures from our order.' He shook his head sorrowfully. 'And many historical records, dating back to 1581 from when we first came to these islands, were damaged or destroyed.'

'But you salvaged a good number I believe?' Declan's voice was hopeful.

Father García crossed himself. 'Yes, we did. And I've dedicated what remains of my life to restoring and documenting them properly, so we have a comprehensive record of the positive impact our order has had, in God's name, on his beautiful island people.'

'Did the Dominicans have missions on the outlying islands back then?'

'Your question's interesting,' replied the old priest, his eyes sprightly and alert. 'As you intimated, the Spanish had difficulty controlling the outlying islands against attacks from Moros, the native Muslims, and from Chinese pirates who roamed the archipelago. So, they constructed forts on some of the larger islands to combat the threat.

'Because of these threats and the logistics of living on the outlying islands, most Catholic orders, like ours, focused on Manila and Luzon, although we had some missions in the northern provinces of Pangasinan and Bataan.' The old man smiled. 'However, the Jesuits, who were a lot more adventurous, built missions on various outlying islands to try and convert what they regarded as the animalistic natives.'

Declan didn't like the direction this was heading, but listened attentively to the affable priest.

'However, I recall an interesting exception I came across in some correspondence.' Father García frowned as he tried to recall the circumstances. 'A Dominican priest I read about with some fascination, who wanted to convert the natives of Palawan to Christianity. A man with a passion for cartography, inspired by the Jesuit, Velarde. As you may or may not know, our order was adept at learning local languages to facilitate evangelising local tribes and spread the word of God.'

'I didn't. That's interesting,' said Declan having caught the scent, cocking an eyebrow. 'Do you remember his name?'

Trying to summon the name, the priest stroked his chin between thumb and forefinger as he walked over to a row of cabinets. 'Fernando ... Fernando ...' He opened the door of the middle one, haphazardly jammed with manuscripts and journals, and rummaged through the pile, eventually extracting a thin plastic folder containing sepia-coloured sheafs of paper. 'You're in luck, Mr O'Connor. The document in question's here.' He held it up proudly.

'Now, let me refresh my memory.' He flicked through the fragile papers. 'It's correspondence between the Archbishop and ... ah, yes, I remember now ... Father Fernando Trujillo.' He looked up at Declan with a smile.

Selecting the relevant page, he summarised the contents. 'It seems he promoted an initiative to set up a Dominican mission on one of the outermost islands of the archipelago, to extend God's work. He was particularly interested in Palawan province, much to the consternation of the more conservative members of the brotherhood, who wanted the order's focus to remain on Luzon.'

Father Garcia scanned through the document with a practised eye. 'Ah, here it is. Trujillo was given special dispensation by the Archbishop to set up a mission on an island in the north of Palawan province. If successful, he would contemplate allowing Trujillo to do the same in the Visayas, the rationale being they wanted to bring islanders together by creating a sense of religious community, which they'd seen the Jesuits do successfully through classical music.'

Declan felt his pulse racing. This was gold dust! 'So, you have a record of where the mission was located then, Father?'

'Let me see ...' Father García squinted through half-moon glasses as he scanned another page.

'Ah, here we are. Permission was granted to explore two locations.' He looked up at Declan. 'I'm sorry, but it doesn't specify which was selected.'

'Does it say where they were?' Declan tried to contain his excitement and remain calm as the priest pointed to a reference.

'One potential location was an island called Laputacan.' The priest shook his head slightly. 'I must say I've never heard of it.'

Declan frowned; he'd never heard of it either. 'And the other?'

'It just says northern Busuanga.'

'Do you have other documents connected with this initiative, Father?'

'It's the only one I've come across so far. There are probably more. I'm slowly working my way through piles of mixed-up manuscripts. This batch only came in recently from the archives.' He looked at Declan sympathetically. 'It can't be rushed, you know. They're in no particular order.'

'Would it be possible to have a copy, please, Father?'

'Of course.'

Father García took the pages to a small photocopier in the corner of the room and made copies. He put the original pages on the desk and handed Declan the copies. 'When did you last take confession?' he asked as if, after so many years as a priest, sensing the emotional turmoil within the old Irishman.

'Err, it's been a while, Father.'

'Then come with me.' Father García grasped Declan's arm firmly and led him into the main body of the church and over to the confessional box.

An hour later, Declan hailed a taxi and returned to Intramuros with an inexplicable lightness of spirit, as though cleansed of much darkness.

# CHAPTER 21

## *Bambam*

ack on Bambam, after scrutinising charts of the archipelago, Peter and Sophie had drawn a blank on identifying a butterfly-shaped island, so Sophie focused on ensuring the building work was being carried out properly, which required a constant flow of decisions. Peter, who couldn't do much until they heard back from Declan, went back to his cabin. There he lay in the hammock where he studied a map of the Western Philippines and tried to visualise the route an East Indiaman might have taken and how far off its normal course it could have deviated, knowing it wasn't improbable that one had sailed from Manila into Palawan province instead of heading directly south-west into the South China Sea, which was the normal route back to England.

Perhaps the captain had tried to find a faster route or do a little personal business on the side. The combination of sailing into uncharted waters and being broadsided by a storm would have provided the perfect circumstances for his ship's demise as it smashed into an unseen reef.

The early afternoon air was hot and heavy, the humidity close to ninety-five per cent. Just as he decided he'd go for a swim, Peter heard someone. He looked up and saw Sophie approaching, looking fetching in a tight white bikini top that left little to the imagination, cut-off denim shorts, and a towel rolled under her arm.

'Any news from Declan?' he asked, trying hard to focus on her face.

She shook her head. 'Not yet. What are you up to?'

'Using my intuition to divine where an Indiaman might have sailed.'

'And?'

'I think it's possible that with the right set of circumstances it could have strayed into these waters. But what's bugging me,' he frowned, 'is apart from the difficulty of locating the wreck site of the *Earl of Suffolk*, if that's our ship, which is a major challenge in itself, I don't know how the hell we're going to locate something as small as a diamond unless it's contained in something bigger that's survived the ravages of time. I don't recall Declan mentioning anything about what it was in or where it was hidden on the ship.'

'Me neither. We'll ask him and we can check the diary. I'm sure he'll know.'

'You realise the odds of finding it are a million to one?'

Sophie nodded gently. 'They're long odds, we know that, but now we have these clues, we're one step closer. Let's hope Dad comes up with something in Manila.'

'Well, we do need some luck,' Peter said.

She could tell he needed cheering up. 'Fancy a swim? There's a place I think you'll like. It might help clear your head.'

'Sounds good. I was about to go anyway.'

'Grab your stuff then, and follow me.'

The thought of seeing Sophie in her bikini was incentive enough, so Peter put on his swim shorts, grabbed a towel, and followed her up the trail past the winding path where he'd accessed the channel the first day.

They climbed for another five minutes until they reached a large rocky outcrop, behind which Sophie disappeared. Hidden from view was a steep, twisting, narrow path that they scrambled down, grabbing rocks and tree roots to steady themselves. It turned sharply to the right, where they came out onto a slab of rock that protruded several metres above the water. Below them, further to the right, lay a small beach fringing the main channel opposite a towering limestone cliff covered in exotic vegetation.

Sophie dropped her shorts and stood briefly in a skimpy white bikini that accentuated her golden tan. She gave Peter a broad grin, took a couple of quick steps and dived into the clear sea water below in one fluid motion. He followed her blurred outline as she skimmed over coral into the deeper water of the channel, looking like a model in a holiday advert.

He walked to the lip of the overhang, executed a perfect jack-knife into the water below, leaving hardly a ripple, breast stroked his way underwater to surface beside her.

'It's bloody beautiful,' he said treading water, surveying their surroundings with a broad grin.

Sophie undulated her arms to keep in situ next to him. 'It's my special place. I knew you'd like it. I come here when I want to get away from everyone.'

She swam further into the channel. Peter swam after her, quickly feeling the strength of the current in the deeper water. On one side, he could see the hidden lagoon where yachts sheltered in rough weather, and on the other, a narrow gap between sheer cliffs led out to sea, too narrow, he surmised, for a yacht to navigate.

They swam back towards the hidden beach until they were able to stand.

Sophie's pert nipples showed prominently through her wet bikini top as she wrung out her hair. Peter desperately wanted to kiss her, but was wary of frightening her off. However, to his surprise, she moved closer to him, the water now up to their waists. 'What's the matter?' she asked.

'Just thinking.'

'You think too much, Peter Blake.' She moved closer, the tension between them, electric as their bodies touched and Peter instinctively circled her waist, pulling her close. As she looked up at him with her seductive blue eyes, her blonde hair touching the water, Peter leant forward and their mouths met hungrily, their tongues exploring and savouring the touch and taste of one another. After a while, they made their way to the beach where they lay talking, laughing, and enjoying their new found intimacy.

'This could be complicated,' Peter said, delighting in the feel of Sophie's breasts against his chest as she lay on top of him, her blue eyes shining, her mouth begging to be kissed.

'It doesn't have to be.'

'I don't think Declan's gonna like this.'

'Don't worry. He likes you.'

'I'm betting that could change.'

'I'll handle him,' she said without concern. 'Besides, he doesn't have to know.'

*Good luck with that one*, thought Peter, knowing he couldn't help himself from getting involved, having never been so attracted to anyone in his life.

Time passed quickly. They eventually made their way back to Peter's cabin where they agreed to meet later by the pool. Sophie went to her cabin to shower and change. When she came out of the shower, she saw a missed call from Declan and called him back. He answered immediately, sounding excited as he recounted his meeting with Father García, but seemed somehow different, and Sophie couldn't put her finger on why. However, he was adamant, based on what he'd found out, that they could commence an aerial search without further delay.

# CHAPTER 22

## *Quezon City, Manila*

Jan Bekker had kept a low profile since escaping from Rocky, hiding out under the protection of the Ba-Gong. However, he'd put out scouts in the event Declan, or the others, might return to Manila, and one of them had kept a vigil outside his Intramuros store. The man had followed Declan's taxi to Santo Domingo Church, where he'd sat and watched him accompany the old priest outside the church, reappearing a good while later, taking confession, then leaving.

He'd found out the priest's name and informed Bekker.

The South African arrived at the church an hour later. It was late afternoon and the church was empty. He made his way through the side door to the cloistered corridor and saw a light in a room off it, some way along. Through the door he saw an old priest hunched over a writing desk, squinting through a magnifying glass, poring over a document, his desk piled high with manuscripts whilst soft choral music played in the background.

Bekker coughed and the priest looked up. 'Can I help you?' he asked.

'I hope so,' Bekker replied menacingly, his outline blocking the doorway.

Immediately recognising the man was trouble, Father Garcia said calmly, 'I'm afraid the next service isn't until 6pm.'

'A friend of mine came to see you earlier. I'd like to know what he wanted,' said the ugly man.

Father Garcia shook his head. 'I'm sorry, but I can't divulge private conversations with parishioners.'

'He's not a parishioner. He's an Irishman searching for something. I want to know what he asked you and what you told him.'

'I'm afraid that's not possible.' Father García placed the magnifying glass on the table, covering the page he'd been scrutinising.

'We can do this the hard way or the easy way, Padre. I'm not religious, so it makes little difference to me. I'd recommend the easy way for a man your age. Fire spreads quickly in this climate.'

He shut the door and walked towards the desk, sensing the old fool wouldn't capitulate.

'What did you tell him?' Bekker's eyes were hard and unforgiving, his voice threatening.

'This is a house of God,' said Father Garcia, crossing himself, 'and you must respect that.'

Bekker walked over and hoisted the old man, who was nothing but skin and bones, to his feet, lifting him with one hand.

However, Father García showed no fear.

'Tell me what O'Connor wanted and I'll spare you,' said Bekker, his fetid breath an assault on the old man's senses. Father García shook his head in defiance, so Bekker hurled him against the wall, knocking pictures off their hooks as he hit it. The priest slumped to the floor. With blood seeping from his gashed arm and forehead, his skin aged, thin and bruised, he tried getting to his feet, but Bekker kicked him in the solar plexus, and the old man doubled over, winded, clutching his stomach, and curled himself into a protective ball.

Bekker walked over to the desk, quickly flicking through the papers on it. The one the priest had been studying was one of several fragile-looking pages, dated 1745, on extravagant-looking letterhead, with an impressive official seal. Unfortunately, it was in Spanish, which Bekker couldn't read. So he picked it up with all the other loose papers and slipped them into a plastic folder.

He walked over to Father García, who was hunched on the floor against the cabinets. 'If what I'm looking for isn't here, I'll be back.' He then kicked the old man for good measure and made his way out, shutting the door behind him.

# CHAPTER 23

## *Bambam to Busuanga*

Declan arrived back at the resort later that evening and described his meeting with Father García, showing Sophie and Peter the copies of historical correspondence.

Whilst Peter scanned through the still legible old-style Spanish, Sophie said, 'So, the Archbishop granted Father Trujillo dispensation to set up a mission with two potential locations in mind?'

Declan nodded. 'That's right. Either somewhere in northern Busuanga or on an island called Laputacan.'

Peter said, 'Do you know it?'

'Never heard of it. Have you, Sophie?'

She shook her head. 'Nope.'

'Not a good start,' said Peter.

'Well, it's enough to commence an initial aerial search,' Declan said enthusiastically. 'If it was on Busuanga, it would be near the coast. Any luck locating Butterfly Island?'

'Sadly, no,' confirmed Sophie. 'Though we've scrutinised your maps pretty thoroughly.'

'Well, if we can locate the mission, we'll find the other island and the wreck site,' Declan said adamantly. 'I'm sure of it. Because it's the only one the Dominicans had outside Luzon.'

'Anything coming up? Peter asked Sophie who was searching on her laptop.

'Nada.' She shook her head in frustration. 'Not a single reference.'

'Maybe it's called something different now,' Peter suggested.

'That's quite possible,' said Declan. 'Many islands have been renamed over the years, and some have multiple names you'd think were different places.'

Sophie had an idea. 'Gabe's got family on Busuanga. He could ask around.'

Declan's eyes narrowed. 'That's a good idea. But tell him to be discreet.'

Sophie went to find Gabe, who agreed to make some calls and let them know if his extended family knew anything. He was used to being tapped for his contacts and local knowledge; relaxed and happy-go-lucky, he wasn't the suspicious type.

A few hours later he came to find them, wearing a broader smile than normal.

'Well?' said Declan expectantly.

'One of my uncles thinks there was a village called that on Cabilauan, that his grandparents talked about.'

Declan looked at Peter. 'That's near the Kyokuzan Maru, the wreck of a Japanese army cargo ship and a popular dive site.' He turned to Gabe. 'Good work, Gabe.'

Gabe looked concerned. 'There's something else, sir. Some gang members been asking the same question round Coron and Busuanga.'

Declan's eyes narrowed again. 'Which?'

'Ba-Gong.'

It couldn't be coincidence. Bekker clearly wasn't wasting time.

'Ask your relatives if anyone else is asking, and exactly *what* they're asking, okay? And tell them not to tell them anything. It's really important, Gabe, it's to do with Miss Sophie's kidnapping.'

Gabe nodded, taking it at face value, and left. He knew better than to ask what this was about.

Peter said, 'How did they get onto us so quickly?'

'Excuse me a minute,' Declan replied, as if a sudden realisation had struck him. He went off to one side and made a call, then walked back over looking frustrated. Peter thought he'd probably tried to call Father Garcia to check he was alright.

'Someone must have followed me to the church,' Declan said, clearly annoyed with himself for putting the priest in danger. 'Well, they might know the old name of an island, but they don't know the clues we have and their significance or that one is most likely a butterfly-shaped island. The mission's only one part of the jigsaw puzzle.'

Peter said, 'Then we need to get airborne as soon as possible.'

Declan nodded. 'I suggest you and Sophie fly up to northern Busuanga and check out Cabilauan and that stretch of coast first thing tomorrow.'

'What are you going to do?' asked Sophie.

'More research. We need to know everything we can about the *Earl of Suffolk*. It's a few years since I narrowed it down to her. I need to refresh my memory and consolidate what I found out.'

Sophie frowned. Her father's memory was sharp as a pin, so there was probably another agenda he wasn't letting on about.

'Did you manage to sound out your contacts about a cat?' Peter asked Declan.

'Yes. I made some calls. I'll let you know what's available. You can take your pick. We'll then ensure it's fit for purpose.' He paused briefly, as if still wondering how Bekker and the Ba-Gong had got onto things so quickly. 'José will pick you up first thing in the morning, in a floatplane I've chartered for as long as we need it. Let's hope you can find something.'

Sophie hadn't heard him so excited for a very long time, seemingly having put the danger that Father Garcia was in to one side. Peter had also noticed the change in his demeanour. It was contagious, despite the omnipresent threat from Johansson and Bekker hovering in the back of their minds.

Peter looked at Sophie. 'What's the weather doing?'

'The short-term forecast is good,' she said, clocking Gabe who was signalling from a distance. 'I've got to help with a yacht arrival. I'll catch you later.'

When she was out of earshot, Peter turned to Declan. 'Do you

185

trust José?'

'Yes,' he replied gruffly, 'but at the same time I trust no one. He knows nothing about what we're looking for and I don't want him to. His job's to fly us safely from A to B and he's paid handsomely for it. Nevertheless, we'll use a cover story for good measure.'

He told Peter about the one he'd used with Father García, about writing a history of the islands. There was some truth in it. He'd penned a lot over the years, which was no secret to those who knew him.

*

Talking about the cat reminded Peter he needed to check in with Henry, which in turn got him wondering if Sam was alright. He called her, and was relieved to hear her voice after the third ring.

'What's going on, Peter? I've been worried sick.'

'I can't say much right now. The call could be tapped. I just wanted to check you're okay?'

'I'm fine, but I'm worried about you. When are you coming home?'

'I don't know yet. Things are chaotic after the typhoon. Soon, hopefully.' He rang off after saying he would be in touch.

Next, he decided to email Henry instead of calling. He didn't feel like answering questions; his message was short and to the point:

*Henry,*

*Sorry for not having been in touch, things were hectic after the typhoon and are only just getting back to normal. The resort got badly hit and I've been helping out. Sadly, I haven't found anything further in connection with Harry's quest. It certainly sounded plausible but there's nothing tangible to follow up on. It will have to go down as a cold case.*

*It's been cathartic to be somewhere different and get away from my normal routine and work, so I've decided to stay here for a few weeks to relax. As I haven't used any funds to date, I wondered if you could see your way to covering the cost of chartering a catamaran for a few weeks so I can explore the islands? It would be much appreciated and*

*I'm sure Harry would have been fine with that.*

*I hope all's going well sorting out his estate and look forward to catching up when I get back, so I can finally deal with his study.*

*Yours,*
*Peter*

He hesitated, hit send, then closed the laptop, putting his mind to the preparations for the following day. After an early dinner by the pool, he walked back to his cabin where he lay for a while in the hammock studying the map of northern Palawan. Feeling tired, he went inside and lay on his bed, sweating from the heat and humidity, trying to take advantage of a light breeze that drifted through the open windows.

Closing his eyes, he conjured an image of the Condesa and Sinclair, and reflected on the trail they'd left. Was it destiny? It certainly seemed as if Declan's, his and Sophie's lives were converging with unstoppable momentum.

As he drifted towards sleep, he heard a noise and sat bolt upright, his senses alert, but he relaxed when he saw Sophie approaching. She didn't speak, just slipped her shorts down, peeled off her top, then got onto the bed next to him. He slipped off his shorts and rolled into her and they embraced, enjoying the feel of each other's bodies to the sound of jungle insects and swifts flying high above. Peter loved the smooth feel of her firm athletic body, and the smell and taste of her as their tongues explored hungrily and their hands stroked and searched while they held one other.

After a while, Sophie pushed him back and, straddling him cowgirl-style, he entered her. They moved energetically in passionate synchronisation towards mutual climax, and afterwards held one another, listening to the sound of each other's breathing, drenched in sweat, fully satiated, quickly falling into a deep contented sleep. For once, Peter's dreams were untroubled and he slept more soundly than he'd done for a long time.

He woke to sunlight streaming through the windows, the only sign of Sophie her faint smell on the pillowcase.

It was time to get airborne and see what they could find.

*

They heard the bush plane before they saw it: a classic de Havilland Beaver DHC-2 floatplane that José had sourced through his friends at Horizon Sun Charters, a top charter outfit based out of Puerto Princesa on Palawan. Although it could accommodate six passengers, Peter sat up front next to José, with Sophie in the row behind, both of them donning headsets with microphones, enabling them to communicate over the noisy Beaver engine.

It was a fine clear morning, not a cloud in the sky, as the plane lifted slowly from the calm water off Bambam and headed in a north-easterly direction towards the northern tip of the Palawanian mainland up towards Coron and Busuanga, 130 kilometres away. With a collage of vivid colours spread out below them, Peter reflected on how much he loved the contrast of flying, with a bird's eye view, compared to being on a boat or diving under the ocean, each environment evoking a unique sensory perception. Being able to experience all three was something he never took for granted.

José looked the part in a white short-sleeved cotton shirt with epaulettes, dark trousers and aviator Ray-Bans glued to his face. The very definition of laconic and speaking only when spoken to, Peter judged him to be a good pilot, measured and reliable. They'd briefed him before take-off about the area they wanted to explore. He'd just smiled and nodded, confirming he understood, before carrying out final safety checks. Although the de Havilland was fully juiced up, they had refuelling options on Busuanga if necessary.

They'd agreed not to talk specifics in front of José, except in the context of Declan's cover story of researching historical Catholic missions, which he'd embellished in some detail before they left.

The flight up to northern Busuanga should take around fifty minutes. They initially flew in silence up towards Coron Bay, near where Sophie had been rescued from Johansson's yacht. Peter had a

1:50,000 maritime chart spread out on his lap and scrutinised any large yachts they flew over, with the *Griffin* very much in his mind, and also aware that the Japanese wrecks strewn in the waters below were graveyards in paradise.

Shortly, Coron town disappeared behind them as they flew over the sizeable island of Busuanga, and before long its north coast was visible. As instructed, José would fly its entire westward length, and then back again, further out, to see what they could spot from the air. Peter wanted to get an overall feel for the area, to try and visualise where an Indiaman might have sailed by accident or design. He thought the nautical chart pretty accurate in terms of channels and depths, but there was no substitute for seeing things first-hand.

Visibility was excellent. Although the islands out here were less dramatic and lower-lying than those in the Bacuit, they were nevertheless beautiful.

Peter noted the whole area was heavily reefed as they flew over Club Paradise, one of the pioneering luxury resorts developed by a German in the 1980s.

José maintained an altitude of 3,000 feet, which was low enough to see topographical details of islands, reefs and shoals, while Sophie took scores of photos and Peter cross-checked what he saw against the chart, only picking up some minor inconsistencies.

'That must be Calauit.' He pointed as a large island came into view. 'Keep the same heading. I'll tell you when to turn back.'

José nodded imperceptibly.

Sophie lent forwards and said into her mic: 'The whole island's a game reserve set up by Marcos in the seventies. He flew over endangered African wildlife from Kenya which has thrived.'

'Sounds like Jurassic Park,' said Peter.

'Just giraffes, zebras and gazelles. No dinosaurs.'

'Shame. I liked the book; good concept and actually possible.' He knew the science had moved on, with the potential to recreate extinct animals from their DNA now a reality, the Russians leading the way, trying to resurrect frozen mammoths in Siberia.

As they flew over the island, it was surreal seeing zebras and giraffes lolloping across savannah at the farthest extremity of the Philippines. When they hit ocean again, Peter 'choppered' his arm and José banked steeply, doing a 180 to head back the way they'd come, this time further out.

So far they'd seen nothing remotely resembling a butterfly.

Peter said into his mic, 'Can you fly low around Cabilauan and land on the north side?'

'Can do,' replied José, his expression deadpan.

José flew the length and breadth of Cabilauan whilst Peter and Sophie scanned below for any sign of remains, but saw nothing worth further investigation through the thick vegetation.

José delicately arced the de Havilland, dropping altitude and heading towards a secluded bay where he gently lowered the plane so it kissed the water as he eased the yoke and set her down on her floats. He taxied towards shore, avoiding a small reef, then cut the engine and let the plane drift to a stop on the beach.

Peter and Sophie climbed out onto the left-hand float, jumped into the shallow water, and walked up onto the beach. Whilst José was securing the plane with the intention of lying back for a snooze, Sophie shouted, 'Sorry, José, we need you.'

Without fuss, he checked the plane was firmly beached and jumped down to join them. The three of them walked up the long beach and along the tree line, around a small headland onto another beach. Whilst Sophie explained to José why they needed his help, they came upon a small cluster of huts set back from the beach among palms. Barefoot kids in dirty clothes were playing football with a large fruit while several women went about their chores, pounding mortars and tending a fire.

A couple of wizened old men squatted, smoking, with vacant expressions, facing one another on wooden steps as though time had no meaning. Fighting cockerels strutted and squawked noisily in wire enclosures in the shade where Peter clocked sets of vicious metal spurs hanging on a pole, knowing the savage sport of cockfighting was an obsession in this part of the world.

After explaining to José what to ask for, thinking it better for a local to do the talking, Sophie hung back with Peter. José approached one of the men. Crouching down so he was the same height, he offered him a cigarette and started talking. The old man took the cigarette with one hand, chuckling and gesticulating, and sucked on his own nearly fully smoked fag which was pincered in the other hand. After a lot of banter, he pointed to the other old man across the clearing. José headed over and repeated the process. The man shook his head animatedly multiple times at José's questions, so José got up, thanked them both with a packet of Lucky Strike, and walked over to where Sophie and Peter were standing.

'They don't know of any mission or ruins,' he said calmly.

'Nothing?' Peter looked perplexed.

José shook his head. 'They've lived here all their lives. One's ninety, the other eighty-nine. They've never seen or heard of any Spanish ruins on the island.'

It was the longest sentence Peter had ever heard him speak.

So that was that. The men had no reason to lie. Sophie told José they'd meet him back at the plane, and she and Peter walked around to the next cove. It was secluded, wild and beautiful, with the sound of the surf and fringing palms rustling in the warm sea breeze, and the smell of the sea.

Beyond the bone-white powder sand, azure water stretched into the distance, with a smattering of islands on the horizon. Peter imagined the unmistakable outline of an Indiaman coming into view, its sails billowing as it ran before the wind, thinking how every voyage would have been an adventure for the crew and passengers, with new sights, sounds and smells to titillate their senses, but always accompanied by the nagging fear of a sudden change in the weather or the potential danger of running into a hidden reef, with the ever-present risk of not completing their journey.

Sitting at the top of the beach, Peter looked out to sea with his thoughts and shrugged. 'Well, there are no ruins here and we've seen nothing shaped like a butterfly. Where do we look next?'

Sophie shook her head. 'Jesus, Peter. It's the first day.' She pulled him up. 'Have a little faith.' She peeled off her shorts and T-shirt. 'Come on, let's have a swim.'

They ran over the scorched sand, dived into the sea, and swam out to where they could see José reclined in the Beaver's cockpit in the next bay. As they enjoyed the refreshing water, they heard the familiar sound of a small prop plane and looking up they saw a Cessna flying low enough to see them and the de Havilland as it headed towards the northern shore of Busuanga.

'Come on, let's go,' Peter said, knowing Sophie was thinking the same thing.

They made their way quickly back to the beach, grabbed their clothes, then hurried to the Beaver. Within ten minutes, they were airborne, en route to Bambam. The flight was uneventful although they kept a vigilant eye out for anything resembling a butterfly or the *Griffin*.

# CHAPTER 24

## *Bambam*

When Peter and Sophie arrived back at Bambam, Gabe informed them that Declan had flown to Manila that morning; they wondered what he was up to.

The resort was almost back to normal, with dive bookings rescheduled; Deep Blue's diving expertise was always in heavy demand. Sophie kept a close eye on the building work and interviewed two temporary diving instructors, careful not to repeat the Ramón mistake.

Meanwhile, Peter went and sat at Declan's poolside table, where he spread out a chart of the archipelago under the shade of some palm and banana trees as the distinctive noise of a banca engine carried on the breeze, cutting through the chilled bossa nova music.

Sipping a cold Coke, he watched a group of workers cooling off in the pool as he thought about his father, stepmother, Tiffany, Henry, Samantha and Sophie, and the events of the past few weeks which had been non-stop since Mitch had extracted him from the Kimberley. He also reflected on the fact he'd never been so attracted to anyone in his life as he was to Sophie.

As Bambam's laid-back atmosphere wove its magic spell, Declan's Irish brogue sliced through his reverie.

'I understand you didn't find anything?' he said, sliding into a chair opposite. Like Sophie, Peter thought, he had a habit of appearing from nowhere.

Peter shook his head. 'Nope. Just miles of ocean dotted with tropical islands and reefs. What about you?'

'Running some errands in town. I still have a business to run, you know. Popped in to see Father García.'

'Is he okay?'

'He was badly beaten by that thug Bekker, but he's resilient and will come back stronger. He's a remarkable man is Father García.' Declan shook his head in admiration.

'So now Bekker's got the original documents he showed you ?'

''Fraid so, which is why they've been asking questions on Busuanga.'

Gabe approached, looking apprehensive.

'What is it?' Declan said gruffly.

Gabe shuffled nervously. 'A cousin called me this afternoon.'

'And?'

Gabe said sheepishly, 'One of the elders told him that a long time ago, Linapacan was sometimes referred to as Laputacan. Sorry for the mistake, sir.'

Declan broke into a broad smile, dismissing Gabe's anxiety. 'Nonsense. Tell your cousin I'm grateful for the information, but stress he mustn't tell anyone else.'

'I'll call right away,' Gabe said, looking relieved as he headed off.

Peter located Linapacan on the chart. Around 80 kilometres south of Busuanga, it opened a plethora of questions. Not least, for an Indiaman to have strayed into these waters it would have to have been far off its normal course. But it was possible, and he felt the adrenaline kicking in.

'Trust me,' Declan said, as if reading his mind, 'if it's out there, we'll find it. You know, I always admired your old man. He had an exceptional nose and superb intuition, but his best quality was he never gave up.'

Knowing the comment was aimed at boosting his morale, Peter raised his glass and gave a weak smile. 'I'll drink to that.'

It was obvious Declan had been fond of Harry, despite the vast span of years that had passed since they'd seen one another. Peter realised that, to Declan, his father was still the young adventurer in the black and white photograph, and that his own presence and close resemblance was as good as a reincarnation, helping to mingle the past and present, intertwined with the Condesa's story.

Studying the chart, Peter said, 'I think it's plausible the Dominicans located a mission on Linapacan. It's smaller than Busuanga but there's a significant archipelago of satellite islands and it's close to northern Palawan.'

Declan nodded. 'They could have been attracted by the Spanish fortifications against the Moros. I guess if the Jesuits had a stronger presence further north on Cullion and Coron, then the Dominicans could have chosen to be further south.' He looked at Peter. 'You know, there's still the remains of a Spanish fort you can walk around. It's heavily overgrown by jungle, but gives a real sense of what it was like back then.'

Sophie approached. 'Looks like I missed something.'

They filled her in on the new development.

'Then we'll fly up tomorrow and check out Linapacan,' she said decisively. 'I've a good feeling about this. You'll love it up there, Peter, the water's unbelievably clear.'

Though cautiously optimistic, Peter could still see the potential for Chinese whispers on island names. He nodded. 'Okay. Sounds like a plan.'

Declan said, 'If the Dominican mission was on Linapacan and there's anything left of it, someone will know. Nothing goes unnoticed on these islands. If we can locate it, we'll have a clear indication of which direction an island shaped like a butterfly and the wreck of an Indiaman might lie, and we can then carry out a focused aerial search. The 50 or so satellite islands around Linapacan are well spread out. We could waste a lot of time otherwise. I'll get José to pick us up first thing,' he said, confirming that this time he was going with them.

They split up, Declan and Sophie to deal with more refurbishment decisions, Peter to check his email in the office behind reception. There was a reply from Henry.

*Peter,*

*I'm pleased to hear things are getting back to normal after the typhoon. Sorry to hear they didn't pan out as you'd hoped in respect of Harry's adventurous challenge. The main thing is you tried.*

*Funding's still available given you've followed your father's instructions and taken this to its conclusion. I suggest you take a well-deserved break and get some relaxation so you feel reinvigorated when you return to work. Let me know how much and where to transfer the money, and I'll execute without delay.*

*Yours,*
*Henry*

*P.S. I can't hold Angela off from the study for much longer, she's champing at the bit!*

The note was polite, understanding and to the point. Perhaps his suspicions about Henry were unfounded after all, but he decided to reserve judgement and see how things panned out.

# CHAPTER 25

## *Linapacan*

E arly the next morning, they boarded the Beaver, which had been moored alongside the jetty, given the calm weather.

This time, Declan sat up front with José, and Sophie and Peter in the row behind. Initially they flew in silence, each locked in their thoughts, the constant whine of the engine their only soundtrack. José looked as professional as ever in a freshly pressed, short-sleeved white shirt, his trademark Ray-Bans glued to his expressionless face.

He flew them up over the northernmost part of the elongated mainland of Palawan. Before long, the island of Iloc lay to their east, followed by Calibang lying south-west of the distinctive shape of Linapacan. From the air, it looked like the missing piece from a difficult jigsaw puzzle: all promontories, peninsulas and deep fjord-like inlets, with a western orientation, its satellite archipelago clustered to the west and north, and some smaller islands lying off to the east.

Peter had read that together with Coron, Culion and Busuanga, it was officially part of the Calamianes group of islands. With no airport or regular ferry service, it catered for the traveller wanting a truly 'off grid' experience.

Its archipelago of some 50 small islands lay scattered over nearly 200 square kilometres. Several, like Patoyo and Calibang, were popular day-trip destinations by banca from the main island; others had boutique resorts on them or were privately owned. However, there were a multitude of smaller unnamed islands which were rarely, if ever, visited in this world-class paradise.

Looking down at the glinting water below them, Peter tried to visualise an Indiaman sailing among the kaleidoscope of bejewelled islands and blue ocean. From the air it seemed a lot more credible than staring at a one-dimensional map, however, the sheer scale of the seascape reinforced the relative smallness of even a large ship at the mercy of the elements in these surroundings.

Shortly, Linapacan's small main town, San Miguel, on its north-eastern coast, came into view. José angled the yoke and executed a wide arc to make his approach head-on towards the town. Minutes later, they touched down on a calm sea a 100 metres from the waterfront and taxied slowly to the jetty. Peter and Sophie got out first, then helped Declan, whose leg was playing up after the cramped flight, climb up.

They left José to look after the plane and keep an eye on the weather, and walked into the small no-frills town, the poverty of the local population all too evident. A strong smell of dried fish pervaded the fierce heat. At the waterfront, skinny, dark-brown kids back-flipped off the jetty into the clear water. There were no tourists in sight, just locals scratching a living in whatever way they could, most living hand to mouth, their mainstay, fresh fish, sent by boat twice a week to Manila in return for necessities. The only other source of income was occasional tourists looking for basic accommodation and hiring bancas to explore outlying islands.

Like any standout location in pristine surroundings, Linapacan and its islands hadn't gone unnoticed, their crystal-clear waters cited by esteemed travel publications as being among the world's best.

Peter thought, rather cynically, it was probably only a matter of time before corrupt planning officials enabled stretches of virgin jungle to be cleared for an airstrip, facilitating the construction of resorts and an influx of tourists which would quickly negate its old-world charm. One only had to look at what'd happened to Boracay in the Western Visayas to see the impact of commercialisation. But for now, thankfully, it was a time capsule in a far-flung corner of the world most people had never heard of, let alone come close to visiting.

They headed for what passed as a café and sat around a rickety plastic table on three non-matching plastic chairs under the partial shade of a broken Pepsi umbrella. A mangy-looking group of dogs covered in flies lay against a shack, while cockerels pecked around noisily.

Peter took in their surroundings. 'If Bekker's people are sniffing around, we'll be ID'd in seconds.'

Declan nodded. 'You're right, son, but there's nothing we can do about it. It's a risk we run anywhere. Still, we should remain vigilant.' He stood up stiffly, then walked slowly over to the small shack where he entered into conversation with the diminutive shop owner, a hunched old woman with a wrinkled face and few teeth, who was chewing betel nut. She pointed down the street, muttering in Tagalog.

Declan walked back over. 'This lady knows someone who can take us to the castle ruins. There's no road there so we'll have to go by banca.' The old woman was now giving instructions to a scruffy-looking young boy who ran off barefoot down the street.

Peter thought there was scope for a thriving dental practice as he watched the woman come out of the shack and place three chilled beers and a bottle opener on the plastic table. He levered them open and handed them around. Sophie placed hers against her neck, savouring the coldness of the bottle.

Ten minutes later, the youngster returned with an old man who wore ragged shorts, a dirty white vest and a pair of flip-flops, all of which had seen better days. He had a wiry physique and a permanent grin and, remarkably, an almost full set of discoloured teeth.

Flies buzzed persistently around them as emaciated kittens begged for scraps of food around their feet. Every now and then a noisy 125 motorbike sped past as the sun beat down unforgivingly with little shade.

Declan proffered a chair and the grinning old man sat down. Declan signalled for a beer for their guest, who was soon slurping

San Mig from the bottle, which he downed quickly. Declan ordered another for him. The old man pulled out a crumpled packet of Marlboro cigarettes from his waistband and lit one with a battered Zippo. Peter found his grin unnerving, wondering if the man was playing with a full deck.

Cigarette smoke hung lazily in the humid air, periodically wafting over them as Declan spoke animatedly to the old boy in Tagalog. Sophie seemed to follow the conversation, but Peter had no idea what was being said, though thought it refreshing they didn't need an interpreter as things always got lost in translation. The old man spoke rapidly, like gibberish, nodding his head continually as if to say, '*Yes, yes, that's right.*'

Eventually, Declan sat back in his plastic chair. 'Right, let's go and hire a banca.'

Peter cocked an eyebrow. 'I'm guessing he knows just the person?'

'Just so happens he does.' Declan grinned like a shark, in his element, as he thrust a wad of pesos into the old man's hands so he wouldn't get stiffed by the others.

They followed the old man back towards the waterfront.

Several steps behind Declan and the old man, Peter said to Sophie, 'What did he say?'

'That he knows the way to the old fort at Castleden, which is now overgrown and not easy to find.'

'If you ask me, he's one sandwich short of a picnic.'

Sophie stopped and turned to face Peter with a serious expression, her father out of earshot.

'We've lived here most of our lives. You get to know people and how they react, which varies around the islands. But if you speak the language and invest a little time, you often get what you're looking for.'

With that she walked briskly ahead, deviating only to update José about their plans.

Feeling suitably admonished, Peter smiled. For a normally cool Swede, Sophie had a fiery Irish side that surfaced periodically. She looked even hotter when that happened. He reconciled to go with the flow; there was really no other option.

When he reached the waterfront, negotiations to hire a banca were well underway, the old man and Declan in heated discussion with a third party who Peter assumed was the skipper. Eventually, after some haggling, they shook hands and agreed a deal.

Declan didn't like being fleeced, but he respected the locals and their fragile way of life, and was generous in his dealings, especially given the significance of their trip.

Sophie joined them, standing by the faded light-blue banca with red and white stripes, a medium rig that had seen better days. With terms settled, the skipper climbed in, followed by the old boy, who leapt in with surprising agility. He in turn helped Declan on board, followed by Sophie and Peter.

Just feet from the jetty, shoals of brightly-coloured tropical fish shimmered through the crystal-clear water around the jetty as young boys and girls wearing makeshift masks and snorkels fooled around, some with dangerous-looking spear guns and home-made *Mad Max* goggles.

The skipper fired up the engine and deftly manoeuvred the banca out towards the channel running between Maapdit Island and the small town. He then angled the banca so they were hugging the coastline, heading up towards Linapacan's north-east coast. They were happy to be out on the water with a refreshing breeze as they motored past bancas of all sizes, some decidedly commercial-looking.

'They're pearl divers,' Declan said, pre-empting Peter's question. 'There are lots of pearl farms round here. Oysters seem to thrive in this location.'

*Probably owned by some fat cat in Manila*, thought Peter, given he'd seen nothing to suggest a thriving economy on the island.

Since the harsh midday sun was directly overhead, Peter wore his blue New York Mets baseball cap, its peak angled down, which had travelled with him to all parts of the world and was something of a talisman. Declan and Sophie sported stylish fedoras, Declan looking every inch the aged adventurer, whilst Sophie, in her white top and khaki shorts, looked like a *Vogue* cover model on an exotic travel shoot.

The skipper wore baggy blue nylon football shorts and a blue basketball vest with white trim, 'Harlem Globetrotters' written across it in orange. He stood upright on hardened bare feet, gently guiding the banca with subtle movements of the wheel to counter the current and stiff breeze. Peter guessed he was mid-forties and wondered if he spoke English. The old man huddled next to the skipper, chatting away amicably, both chain-smoking, periodically erupting into uncontrolled laughter.

The banca sliced purposefully through the waves in a south-westerly direction across Linapacan's heavily indented fjord-like coastline, passing other bancas containing locals who waved to them as they went about their business, a scene that was often witnessed around the Philippines.

After thirty-five minutes, the skipper steered the banca towards a large bay, which, as they approached, split into several smaller ones. He steered into one of these, heading for a narrow concrete jetty jutting into shallow water. The jungled hillside beyond the small shoreline gave nothing away as to what might be hidden in its mass of thick tropical vegetation.

Declan grinned as they came to a stop and said dramatically, 'Welcome to Sitio Castleden.'

Peter looked up the hillside, then at Declan. 'You've been here before, right?'

Declan nodded. 'Once, a long time ago. It wasn't so overgrown then ... but even then it wasn't easy to find.'

Peter looked at Sophie. 'Have you?'

'To Linapacan, yes, but not here. It's my first time, although I've heard about it from Dad.'

There was no one around. The place was deserted and quiet, and the sun beat down mercilessly on the shimmering clear water.

The old man leapt onto the jetty and helped Declan up, as ever followed by Peter and Sophie. They walked up to the narrow shoreline where a small stream fed into a well. To its left, a trail snaked up the steep hillside. The old boy forged ahead and they followed him, Declan leaning on his cane for support as they made their way slowly upwards through thick, luxuriant vegetation. It was impossible to make out any discernible path. The climb was deceptively steep, but the old man waded purposefully upwards.

Eventually the jungle opened up and their guide pointed to the other side of the clearing, grinning inanely before lighting a cigarette. Peter wondered if they'd been brought to the right place. All he could see was jungle, but his eyes slowly adjusted and he made out several large blocks of stone in a fragmented line.

'They're part of the outer rampart,' Declan said, bending over and clasping his knees, gasping for breath. 'They're crafted from coral.' Looking beyond the stones towards the bay, Peter gradually made out the outline of a structure, its coral block walls part of the original fort, covered in creepers with large sprawling trees that clung like fig stranglers. The place was eerily deserted, reminding him of images he'd seen of lost ruins in the Mexican jungle.

Forcing their way through thick vegetation, they came to one of two remaining bastions and a thickset stone staircase which they climbed cautiously. Although the ruin was dilapidated and overgrown, there was enough remaining of the fort to appreciate how solidly it had been constructed by the Spanish to protect themselves against Moro raiders and Chinese pirates, and to get a real feel for what it must have looked like. Peter thought that seeing a physical structure from the time of the Condesa's story definitely made everything seem more real.

Although the views towards the sea were restricted by dense jungle, the three of them could see glimpses of blue water and islands in the distance, and each of them wondered the same thing: which one held the key to the sunken Indiaman?

Declan articulated their thoughts. 'It's out there somewhere and we're bloody well going to find it, if it's the last thing I do,' his expression a mask of determination. As he squinted in the bright sunlight, he looked every one of his 78 years and it was clear to Sophie and Peter that he had one more dream to fulfil before he felt his life was complete. This quest, which had eluded him his whole life, was now within his grasp if they could just locate the mission.

They slowly made their way back down the hillside to the banca, and Declan engaged in discussion with the gormless-looking old man, who continued to spit, laugh, smoke and gesticulate animatedly.

When they arrived back at the jetty, Peter said, 'So what now?'

Declan smiled conspiratorially. 'Our friend here knows some similar ruins. So, we go take a look.'

Standing with her hands on her hips, Sophie gave Peter a pointed look before following Declan into the banca.

The skipper fired her up and motored out of the large bay into open ocean. As the vessel sliced through the waves and they tracked the jagged coastline in the refreshing breeze, Peter reflected that a banca's design wouldn't have changed much since Sinclair's time, the only difference being they were now motorised.

They passed another large bay that split into a multitude of smaller ones before rounding the peninsula at the north-western tip of Linapacan and heading down the western side. Thirty minutes after leaving Castleden, the skipper slowed the engine as the old man, pointing at the shoreline, turned to face them, his perma-grin intact, nodding his head vigorously with enthusiasm.

Between two headlands on the rugged coastline lay an easily accessible beach, fringed by a rocky, jungled hillside.

The skipper drifted the banca into shallow water and beached it with the old man's help. By the time Sophie and Peter had helped Declan onto the beach, the old boy was at the top left-hand corner of it, beckoning animatedly for them to join him.

Through gritted teeth, Declan said, 'You go ahead. I'll follow at my own pace.'

It wasn't worth arguing, so Sophie and Peter walked up the beach to where the palms bordered the jungled undergrowth; here, they made out a narrow path. The old man was nowhere in sight. It was obvious no one had been there for a long time, the path barely discernible. As they pushed through the undergrowth, they heard a yell from above and looking up saw the old boy waving both arms to follow him up, another fag dangling between his clenched lips.

Peter took the lead. When he came to a fork, he took the left path through a narrow passage between large boulders, which led up to where their guide had waved from. But when they arrived, yet again the old man was nowhere in sight.

Thick jungle grew almost to the edge of the elevated headland which had a magnificent view westwards of open ocean and a smattering of small islands in the distance. They spotted another faint track which they followed, pushing their way through thick lush vegetation until it abruptly opened into a large clearing.

On the other side, the old man squatted on a low rock, cigarette tightly pincered between thumb and forefinger. Muttering to himself, he swept his arm in an arc, his perma grin unnerving.

Large stones, similar to those they'd seen at the Spanish fort, lay scattered throughout the vegetation.

'Well, there was definitely a structure here,' Sophie said excitedly, grabbing Peter's arm as he brusquely pushed through vegetation. 'Careful! There are poisonous snakes here.'

'Any in particular?'

'Cobras and coral snakes,' she said casually. 'Both highly poisonous.'

'Spiders too, I'm guessing?'

'Tarantulas and large bird-eating ones that really pack a punch if you piss them off.'

'Great.' Peter felt safer under water.

As he pulled a tangle of vines apart, a low line of large square stones appeared, worn down like a set of lower teeth, moss-covered but recognisable as man-made. Parting more vegetation, they were able to make out the rectangular footprint of a structure. Could it be the remains of the Dominican mission, they wondered? Once again, Peter was reminded of Aztec ruins in Mexican jungles from the way the stones lay scattered, however, there was nothing to indicate their purpose or ownership.

Sophie looked at him expectantly. 'Well, it's possible, isn't it? They're foundations.'

Peter nodded. 'It's certainly possible.' He made his way around the rectangular shape and found more stones. 'We need something tangible to identify it.'

Sophie said, 'I'm going to get Dad. He needs to see this.'

Peter looked around for the old man but he'd disappeared again. 'I'll come with you.'

They made their way back out onto the headland where Declan sat looking reflectively out to sea, the way old people do when caught up in memories over an ocean of time.

He turned as they approached. 'Just taking a breather. Damn leg's playing up. Any luck?'

They told him what they'd found. He agreed it was encouraging, but without anything to positively identify it, it would just be speculation.

'Have you seen the old man?' asked Sophie.

Declan shook his head. A noise above made them look up. About 20 metres to their right, the old boy was standing on a rocky outcrop, yet again waving for them to join him.

'Jesus,' said Peter. 'I'll go and see what he's up to.'

Peter made his way over to where the man was pointing and found the route up, scrambling up some jumbled rocks until he reached a small area of flat land, hemmed in on two sides by large boulders with thick jungle behind. The slight elevation gave another spectacular view out to sea. As Peter got his breath back, he turned to see their guide squatting on what look liked a small plinth, just large enough to accommodate his modest frame.

Peter's heart skipped a beat. Perfectly chiselled into the smooth, flat face of the boulder behind the old man was an easily recognisable, though heavily weathered, Dominican cross. He looked affectionately at the uncomplicated old man, who knew his island and had delivered what had been asked of him, his grin expanding as he witnessed Peter's reaction.

Peter let out an almighty 'Whoo hoo!' as he walked over to the edge of the rocks and signalled to Declan and Sophie below, who instantly realised he'd found what they'd been searching for. They made their way cautiously up the rocks, Declan determined to see it for himself. Before long, they stood next to Peter, staring at the Dominican symbol. The old man remained squatting off to one side, grinning and chuckling inanely, knowing he'd done something good but not understanding what all the fuss was about. What excited these white people was very different to what excited him and his people. Hawking phlegm, he gobbed in the dirt, got up smiling and disappeared down the path towards the beach.

Sophie reeled off photos as Declan sat down and caught his breath, whilst Peter stared at the symbol, digesting the significance of the find, each of them knowing they were now one step closer to finding the *Earl of Suffolk*.

Declan turned and looked out to sea, and Sophie and Peter went and stood either side of him, following his gaze. A stiff onshore breeze had developed, which was a welcome dilution of the afternoon heat. They looked towards the horizon beyond the chain of little islands, knowing that was the direction in which they would commence their search for an island shaped like a butterfly.

'Well, time waits for no man,' said Declan, setting off with renewed vigour towards the path down, followed by Peter and Sophie who helped him navigate the rocks back to the beach.

When they arrived at the banca, they found the skipper flat out, snoring heavily under the shade of the canopy, and the old boy squatting in the prow, sipping a Coke and smoking.

Declan yelled in Tagalog and both men jumped quickly to their feet, helping them into the boat, cigarettes dangling dangerously just feet away from a jerry can of diesel. The skipper fired up the engine, which spluttered into life, and reversed into deeper water, where he angled the banca in the direction they'd come from, the sea now choppy.

They savoured the cool air that flowed over them as the boat motored at a steady clip back to San Miguel, Peter marking the exact location of the mission ruins on a map, knowing they could now initiate an aerial search of outlying islands, and grateful that at last they had something tangible to work with.

*

Back in San Miguel, under the shade of a Pepsi umbrella, a youth in his early twenties sat watching the waterfront. He'd arrived that afternoon on the ferry from Tay Tay, with precise instructions what to look out for, and had chatted to locals, telling them he was scouting ahead for his boss to facilitate a trip.

He'd picked up that the tourist trade was quiet. However, three Europeans had arrived that morning on the de Havilland float plane moored by the jetty. He tracked down the old women at the café, who told him they'd hired a banca to visit the old Spanish fort.

As a fully paid-up member of the Ba-Gong, the youth was lethal with a knife and good with his fists, having learnt the martial art of Kali in Manila City Jail where twelve rival gangs, left to their own rule of law, fought for dominance in the world's largest prison. But he was also patient, and much of what he did was waiting, looking, assessing and reporting back; that's what he was paid for.

With low expectations when he'd arrived, the gang member quickly realised his good fortune at hitting the jackpot from the get-go as he watched the multi-coloured banca head towards the jetty, two Filipinos in the front and three Europeans at the back, one a blonde woman who'd been described to him in detail.

He watched them disembark the banca and walk across to the floatplane. Minutes later, the de Havilland taxied to open water, skimmed the choppy water for 300 metres, then rose slowly but surely, climbing then banking in a large arc over Linapacan in the direction of Palawan.

After writing down the plane's tail number, the gang member's weapon of choice for once was cash, and he handed a wad of pesos to the old man and brought him to sit with him. Unconcerned that the youth was a gang member, which was obvious from his tattoos and demeanour, the old man willingly drank the beer he was brought and, thinking it was his lucky day, was happy to tell him about the Europeans' excitement at the ruins he'd shown them, confirming he'd be happy to go again for the right price as he sipped the cold stuff, a cigarette pincered between his thumb and forefinger. Easy money.

*

Bekker took the call while having a soapy sandwich with two naked Filipina women. Things were falling into place nicely. All he had to do for now was watch, follow and assess. The main question being, should he involve Johansson?

*

There was no sign of the ruins from the air as José flew over Linapacan. The journey back to Bambam was uneventful, however, there was a renewed energy between them. Even José had a broad smile etched on his craggy face. Like Gabe, as one of Declan's faithful retainers who loved his job and liked his boss, he knew when things were going well and when they weren't.

# CHAPTER 26

## *Butterfly Island*

The next morning, Declan elected to stay on the island. The stiff breeze of the previous evening hadn't materialised into anything more sinister, and the ocean was flat and calm as the sun slowly increased its intensity and the humidity rose. With the smell of the tropics heavy in the air, Peter and Sophie set off early in the Beaver with José.

This time, Sophie sat up front with Peter behind her. José followed the same route as the day before. Before long, they'd left the Palawanian mainland on a heading for Linapacan, their route westwards from the previous day as they flew over Darocotan Island and tracked up west of Calibang. The logic being that, based on the narrative in the Condesa's diary, they would initiate their aerial search to the west of the Dominican mission ruins.

True to form, José didn't enter into conversation, keeping his thoughts to himself, even if he was secretly curious as to what they were looking for. They were clearly on a mission for something. One of his pilot buddies had told him someone had been asking questions in El Nido about the de Havilland and its owner, which he'd report to Declan.

At 3,000 feet, visibility was excellent. Small islands dotted the vast expanse of blue ocean, periodically slashed by strips of bone-white sand, as bancas zigzagged the area, ferrying goods, supplies and people to the outermost reaches of Linapacan's satellite archipelago.

Glued to the windows, Peter and Sophie scoured the seascape

which looked as if an artist had taken a giant paintbrush using the most exotic colours in their palate. They spotted the ferry from Tay Tay as the de Havilland approached Malubutglubut, Naga and Cacayatan, exquisite little islands with fringing reefs, popular with day-trippers from the main island.

A large motor yacht heading south-west caused Peter to do a double take, but he quickly dismissed it as a potential threat.

Given most of the islands were low-lying, Peter and Sophie knew the island they were looking for would need sufficient elevation for Sinclair to have made the comparison with a butterfly all those years ago.

Peter cross-checked the chart as they flew over a private island with a small cluster of huts near the beach, knowing there were still a few scattered islands on the horizon to check out. He asked José to maintain his heading, knowing if they drew a blank they would have to then search the northern islands, which would negate their theory about the location of the island relative to the mission.

The de Havilland's engine droned noisily as José flew low over a couple of tiny islands with nothing but palms. Peter was about to ask him to turn back when Sophie leant between them and said excitedly: 'Look, over there!'

Squinting through the shimmering haze, Peter made out the outline of a small island with two hills that tapered either side. It was the first time they'd seen an island with some height to it.

Within minutes they had a bird's-eye view.

'Holy shit!' Sophie shouted into her mic in awe, as the full panorama unfolded beneath them: the impression of an exotic butterfly unmistakable.

The two hills were almost identical in size and shape, tapering on either side, with a peninsula of bone white sand extending between them beyond a stand of palms, bisecting two almost identically-shaped reefs. The image of the butterfly comprised the two green tapering hills which were the upper set of wings, the extended strip of bone-white sand its abdomen, and the reefs either side its lower set of wings.

Looking down at the contrasting blues where the reef shallows met deeper, darker water, Peter was certain this was the island they'd been searching for and he asked José to circle it. Sophie reeled off photos while he cross-checked the map on his lap, realising the island hadn't been properly drawn, just shown as a smaller island with a limited surrounding reef in a lighter colour, nothing resembling the actual shape of the island or shape of a butterfly when taking the island and surrounding reefs together.

After flying a full 360 of the island, José angled the Beaver and brought her down gently onto the sea below, slowing and then taxiing 100 metres to the edge of the sandy peninsula – the imaginary butterfly's abdomen – where he cut the engine. Peter and Sophie climbed out and jumped into the shallow water, reluctant to talk until out of earshot, despite trusting José like family.

They walked up the strip of hot sand to the shade of some palms fringing jungled undergrowth where a group of massive smooth boulders lay scattered, as if randomly thrown down by a giant, similar in appearance, thought Peter, to photos one often saw advertising the Seychelles.

Looking up the hillside, he was confident there was enough elevation to enable a panoramic view of the whole island. 'This has to be it,' he said.

'Well, there's only one way to find out,' Sophie said, walking to the base of the hillside, assessing the best place to start a climb through the jungled undergrowth, and making a start.

Scrambling after her, Peter thought about the parameters for this being the final resting place of the *Earl of Suffolk*. Although the island was about 35 kilometres from Linapacan, a sailing banca in the eighteenth century would easily have been able to go the distance, most likely attracted by rich fishing grounds. He thought it more logical for an East Indiaman to have been sailing on the fringes of the archipelago when hit by a storm, rather than closer in.

The climb was hard going from the outset, with exotic plants designed by evolution to cut, tear and generally thwart movement. They scrambled slowly up, making steady progress, stopping halfway to catch their breath and drink plenty of water.

Even from that height the Beaver, way below, looked small against the turquoise and navy water as the image of an exotic butterfly began to take shape. As they climbed, Peter and Sophie hardly spoke, saving their breath, imagining what it must have been like for Robert Sinclair and the other survivors of the *Earl of Suffolk* doing the same climb in shredded clothing and footwear, with little protection from the sun.

It certainly put things in perspective.

After twenty-five minutes, they reached the summit where a group of boulders obscured their view down towards the plane.

Peter helped Sophie climb up one and she stood shielding her eyes as she did a 360 of the island and its surrounding reefs.

'I see wonderful things,' Sophie said as she looked out to sea, mimicking Howard Carter after discovering Tutankhamen's tomb. 'Climb up and see for yourself.'

Seconds later, Peter stood beside her, awestruck at the panorama beneath them. The impression of an exotic butterfly was as unmistakable as it had been from the air and there was not a doubt in their minds that this was their island.

Peter hugged Sophie tightly as they looked down at the white sand and turquoise reef shallows way below, towards the demarcation to deeper water where the Beaver was beached. He thought Sophie looked incredibly beautiful, a child of these exotic islands, the product of passionate adventurers, living her carefree existence far from the confines of big city life. He watched as she gazed into the distance, her hair trailing in the wind, knowing she was trying to visualise where the lines from the writing boxes intersected on the outer reaches of the lower right butterfly wing, the probable location for the wreck.

She looked at him. 'How would you start the search? I mean, this is what you do, right?'

Peter nodded. 'Yup, it's what I do. We'll charter a cat and sail up here, then we'll dive recce the area on the QT. Once we see how the reefs are formed, how they adjoin open water, and the currents flow, I'll have a better idea of where she might've gone down. And hopefully we'll find some evidence,' he said, excited at the prospect of sailing and diving here alone with Sophie.

'Well, let's get going then,' Sophie said, jumping off the rock and leading the way down. As they carefully picked their way down the hillside, Peter made a mental note to read all he could about the *Earl of Suffolk* and other Indiaman from the same period, and to check the Condesa's diary for anything Declan might have missed.

Despite his excitement at their finding the island, he wondered how in the hell they were going to find something as small as a diamond even if they did manage to locate the wreck. They had to pray it had been put into something protective and durable that could have withstood the ravages of time, given the probability of finding it at all was one in a million and in view of the thousand ways a ship could break up and scatter over time.

He knew from experience that unless a wreck remained in relatively shallow water, the only way they would stand a chance of finding anything would be through a full salvage operation, as any remains would likely have been scattered into deep ocean by currents and storms, which could take years to locate, if at all.

Anyway, first they had to find evidence of a wreck. Nirvana would be to establish the provenance of an actual named Indiaman, which would enable them to stake a formal claim with the authorities and initiate a legitimate salvage operation.

However, despite all these valid concerns the greatest 'if' of all was whether the captain's account to Sinclair as he lay dying, delirious with fever, was the confession of an opportunist who'd come close to pulling off the heist of the century, had it not been for mother nature or the rantings of a dreamer.

Nevertheless, Peter thought the facts compelling: Sinclair was historically documented as the official liaison with the local Spanish population during the British occupation of Manila in 1762; a Condesa de la Cruz was recorded as having been engaged to one Pedro Vásquez, from a prominent galleon family; the Blue Moghul was a documented legendary diamond, detailed by Tavernier in his celebrated *Six Voyages*; and the *Earl of Suffolk* was on record as an East Indiaman that had disappeared after calling in at Manila on its way back from China at the right time. The matching writing boxes seemed to cement the story beyond reproach.

Looking at the spectacular panorama around him where verdant jungled vegetation contrasted with vivid blue water, serendipitously shaped like an exotic green and blue butterfly, Peter thought a quest to locate a legendary diamond called the Blue Moghul befitting.

*

Back in Manila, Bekker sat on the first-floor balcony of a heavily protected villa, looking out over a freeform swimming pool that was surrounded by half-naked women and tattooed gang members.

It was 11am. He'd had a massage and cracked open his first beer of the day. With a white towel wrapped around his huge girth, his sunburnt flab contrasted with his ginger hair as he gripped his mobile in one hand and sipped beer with the other, thinking things were coming together nicely. Much faster than anticipated.

A Swedish calm settled over the airwaves, the voice as measured and methodical as ever: 'Where exactly is this island?' it said.

'About 35 kilometres west of Linapacan.'

'Does it have a name?'

'Not that I could see from the map; it's just a small island on the periphery of the archipelago,' Bekker answered patiently, fed up with the Swede.

'You're sure they don't know they're being tracked?'

'I'm sure,' replied Bekker, not having believed his luck that one of the Ba-Gong had spotted the three of them on their Linapacan excursion, after which it'd been simple to trace the floatplane upon which one of his people in El Nido had installed the radio transmitter. Piece of cake.

'Where are *you* now?' Bekker asked, knowing Johansson was somewhere in the vicinity. For the time being, they needed each other. However, much to his chagrin, he had no idea what O'Connor had been able to ascertain from possessing the two writing boxes except the probable location of a ship wreck site, but no details of what the treasure might be. He was, though, all too aware of Johansson's majority ownership of Global Salvage Inc., with dual listings on the New York and Hong Kong stock exchanges, and for that reason alone knew it must be highly valuable.

'It doesn't matter where I am,' said the Swede. 'Suffice it to say, not far away.'

'And your recommendation?' Like he gave a shit.

'Watch from a distance. Do nothing. Let them do the heavy lifting. Logically, they'll go up by boat and do some exploratory diving. Chances are it'll be totally speculative as to where they commence a search. You'll need to find out what sort of boat they choose, which I'm assuming's within your capabilities?'

'I think I can do that,' said Bekker, failing to hid the growing irritation in his voice. Johansson didn't seem to appreciate how the parameters had changed since he'd ditched him. The fact Johansson looked down on him really pissed him off.

'Keep me informed,' said Johansson dismissively. 'It's only worth moving in if and when the time's right.' The line went dead.

'Fuck you,' muttered Bekker into the phone, helping himself to another beer, and relishing the prospect of melting the Swedish iceman soon. He leant over the balcony and beckoned up one of the girls who was sitting on the edge of a sunbed slapping on sun cream. She was surrounded by scrawny, bare-chested, wiry-looking Filipinos, who were stripping and cleaning a selection of semi-automatic pistols and carbines, cigarettes dangling from their mouths, in preparation to hit one of Rocky's clubs and start some fireworks. *Should be a fun evening*, thought Bekker who was sick of being cooped up, and had been promised he could personally deal with Rocky when he got the chance.

If things panned out as planned, the whole journey just might have been worth it, he thought. What was the saying? Life's ten per cent how you take it and ninety per cent how you make it. Knowing it was supposed to be the other way around, his version always made him chuckle. He laughed so hard he got a coughing fit, and when he got his breath back, he called Dakila.

'Your man still active in El Nido?' he asked.

# CHAPTER 27

## *Bambam*

With most of the rebuilding work completed, the first party of guests had checked in that morning and a chilled tropical vibe pervaded the pool area, with conversations, light music and laughter.

It felt good to be operating as a dive resort again, rather than a building site, as Declan, Sophie and Peter convened around the table at the far end of the pool in the early evening.

Declan flicked through Sophie's aerial photographs. 'Sweet Jesus!' he said, shaking his head in disbelief. 'So, it really does exist.'

For an instant, he reminded Peter of an elderly Al Pacino, with his dark soulful eyes and characterful face. Sophie rubbed her father's shoulder lovingly, instinctively knowing he was thinking about her mother who had loved the romance of the story. It had been their dream to one day locate the Indiaman together. Sophie couldn't help but wonder if it was fate or just a random sequence of events that had brought the three of them to this moment in time.

After a moment of silent reflection, Declan said, 'I've revisited my research and I'm convinced it's the *Earl of Suffolk* we're looking for. I couldn't find any other unaccounted Indiaman that season.' He bent down and extracted a brown leather-bound journal from a satchel by his feet, which he handed to Peter. 'Here's the Condesa's diary you asked for. I'm assuming you read and write Spanish?'

'*Por supuesto*,' said Peter, having lived with his mother in Madrid until his early teens before being sent to boarding school in Australia.

'There's nothing like reading her account first-hand,' said Declan. 'You'll be able to sense her emotions and state of mind; it'll transport you right back there, believe me. It's a long time since I first read the whole thing but when I did, I was blown away. When you read what she wrote in the context of the writing boxes, and what you've now seen at the island, you won't have any doubts. Except what's still left to find.'

Handling the soft Moroccan leather carefully, Peter undid the tie and opened the dairy's first page. Expertly bound, it looked like an original antique, with fluid, symmetrical handwriting, the letters carefully inked and the spaces between the lines as if measured with a ruler. Although the writing was flamboyant, the words were easy to make out. At the top of the page was the Condesa's coat of arms. Underneath was her full title and the date of her first entry: *El Año de Nuestro Señor, 1763.*

Declan said, 'I suggest you go somewhere quiet to read it. Then summarise the relevant parts for Sophie. I can't recall anything that would give you more information other than what I've already told you but as I said, it's been a long time.'

Reaching again into his satchel, he extracted an iPad which he handed to Sophie; he looked tired, as if handing over the baton. 'I've uploaded copies of everything I've got on the *Earl of Suffolk*, including all Indiamen recorded as calling into Manila around that time. All my research is on here, too.'

Sophie and Peter both realised the significance of what he was doing.

'Did you speak to your contact about cats for charter?' asked Peter.

Declan nodded. 'I've emailed you a link with various ones he can charter at a favourable rate, most of them located in Manila. However, there's a Leopard 40 in El Nido that had to curtail its charter yesterday because a man had a heart attack. It'll be sailed back to Manila if it's not rechartered. Personally, I think it'd do the job.'

Familiar with the South African-designed catamaran, Peter thought it would be ideal. The fact it was so readily available enabled him to make a quick decision. 'I'll take her, subject to checking her out. And I'm paying,' he added, before Declan could say anything.

Declan looked pleased. 'Great. I'll confirm you want it, subject to an inspection. Why don't you both go across in the morning, sort out the paperwork if its suitable, and get the supplies you need.'

Peter said, 'Well, apart from hiring a cat to sail there, the most important thing's the diving equipment. We need a good selection of scuba tanks, a small compressor and the option to dive with nitrox if we need to go deep.'

'We've got all that,' Sophie said. 'I'll start sorting what we need with Gabe. Then we can make a list of the provisions we should take.'

Declan's mobile rang. He fumbled in his pocket, answering after a few rings. It didn't have to be on loudspeaker for Sophie and Peter to know it was Rocky. His unique pronunciation of his favourite word was clearly discernible in the humid air.

Declan listened intently then said, 'There's been no sign of him, but that doesn't mean he's not lurking around.'

Sophie and Peter heard various other expletives before the call was terminated.

Declan raised his eyebrows. 'Rocky's nightclub got hit last night by the Ba-Gong. Looks like it's out-and-out warfare.'

'And Bekker's the catalyst?' said Peter.

Declan nodded. 'Apparently he left Rocky a calling card, which has really wound him up.'

'What sort of calling card?' asked Sophie looking worried.

'Sliced up his favourite bar girl, then dumped her body outside Rocky's property with a note pinned to it. She's alive but severely disfigured.'

Peter thought back to the girls by Rocky's pool. Bekker was a sick fuck. The fact he was loose worried him. They all knew that it was odds-on he'd turn up sooner or later, so they would need to be prepared.

After Sophie excused herself to help some guests, Peter turned to Declan, and said quietly: 'We're going to need some firepower. If we get into trouble at the island, there won't be time to call for back-up without serious consequences.'

'I'm on it,' Declan confirmed as though it was a run-of-the-mill victualling request for any sailing trip from Bambam. He winked. 'Don't worry, I'll have what you need tomorrow.'

Declan knew the risks involved in being on the remote island by themselves, but thought the approach by cat made sense under the circumstances. He was conscious it wasn't just Bekker and Johansson they had to be careful of. There were the Filipino authorities to worry about, too. If they got wind of a search for a treasure ship, it could scupper everything, quickly turning into a bribing contest to access the island and surrounding reefs with politicians and gangs involved, under the guise of the National Museum. It didn't bear thinking about.

After the relevant dive equipment had been earmarked for their trip and separated from the rest, Sophie and Peter made a list of provisions they'd need, after which they went their separate ways.

Peter went back to his cabin where he lay in the hammock and started reading the Condesa's diary, his tiredness dissipating as he read her captivating words.

She wrote well, setting the scene and atmosphere of the times, carrying him effortlessly to eighteenth-century Manila, just as Declan had said she would. It was as if he was sitting in her house in Intramuros as she recounted the story, from when she'd arrived in Manila for her betrothal to Pedro Vásquez to when she first met Robert Sinclair. Peter could almost hear the carriages clattering over the cobblestones and cannon firing salutes to arriving ships in Manila Bay.

As he read about the Vásquez family, Sophie quietly approached. 'You look engrossed.'

He looked up. 'I am. It's a captivating story, though it's tinged with sadness.'

'Have you reached the part about the shipwreck?'

'Not yet.' He patted the hammock next to him. 'Come and lie with me. We can read it together.'

She went and lay beside him in the dim light. Mosquitoes buzzed around the solitary light bulb. A cacophony of noise emanated from the undergrowth. Swifts darted high above as bats weaved in and out of the palms.

Peter thought the smell and feel of Sophie as she lay beside him lent even greater poignancy to the Condesa's love story, set against the backdrop of these magical islands. He flicked the pages to the Condesa's second-hand account of the typhoon, which he summarised in English.

Sophie said, 'Is there any reference to the ship's name?'

Peter shook his head. 'Nothing. She just refers to "The Indiaman", saying Robert Sinclair and the other three survivors, which included the commander, made their way across the reef to a small tropical island. There, they waited several days, desperate for food and water, until they were rescued.'

'Is there any description of the island?'

'Only a mention of a vantage point from which Sinclair spotted two fishermen in a banca after the two crew members had perished trying to leave the island.'

Peter flicked to the next page. 'Here's the part about being taken to the mission,' he said, translating word for word:

*'My darling Roberto and the commander of the ship were rescued by two native fishermen in a sailing banca, who chanced to be passing the island. Roberto was weak, but in the best physical condition. The commander was delirious and in and out of fever as the fishermen sailed the banca in an easterly direction, eventually arriving at a tropical beach onto which they collapsed. The fisherman returned some time later with a Catholic priest, who took them to his mission where he looked after them, for which I shall ever be thankful. In the year of our Lord, 1763.'*

Sophie said, 'And no mention of the mission's denomination?'

'None.'

'Then it's intentional,' she said conclusively. 'I'm sure she knew the name of the ship and the commander, the denomination of the mission, the name of the priest, and the approximate distance from the island to the mission.' She paused. 'Is there any mention of how long they took to sail there?'

'No. Just the implication they arrived later that day. Nothing about sailing in the dark or spending the night anywhere en route.'

Sophie looked frustrated. 'Why's she not giving details? Sort of contradicts writing an account of everything.'

Peter grinned mischievously. 'Because she was a romantic and because of the writing boxes she commissioned. She knew when she never heard from Sinclair again that unless the boxes could be reunited, the wreck would never be located unless somehow fate were to bring them together. In which case her story would be understood and her love for Sinclair solidified – the Blue Moghul being the prize.'

'Excuse me, but who's the romantic here?' Sophie propped herself on an elbow. 'Can you read me the part when the commander told Sinclair about the diamond?'

'Sure.' They both knew the whole quest hinged on this. Peter found the relevant passage, and translated:

'Since arriving at the mission, the commander had been in and out of fever, most of the time delirious. But after a few days of natural plant remedies administered by the priest, he appeared to make a little progress with periods of lucidity, during which Roberto would offer words of encouragement. It was during one of these, knowing that he was dying, that the man told Roberto about a priceless diamond he had smuggled onto the Indiaman. A legendary diamond, as big as a small clenched fist, known as the Blue Moghul, which had been stolen from the Nawab. A diamond famous enough to have been documented by the famous French jeweller, Jean-Baptiste Tavernier, who travelled India in search of the finest diamonds on behalf of Louis XIV.

'When the commander once again lapsed into a fever-ridden delirium, Roberto went to fetch the priest, knowing the man was close to death. But when they returned, the man had died.'

Sophie said, 'I'm assuming there's no reference as to what the diamond was hidden in?'

Peter shook his head. 'None.'

'You know what?' Sophie looked into Peter's hazel-green eyes. 'Why on earth would a dying man make up a story like that? I mean, the effort it must have taken. So, unless the Condesa fabricated the whole thing, which seems unlikely, this has to be for real.'

Peter closed the diary and placed it carefully on the floor, manipulating Sophie to roll on top of him. They lay for a long time looking at the stars, wedged close to one another, discussing the story and more intimate things before sleepily making their way to bed and each going out like a light.

They dreamt of diamonds, Indiamen and Moghuls against the backdrop of eighteenth-century Manila. In his dream, Peter was Sinclair and Sophie the Condesa.

# CHAPTER 28

## *The Santa Maria, El Nido*

The following morning, Jovy took Peter and Sophie over to El Nido in a rib. As they entered the bay, Peter spotted a Leopard 40 among several other yachts.

'She looks in good nick,' Sophie shouted above the wind.

It was good news. If she checked out, it would save them a trip to Manila and meant they could start sailing up to 'Butterfly Island' without delay.

Jovy dropped them at the waterfront and they walked up to Davilo's where they'd agreed to meet the charter rep.

'Hey, man, good to see you again!' shouted Davilo from a corner table where he was going through accounts. 'You heading back to Oz?' he said, walking over.

Peter reciprocated his strong bro' handshake. 'No, I'm sticking around a while. We're meeting someone here.'

Looking Sophie up and down with a practised eye, Davilo gave Peter a knowing wink. 'Didn't I tell you, man, these islands would blow your mind?'

'You're a visionary, Davilo!'

Scarcely able to keep his eyes off Sophie, Davilo said, 'What can I get you guys?

Sophie's ice-blue eyes lasered his, and he reluctantly averted his gaze, showing them to a table by the balustrade where they sat down while Davilo sorted two mango juices; it was too early for beer. Peter reflected on how much had happened since he'd been there last. He was also aware it'd been a while since he'd sailed a cat, and hoped everything would come back quickly.

'Mr Rodriguez?'

Peter looked up and then back down again as a diminutive, chubby Filipino with a friendly smile approached them.

'You from Island Marine?'

The man extended his hand. 'Yes, sir, that's me. Manuel Fuentes,' he said affably.

Peter shook it. 'Please, take a seat. I'm Peter. This is Sophie. That's the Leopard out there, right?'

'Yes, sir.'

'She's got fine lines.'

'New this season,' the rep said proudly.

'How's the gentleman who had the heart attack?' asked Sophie.

'He's been medevac'd to Manila and is stable, thank goodness.' The rep wiped his brow, sweating profusely.

'That's a relief,' said Sophie.

Davilo pretended to go through paperwork, but watched the meeting from his corner table with keen interest, not missing a trick.

Peter flicked through the English version of the charter contract. It wasn't great, so he asked Sophie to run though the Filipino version. Apparently that wasn't great either, so they suggested some amendments for clarity, which Fuentes accepted in principle.

Peter said, 'I can sign this and have the money transferred today, but I'd like to check her out first.'

'Not a problem, sir,' Fuentes replied, clearly scarcely unable to believe his luck at chartering the catamaran out again so fast, and making a double commission in the process.

'Our rib can take us over,' Sophie said, leading the rep out of the bar into the street.

Peter signalled to Davilo that they'd like to settle up. Davilo walked over and put his arm round Peter's shoulders. 'Looks like you hit the jackpot, man.' He shook his head from side to side with a knowing look. 'Even better than her mama, God bless her soul. She's one hot chick, man. You know, a lot of people been trying to crack that coconut for a long time. You'll have to share your secret one day. You obviously got the magic.'

'It's a date.' Peter grinned, slapping Davilo on the back, then headed down to the jetty where he joined the others waiting by the rib.

Jovy drove them across the bay and a couple of minutes later, the rib bumped gently alongside the cat – the *Santa Maria* – and they climbed aboard. First impressions were good: everything was brand spanking new. Peter knew charter yachts generally got thrashed, but there hadn't been time for that. He and Sophie scanned the saloon, then each of the four cabins in turn, followed by the heads and storage areas. Everything seemed in good order. Tastefully decorated and well laid out, one of the main attractions for Peter was the spacious open-plan saloon which opened onto a wide rear deck with plenty of room to store the compressor and diving equipment. He wanted to use a cat because it gave them better stability for what they intended to do and was more spacious than a single-hulled yacht, ideal as a living and diving base.

He fired up the inboard 29hp Yanmar engines, which were in good condition and would be critical if there wasn't enough wind or they had problems with the sailing equipment. Satisfied with what he saw, he had a quick word with Sophie about tweaking the terms, suggesting a final squeeze on price. After all, the company had a chance to make double money with the previous charter cut short, and someone would have to sail it back to Manila if they didn't take it. The efficient rep met them halfway; everyone was happy.

Jovy took Fuentes back to shore in the rib with a list of provisions to stock up on while Peter and Sophie rigged up the cat to sail to Bambam.

*

The same gang member who'd kept tabs on Peter when he'd arrived in El Nido spotted them coming ashore and watched with interest as they disappeared into Davilo's then re-appeared, motoring over to the catamaran. A quick call to Dakila earnt him some easy cash.

*

Peter hadn't thought to check Sophie's sailing credentials, but it was quickly apparent she knew what she was doing, seemingly at home on anything connected to the ocean, and he relished the prospect of sailing with her up to Butterfly Island, whatever the risks.

After raising and setting the main, they sailed out of El Nido bay as a crew very much in sync.

Peter stood tall, tanned and barefoot at the helm, sporting two days' worth of stubble, his Bermuda shorts and dark blue baggy T-shirt billowing in the wind. His thick dark hair had grown quickly in the sun. Sophie stood beside him in white bikini bottoms and a T-shirt that Peter thought highlighted her assets to perfection, her hair in a ponytail. Also barefoot, her right ankle displayed a new array of colourful ethnic friendship bracelets.

A steady easterly breeze enabled them to give the cat a good workout. She handled well and was responsive, and although the sailing experience was different to a single-hulled yacht, Peter was confident they'd master the art quickly.

As they stood beside one another at the elevated helm station, trimming the sails to facilitate a broad reach, they savoured the freedom and exhilaration of sailing the cat as they raced through time and space to Bambam.

Appearing from seemingly nowhere, a pod of spinner dolphins arched in and out of the cat's wake to starboard, an echo of their first meeting which bode well.

The midday sun bore down from a cloudless blue sky onto azure water through which the cat sliced effortlessly as the colours of the sky, ocean and rugged jungled islands they navigated around played past them as if in vivid Technicolor.

Although Peter knew there was a lot to be grateful for, he also knew it was a fragile balance with the players involved in the race to locate the wreck of the Indiaman and its hidden secrets, and he felt that if his father was watching over them, he would be smiling, envious of the thrill of the chase, this being exactly the sort of adventure he would have wanted him to embark upon, even with the associated risk and, ultimately, the prize potentially there for the taking. Out here, Peter felt truly connected to his father.

And being with Sophie, the adventurer daughter of Declan O'Connor, he knew, without a shadow of doubt, that this was where he was supposed to be, right here, right now, in the race to locate the Blue Moghul and complete the circle put into play over 250 years earlier.

Perhaps Sinclair and the Condesa were watching over them, he thought, reunited in the afterlife and hoping now the boxes had been reunited that Sophie and Peter would locate the wreck and find the Blue Moghul, thereby fulfilling their dream.

It was a thrilling prospect. If they could locate the diamond, then he knew that many ghosts, past and present, would be laid to rest.

\*

Johansson listened to the guttural South African on the other end of the line. He didn't like or trust Bekker, but he was efficient and the Swede felt confident he could handle him to achieve his objective. Re-engaging Bekker's services enabled him to stay out of sight for as long as possible, taking into account Rocky's unambiguous message to stay away from the islands.

'And there's just the two of them?' asked the Swede.

'At the moment,' Bekker replied matter-of-factly. 'They'll be heading to Bambam to kit her out, then up to the island.'

'How do you intend to track them?'

As the South African outlined his plan, Johansson had to admit it was a good one. He was an intelligent thug: a dangerous combination.

'Whatever you do, Bekker, don't frighten them off or our relationship will be terminated with immediate effect. And don't think for a second about going it alone. Your very existence in these islands depends on my patronage. Don't forget it.'

Bekker smiled. He'd reached this juncture in previous

relationships where his unique talents had been engaged. It had never presented an issue to go it alone at the appropriate time before, so why would it now?

It was a game of chess: the moves you made depending on the other person's as much as your own. Now he had connections, he stood to gain far more working with the Ba-Gong rather than with the pedantic Viking. Always better to cut out the middleman.

Grinning lopsidedly, he fumbled a crumpled soft pack of Marlboro red, extracting the last bent cigarette which he straightened and lit, sucking the strong aromatic smoke deep into his lungs like an addict.

His rheumy pale blue eyes, red with abuse and lack of sleep, darted dangerously, as he projected what he was going to do and how he was going to do it. He chuckled as he thought about who would be the winner in all of this, which catapulted him into a coughing fit as he reached for a bottle opener and levered open another beer.

*Fuck Johansson!* he thought. The Swede may reckon he was the master puppeteer, but would soon find out who was playing who.

# CHAPTER 29

## *Bambam*

Back at Bambam, Peter and Sophie moored the cat between Home Reef and the beach as the jetty was occupied by outriggers and ribs.

After locating Declan, they reconvened by the pool and systematically ran through everything they would need for the initial search: dive equipment, research information, comms and provisions of food and water. There was a lot to organise before they set sail for Linapacan the following morning.

Of course, José could always fly something up by plane if necessary, and Declan intended to join them as soon as they found anything.

Knowing that staff on the island talked and had connections, they agreed a cover story that Peter and Sophie were sailing up to Coron to dive on some Japanese wrecks.

After a couple of hours, Declan sat back and rubbed his eyes wearily. 'I think that covers everything. You'll be able to operate effectively for at least ten days, with back-up from the floatplane whenever required, weather permitting, and we'll be in regular contact.'

Peter could tell he was anxious, the ever-present threat of Johansson and Bekker clearly weighing on his mind.

'You've got maritime charts, schematics of the *Earl of Suffolk* and other similar Indiamen,' said Declan. 'The official manifest from when it set sail from England, as well as a record of what was taken on board in Bengal to trade for tea and porcelain in China. I got that from the India records,' he added proudly. 'Went through them with a fine tooth comb – recognising something, however innocuous it might seem, is the key to locating this ship.'

Although he was preaching to the converted, it was obvious Declan was disappointed not to be going with them, wanting to help in whatever way he could. The success or otherwise of what now lay ahead was firmly in Peter and Sophie's hands. He couldn't do more other than try to keep them safe and provide the necessary back-up.

As he looked at Sophie, Declan felt his heart wrench. She was an ever-present reminder of Ingrid, with the same natural beauty, strength and determination that she had had. But he knew Sophie had also inherited his toughness and was streetwise, able to handle herself better than most women in difficult situations.

As far as Peter was concerned, he thought him capable, tough, dependable and level-headed, and was confident he'd take care of Sophie as best he could. Though nothing had been said, it was obvious they were an item. He thought them a good match, and knew Harry would've agreed. Perhaps the possibility had even crossed the old bugger's mind when he left Peter his final quest; although Harry had never met Sophie, he knew all about her mother.

Looking up at the clear blue sky, thinking about Ingrid and Harry, Declan crossed himself, remembering Father García's comforting words during confession. Perhaps he would find some inner peace after all, despite events converging in an uncontrollable fashion. They were in God's hands now, their fate sealed by a roll of the dice some 250 years earlier, the gamblers selected for whatever reason. Things must now play out.

Declan's actions hadn't gone unnoticed. Peter and Sophie had both perceived a change in him since his meeting with Father García.

Emerging from his reverie, Declan said, 'Have you decided where you're going to start the search?'

Sophie nodded. 'Logically, as close as possible to where the lines on the writing boxes intersect, cross-checking with what we can see from the aerial photos.'

'Makes sense. You'll know as soon as you get underwater whether it's plausible.' Declan paused, as if looking for the right words. 'You know, I've full confidence in you both. You've got the diving experience, and you've got the same nose as your father.' He looked at Peter. 'There's no one better qualified.'

'Thanks for the vote of confidence,' said Peter.

Sophie threw her arms around her father and kissed him on the cheek.

'I've said enough,' he said gruffly, kissing her back.

Sophie excused herself to brief Gabe and the other instructors, keen everything should operate properly in her absence; after all, they had a business to run and a reputation to maintain.

Declan turned to Peter. 'I've got what you asked for. I'll bring it down to the cat later. We can't afford to take any chances with Karl or Bekker. Word travels like wildfire around these islands and bad pennies have a habit of turning up when you least expect them. You'll be exposed out there and need to keep your wits about you.'

'We'll be as vigilant as we can,' Peter said calmly.

Declan looked serious. 'This is the protocol if you run into trouble. God forbid you have to make a call under sufferance.'

Peter committed it to memory and they split up, agreeing to meet later at the cat.

Back in his cabin, Declan heard on the short-wave radio that a full-blown turf war had erupted between rival gangs in Manila, with a series of revenge killings and targeted attacks.

Peter went to re-check the dive equipment to take up to the island, and suddenly felt guilty he hadn't been in touch with Samantha. Glancing at his Tudor Snowflake, he calculated it was 11am in Perth, so he diverted to the office behind reception and tried her mobile. There was no answer but he left a voice message and sent a WhatsApp, hoping she was okay.

He then swam out to the cat and brought her alongside the jetty so they could load up and get prepared. The sun was setting into a blood-red ball on the horizon, casting its magical spell over the island as the heat of the day dissipated, and there was a welcome offshore breeze. Peter set about organising the master cabin to the comforting sound of water lapping against the hull when Sophie appeared in the doorway with a serious expression.

'What's wrong?' he asked.

'I'm worried about Dad. He's not normally so anxious.'

'He's just getting old,' Peter said gently. 'The past couple of weeks have taken their toll. Remember, he's lived with this story for many years. Now it's looking like he might finally be able to lay some ghosts to rest. He's also worried about you after what happened with Johansson.' Then, without thinking, he added, 'And probably thinking of your mother.' He regretted the words as soon as he'd uttered them. 'I'm sorry,' he said quickly. 'I didn't mean to speak out of turn.'

'It's all right,' Sophie said softly, sitting on the edge of the bed and placing her hands in her lap. Staring quietly ahead, her eyes not fixed on anything in particular as if in a trance, she said slowly: 'There were four of us. Mum, Dad, myself and a diving instructor called Diego. It was a clear blue day and we were happy.' She gave a wan smile. 'More than anything, I remember that we were happy. Mum and Dad up front. Myself and Diego at the back of the banca.'

Peter stood rigid.

'Some fishermen had told Dad about a wreck they'd come across. He wanted to check it out with a view to diving on it with clients.' Pausing, she took a deep breath. It was clearly painful, but she knew she had to get it out. As much for herself as for Peter's benefit. This had been buried deep within her for too long, and she needed to exorcise the darkness.

Peter sat gently beside her.

Still staring ahead, Sophie said, 'It was the first time Mum and Dad had been on a dive together for a while. The running of the resort and Dad's business took up all their time. It was a spontaneous trip.' She gave a weak smile. 'They were always spontaneous,' she said wistfully, looking ahead as if transported back in time, the images imprinted in her brain. Images that must have played like a loop, over and over, thought Peter, who kept silent, knowing this had to be in her own time and at her own pace.

'We arrived at the dive location,' she said quietly. 'Conditions were calm. Visibility was excellent. We buddied up. Mum with Dad. Me with Diego.

'It was just a recce dive to check out the wreck ... the last time the three of us were together. I remember laughter and happiness ...'

Peter thought it was obviously an image she desperately wanted to cling to as Davilo's words reverberated around his head, and the rumours that had circulated about Ingrid's death.

Sophie fidgeted nervously with her emerald necklace, twirling it back and forth between forefinger and thumb: a tangible connection to her mother. 'Mum and Dad went down first.' She swallowed hard and took a deep breath. 'That was the last time I saw her properly. I remember her smiling, happy, full of laughter as she put her mask on and back-rolled into the blue after Dad.'

Peter stayed silent, conveying as much sympathy and encouragement as he could through the slight pressure of his hand on her shoulder.

'The outline of the wreck was clearly visible at about 25 metres.' Her voice was emotionless. 'It was a 1930s Hong Kong tramp steamer.

'After a good dive around the outside and inside the ship, Diego and I headed topside and Dad indicated he and Mum would follow shortly. It was only when he surfaced about fifteen minutes later, in a blind panic, we knew something was seriously wrong.'

Sophie paused, the trauma clearly replaying in her mind, and she took deep breaths as if short of air. 'Dad said an oceanic whitetip had appeared from nowhere, becoming unusually aggressive, cutting Mum off from him. Already low on air and about to head up for their safety stop, Mum headed into the bridge for protection while Dad banged his tank to draw attention away from her. But the shark kept her pinned down.

'Dad saw her signalling desperately that she was out of air, grabbing her pony. He couldn't get past the shark to enable her to buddy breathe with what little was left in his own tank. Then, from nowhere, a second oceanic whitetip appeared, focusing on Dad. He said it was like they were working in tandem.'

Peter's body tensed as she recounted the story; tears cascaded down her tanned cheeks, her voice quivering.

Wiping the tears away with the back of her hand, she said, 'We always carried a pony back then, and still do on dangerous dives. They'd all been checked that morning. But although it was full, it malfunctioned and she couldn't breathe the air inside.'

Sophie's face was a mask of incomprehension and her blue eyes swam with tears. 'Mum's body was recovered the following day.' She gagged momentarily, then blurted out: 'Dad found her floating on the roof of the wheelhouse.'

As she looked at him, Peter felt the pain etched over her distraught face.

'She ... was ... our world,' Sophie said, struggling to get the words out, 'and nothing's been the same since.' She instinctively turned into him and buried her head in his chest, sobbing uncontrollably as he held her tightly.

They stayed like that for what seemed like an age. Not speaking. Just holding one another. Peter had tears in his eyes as he thought of the pain she and Declan had endured. There was no way of asking the question that was nagging at him: had the pony been tampered with, as Davilo had suggested, or was it just a tragic malfunction?

Eventually Sophie lifted her head, wiping her eyes, emotionally exhausted. As if reading his mind, she said, 'Dad's convinced Johansson interfered with her pony.'

'What do *you* believe?' Peter asked gently.

'I don't know what to believe. Maybe it was a freak accident.' She paused briefly. 'But I can't help thinking it was him, now I've seen what he's capable of.'

Peter knew that the only way they'd ever know was if Johansson admitted it. Now he understood Declan's uncontrollable rage back on Johansson's yacht and wondered if, under the same circumstances, he'd have been able to let him go. One thing he knew for sure, though, was that if Johansson fucked with them again, he was a dead man.

There was a knock on the hull. Declan stuck his head down the hatch and said cheerfully, 'Permission to come aboard!' – clearly he was in good spirits.

When he saw Sophie's face, it was as if his intuition told him what'd happened. He exchanged a look of acknowledgement with Peter as she made an excuse about fetching something, brushing past him to go up on deck where Gabe and a colleague were loading scuba tanks and other diving equipment.

Declan carried a canvas bag into the cabin, and took out two SIG P226s and a SIG P230 sub-compact, all 9mm, with numerous packets of bullets and spare mags.

'Thanks,' Peter said, knowing better than to ask where they were from.

'Let's hope they're just insurance.'

Peter nodded, and secreted them temporarily in one of the lockers in the second cabin.

An hour later, they had pretty much everything ready to leave first thing in the morning. Last on board was the compressor, which Gabe and an old-timer handyman securely fixed in situ, the back of the cat having been modified when constructed to accommodate one. They then made minor modifications in the cabins at Declan's suggestion.

When everything had been completed, they had a quiet early dinner, each locked in their thoughts about the forthcoming trip. Shortly after, they turned in for an early night, Peter electing to sleep on board the cat as they couldn't risk anyone breaking in at this stage in the game.

*

They rose early the following morning. Peter met them ashore where they ate a full breakfast and made final checks. At 9am, they were ready to roll; the sun well up, the heat of the day escalating predictably.

They didn't prolong their goodbyes. Declan hugged Sophie tightly, telling her he loved her very much. He then placed a firm hand on Peter's shoulder. 'She's my life, Peter. Part of me and Ingrid. Guard her with yours and take good care of yourself, you hear me?'

He made to leave, then turned back. 'And good luck.' A flash of the old Declan smile before he walked slowly back up the jetty to hide his emotions, turning one last time as he enviously watched the catamaran pass Home Reef and sail off until it was just a speck on the horizon.

The dice had been rolled. The roulette wheel was spinning; where the ball would land was anyone's guess.

# CHAPTER 30

## *Bambam to Butterfly Island*

Peter and Sophie were relieved to finally be underway as they sailed around the southern extremity of Matinloc, up past Miniloc, then up between Inambuyod and Dilumacad before heading up the west coast of Cadlao and past Cauayan into open water.

The *Santa Maria* sliced through the glinting blue ocean as Peter helmed at a respectable seven knots, tracking up the north-west coast of Palawan. He knew sailing a cat was a trade-off between speed and space, and thought the Leopard 40 an ideal compromise for their purpose.

They'd allowed themselves two days to sail to Butterfly Island, taking a roundabout route to ensure they weren't being followed. To the casual observer, they were just an attractive young couple sailing the islands, exploring this tropical paradise.

With Johansson and Bekker firmly at the back of his mind, Peter scrutinised every sail or motor vessel they passed, but in favourable conditions they made good time, happy to be out on the water in each other's company.

After a couple of hours hugging the coast, Sophie pointed out the partially hidden entrance to a rarely visited lagoon, well beyond the range of day trippers from El Nido. Reducing sail, Peter steered the Leopard slowly into the natural amphitheatre, encircled by limestone peaks. As the cat slowed to a virtual stop, he released the anchor, engaged the twin engines and reversed slightly until it was secured.

Sophie wasted no time discarding her T-shirt and diving into the crystal-clear water, swimming with firm strokes under the shimmering water, scattering shoals of tropical fish.

Surfacing midway to the beach, she shouted, 'What are you waiting for?'

Peter checked the cat was secure then dived in, surfacing beside her.

They trod water in paradise, the sleek white catamaran bobbing gently on the azure water, surrounded by rugged limestone and tropical vegetation. Beyond them, a small crescent-shaped beach, fringed by palms, lay nestled in the curve of the lagoon.

They swam to it and made their way to some shade under a stand of palms where they sat side by side in idyllic contemplation.

'This was one of Mum's favourite places,' Sophie said, shading her eyes from the sun, her voice even and firm.

'Well, she had great taste.' Peter had noted the positive change in Sophie from the evening before. Telling him about her mother seemed to have done her the world of good, but it had also given them a bond, showing she trusted him.

Whilst they savoured their surroundings in reflective silence, the palms behind gently rustling in the tropical heat, the angular prow of a white yacht appeared at the cove entrance.

'You've got to be kidding!' Sophie said in astonishment.

'Well, like it or not, we've got company.'

As it emerged, Peter identified it as a Swan 40. It cruised slowly before coming to rest 10 metres from the *Santa Maria*.

'Ahoy, there!' shouted a man's deep voice. Two people were waving at them.

Sophie stood up, brushing off sand. 'Can you believe it? I haven't been here in seven years and this happens.'

'They've as much right to be here as we have,' Peter said diplomatically.

'Let's leave. I don't want to share this place.'

'Sure,' he said, getting up.

They walked down the beach and into the water, picking their way carefully as the couple dived off the Swan and swam towards them.

They were waist deep as the strangers approached, their faces now clearly visible. The man was a similar age to Peter – mid-thirties. Well-built and muscular, he had short-cropped blond hair and designer stubble on a large angular face. The Eurasian woman was pretty and tanned, maybe late twenties, thought Peter. Finding their feet on the shifting sand they stood facing Peter and Sophie, gently wafting their arms to retain balance.

'Didn't mean to crash your party,' the man said with a strong South African accent, 'but couldn't resist coming in.' He looked around the cove. 'Love the cat, man.'

The woman kept quiet, acknowledging them with a weak smile, deferring to the man. Sophie and Peter each made swift judgements of their visitors.

'Nice looking yacht you've got yourself,' said Peter. 'Where's she from?'

The man scrutinised him. Although his broad grin was friendly, his eyes weren't. 'Chartered her out of Coron, a week ago. Yahh, she's a fin wessel, quick, too. You're Aussie, right?'

'Right.'

'On holiday?'

'Yeah. Sailing and diving.'

'Where d'ya pick up the cat?'

'Puerto Princesa,' lied Sophie.

'On your way back?'

'Not yet.' Peter watched the man processing the conversation as if X-raying them both with hard brown eyes. 'You from Jo'burg or Cape Town?' he asked.

'Durban. You?'

'Sydney,' lied Peter.

'I'm Lars,' the man said, holding out his hand, which Peter shook. A strong hand, but one that gave only thirty per cent. 'This is Nenita.'

The woman gave them each a limp handshake.

'I'm Tom. This is Janet,' lied Peter, thinking the man a dead ringer for Jannie du Plessis, the Springbok prop forward: large, solid, and tough, with that distinctive Afrikaner appearance he'd come across before.

'Well, enjoy the islands,' Peter said.

'Thanks, man. Who knows, perhaps we'll see you again.' The man's eyes remained rock steady with a hint of menace.

Peter grinned. 'You never know.'

Peter and Sophie swam back to the cat. Five minutes later, they motored slowly out of the cove, and Sophie got to work with her Nikon and a powerful 600mm zoom lens. Once into open water, away from the protection of the cove, the cat's sails filled with a strong westerly breeze and they continued their journey up the north-western coast of Palawan.

Standing next to Peter at the helm, Sophie said, 'He's trouble.'

'Agreed.'

'Do you think he's working for Bekker or Johansson?'

'Perhaps.'

He'd met many types like Lars, which he bet wasn't his real name; hard cases who ended up in these kinds of locations, bumming around, crewing on yachts, taking sail boats between destinations for charter, smuggling booze, drugs, money, weapons – anything for a fast buck. Sophie watched as Peter weighed up the danger.

'Was she a hooker?'

'Not your average bar girl. Look, we just need to keep our eyes open, be careful and stick to the plan.'

'I'll ask Dad to run a check,' Sophie said, sounding like a CIA field officer reporting to Langley.

Peter nodded. 'Let's make for somewhere easy tonight. We'll circumnavigate Linapacan tomorrow to make sure we're not being followed. If everything's okay, we'll head up to the island.'

'Sounds good.'

Any suggestions?'

'Calibang. It's a beautiful little island and well situated.' Sophie pointed it out on the chart and Peter saw it was more or less equidistant between Linapacan and the northern tip of Palawan.

'Perfect,' he said, smiling reassuringly as he coaxed the wheel first to port then to starboard to maintain their course.

A couple of hours later, they spotted the island.

Sophie said, 'It's a Tagbanwa tribal sanctuary which means you're supposed to have permission from the Barangay Captain or tribal council to visit.'

'Is that a problem?'

She threw her head back, laughing. 'Not for us. We've been here loads of times and have a free pass. Though it never does any harm to check in with one of the elders,' she added.

*

They anchored the *Santa Maria* off a sheltered bay on the south side of the island and took it easy; swimming, snoozing and reading. There was no further sign of the couple they'd met earlier, but Sophie radioed Declan and described them and their yacht.

'Sounds suspicious,' he said, taking down the yacht's details. 'I'll check him out and get back to you.' They agreed to speak again when they arrived at Butterfly Island unless he found something out first.

They ate a simple fish and salad dinner, then retired with a couple of cold San Migs in coolers to the sofas at the stern where they started sifting the ream of information Declan had uploaded on the iPad.

Darkness fell quickly and they sat alone in their own small pool of light surrounded by inky blackness apart from a few lights twinkling in the distance, Sade's distinctive voice playing soothingly in the background.

Peter said, 'If the *Earl of Suffolk*'s our ship, and the evidence certainly points to it, she was built in 1748 by Perry & Co in Blackwell, on the north bank of the Thames in London. At around 600 tons, which was typical for ships at the time, she was 105 feet on the keel and 33 feet 4 inches amidships.'

'I thought they were smaller,' said Sophie knowledgeably.

'They got larger with the expanding China trade.'

'Presumably constructed of oak?'

Peter nodded. 'Yup. From the Weald of Kent. It wasn't until the late eighteenth century that the Parsees used Indian teak, which was a lot more resilient.'

'Well, sadly it will all have rotted away by now, won't it?' Sophie said, philosophically.

'Most likely.' Peter knew the best-preserved wrecks lay in cold water, under layers of protective mud. 'But plenty of things on board would have survived, as categorised in your father's research.'

Sophie lay back and put her hands behind her head. 'Can you talk me through some of them?'

'Sure. Well, broadly speaking there's clothing and fashion accessories; personal items, such as pocket watches, lockets, writing bureaux, boxes and chests, and ordinary and fine dining ware made of silver, copper, brass, porcelain or china.

'Then items specific to the ship like its custom-made bell, the anchor, large metal lanterns that were installed on the quarter deck, the iron staircase that connected decks, and a carved wooden figurehead on the prow, although that would probably have rotted.'

Peter glanced up at Sophie who was looking up at the sky, clearly concentrating on what he told her. 'Their navigational equipment consisted of octants, dividers and compasses, and weaponry included cannon, carronades, muskets, flintlock pistols and swords,' he continued. 'They would most likely have carried significant bullion and coinage and, of course, the ship's holds would have been packed with tea chests and porcelain which were the commodities that were the whole *raison d'être* for the China trade.'

He looked over at Sophie, who met his gaze and said, 'That's quite a list.'

'Well, given that the full complement of an Indiaman of this size was around 150 officers and crew, as well as passengers, that's potentially a lot of stuff scattered over the seabed, which increases our chances of finding something.'

'Presumably items like cannon or the anchor are easier to locate?'

suggested Sophie.

Peter shook his head. 'Not necessarily. They often become part of the reef structure, making them hard to find or identify.'

'How many decks did the *Earl of Suffolk* have?' Sophie was clearly trying to visualise the ship in all its splendour.

'Three. The main triple-height cargo hold and lower and upper decks. At the rear was the roundhouse, the captain's cabin, which was below the grand cabin shared by billeted officers. Above that were the quarter and poop decks.'

'You mentioned cannon. What was her firepower?'

Peter scanned the stats. 'Twenty-eight guns, positioned on the upper deck. Interestingly, although the Indiamen were merchant ships, they resembled navy frigates, which confused the enemy and helped protect them.'

'What would the officers have worn back then?'

'They dressed flamboyantly. Their uniforms emulated those worn by the Navy: long coats worn over waistcoats, with breeches and buckled shoes. You have to remember,' reinforced Peter, 'these guys had the best of both worlds: accessorising the fashions of Georgian England with jewels and craftsmanship from India, China, Burma and Ceylon. Many would have commissioned intricately designed swords and pistols set with precious stones and engraved with coats of arms or initials.' He handed Sophie the iPad. 'Take a look at these.'

She sat up and flicked through the photographs Declan had taken at the National Maritime and Victoria and Albert Museums in London, showcasing the dress and fashions of the day. 'Wow,' she whistled, 'they sure lived in style.'

Peter nodded. 'Yes, they did. Remember, East Indiamen were the most luxurious ships of their day, even though predominantly cargo carriers, and their officers were wealthy men.' He shook his head in admiration. 'I have to say, your father's research is first class. He's not left a stone unturned.'

'Which is why he successfully located two Manila galleons,' Sophie said proudly. 'You know, he spent three months living in Seville, sitting in the Archivo de Indias every day until he'd exhausted all possible sources of historical evidence. That's why he was able to identify pieces from both wrecks.'

'Well, let's hope he'll work his magic again, even though we'll be the ones underwater.'

'I'll drink to that.'

The music switched to Jack Johnson's chilled vocals as they sat in the small pool of light at the cat's stern, water lapping soothingly against the hull.

Peter said, 'We'll need to find items that can identify the ship and the period. Ideally, things with makers' marks, coats of arms, initials or branded items. The East India Company chopped their tea chests, which would've disintegrated long ago, but they also marked more durable items that might've survived.'

He got up and walked into the saloon. 'Fancy a nightcap?'

Sophie shook her head. 'No thanks. You go ahead.'

He sprinkled some ice cubes into a tumbler and poured a generous measure of Don Papa, Declan's favourite rum from the island of Negros, which seemed the perfect accompaniment to their discussions.

He went back and sat next to Sophie, picked up the iPad and flicked through various screens until he found photos of antique coins. 'One of the best identifiers is currency. As well as having stamped silver bullion on board, they would almost certainly have had Spanish Reals, also known as "Mexicans" or "Pieces of Eight", which were the international currency of the day. The East India Company also minted its own currency in various presidencies. Finding any of these coins would be some of the best identifiers of all.'

'Ideally we need to find something specific to the *Earl of Suffolk*,' said Sophie, 'so we can cross-check it with the ship's manifest and recorded details of the officers and crew.'

Peter nodded. 'That would be nirvana and definitely give us the provenance we need.' He yawned. 'I'm bushed. Shall we turn in?'

Sophie didn't reply, but got up and walked to the music system and hit some buttons. She turned to face him as Joe Cocker's *You Can Leave Your Hat On* started playing and, moving seductively to the rhythm, peeled off her T-shirt which she flung at him, revealing her firm, pale breasts which contrasted with her golden tan.

'Just how bushed are you, Peter Blake?' she said in a husky voice. 'Or is that Pedro Rodriguez?' she teased.

Gyrating some more, she wiggled out of her bikini bottoms, spun them around her finger, then flung them at him. 'Still tired?' she shouted as she ran into the saloon and below decks.

'Not as bushed as I thought!' Peter yelled, ripping off his T-shirt and shorts then running in a coordinated lollop across the saloon. Taking the stairs in a controlled jump, within seconds he stood in the main cabin, stark-bollock naked. Sophie lay on the bed in the dim light, her blond hair and breasts splayed, her expression sexy, her blue eyes invitingly playful.

Peter got onto the bed and gently straddled her, bending his head to hers, and their lips met one another hungrily as he slid into her. After making electric frenzied love, heightened by their solitary location and the adrenaline of the whole adventure, they fell into a deeply contented sleep in one another's arms.

# CHAPTER 31

## *Butterfly Island*

They rose early the following morning, motivated by the search ahead and keen to set sail up to Butterfly Island. Declan's voice faded in and out over the radio as Peter brewed coffee.

'Repeat, over?' Sophie said into the mic.

Declan's voice had an edge. 'Some of Gabe's relations got roughed up pretty bad yesterday. Thugs came asking more questions ... but they didn't tell them anything.'

Peter handed her a cup of coffee. 'Any sign of Bekker or Johansson?' she asked.

'Not yet. If Johansson returns, he wouldn't be stupid enough to come in the same boat. But it's odds-on he's in the vicinity, closing in like the fucking hyena he is.'

They thanked him for the update and agreed they'd radio in when they reached the island unless he got any information on the South African beforehand.

Shortly, they set sail, circumnavigating Linapacan to check they weren't being followed before setting a heading for Butterfly Island. The weak breeze had veered from the day before, so they patiently tacked their way westwards, passing bancas, the odd ferry and the occasional yacht or motor launch.

Watching Sophie at the helm with a steady grip on the wheel, her blonde hair trailing, Peter thought she looked as much in control as when they'd first met and she'd powered the rib over to Bambam.

The wind picked up and the *Santa Maria* clipped along at a purposeful seven knots as they zigzagged over the changing blues of the ocean. Big skies. No clouds. Blazing sun.

Peter periodically swept the surrounding ocean through binoculars, half expecting to see the Swan, but it was nowhere in to be seen.

By mid-afternoon, Butterfly Island was in sight. Terns wheeled and dive-bombed the water like missiles, hitting large shoals of fish. The twin hulls of the *Santa Maria* glided through the waves as they raced to uncover the island's hidden secrets.

About a kilometre from the eastern side of the island, Sophie shouted, 'We'll sail round the northern end!'

'Sounds good!' Peter shouted back, heading towards the bow. 'That'll enable us to take a good look at the topography. I'll keep an eye out for reefs.'

About a 100 metres from the island, Peter signalled to Sophie to veer to avoid a bulging reef, motioning for her to slow down, finding it difficult to judge the depth of the shimmering water.

'I'm going in under engine!' she shouted, pushing a button to take in the mainsail. Once secured, she engaged the twin Yanmars, which throbbed into life, and they chugged slowly around the reef at a cautious three knots.

The water was unbelievably clear, the rays of the sun, at its zenith, reflecting off its surface like laser beams, and the sand on the sea floor sparkling.

Through polarised sunglasses, Peter recognised an exotic array of soft and hard corals teeming with brightly coloured fish. Keeping a close eye on the water depth, he spotted a hawksbill turtle swimming lazily to starboard which, despite its chilled appearance, reminded him of Bekker's ugly, menacing face.

Closer to the island, blacktip sharks opportunistically cruised the reef shallows, their fins periodically breaking the surface as seabirds wheeled high above. Beyond the narrow strip of sand and rocks on the foreshore, a smattering of palms abutted the jungled hillside.

As they sailed towards the northern corner of the island, jagged rocks forced them further out where the sharply contrasting delineation between shallow turquoise water and deeper blue ocean beyond looked like a vivid painting. Shoals of silver fish skidded below the surface, glinting in the sunlight as they raced ahead of the bow.

Declan's staccato brogue suddenly cut through the noise of the engine and wind as the radio crackled into life.

Sophie swiped the mic and eased the throttle as Peter joined her in the cockpit. There was a lot of static.

'... coming up...'

'Can you repeat, over?'

'... chartered a week ago... clean South African passport ... no red ... repeat ... no flags ... Looks clean. If ... differently ... ... know.'

'Roger that.' Sophie placed the mic back in its holder and looked at Peter. 'You're not convinced?'

Peter shook his head. 'Perhaps he's not with Bekker, but either way he's bad news. We need to keep a careful eye out for any sign of him.'

Sophie re-engaged the engines and they resumed their navigation around the northern corner of the island. In no time the full majesty of its western side came into view. Peter reflected that no two islands were the same, unique as fingerprints, as he made out the lower wings of the imaginary butterfly from the outline of the fringing reefs either side of the narrow strip of bone-white sand: the insect's abdomen.

Sophie skilfully guided the *Santa Maria* around the bulging edge of the first reef, around the protruding sand bar, heading for the furthest part of reef beyond, where they intended to start their search.

Peter tried to visualise the *Earl of Suffolk* caught in a typhoon here, thrust against the reef in monstrous seas as the commander, officers and crew, unable to save the vessel or indeed themselves, abandoned ship. The place was certainly remote, reinforcing just how isolated he and Sophie were, despite the luxury of mod cons and comms. He could only imagine how the handful of survivors had felt as they made their perilous way to shore, drained and exhausted, searching for any type of cover they could find until the storm abated.

Looking at the reef's outline, Peter knew that if this was the correct location, the ship wouldn't have stood a chance. The island wouldn't have been on any chart, appearing from nowhere through the chaos of the storm, and leaving no time to avert the inevitable.

While he pondered all this, Sophie kept the *Santa Maria* a sensible distance from the reef, motoring slowly towards the grid reference they'd programmed into the GPS. It wasn't difficult. The island was small but they wanted to be as precise as possible. Before long, she said, 'Okay, we're on it.'

'What's the depth?'

'Give or take, 15 metres.' Deftly manoeuvring the vessel, she released the anchor. Peter waited for it to hit the sandy bottom, gave the thumbs up and Sophie reversed until it gripped securely, then cut the engines.

It was 3pm. There was a gentle breeze. Surrounded by a kaleidoscope of colours, with the sun blazing and glinting gently on the undulating water, and four hours until sunset, they could at last get underwater.

They wasted no time kitting up. Peter peeled on his blue wetsuit and Sophie her black and pink one. Peter removed two scuba tanks from their bungees, securing their BCDs, while Sophie fetched masks, snorkels and fins; they were two professionals, going about their business, checking their equipment and kitting up as efficiently as soldiers stripping, cleaning and assembling weapons before an assault.

Peter purged their regulators to ensure they were working properly, breathing through each, checking the air came through nice and easy, just as it should. He never took shortcuts. He'd seen people who had. Some of them weren't around anymore.

Sophie said, 'Wouldn't it make sense to snorkel first?'

'Probably, but I prefer to dive straight away.' He wanted to make sure there were no issues with the equipment, plus it would save time if they didn't snorkel first. He thought it the best way to get into the right mindset.

'Okay,' she said, acknowledging his switch to work mode.

The cat was stable in the current and a gentle breeze tempered the extreme heat as Peter swept the horizon through the binoculars, seeing nothing but empty ocean which served to enhance their sense of isolation and the protection afforded by the island.

They helped each other into their integrated BCDs with scuba tanks attached, checking everything was secure. Sophie then walked backwards to the edge of the transom, turned and jumped feet first into the azure water, legs scissored, one hand holding her mask in place, the other across her chest, closely followed by Peter.

Bobbing on the calm water, they okayed one another then deflated their BCDs, slowly submerging below the surface and levelling off at 3 metres. The shadow of the *Santa Maria's* twin hulls shimmered reassuringly above them as bright shafts of sunlight pierced the clear water.

After checking the anchor was secure, Peter made the okay sign and Sophie reciprocated. They orientated themselves, assessing the topography of their underwater surroundings, taking in the shallow reef, the drop-off and the open ocean beyond, with the *Santa Maria* anchored at the edge of the lower right wing of the imaginary butterfly where turquoise water met deeper navy blue.

The reef extended in relatively shallow water over the majority of the imaginary wing, but near its furthest extremity, just beyond where they hovered, it dropped off rapidly. Peter imagined the hull of the Indiaman slicing into it, its cargo hold splitting open, fully laden with tea, porcelain and other products from China, knowing the coral head would have been smaller back then, but just as deadly.

Movement below caught his eye. An eagle ray raised itself off the sandy bottom, hovering momentarily before zipping along the reef where a blacktip shark swam lazily near the surface. A couple of lionfish protected their territory near some fan coral while a large grouper swam close by him, seemingly oblivious. Further along, an ugly bumphead parrotfish systematically munched coral for algae with its powerful beak-like incisors.

A shoal of brightly coloured goatfish enveloped them, then dispersed, while further out, in deeper water, a large shoal of chevron barracuda held formation in the current, their predatory torpedo-shaped silver bodies shimmering in shafts of sunlight.

With visibility at least 25 metres, it was obvious the mature reef system had formed over many years. Peter finned slightly behind and to the right of Sophie as they made their way around the reef edge, propelling themselves along the lower right-hand side of the imaginary butterfly's wing, back towards the main body of the island. A posy of bluefin trevally hovered at the edge of the dark blue, as if eyeing them, holding sentinel.

A flash on the sandy sea floor below caught Sophie's eye, so she swam down to the edge of some fan coral and picked up an object. It was a large oyster shell, its inside smooth mother of pearl. Dropping it back to the sea floor, she grinned at Peter, knowing the chances of finding something that quickly were remote.

They turned and headed back the way they'd come.

Peter admired Sophie's athletic body as she finned efficiently ahead of him, beckoning for him to follow her over the edge of the wall into deeper water, which he did. Hovering in the strong current, they found it difficult to stay in situ without compensating heavily with fins and hands and, in the process, consuming more air.

Below them a giant clam, several feet across, lay partially open, like a picture in a story book, its exterior covered in orange and red corals, its undulating sides displaying a soft bright and dark blue interior. Peter couldn't help grinning, thinking it looked like a giant labia.

Looking back, he thought the reef looked ominous as he tried to imagine a wooden-hulled Indiaman approaching at speed towards the jagged, angled and deadly mass of exoskeleton. It was iceberg syndrome: what lay below the surface, the mother lode, was as sharp as a surgeon's scalpel on a carefully crafted oak hull.

He checked his depth: 10 metres. Then air: 70 bar. The strong current was pulling them forcefully at an angle from the reef, so he signalled to Sophie to head back to shallower water where they made their way back to the *Santa Maria*.

Peter surfaced first, closely followed by Sophie, slipping out of his partially inflated BCD and climbing the narrow ladder, hoisting his tank onto the transom, then lifting hers, which she passed up to him.

Sophie looked up, her mask propped on her forehead, water droplets sprinkling her tanned face, her blue eyes expectant. 'Well, what do you think?'

Peter gave a characteristic grin. 'I think it looks promising.'

Sophie climbed the steps and sprang athletically onto the transom.

They peeled their wetsuits down around their waists, feeling the familiar tightness of salt on their skin and its taste on their lips as the sun's rays warmed them.

Wringing out her hair, Sophie said,' That's one hell of a current.'

'Not ideal,' Peter said matter-of-factly. 'If a ship hit here, the likelihood is she broke up and was swept into deeper water, potentially over a huge area.'

'So, you think it could have gone down here?' Excitement in her voice.

'I do,' he said confidently, securing the equipment. 'It's just the sort of small, hidden but very dangerous reef that wouldn't have been spotted until it was too late. Reefs like this have been responsible for the demise of many East Indiamen, galleons, caravels, naos – you name it.'

Sophie took a couple of Cokes from the fridge and handed him one. 'I'm going to call Dad.' She picked up the mic and depressed the transmit button.

'Cat One to Cat Two, do you read, over?'

Declan answered almost immediately. 'And? What does it look like down there?' They could picture him bent over the mic trying to visualise their situation.

'It's a plausible wreck site,' Peter confirmed, describing what they'd seen.

'Sounds promising.' There was a pause and some heavy breathing. 'Damn, I wish I was there with you.'

'As soon as we find anything you can fly up,' said Sophie. 'Tomorrow we'll initiate a grid search.'

'Keep your wits about you,' Declan advised. 'Above and below the water. The weather's changing. A low-pressure system's moving in, which I'm keeping an eye on.'

'Roger that. We'll give you an update tomorrow, Dad.' Sophie placed the mic back in its holder.

The sun had commenced its steady descent, a large ball on the horizon, more dramatic by the minute as orange turned to gold then into a deep fireball of red, reflecting off the wide expanse of open ocean, changing the ambience of their isolated setting. Before long, they were only illuminated by light from the stern and saloon in what was otherwise a pool of inky blackness.

After a light dinner, they sat at the back of the cat, looking through Declan's research, studying photos of everyday items on an Indiaman as well as cargo, clothing, ornaments and personal effects, trying to commit them to memory.

Bebel Gilberto's laid-back Brazilian vocals permeated the night air on the speaker system, blending with the gentle sound of water lapping against the twin hulls. Super peaceful, they felt a million miles from anywhere. However, Peter felt a pang of guilt that he hadn't managed to get hold of Sam and hoped she was alright.

Looking at Sophie with her long, tanned legs curled beneath her on the comfortable padded bench, Peter's thoughts turned to his father, grateful he'd sent him on this quest which had turned into one hell of an adventure.

Feeling his gaze, Sophie looked up.

'I'm curious,' Peter said. 'Do you consider yourself Swedish, Irish or international?'

'I could ask you a similar question.'

'Well?'

'I'm the sum of my parts. Part Irish, part Swedish, part of these islands,' she said, somewhat philosophically. 'What do you feel?'

'More Australian than Spanish, but my Spanish family's a strong part of me. I guess most of us are mongrels of some description.' After a brief silence, he said gently, 'Tell me about your mother.'

Sophie didn't answer straight away, then said calmly, 'She was graceful and beautiful in a striking way, turning heads wherever she went ,and could easily have been a model but she shunned the superficial lifestyle. She was naturally curious and adventurous, but above all she was passionate, and she adored my father because he was passionate, too, with similar interests despite them coming from very different backgrounds. They somehow just connected, Mum's Swedish reserve perfectly countering Dad's Irish impulsiveness and temperament.

'I've got traits from both of them,' she said, as if only just coming to the realisation. She paused, then said, 'I think everyone's a unique product of their genetic make-up, upbringing, environment, personality and experiences.'

'There's no doubt about it,' Peter agreed, standing up.

They were both exhausted. It'd been a long day and they had to make an early start in the morning. So they shut everything down and headed to bed. Sophie fell asleep almost as soon as her head hit the pillow. Peter lay for a while watching her before covering her with a sheet and falling into a troubled, fitful sleep.

He tossed and turned as different faces entered his dreams: Rocky, Declan, Harry. Ingrid floating against the roof of the tramp steamer's wheelhouse; Harry sitting in his study, writing his last words to him; Harry in his hospital bed, the effort of his last words ... Suddenly they were all in eighteenth-century Manila being chased by the Springboks, surrounded by redcoats with muskets. Peter, running for his life, holding Sophie's hand, and under his other arm the Condesa's writing box, except it was a fake. He woke several times during the night, drenched in sweat, unable to get back to sleep. Sophie murmured a few times, but his constant movement didn't wake her.

Eventually he got up and made some tea, then went to sit at the back of the cat where he read more about the *Earl of Suffolk* and the legend behind the Blue Moghul. He couldn't help but feel they were clutching at straws, at the same time knowing that was what this business was all about. Sometimes the straw you tried to clutch was actually made of sterner stuff and connected to what you were looking for. He checked the weather: the low-pressure system was moving over Luzon, with the likelihood of bad weather increasing.

After a while, he dozed off on the cushioned seat.

*

He woke a couple of hours later to the sound of Sophie making breakfast.

'You look unhealthily refreshed,' he said, sitting up as she came over with a mug of steaming coffee.

'Slept like a log. I take it you didn't.'

He knew she'd clocked that he often had trouble sleeping, and guessed she was wondering what the reason was, not wanting to pry but confident she'd find out soon enough.

Peter got up, stretched and sipped his coffee appreciatively, surveying their surroundings. The sea was calm. The sun was already well up and it was getting hotter as a pleasant sweet smell wafted over from the picturesque island.

Still worried about the South African, Peter swept the horizon with binoculars but saw no other vessels, just seabirds circling shoals of fish.

He went to retrieve Sophie's aerial shots, then spread them out on the table at the back of the boat. She came and sat next to him.

'I think we should cover this area first,' he said, pointing. 'We're here. This is where we dived yesterday' – tracing a line with his finger – 'Let's begin on the outer edge of the butterfly's wing and work our way back around the reef.'

Sophie nodded. 'Sounds sensible.'

He updated her on the weather situation, telling her they were fine but needed to keep an eye on it. He took out fresh scuba tanks from the bungees. This time they would take scavenger nets and prodders, and they'd each have a dive knife strapped to their ankle.

Peter scissored into the blue, feet first, closely followed by Sophie, the reef a kaleidoscope of colour, reflection, refraction, luminescence and pulsating life. His tiredness instantly dissipated as he looked around him, then at Sophie, whose broad smile mirrored his own at the pure pleasure of being in such an unspoilt marine environment.

It didn't get much better, he thought, savouring the moment. Indicating they should head along the reef, they finned purposefully towards the point from which they had agreed to commence their formal search, at a depth of 6 metres according to his Suunto dive watch.

Surrounded by an abundance of tropical fish, Peter identified angelfish, butterflyfish, damselfish, pipefish and sweetlips mingled among the coral head, while out where the current was stronger, a shoal of young silver barracuda held position along from a shoal of trevally. Hard corals thrived in the sun-blazed shallows, whilst soft corals preferred the shadier, deeper water near the drop-off, extending their tentacles to filter the current for plankton. Peter couldn't recall a healthier marine system, noting positively that he hadn't seen any plastic drifting along the sea floor.

After ten minutes of lazy progress over the reef edge, they reached the point from which they'd agreed to start their search. From there, they swam in parallel, 5 metres apart, exploring the edge of the reef closest to the drop-off and the edge of the sloping wall, with all its nooks and crannies extending to the sea floor.

Peter watched an octopus rapidly change colour as it moved from sand to rock, becoming invisible. A moray eel stuck its head out of a crevice, exposing razor sharp teeth, its mouth opening and closing as it pumped water into its gills, and the white sand of the sea floor, the product of ground coral over hundreds of years of wave action, glinted with the sun's penetrating rays.

As he watched several pairs of orange and white clownfish

darting around the tentacles of their brightly-coloured sea anemone hosts in biological harmony, Peter had to remind himself he wasn't there to admire the marine life, but to search for the remains of the *Earl of Suffolk*.

He tracked Sophie's outline, her pink fins propelling her forwards, and saw a large school of jacks undulating in the current near deeper water. Once again, he tried to envisage an Indiaman approaching in a raging storm, the captain, officers and crew squinting through wind and rain, and most likely darkness, spotting the reef when it was too late to avert a collision. Assuming this was the wreck location, he wondered whether it had hit head-on or broadside.

He swam further out, and within metres he hit the strong current again which was clearly a permanent phenomenon, like an invisible conveyor belt. However, he thought that at least it would give them something to work with on potential wreckage scatter if they could find some initial evidence.

He worked his way methodically along the wall for another forty minutes, prodding and probing until, seeing nothing of note, he converged to where Sophie was and signalled to head topside.

Back on board, they shed their gear and sat on the transom of the *Santa Maria*, feet dangling in the water, facing the island. Peter was relaxed. 'If it went down here, we'll find something,' he said. 'Perhaps we should climb the hill again to get a better look at what they would have seen. We didn't spend long up there. I think we need to explore the island a bit more. After all, the survivors had several days on the it.'

'Sure, but let's wait until it's cooler,' Sophie suggested.

Peter got up and bungeed the empty tanks separately from the full ones. Disappearing into the saloon, he reappeared with an A3 sketch pad and went and sat at the stern table where he started sketching the reef in section, detailing the areas they'd covered.

Sophie went and joined him. 'You've a good eye.'

'It's a habit. My mother's an artist. She taught me.'

Peter always sketched out a dive site on any search, regardless of digital or 3D drawings constructed by software, and always annotated his drawings. It helped him connect and remember things, especially if there were time lapses between searches on remote well-funded dives. He also found it therapeutic; a good way to kill time between dives, waiting for the nitrogen to exit the bloodstream. He would then transpose his annotated sketches to his Mac and religiously back everything up.

After the requisite time out of the water, they were safe to dive again. Twenty minutes later, they were back underwater, finning towards the right-hand side of the imaginary butterfly's lower right wing where they intended to cover the next search leg in a similar way. The reef close to the island was in shallow water, but further away it shelved so that its flank which ran to the tip of the lower right wing comprised a small cliff covered in soft corals, sponges and colourful algae.

This time Sophie took the lower section and Peter the upper. As before, there was an abundance of marine life, with visibility of at least 25 metres. Shoals of damselfish and sweetlips flashed this way and that, in perfect synchronisation, as though a central brain was sending impulses to an army of foot soldiers. Smaller fish were harried by larger predators, who in turn kept an eye out for those higher up the food chain. They saw turtles, rays, parrotfish, angelfish, butterfly fish, and a whitetip shark holed up at the base of the cliff wall, its large eyes glazed over. Further out, a swarm of jellyfish drifted by ethereally, then disappeared.

They inspected every inch of coral, rock and sand they swam over, expertly controlling buoyancy, keeping as aerodynamic as possible as they moved horizontally, one arm on top of the other, to the otherworldly sound of breathing through regulators as their bubbles streamed up to the surface.

Peter was watching a perfectly camouflaged frogfish snap its prey at lightning speed with its antenna lure when he heard a metallic banging. Looking over, he saw Sophie rapping her tank with her knife to get his attention. He quickly finned over, scanning for potential threats, double-checking they were on their own.

She was 5 metres down a small cliff face, hovering horizontally, neutrally buoyant, her blond hair trailing in the slight current. As he drew level, she pointed at the base of the cliff face to an indentation where the reef wall jutted out.

Swimming down to take a closer look, Peter focused on a dark patch of coral and his face erupted into a broad grin as he recognised a familiar shape. Within the consolidated mass was the distinctive curve of a cannonball. He felt his heart race. Having dived hundreds of wreck sites, this meant one thing. He reached out and touched it, a tangible connection with the past, the initial evidence they'd been hoping for.

He jabbed the mass from various angles with his dive knife but it was rock solid, cemented into the reef structure. Sophie's eyes sparkled through her pink Tusa mask as she looked at him; he indicated with an upturned thumb to make for the surface, which they did at the requisite rate of no faster than a foot a second.

They broke the surface at the same time, leaving the silence of the undersea world, pushing their masks onto their foreheads.

'She's down there, isn't she?' Sophie gasped excitedly.

Peter gave a broad grin. 'Well, there's definitely a wreck down there. That was well spotted. Let's head to the cat and take stock.'

They swam slowly on their backs over to the *Santa Maria* as the sun beat down on this remote patch of paradise. Back on board, they shed their diving gear. Peter went and sat at the table where his books and the sketchpad were spread out, keen to update his drawing with the location of the cannonball while it was fresh in his mind, trying to envisage how the wreck might have hit, broken up and scattered.

He looked at Sophie. 'You know, the *Atocha*, found by Mel Fisher off Florida, was hit by multiple cyclones over many years, its wreckage scattered over ten miles.'

Sophie, familiar with the story of the Spanish galleon, one of the most valuable treasure finds of all time, said pragmatically, 'Every shipwreck's different. You know they can disperse in a thousand ways.'

'It took a team of experts years to find the mother lode,' Peter persisted. 'The likelihood here, with that current, is that most of the wreckage would've been dragged into deeper water, beyond here.' He pointed at one of the aerial photos. 'Further out from the tip of the butterfly's wing.'

'Let's not get ahead of ourselves,' Sophie said calmly. 'We've made a good start. It looks promising.'

'I agree. I'm not trying to put a dampener on things, just be realistic.'

They parked the idea of exploring the island for another time. Instead, they read, relaxed and went to bed early after updating Declan. Tired from the physical exercise and adrenaline rush from their discovery, and with the anticipation of the search ahead, they both slept deeply.

*

Next morning, they made an early start, the sun not yet up. They finned to the section of drop-off containing the cannon ball and focused their search on the immediate vicinity, poking coral and rocks with prodders and knives, surrounded by tropical fish of all shapes, sizes and colours, some in pairs, other in shoals, as they methodically worked their way along the sea floor, skirting this section of reef wall.

Peter signalled he would look further out. Sophie okayed him, continuing to search the reef edge, double-checking the area she'd covered the day before.

As he swam into deeper water, Peter felt the full force of the current running parallel to the reef. Further out, the sea floor comprised large and small areas of isolated reef, like islands, interspersed by wide areas of sand, some rising like sea mounts, or bommies, from the ocean floor, stopping metres shy of the surface and more than capable of slicing open a ship.

Floating horizontally, neutrally buoyant, midway to the surface in

10 metres of water, he watched an eagle ray move across the sea floor like a hovercraft, its white spots contrasting against dark skin, its long slender venomous tail trailing behind, whilst a solitary grey reef shark came into view ahead of him, easily recognisable by its shape and the black edge to its tail, though seemingly uninterested.

He looked towards deeper water where a pair of manta rays glided gracefully into view, their giant mouths sieving millions of plankton, their large bat-like wings propelling them silently through the blue expanse. As they disappeared into the distance, a hawksbill turtle swam towards a standalone outcrop 20 metres away.

Checking his air was good for another fifteen to twenty minutes on current consumption, he was about to go and find Sophie when his eye caught the glint of a shoal of young barracuda holding the current, like the day before. *Probably the same shoal*, he thought.

His eye travelled to where the turtle had settled on a coral outcrop, then down to a dull green colour at its base, distinct from the rest of the coral. Curiosity got the better of him and he finned over. The turtle quickly headed to deeper water.

Surveying the outcrop with a practised eye, Peter made out familiar shapes, and his heart beat faster.

There were two of them, encrusted in coral, their ends crossed over, one lying diagonally across the top of the other at the base of the outcrop. Not a doubt in his mind they were cannon. Waving sand from the edges with his hands, he prodded the rock base. Sensing movement out of the corner of his eye, he turned to see Sophie heading towards him, pointing at her watch. It was time to head back. He okayed her, pointing repeatedly at the cannon. She acknowledged him with a killer grin, and they made for the cat.

Back on board, their excitement was palpable.

'We need an hour on the surface.' Peter looked at his dive computer. 'Then we'll head back down again.'

'Maybe it didn't scatter over such a large area after all,' Sophie said optimistically.

'Maybe.' He smiled. 'It's definitely a good sign. Clearly a ship sank here, but whether it's the one we're looking for remains to be seen.'

'What are the chances of another one?'

'Higher than you might think. Also, not wanting to put a dampener on things, I've worked on plenty of wreck sites where you find a few things quickly, then it's a long time before you find anything else, and that's if you're lucky. I'm not saying that's the case here. Just warning you, that's all.'

'I'm a big girl, Peter. I can take it.' She looked at him expectantly. 'So, what's the plan?'

'We explore the area around the cannon with a toothcomb. There's plenty of coral heads further along where stuff could have lodged.'

They remained quiet, lost in their thoughts as they enjoyed the sun's warming rays and drank water to keep hydrated. Itching to get back under water, time passed slowly.

Eventually, Peter's Suunto beeped.

'Okay. We're good to go,' he said.

They wasted no time kitting up, jumping off the transom and submerging once again in the crystalline blue waters.

Visibility had dropped slightly, which Peter took as a sign the weather was changing. Although the marine life was still prolific, there was no sign of the grey reef shark he'd seen earlier, just a couple of blacktips opportunistically cruising the shallows.

When they reached the outcrop holding the melded-together cannon, they sank to their knees, carefully scraping sand and loose material from under and around it. The coral head was significantly more substantial than it had looked from above, and went deep.

One of the cannon was more exposed than the other, but both were heavily encrusted, with no visible branding on what could be seen. Peter knew the likely location of a coat of arms or a crest would be under the hard growth, which would require professional salvage equipment to shift.

Sophie signalled she was going to explore further over, and finned around the outcrop, disappearing from view.

Given the complicated nature of the site, Peter thought there was a good probability heavier items and parts of the ship could have lodged in the vicinity, while others would undoubtedly have been flushed into deeper water once they'd made contact with the strong current.

He finned around the outcrop on the opposite side from Sophie, hugging the sea floor, combing away sand and loose rocks. A host of colourful fish living in cracks and crevices darted in and out, protecting their micro habitats, evading potential danger, and pairs of 'Nemo' clownfish swam among the swaying tentacles of their brightly-coloured hosts.

Moving methodically, breathing evenly to conserve air, Peter expected to see Sophie any minute. The outcrop shelved into deeper water and looked a lot more substantial from this angle. He followed the contours down, spotting a couple of whitetips dozing under a deep overhang, their large dead-looking eyes watchful while above, a small group of big-eye trevally hovered, gleaming iridescent silver.

Scanning the area where the whitetips lay, his intuition told him to search the overhang they were under. He approached cautiously, his shark stick extended, gently prodding the nearest, which snapped aggressively. He hassled them until they reluctantly moved further along the outcrop.

Peter cautiously entered the long, narrow cave-like space, careful not to snag his scuba tank on the coral roof. Three metres in, the ceiling dropped, narrowing towards its apex. A stingray startled him as it shot out from beneath him but he maintained his composure, trying not to stir up sand. A scorpionfish arched its poisonous fins and brushed his arm and he shifted position to let it pass. As he prodded the cracks at the furthest recesses of the cave, he realised his tank was dangerously close to the ceiling.

In the confined space, the sound of his breathing seemed louder. Hearing his tank scrape the roof, he slowly reversed, unable to turn, wafting both hands to propel himself backwards as clouds of sand billowed and swirled. At that moment, something caught his eye: a dull metallic colour, not coral or rock, in the furthest left-hand corner. Unable to reach it with his tank on, he calmly unclipped and slipped out of his BCD, then laid the tank in the sand, his regulator still firmly in his mouth, his breathing even, no change from before; he'd done this countless times in various situations, one of the skills that separated a professional diver from a hobbyist.

Peter checked his dive time and air supply; both were good. Gently edging his tank alongside him, he made his way slowly in again to the rear of the narrow space, scuffing up more sand. Placing his tank to one side, he waited for the sand to settle, breathing slowly and evenly.

As it drifted and settled, he wondered if his eyes had tricked him, then saw what had caught his attention the first time: a mass, about the size of a small teapot, with a dull sheen about 2 centimetres wide on one side. Having seen similar examples many times on wreck sites, he was certain it was an amalgamation of coins, welded together over the centuries by the chemical reaction of seawater and metal alloys to form a hard crust.

Initial jabs with his knife proved fruitless, but after ten minutes he managed to prize part of the ball from the coral, lifting it carefully and placing it in the net attached to his weight belt. Using his hands to waft away more sand, he saw something long and flat wedged in a crevice, and reached for it. It wouldn't budge. Breathing heavily, knowing he was consuming air at a faster rate, he worked his knife under the item, eventually prying it free. Slipping it into his net, he checked his dive watch. Time had passed quickly. He should head back.

He reversed out of the cave slowly, half-carrying, half-shoving the tank, careful not to stretch the junction with the air hose. At the entrance, he knelt in the sand and with practised ease slipped it back over his head and snapped the plastic buckles securely on his BCD. As he set off to find Sophie, she appeared above him, pointing excitedly at her trailing net, seeming to also have found something. Peter signalled they should surface and they made their way back to the *Santa Maria* as fast as safety would allow.

*

They broke the surface and bobbed next to one another, kept afloat by their BCDs. Sophie hefted her net up excitedly. 'I found some porcelain. I think they're plate fragments. What about you?'

'A mass of coins,' Peter replied, looking up at the ominous sky, not mentioning the other object he'd retrieved. Large clouds scudded high above, blocking the sun.

'Dad's gonna be really excited,' Sophie said as they swam to the rear of the cat.

'He's not the only one.' Peter's expression was suddenly serious as he looked beyond her, towards the corner of the island they'd navigated two days earlier. 'Shit, we've got company.'

Sophie followed his gaze, immediately computing the danger.

'We need to move fast,' Peter said, wasting no time in discarding his BCD and climbing onto the transom. Sophie handed him her haul and tank which he hastily stashed to one side before helping her up.

'Let's get this stuff hidden.' He grabbed their nets and ran down to the lower deck, stuffing the items into a locker in the port-side fore cabin. Back on deck, Sophie gathered up the papers, books and research material, hiding them from prying eyes in a locker in the main saloon. They shed their wetsuits and donned T-shirts and shorts.

'What do we do?' asked Sophie.

'Play innocent and move on,' Peter replied, opening a cupboard, untapping one of the semi-automatics he'd hidden, shoving it into the back of his shorts and pulling his T-shirt down over it.

The Swan 40 was clearly identifiable now, as were 'Lars' and 'Nenita', heading straight for them.

Peter hefted the tanks, securing them next to the others. 'I'm going to try Declan,' he said, grabbing the mic and depressing the transmit button:

'Cat One, do you receive, over. This is Cat Two, over. There's a fox in the coop.'

He repeated the call sign several times, but there was no answer.

'Shit. Murphy's law. He sits by the bloody machine for days and isn't there when we need him.'

Sophie rolled her eyes.

As the Swan approached, the big South African waved, his broad smile and muscular shape easily discernible like a solid piece of granite. The yacht slowed as he angled it round so it was parallel to the *Santa Maria*'s stern, and with only a metre between them he dropped anchor.

'Seems we're attracted to the same places,' he shouted over.

'No shit,' Sophie muttered under her breath.

'Nice and friendly,' Peter said out of the corner of his mouth, continuing to secure equipment. 'We didn't expect to see anyone out here,' he shouted back.

'I was just saying to Nenita, I had a strange feeling we might run into you again. Almost a premonition. Mind if we come aboard? I'd lick to pick your brains, man.'

Peter shook his head. 'Sorry, but we're heading off. We're late for a rendezvous.'

'Won't take long,' the South African replied, jumping onto the *Santa Maria*'s transom without invitation, closely followed by his companion. 'You look like you know the area well.' The same menacing smile, the hard eyes flicking searchingly over the cat, missing nothing as they climbed the steps up to the stern deck.

Ironically, thought Peter, the man wore a green Springboks singlet with yellow trim, his muscles bulging, not an ounce of fat.

Taking in the scuba tanks, Springbok said provocatively, 'That's some serious equipment. How's the diving?'

'Not as good as it looks.'

'Looks pretty good to me.' He grinned broadly. 'You're searching for something?'

Peter smiled. 'Solitude and fine diving. Look, mate, we don't mean to be rude, but we're meeting friends in Coron and running late.'

The man approached Peter so he was standing close; marginally shorter but much broader.

'I heard there's some old wrecks up here only a few well-informed people know about,' he said, his expression intimidating.

Peter stepped back to retrieve his personal space. 'What sort of wrecks?' He tried sounding casual but there was an edge to his voice the man evidently picked up on.

The man's eyes were unforgiving, the smile gone. 'Ones that some people would kill to find.'

Sophie laughed. 'If you mean Manila galleons, you're way off base. They sailed the other side of the Philippines. There's no treasure ships out here.' Pitched just right with the appropriate ring of authority.

The South African grinned like a great white. 'Is that so?'

Sophie nodded. 'Anyone who's read the history of the islands and likes diving knows the stories.' As her father always said, a little bit of truth goes a long way. 'Sounds like you're the one searching for something?'

'Always,' he replied. 'Any chance of a glass of water?'

Seeming to relax marginally, he backed off from Peter, less confrontational, more conciliatory.

'You want one, too?' Sophie asked the woman.

'No,' she replied, her face expressionless, her oversized black sunglasses giving her the incongruous appearance of a bat.

Sophie returned and handed a glass of water to 'Springbok', which he downed like a shot, the glass tiny in his ham-like hands.

Smiling affably, Peter said, 'Well, we need to get going. Enjoy the island.'

Springbok moved towards him. 'What's the rush?' He asked, their faces inches apart.

Peter looked him in the eyes. 'We don't have to explain ourselves to you.'

Meeting Peter's gaze full on, the South African reached behind him and in one smooth movement extracted a large semi-automatic. 'I can't let you do that, man.'

'You Bekker's whipping boy?'

'Search him,' Springbok instructed the woman. She quickly found Peter's semi and spare mag, and took them.

'Move over there.' Springbok motioned with his gun towards the padded bench. 'Both of you. Sit.'

The woman stuffed Peter's SIG into her shorts, then produced two sets of plastic ties.

Waving the semi, Springbok said, 'Put your arms out wide. Feck about, I'll not hesitate.'

They believed him.

The woman plastic-cuffed Sophie first, then Peter.

'I'm surprised you made it so easy,' Springbok sneered.

'You're wasting your time,' said Peter.

'I don't think so. Found what you're looking for?'

Springbok turned to his companion and flicked his head towards the saloon. 'Start searching.'

The woman flung open cabinets and drawers, soon finding the sketchbook which she brought over and laid on the table: the cross-section of the reef in all its glory.

Springbok shook his head in amusement. 'This just gets better and better. And I thought you were professional and potentially dangerous. What was he thinking?'

The woman went through everything. Anything deemed unimportant was flung across the floor. Next she picked up a book on East Indiamen, which she held up.

'Not galleons, but Indiamen,' Springbok said, clearly loving this. 'Makes sense. I have to say I couldn't figure it out. But then I don't have all the facts.'

'Generally, the hired help's the lowest member of the food chain,' Sophie snapped, which immediately riled him. He walked over and unceremoniously pistol-whipped the side of her head, drawing blood. Peter jumped up, but the man was quick, lashing out at him too, winding him with a blow to the stomach. The guy was a power machine.

It wasn't long before the woman found the items from their last dive in the guest cabin. She brought them up and placed them on the saloon table.

Their captor's wide grin returned. 'So, not only have you been looking for a shipwreck, but it seems you've found one.'

Peter wondered what would happen now. This guy was working for either Bekker, Johansson, or both, and would logically call them in. The sun had disappeared. The sky was now a dull gunmetal grey, and there was a palpable drop in air pressure. He inwardly cursed they hadn't been able to get hold of Declan and could only hope that he'd realise something was wrong when he didn't hear from them, especially with the weather closing in.

Peter looked at the thug defiantly. 'So, what's the plan?'

'We're gonna wait until my friends arrive. In the meantime, we can have a little chat.'

'I don't feel chatty,' Peter said with a poker face.

'Oh, believe me, you'll talk.'

The boat rocked in the significant swell that had developed since they'd surfaced.

Sitting across from them, Springbok examined Peter's sketch. 'So, you've found items in two locations. I'm impressed.'

Peter thought about charging the guy but with his hands cuffed and an opponent as strong as an ox, it made no sense. He couldn't risk him hurting Sophie. They would have to play this out.

'What was on the manifest?

'We just got lucky,' said Peter. 'We heard a story from some fishermen on Linapacan and thought we'd check it out. Never thought we'd find anything. We've no idea what wreck they're from.'

'You think I'm a fecking idiot?'

'You look like one,' Sophie said.

'You're pissing me off, lady.'

She looked at him without fear. 'That's good, then.'

Peter gave her a look that said: *Don't rile this guy.* She got the message. He wondered what she'd said to Johansson when she'd been kidnapped. He'd love to have been a fly on the wall as she sure as hell didn't buckle under pressure.

'Is it gold or silver bullion?' persisted Springbok.

No mention of diamonds or jewels. So Bekker didn't know, or if he did, wasn't telling the hired help. Made sense. Also, why would Johansson tell Bekker what he was really after? There was potential for double-crossing at every level of the food chain.

'As I just said, we've no idea. We just got lucky.'

'Real lucky, I'd say. Heading up to a remote island on the edge of the Philippine archipelago, diving for two days and finding evidence of a shipwreck. What are the chances of that?'

Peter's eyes narrowed as he calculated his best approach. This man seemed violent but measured, like Bekker. Maybe Afrikaans special forces. He certainly looked like a mercenary.

Springbok's expression became serious. 'I'll ask you again, nicely. What are you searching for?'

They just stared at him, neither answering.

Springbok fired his pistol to the left of Sophie's midriff and part of the gunwale fragmented.

Sophie and Peter both flinched.

'Next one's into flesh.'

Peter knew he had to give the man something. 'It's silver bullion,' he said. 'Lots of it, if the story's true.'

He saw a flicker in the man's eyes, as if congratulating himself on extracting the information.

The cat was rocking uncharacteristically in the now choppy sea as the sky darkened by the minute. 'You better make some decisions,' Peter said. 'There's a serious storm coming.'

As if noticing for the first time, the thug looked at the ominous sea which was now a uniform colour with no distinguishing boundaries between blue and azure; just grey with white horses further out.

'We'll ride it out,' he said dismissively.

'And we're just going to sit here with you pointing a gun at us?' said Sophie. 'You're thicker than I thought.'

This time it was the woman who stepped forward, lashing out at Sophie, her eyes gleaming. Peter realised she was a sadistic bimbo, not just cover but someone who enjoyed inflicting pain. But he also knew Springbok had a dilemma. This looked like a major storm that could cause serious damage, one ideally they should head to the safety of a natural harbour to protect themselves from. Out here they were exposed, with two yachts and either one or two skippers – although he wasn't banking on the woman's capability – given he and Sophie were out of action, at least for the time being.

Springbok waved his gun towards the saloon entrance. 'Get up, nice and slow. Walk down to the lower deck. Try anything, I promise I'll blow your knee caps off. I'm an excellent shot. I've been told to keep you alive. No one said anything about anything else.'

Smiling at his ingenuity and waving the semi-automatic, he said, 'You first, bitch.'

Sophie got up. As she walked past him, she spat in his face.

The woman smashed a fist into her side, and Sophie doubled over but still she didn't cry out. Peter followed cautiously, trying to come up with a plan. The storm could provide an opportunity or it could be their downfall, depending on how this played out. He'd been through enough to know you needed all hands on deck and all your expertise to safely ride out a big one, and that needed full concentration, staying power and no diversions.

'Keep them apart,' Springbok instructed the woman.

First she tied Peter up in the starboard fore cabin while Springbok trained his gun on both of them. Sophie was then ushered out and Peter's door slammed shut. She was taken up into the saloon, then across and down the staircase on other side and into the portside fore cabin where she was tied up.

After shutting her door, their captors retreated back up to the saloon where Sophie and Peter could hear them in animated discussion. After a few minutes, Peter couldn't hear anything and guessed one of them had returned to the Swan to radio Bekker or Johansson.

He had to do something quickly; they'd be in a death trap if they were left tied up when the storm hit. Shuffling upright, he peered through the porthole at the Swan, but without a direct line of sight couldn't tell who was on board. If it was Springbok, they had a chance.

He decided to risk it, despite the potential consequences. 'Hey, can you come down?' he shouted.

No answer. He shouted louder.

Sophie shouted, 'Are you all right?'

'Fine, just leave this to me.' He heard footsteps down the stairs and corridor, and the woman appeared in the doorway.

'So, you wanna be gagged?' she said in a whining Filipina-American twang.

'I need the toilet. I don't want to piss myself.'

'I tell Franz,' she said. 'But don't think he care you piss your pants or not.' Laughing, she closed the door, and Peter heard her footsteps receding back up to the saloon. That told him two things: Springbok was on board the Swan and his real name was Franz.

This was his chance.

Manoeuvring himself around on the floor, he elbowed part of the skirting abutting the back corner of the bedroom until a knife with a finely honed six-inch blade sprang out at ninety degrees – Declan's idea. Aligning his bound wrists, he carefully sliced through the plastic ties, then untied his feet.

Once free, he retrieved the other SIG P226 and the smaller SIG P230 sub-compact from under the base of one of the lockers. Checking they had full magazines, he stuffed a spare in his shorts, then carefully opened the cabin door. He cautiously made his way up the steps to the saloon and, poking his head around the corner, spotted the woman at the stern talking over to the South African on the Swan. He moved stealthily across the saloon, keeping low, then ran down the steps the other side, opened the fore cabin door, cut Sophie loose and handed her the SIG P230.

'Follow me,' he whispered, finger to his lips. He cautiously climbed the steps to the main saloon, half-expecting the woman to be waiting at the top, but halfway up he saw she was still at the stern. It was now or never.

He whispered to Sophie. 'You take her. I'll focus on him.'

She nodded. Declan had told him she could shoot. Now was the time to prove it.

The woman spotted them as they entered the saloon. Peter dived to one side as she fired her pistol at him. Sophie dived onto the floor, firing two shots in quick succession, a 'double tap' in army parlance, hitting the woman in the lower leg and throwing her off balance so her own shots went wide, splintering the designer woodwork to the left of the stairwell.

Seizing the initiative, Sophie and Peter rushed forward. The woman lay awkwardly against the padded seating, one leg stretched out, resting on her elbows. As she raised her pistol, Sophie delivered a merciless kick to her firing arm, and her weapon flew across the deck.

Holding his SIG firmly in both hands, stretched out in front of him, Peter anticipated Springbok's athletic presence imminently. As Sophie pinned her opponent down and pistol whipped her face, quid pro quo, he saw the South African about to catapult himself over from the Swan.

Firing several shots in quick succession, Peter halted the man in his tracks. If there was one thing he unambiguously understood, it was the power of weaponry – that a bullet was entirely ruthless and unselective in who it maimed or killed.

'Stay the fuck over there!' Peter shouted. 'Raise your hands where I can see them. Drop the weapon overboard.'

Thankfully, and to Peter's surprise, the thug stayed on the Swan, dangling the Glock 17 upside down from his forefinger, his defiant dark eyes hard and menacing even from this distance. Peter fired a shot to the man's left. Flinching, Springbok dropped the pistol overboard. Peter knew that if he dived into the cabin, he would grab another weapon.

'Get over here, *now!*' he yelled. 'Nice and slow.'

Springbok didn't move, his eyes locked onto Peter's, a cruel, teasing smile on his face. Peter fired another shot. This time closer to his body, the bullet shattering the hull behind him.

'I'll not ask again!' Peter shouted. 'Nice and easy, no sudden moves, or the next one goes through you. Keep your hands in the air,' he said, stepping back to allow him space.

Springbok stepped onto the *Santa Maria*, sure-footedly, like a large predatory cat. With his SIG aimed at him, Peter maintained his distance, motioning the man towards his companion on the sofa bench. As a solid chunk of hugely dangerous potential energy, it was their priority to tie him up. Only then could they determine their best course of action.

The sky was now the colour of lead, dark and ominous, and a large swell rocked the normally stable cat.

'Throw your ties over,' Peter said to the woman.

With an obstinate look on her face, she reluctantly obliged. Her swollen, bruised left eye gave her a more threatening appearance.

Sophie cautiously bent to pick them up, keeping her eyes and her semi pointing at the woman.

'Move apart. You this side, you that,' Peter commanded.

'Tie her up, hands first,' he said to Sophie. 'If either of them makes a move, I'll kill them.'

Sophie cuffed the woman first. Her wrists were slim and it was easy to ratchet home the ties.

'Now Franz!' Peter spat the name. 'Hold your arms out, wrists together, no sudden moves,' he said. He nodded at Sophie who approached cautiously, careful not to come between Peter and the South African. Springbok obliged, but his eyes taunted, showing no fear, like a coiled Cobra that could strike any second. Even so, Sophie managed to secure two of the ties around his wrists, but only just. They were thick and powerful. She pulled them as tight as she could.

'What you gonna do now, sport?' Springbok said grinning. 'I'd say you're the one with a few decisions to make'. He indicated with his eyes at the sky as it began to rain heavily, drumming the roof of the canopy like machine gun fire.

With limited visibility, their surroundings now looked anything but tropical.

Peter wasn't a killer, but he was conflicted, resolved he would do whatever it took to protect Sophie. If he put the couple on the Swan, it would solve nothing. Leaving them on the island also had negative implications, given Springbok would no doubt have already radioed Bekker or Johansson who'd soon arrive with back-up, weather permitting.

He made a decision. Waving the SIG, he said, 'Both of you get up. Move slowly into the saloon.'

Springbok slowly got to his feet, his face locked in a smirk as he edged out from the sofa bench, his hard eyes never leaving Peter's. Peter stepped back to put more space between them, his arm fully extended, the SIG aimed at the man's chest.

The South African walked slowly into the saloon, his bound hands in front of him, his every movement packed with latent threat. Peter shoved him in the back. He staggered forwards, tripping onto the floor. Peter moved slightly so the woman could to go alongside her companion, his SIG never wavering from the South African.

'Get the rope out of the cupboard,' Peter said to Sophie. 'I've got them covered.'

'Sit on the floor,' he ordered them.

Then to Sophie: 'Tie their hands and feet to the table. This fuckhead first.'

He waved the SIG at them. 'Any moves, I shoot to kill. On the floor, now.'

As they sunk to the floor, Springbok's eyes were still locked onto Peter's.

Sophie bent down warily, tying his legs first, then his wrists, as securely as she was able to the table leg soldered into the floor. She then did the same with the woman, backing off with her semi pointed at them when she'd finished.

Peter walked over and checked the knots. He was impressed: they were solid and tight.

He ushered Sophie to the stern and slid the saloon door shut after them so they were out of earshot. The cat was rocking heavily now, the sea and gunmetal grey sky now one threatening entity as waves crashed onto the reef and huge plumes of spray were forced up through the rocks along the shoreline, like geysers. Rain sheeted down relentlessly as the wind gathered strength and coconut palms whipped along the beach.

Looking across at the Swan, Peter tried to determine their best course of action. 'We'll keep them where we can see them, it's better that way,' he said decisively, picking up the mic. 'I'll try Declan again.'

Still nothing but static.

'You're fecked!' Springbok shouted from the saloon. 'Really fecked.' His mocking, deep-throated chuckle carried threateningly on the wind.

'Don't take your eyes off them for a second,' Peter said to Sophie. 'I'm going to disable the Swan. We'll then head somewhere safer.'

She nodded. Although Peter knew she was anxious about their predicament, she hadn't panicked and he knew he could count on her.

With careful timing, he jumped onto the Swan which was pitching violently. He disabled the engine and electrics, smashing the VHF and GPS and then disconnected the steering. He slashed the sails and halyards for good measure and lastly he cut the anchor loose before jumping back onto the *Santa Maria*. The Swan soon drifted swiftly towards the island, carried by wind and current.

He went into the saloon to double check their prisoners were firmly secured, all too aware of Springbok's capabilities, while Sophie kept her SIG trained on them. They seemed secure so, sliding the saloon door shut, they went up to the elevated helm station.

Given the conditions, Peter elected to motor sail, using the headsail and the engines in unison. He thought they'd be safer moving location as Bekker and or Johansson would most likely be heading for the island in a sizeable motor vessel better able to handle the rough weather, and he and Sophie would be sitting ducks. As he sat in the helmsman's chair with Sophie next to him, there was a good view of their captives through the glass.

'We'll make for Linapacan,' Peter said decisively, 'but we'll need to deviate from the direct route as that's where Bekker's men will most likely be coming from.'

The helm was less responsive than usual. The cat sailed awkwardly, requiring constant correction, however, the combination of sail and twin engines allowed them some control. Heading into wind towards the southern tip of the island, they saw the Swan near an outcrop of rocks, keeling at 90 degrees as it took on water.

Drenched by spray, it took all their concentration to see where they were going and to avoid the reef. Rain lashed the cat and waves surged on board, a full force nine storm having developed.

On the shoreline, waves crashed onto the beach and spray spumed from rocks. Stands of coconut palms lining the edge of the jungled hillside flexed over like giant catapults.

Glancing into the saloon, Peter's heart skipped a beat.

Springbok was gone.

'The fucker's escaped!' he shouted to Sophie above the wind. 'Here, take the helm. Guide her as best you can. Head out to avoid the reef.'

'What are you going to do?' Sophie shouted.

'Disable him.' Peter's face was a mask of determination as he grabbed the SIG from his waistband and slid the action. He entered the saloon. Thunder rumbled loudly. Fork lightning streaked the sky, illuminating the vast emptiness of the ocean and reinforcing their isolation.

Peter wasn't sure if he was the hunter or the hunted. The woman taunted him with a twisted smile on her bruised face, but said nothing. She looked securely tied. There was no sign of Springbok. Just limp rope and broken cuffs where he'd been tied up.

Sophie suddenly screamed, 'Behind you!'

From seemingly nowhere, the prop forward rammed Peter at full pelt, the momentum propelling them onto the stern deck so that they crashed against the table and wraparound sofa benches. He felt a crushing pain in his shoulder as his SIG flew across the deck towards the transom. Springbok, momentarily disorientated from hitting his head, staggered to retain his balance, allowing Peter in one fluid movement to dive and grab his pistol. The South African got to his feet, shaking his head and grinning, blood trickling down his face as though he was in a good rugby scrap.

Like an express train, he lunged at Peter, who fired two shots into his thigh. But he kept on coming, pinning Peter against a stanchion. Peter shot blindly and his opponent screamed in pain, instinctively clutching the right side of his ribcage and releasing his grip on Peter. As he lunged again, lightning fast, Peter sidestepped and tripped him so that he crumpled onto the transom.

Charging as fast as he could, and summoning all his strength, Peter upended the powerful South African into the grey, turbulent water, watching his face submerge out of sight. He ran over and turned his attention to Sophie, grabbing the wheel and angling the cat hard to starboard, towards open water, but it was too late. They heard the unmistakable sound of coral crunching into the left hull.

Instead of glancing off the reef, the cat ground hard into it with the full impetus of the current and gale-force wind. Peter rushed below to inspect the damage – water was gushing into the master cabin, already nearly a foot deep, far too extensive for any temporary repair. He ran back up to the helm station where Sophie was trying to reverse off the reef, the engines straining at full throttle. But they were firmly wedged.

'Did you kill him?' she screamed through the wind and sheeting rain.

'No,' he shouted back. 'But chances are he'll drown or become shark fodder.'

He'd seen Springbok was bleeding heavily and seriously wounded as he tumbled into the angry sea, but equally he knew the man couldn't be written off unless they had evidence of his dead body.

Wiping water out of his eyes, squinting against the wind and rain, Peter shouted, 'We'll have to swim to the island. Put your wetsuit on. Shove anything useful in a waterproof pack. She won't sink, but she may capsize.'

'What about the bitch?'

'We'll cut her loose. She can take her chances.' Peter ran into the saloon and cut through the woman's ties and cuffs. Without a weapon and the support of Springbok, she looked harmless enough. He marched her outside and gave her the good news, handing her a life jacket. As she massaged her arms and legs to get the blood flowing, he pushed her towards the transom. 'You're on your own. Swim for the shallows.'

Expressionless, she said nothing, just jumped in and started swimming frantically.

Peter turned his attention to Sophie. 'Where are the items from the wreck? I can't find them,' he shouted, realising Springbok had probably taken them onto the Swan; he cursed himself for not checking.

They hastily scoured the cabins but drew a blank. The cat was listing heavily now, large waves pushing them further onto the reef, ripping out more of the hull. They quickly put on their wetsuits and shoved a few essentials into waterproof packs, then abandoned ship and started swimming the 200 metres to the island as lightning zigzagged and thunder rumbled, the sea periodically illuminated as if by a stroboscope. Peter thought history was repeating itself as he imagined the *Earl of Suffolk* in similar circumstances, holed on the reef, listing, filling with water and sinking as men abandoned ship, trying to swim to shore, most drowning, trapped in a watery grave far from home on the other side of the world.

They struck out towards the island as the cat lurched heavily to port, its left hull now two-thirds submerged, as angry grey waves rolled over the stern, flooding the saloon. Through the driving rain they made out the woman crawling up a small spit of sand sandwiched between rocky outcrops on the island, and wondered what had become of Springbok.

They couldn't avoid minor cuts from the razor-sharp coral although their wetsuits afforded them some protection; they just hoped they wouldn't attract any sharks. Halfway to the island, the conveyor belt strong current pulled Sophie towards open water, and

Peter had to swim hard to pull her back, knowing that if they got stuck in it, they'd be swept out to sea.

After a strenuous swim, they made it to the shallows and staggered out of the water, up the beach to the line of palms. There was no sign of the woman or Springbok. Looking towards the outer edge of the reef, they saw the *Santa Maria* was now half submerged, being lashed by waves in the sheeting, relentless rain in gale-force winds.

They took stock of their cuts and scrapes, which were painful, but not serious.

'We need to find shelter,' Peter yelled through the howling wind. 'Let's head for the boulders where we climbed the other day.'

He held Sophie's hand tightly as they fought their way along the top of the beach under the swaying palms which fringed the lower reaches of the hill, dodging flying coconuts and debris. Peter was grateful that unlike Robert Sinclair and the other survivors of the *Earl of Suffolk*, in almost identical circumstances all those years ago, at least he and Sophie knew where they were.

When they reached the cluster of huge boulders, they found a narrow passage leading to a small covered area, which, while not quite a cave, at least afforded some protection from the elements in a deep cleft with a rocky overhang. Crouching, Peter checked the inner pouch of their waterproof packs, sighing with relief that the two SIGS, spare mags, a flare, torch and binoculars were dry.

He slumped next to Sophie and they huddled close, shivering from the wet and cold, emotionally and physically exhausted, their only option to ride out the storm and hope that Declan would bring help.

\*

It was a long, uncomfortable, noisy night as the wind howled and debris flew about but eventually, in the early hours, the storm abated and they fell into a fitful, troubled sleep.

Peter woke to daylight, realising the wind and rain had stopped. It was eerily quiet. He gently prized himself from Sophie and propped her against the rock, cushioning her head with a T-shirt. He threaded his way through the boulders out onto the beach, looking at the devastation as he walked diagonally down to the shore. The normally picture-perfect island was a tangled mass of vegetation and other debris which lay strewn across the sand with a wide band of flotsam and jetsam demarcating the high water line. The sea was still a uniform grey-blue, stretching from the shallows into deeper water where the upturned twin hulls of the *Santa Maria* were jammed on the reef head. The Swan was nowhere in sight.

Heading back up the beach to wake Sophie, Peter stopped in his tracks at the top, near the passageway into the rocks. From the left, a clear set of large tracks joined his own going the other way: one elongated, as though someone or something was being dragged, the other a normal but large human footprint. His heart skipped a beat. They weren't women's prints, which meant one thing: Springbok was alive. He reached behind him for his SIG and cursed, remembering it was in his backpack. Stupid. As he ran quickly into the passageway between the boulders, Sophie gave a piercing scream.

Peering cautiously into the narrow space where they'd taken shelter, Peter saw Springbok was sitting with Sophie in front of him, holding her in a vice-like grip with a serrated hunting knife to her throat. His face was heavily swollen and covered in cuts. One eye was completely closed. Clearly in trouble, with a blood-soaked ragged tourniquet around his left thigh, his legs were a pulpy mass of wounds, presumably from being pounded against the coral. How he'd made it ashore was anybody's guess. But he was a survivor.

For once, Sophie looked terrified. They both knew this natural-born killer had nothing to lose.

Grinning, Springbok said with menace, 'You feck me, I feck you.'

'Don't hurt her!' Peter yelled as he took in Sophie's stance and position in relation to the South African, as well as their packs. 'Whatever you want, it's yours.'

'What I was promised,' snarled the man, clearly in agony, 'and I'm gonna get it, whether you both die or not. Where's your gun?' He grimaced through gritted teeth.

Peter didn't answer.

'I'm sitting on two packs. Inside there's gotta be a gun,' hissed the South African, shuffling sideways, his grip on Sophie unwavering as he used his feet to sit more upright away from the packs.

'Empty them out. Try anything, she's gone,' he said. 'Move slowly, empty one at a time.' His knife was tight against Sophie's throat.

Peter emptied his pack first, shaking out a torch, a map, a SIG P226 and a spare mag onto the hard ground.

Springbok smiled through his broken face. 'Throw the gun, nice and slow,' he said, increasing the pressure on Sophie's neck.

Knowing he wasn't quick enough to try anything, Peter obliged, the semi-automatic landing at Springbok's feet. The man pushed Sophie in front of him, and she sprawled in the sand. In one swift movement he picked up and racked the semi-automatic, aiming at each of them in turn, a crazed look on his face.

He waved Sophie towards Peter. 'Empty the other pack.'

She obliged. Some fruit bars and a water bottle fell out, but no pistol.

'Throw me the water,' he said.

She flung it over. He caught it, deftly unscrewing the lid one-handed, keeping the gun trained on them with the other, drinking the contents greedily as water cascaded down his chin.

A sustained burst of automatic gunfire shattered the still air from the direction of the beach, momentarily distracting Springbok. With lightning reactions, Sophie reached behind her, drew her SIG sub-compact from her waistband and fired multiple shots in quick succession into the South African's face and chest. His head slumped, its weight keeling him sideways, and his broken face hit the dirt. Just one more soldier of fortune who'd met his fate.

Sophie started shaking. Peter kicked the prone figure to check he was dead. It wasn't in any doubt. He put his arm around her. 'You did great, Sophie, but it's not over. Stay out of sight and I'll see what's going on.' Shaking, she nodded in acknowledgement.

Peter wove his way cautiously through the boulders until he had sight lines across the beach to the reef. Streaked gunfire was being exchanged between two large white motor yachts, about 50 metres apart, a 100 metres or so beyond the cat, automatic bursts clearly visible and flashing between them like tracers.

Peter watched in fascination until the motor yacht furthest away slowly turned and headed out to sea, and the gunfire ceased. Minutes later, a rib loaded with armed men sped towards shore from the remaining yacht. He swept his binoculars over the motor yacht's upper deck and breathed a massive sigh of relief at the unmistakable squat shape of Rocky, his trademark burner firmly clenched between his teeth.

The other vessel must have been Bekker's or Johansson's, Peter thought, as he quickly made his way back to Sophie. But she wasn't where he'd left her. Glancing at Springbok's spent body, he looked along the narrow passage and shouted her name.

'I'm here!' she shouted from somewhere behind where they'd taken shelter. Peter squeezed his way further back between large boulders, not having realised they went back so far, and reached an enclosed area where to his relief he found Sophie safe and well. He quickly updated her on their situation, reinforcing they should proceed with caution, fearing Rocky's men might shoot first and ask questions later.

'What are you doing back here, anyway?' he asked.

'I needed to relieve myself. As I squatted, I looked up and saw those.' Her eyes indicated a point behind him and he turned to see a large boulder with a flat surface upon which four sets of initials were crudely carved: *RJS, TNH, PM, SJ*

And underneath: *ES 1763*

'Jesus! This is fantastic, Sophie! It proves we've got the right island, but we need to deal with Rocky's guys first and get to safety. Come on!' He grabbed her arm and led her back out towards the beach where a line of men brandishing assorted weaponry were marching up the beach towards them, pointing and shouting. Taking no chances, Peter and Sophie put their hands in the air, however, when Sophie shouted something in Tagalog, the men visibly relaxed and one of them handed Peter a walkie-talkie.

'Magandang umaga. Good morning, Pedro,' came a voice through the static. 'Looks like I got here just in time. Motherfuckers ...'

Peter grinned, never thinking he'd be so pleased to hear Rocky's voice. 'Is Declan with you?' he asked.

'No. But it's thanks to him I'm here,' said Rocky. 'He's on his way. My men will bring you over.'

Peter handed the walkie-talkie back to the Filipino, who wore a black bandana and had an AK-47 casually slung across his chest with spare mags tucked into his waist band. Thinking the man looked like a fully paid-up member of Abu Sayyaf, Peter was glad they were on the same side.

The man held the walkie-talkie to his ear and listened as Rocky fired instructions while two similarly dressed men walked across the beach towards them, dragging a lifeless body between them which they dumped at their feet. It was Nenita. Her throat was slit and she looked as if she'd bled out. Flies swarmed her face. Peter and Sophie recoiled from the shocking image and smell, covering their noses as they walked down the beach to the waterline where they boarded the rib to take them over to the motor yacht.

*

As it bumped against the transom, Rocky grinned down at them, his toupée slightly askew.

'You picked a nice spot for whatever it is you're up to, Pedro,' he said teasingly as he helped Sophie up with a strong tatooed forearm.

Peter climbed up behind her. 'Who were you shooting at?'

'Motherfucking Ba-Gong.' Rocky spat over the side in disgust.

'Did you see Bekker?' asked Sophie.

'Yeah. I saw the motherfucker.' Rocky's eyes narrowed. 'Any luck, he got hit.'

Clocking the firepower on the motor yacht, which looked more like a naval assault vessel than a gin palace, Peter said, 'Do you think they'll come back?'

Rocky nodded grinning. 'No doubt about. But we'll be ready for them and there's back-up on the way.' He smiled. 'Let's get Declan on the line.'

Rocky picked up the VHF mic and shook his head as he looked at Sophie. 'You know, you're just like your pappy, always getting into trouble.' He turned to Peter. 'And Pedro, here, he no better.'

He chuckled as he depressed the transmit button and within seconds Declan's welcome brogue came over the airwaves through the crackling static, confirming he was half an hour out in the de Havilland and mightily relieved they were safe.

Sophie and Peter went to clean up below decks, trying to avoid Rocky's questions. They were in his debt, but his presence complicated things. They would leave the explanations for Declan.

The sun had finally emerged and the sky was now a brilliant cobalt with not a cloud to be seen, the tropical colours of the island and its surrounding reefs having been reinstated, and the heat and humidity once more settling like an invisible blanket over it. The only evidence of the storm was the debris on the beach, the upturned cat and the unusually stirred-up water.

Sophie and Peter went up to the upper deck and sat in the shade, sipping iced Coke and savouring their newfound circumstances when they heard the familiar sound of the de Havilland. Sophie spotted it first as it grew from a midge to a gnat to a fly, circling for the best angle to land before José made one of his textbook landings into wind, taxiing to a standstill alongside the ladder leading up to the transom of the motor yacht.

Declan was helped on board and made a beeline for Sophie. His huge relief at seeing her unharmed was written all over his face. They hugged and he kissed her forehead lovingly, then walked over to Peter and gave him a man hug along with a look that said many things.

Rocky diplomatically hovered in the background, clearly desperate to get the low-down on what this was all about. Whatever it was, he knew it involved this island and that dangerous people were prepared to kill for it.

Declan thanked Rocky profusely, then told him they needed some privacy, which Rocky reluctantly accepted. The three of them went up to the upper deck where Peter and Sophie filled Declan in on what had happened over the past 24 hours. Declan, in turn, told them the disturbing information he'd received too late about the South African. Unable to contact them, he'd wasted no time engaging Rocky's help, who by good fortune, had been near Coron on his motor launch carrying out some illicit business which was why he'd been able to get to the island so fast, despite the storm.

'Where are the pieces you found?' Declan asked.

'Most likely on the Swan,' said Peter, clearly frustrated. 'Things happened fast. We didn't have much time.'

Sophie told Declan about the initials they'd found.

'Well, looking on the bright side, you've located a wreck site and we know it's the right island,' Declan said, trying to be encouraging. 'But we'll need to establish provenance if we're to stake a claim and implement an official search or salvage operation.'

'Then we have to try and locate the items we found now,' Peter said decisively, standing up. 'They're the only ones we've got apart from the cannon.'

There was no argument. 'Let's kit up then,' said Sophie.

Declan used his cane to stand up and looking every one of his seventy-eight years, said quietly, 'I need to feed Rocky a line or three.' Then, projecting his voice: 'Where are you, Rocky, my old friend?'

He winked at Peter and Sophie, and whispered out of the corner of his mouth, 'This is going to cost us!'

Fifteen minutes later, one of Rocky's men took Peter and Sophie the short distance over to the *Santa Maria* in a Zodiac. The cat lay awkwardly, largely submerged, only kept afloat by air pockets in its cracked hull.

They snorkelled around her, free diving at intervals to check the damage with visibility down to a few metres. Peter clambered onto her left hull, which was firmly embedded on the coral head. He made his way chest-deep into the saloon, methodically checking cupboards, drawers and any places the wreck items could have been put or lodged. Possessions and research materials bobbed and floated around him, books, iPad and electronic gear all ruined. No sign of what he was searching for.

He clocked the scuba tanks and compressor, still firmly secured to the gunwale, as he made his way out.

'The bastard must have taken them onto the Swan,' he said to Sophie with frustration as he trod water next to her.

'Let's find it, then. It can't have gone far.' With that, she snorkelled out and up, along the right-hand side of the imaginary butterfly's lower right wing towards the island, with Peter following.

Although things above water had normalised, the reduced visibility caused by the storm gave the underwater realm a whole new vibe and the resident blacktips were taking full advantage of disturbed conditions, whipping deftly through the shallows and along the reef edge, searching for disorientated prey.

Peter and Sophie snorkelled towards deeper water where visibility improved as the current flushed debris, conveyor-belt fashion, out to sea.

She tugged Peter's arm and with two fingers pointed at her eyes, then in a diagonal away from the reef edge towards deeper water. Following the line of her finger, at first he saw nothing but then spotted the Swan lying at a 45-degree angle about 80 metres away, in around 20 metres of water. It was wedged into an isolated reef outcrop, connected to the island by low-lying rocks. Beyond it, open ocean on the other side plummeted into the depths where grey reef sharks patrolled the divide.

Breaking the surface, they positioned themselves upright and beckoned Rocky's hood over in the Zodiac. He motored quickly over. They pulled themselves into the boat, kitting up with scuba gear before back-rolling back over the side and finning down towards the Swan, which didn't take long to reach. Visibility was frustratingly variable as reef sharks circled the yacht and tropical fish clustered around it for protection.

Judging by the angle it lay, they surmised it must have drifted beyond the reef shallows into deeper water before ripping open as it hit this section of isolated reef, sinking quickly, its mast now wedged between it and the low protruding rocks jutting out from the island.

They swam towards the Swan's stern, giving wide berth to a pair of deadly black and white banded sea kraits that spiralled between them. Four reef sharks were now patrolling the reef edge, every so often accelerating in towards the Swan, then heading back out again.

They'd agreed Peter would enter the yacht while Sophie kept an eye out for trouble. Peter knelt on the sea floor and, keeping one eye on the sharks, he lifted his tank over his head and detached his pony from his BCD, inserting it into his mouth, breathing evenly and calmly. He gave an exaggerated grin to Sophie, raising his eyebrows comically up and down as he made the okay signal which she reciprocated, her blond hair trailing in the current, her blue eyes sparkling through her pink Tusa mask.

As Peter finned towards the yacht, an eagle ray with a long dangerous tail shot out from under him. He entered the vessel, which lay at an angle, cautiously, careful to avoid becoming entangled in anything, brushing aside a woman's handbag with an open Durex packet stuck in its strap, then swimming through a shoal of tiny orange fish that had taken refuge in the hatchway, along and down the steps which lay at an angle and led into the saloon. He swept away a collapsible holdall and some female clothing, noticing a cluster of empty beer cans floating in an air pocket.

He scanned the confined space, checking every inch with his torch beam, until at last he saw what he was looking for. Wedged beside the built-in table was the nylon bag containing their findings, which he grabbed before carefully making his way out of the Swan into open water. He handed it to Sophie who grasped it tightly with a broad smile and gave a thumbs up.

Peter put his scuba tank back on, securing the buckles, then re-attached his pony and indicated it was time to head topside. Sophie okayed him and began her ascent. He watched her pink fins waft up to the surface and then took a minute to scan the area, looking along the yacht's mast towards the rocks where it was tightly jammed.

Glancing up, he saw Sophie at the surface looking down at him, probably wondering why he was taking so long. Looking towards the hull of the Swan and the drop-off beyond, he quickly computed the danger he was in as a grey reef shark, its body hunched, its pectoral fins angled down, swam towards him in pronounced jerking movements: an unmistakable warning display which Peter knew from experience was a precursor to an attack.

Although his natural instinct was to swim as fast as he could upwards, he controlled himself, instead finning slowly, keeping low to the sea floor along the length of the mast towards the rocks. Once he reached them, he looked up and saw Sophie watching from the surface. The shark was now in a frenzy, making figures of eight and runs at him, closer each time. Peter checked his air. He had no more than a few minutes left, given the tanks hadn't been full to begin with, plus whatever was in his pony.

Another reef shark started exhibiting the same aggressive behaviour and Peter saw beyond the Swan at least ten more sharks were now swimming along the reef edge. With no idea of what he'd done to piss them off, he pushed himself into the rocks and tried to make himself as non-threatening as possible as the lead shark made another pass. Coming within a few feet of him, it flicked its tail then turned on a dime, closely followed by a rapid run at him from the second shark.

He grabbed the Swan's mast firmly with his left hand to hold himself in place and pushed his right hand into the sand under the base of the rock. Keeping his eyes on both sharks, he slid his hand to get better purchase and encountered something smooth. He kept his eyes locked onto the closest shark which, with a flick of its tail and a turbo burst of speed, lunged to bite him, his only defence being to use his left hand to deflect its snout as he'd done in other dangerous shark situations he'd experienced over the years.

In preparation for the shark's next approach, Peter backed into the rock. But there was nowhere to go. Leaning on his right hand, he clutched the sand tightly for better purchase and felt something sharp, yelping into his regulator. Both sharks were now zigzagging frenetically between him and the yacht, getting closer on each pass. Brushing sand away, he glanced down to see what had hurt him and saw the dull sheen of crumpled metal wedged into the rock.

He tried to pull it, but it didn't give. He jabbed it hard with his diving knife, trying to loosen it, with one eye on the sharks, conscious this would piss them off even more. Blood trickled from his cut hand. *Not ideal*, he thought.

He sucked another breath of air but nothing came through his regulator. His tank was empty. In one swift movement, he unclipped his pony and sucked hard on its small regulator, thanking God there was some air left in it. His was breathing fast now, not his normal calm self. Trying to control himself, he turned and tried to prise the object out with his knife, but twisted so hard the blade broke. However, it was enough; whatever it was had come loose. In the pause between attacks, he managed to yank it out. It was a sizeable trophy of some sort, with some weight to it. The type used to commemorate events or sporting achievements. Holding it tightly, he sucked in another breath, but this time nothing came out: the pony was empty. He looked at the weaving sharks preparing for another assault.

He had one option left and without a second thought, finned upwards as fast as he could in an emergency ascent, holding the trophy tightly, all the while exhaling what little breath he had left to avoid damaging his lungs as they expanded with the reduction in pressure.

Sophie and Rocky's man were banging the water in an effort to distract the sharks as Peter broke the surface, his lungs bursting as he gasped fresh air. Checking under the water as the rib sped over, he saw one of the sharks torpedoing up towards him. Trying to stay calm, he timed it carefully so just as it got to him, he smashed his fist into its snout, deflecting it sideways which gave him the seconds he needed for Sophie and the hood to heave him roughly into the rib.

'Jesus, that was close,' Sophie said, visibly shaken.

'You're not kidding!' he replied, gasping for breath. He could try to make light of the situation but they both knew how lucky he'd been. 'But hopefully worth it,' he added, quickly secreting his find in their gear. The tattooed gang member, fag in mouth, AK-47 firmly strapped across his chest, narrowed his eyes, squinting in the bright sunlight, angling the rib towards the motor yacht.

*

Back on the motor yacht, they made their way to the main saloon. Rocky sat with his legs apart, his arms outstretched either side of a sofa, a big cigar clenched in his teeth, grinning inanely. Opposite, Declan reclined in an easy chair, looking relaxed, his fedora on the glass table in front of him, his walking stick propped alongside.

'Declan's filled me in,' Rocky said with a look of satisfaction, exhaling cigar smoke dramatically.

Peter and Sophie clocked Declan's expression.

'An East Indiaman,' Rocky continued, 'not a *galleone*'. The implication that he'd been onto them from the start. 'So, what you found so far?' he asked as though suddenly part of the inner circle of trust.

Peter shook his head. 'Nothing significant. Just broken pieces of porcelain and some old coins. Evidence of a wreck, but whether it's the one we're after is anybody's guess.'

'Just broken plates, then?' Rocky said dismissively. 'No sign of the silver?'

Sophie tried to keep a straight face. Declan bit his tongue.

'Not yet.' Peter played along. 'But if it's out there, we'll find it.'

Declan grabbed his cane and stood up, placing his fedora rakishly on his silver mane. 'We should head back to Bambam. There'll be all sorts of bureaucratic bullshit to sort out with the cat.' Adding as he looked at Peter and Sophie in turn, 'I hope to God it's properly insured.'

He turned to Rocky. 'It's imperative you keep the island protected until we can set up something more substantial.'

Lounging back, every inch the capo and puffing thoughtfully on his fast-diminishing burner, Rocky said, 'Don't worry, Declan. No one going near this island. I'll see to it.' He winked. 'But for a good cut, right?'

'Right.' Declan rolled his eyes as he turned to leave.

Sophie said, 'We owe you our lives, Rocky. Thanks for everything.'

'She's right, we owe you big time, Rocky,' said Peter. 'We're in your debt.'

Looking like a squat toad, Rocky put his arms around them both. 'If you can't rely on Uncle Rocky, then who can you rely on? And don't worry, Declan, I got reinforcements coming.'

As they made their way down the ladder to the transom and boarded the de Havilland, Peter clutched Declan's holdall containing the items they'd retrieved. José hit the ignition and fired the single prop into life, slowly turning the plane around and taxiing towards open water. Gunning the engine, he gently pulled back on the yoke as they scudded across the sea surface, gradually lifting into the air, then banking smoothly so they had a bird's eye view of the island.

Looking down at Rocky's diminishing white motor yacht against the now blue ocean, the image of an exotic butterfly was undeniable. The sun glinted off José's Ray-Bans and he levelled off at a cruising altitude of 3,000 feet on a heading for the Bacuit.

Things had got complicated, but then they were always going to be. By tacit agreement, they kept the conversation to banalities, not wanting to expose José to their true purpose. There would be plenty to talk about when they got back.

# CHAPTER 32

## *Bambam*

They arrived back at Bambam after an uneventful flight. José taxied the de Havilland to the jetty, past a couple of new yacht arrivals anchored near Home Reef. Across the jetty, a banca was being loaded for a late afternoon dive.

Swifts darted high above the limestone peaks and palm trees swayed gently in the afternoon breeze as the sun began its gradual descent and Declan, Sophie and Peter made their way up to the clubhouse, passing a group of smiling and laughing young divers heading to a banca. It was a refreshing sight after the stresses of the past 24 hours. *French*, thought Peter, judging from their accents as he tightly clutched the holdall containing their precious finds: items most likely from an eighteenth-century East Indiaman.

In the clubhouse, a couple sat with drinks, leafing through magazines, while a female member of staff helped a young woman send a message. Out by the pool, people lounged on sunbeds or swam as chilled Brazilian samba music drifted seductively over the resort.

Leaning on his cane, slightly hunched and looking tired, Declan said, 'I've got some calls to make. You better call the marine agency and give them the good news. Speak to Walter. Tell him I'll call him later. The insurance should cover it … Act of God and all that … See you by the pool in an hour.' He gave a weak smile, then headed off.

Sophie waved Gabe over. 'Where's *La Señora*?' she asked.

'In the channel, Ms Sophie.'

'And those yachts?' She pointed towards Home Reef. 'Who do they belong to?'

'One belong to Eduardo Vilar, the cigar tycoon from Cebu.' Gabe smiled reassuringly. 'Declan know him.'

'The other?'

'A French couple who arrived on a charter from Puerto Princesa this morning.'

'Were they booked in?'

'No, but we have capacity.'

'Can I see copies of their passports?'

Gabe pulled a folder from behind the counter and produced them.

Sophie scrutinised the paperwork. 'They seem to be in order,' she said, handing them back. 'But we can't take any chances. Can you arrange a staff meeting at 7pm and ensure everyone attends?'

'Yes, ma'am,' Gabe replied, clearly noticing the edge to Sophie's voice.

'Why don't you get cleaned up?' Peter said to Sophie.

'That's a good idea. Let's meet by the pool in half an hour.'

She made to head off, then turned and kissed him on the lips before she left.

Peter stood still for a minute, pondering the mystery of women.

*

Peter didn't bother going to his cabin but took the bag of wreck items and headed for Declan's table at the far side of the pool. He sat down, wanting to take a breather. It had been a stressful 24 hours and there was still a lot at stake.

Declan's table was strategically placed, screened by palms and a stand of banana trees, sufficiently far away from the guests to discuss private matters.

Half an hour later, Declan and Sophie joined him and Gabe brought over a tray of soft drinks.

With an intensity in his eyes, Declan said, 'Well, let's see what you've found, then.'

Peter opened the bag, and extracted the items, placing them carefully on the table.

There were several pieces of broken blue and white porcelain, two about the size of half a side plate, three that looked as though they were from the same bowl. Then the conglomeration of melded-together coins about the size of a small teapot. By its side was an encrusted object, about nine inches long, with two inches of what might be metal protruding from it. And, last but by no means least, the crushed trophy Peter had recovered earlier that day.

It was the first time they'd had a chance to assess their finds properly.

'I'm impressed,' said Declan, 'It's a great start.' He hefted the encrusted object Peter had found under the overhang.

'It's part of a sword hilt,' he said confidently, 'the pommel solidified and the quillons damaged.' He prodded the cluster. 'These are obviously coins, which are always good identifiers of time and place.' He picked up one of the porcelain pieces and examined it. 'These are Qing Dynasty, from the right period.'

Lastly, he lifted the large crumpled cup, holding it up and turning it. One of the two original handles had snapped off. The face was solidly encrusted, prohibiting any clues as to what might be engraved beneath. It looked robust enough, but depending on the material it was made of – silver or some alloy – could become unstable after being underwater for so long and now exposed to air.

'Well, it's obviously a trophy of some kind,' Declan said, his mind clearly wondering what it might have been for.

Peter told him how he'd come across it.

Declan said, 'There's no accounting for storm activity over 250 years. Who knows, it might even give us our provenance. We need to get these into chemicals so we can clean them up and see if there's anything on them.'

They knew he was right: depending on who it had belonged to and its purpose … who knew …?

Sophie said, 'Is everything set up?'

Declan nodded. 'Yup, it's all ready. The sooner we get these things into solution, the sooner we might find some clues.'

They knew the soaking and cleaning process could be lengthy, depending on the composition and condition of the metals and how they reacted with the chemicals. But time was of the essence if they were to log the wreck site with the authorities and stake a claim on a specific ship.

Sophie told Declan about the security briefing she'd arranged, which he concurred was a good idea.

Peter had noticed several new faces on the island, who were clearly not guests, looking more like friends of Rocky, and wondered what Declan was up to.

'Come with me. I'll show you what I've set up,' Declan said, making his way round the pool, with a 'hello' here and a 'how's it going?' there as he walked past guests who were none the wiser as to who he was or the adventures he got up to.

Sophie and Peter followed him around the back of the clubhouse, past the diving equipment storage rooms to a newly constructed hut with steps leading up to it, which he'd designed and had constructed as part of the rebuilding programme.

He unfastened a large padlock and ushered them into the small space, flicking on a light switch. Occupying the middle of the room were two open tanks in parallel, each about half the size of a cow's water trough, filled with liquid to around three inches shy of their lips.

Familiar with the process and admiring the set-up, Peter said, 'I'm impressed,' as he took in the workbench that ran along the back wall, containing all the tools and equipment one would associate with salvage and cleaning for smaller shipwreck items.

'Put the coins and sword hilt in that one.' Declan pointed to one of the troughs. 'And the trophy in the other. Then we'll let science work its magic.'

Peter obliged, using a pair of tongs. Then they left the room and Declan locked up.

They walked towards the clubhouse, passing Gabe accompanied by a short, tough-looking individual in an ill-fitting resort uniform, who Peter noticed was armed. He raised a quizzical eyebrow. 'One of

Rocky's?'

Declan nodded, his expression serious. 'Uh huh. They'll take shifts. We can't take any chances after what's happened.'

It reinforced just how vulnerable they were on the island. He thought if the guests got a remote whiff of what was going on, they wouldn't be chilling by the pool, they'd be on the first plane home.

Although it was early, they were physically and emotionally drained after the events of the past 24 hours.

Declan excused himself and Sophie said to Peter, 'Let's call it a night, we're all exhausted.'

Peter nodded. 'That sounds sensible.'

As if reading his mind, she said, 'I need to keep an eye on him.'

He smiled. 'Don't worry. I understand.'

She pecked him on the cheek then went to look after Declan. Peter went and ordered a club sandwich by the pool, then made his way up to a newly renovated Swift View.

The cabin looked even better than before, kitted out in a similar, but updated, blend of Filipino and Scandinavian ethnic cool. He lay on the bed under the lazily circling ceiling fan and opened a book to read. However, overwhelmed by tiredness, he shut his eyes and conked out, falling into a deep sleep until woken by bright sunlight streaming through the open shutters the following morning.

*

Feeling unusually well rested, Peter got up, splashed water on his face, then dressed in shorts and a T-shirt. Instead of going for a swim, he went straight to the clubhouse. It was 8am. He felt alive. Ready for whatever the day would bring.

On his way to breakfast, he took a detour by the new salvage hut. A similar-looking individual to the night before sat outside the padlocked door, alert and vigilant, a semi-automatic plainly visible in a shoulder holster. The man wore a resort polo emblazoned with the 'Deep Blue' diving logo, his muscled forearms displaying full-sleeve tattoos, his lank black hair greased back rocker-style. Peter acknowledged him, but wasn't acknowledged in return. The man simply tracked his movements. Pleased the guy was on their side, not Bekker's or Johansson's, Peter knew they had plenty to match him.

After a good breakfast by the pool, feeling ready to attack the day, he spotted Sophie talking to some dive instructors on the jetty who were about to set off with a banca full of divers. He thought the distraction would be therapeutic for her after what had happened. Although Springbok had been a scumbag that no one, except perhaps his mama, would miss, Sophie had been affected by what had happened. It was quite a thing to kill someone, Peter reflected, having never killed anyone himself, although he knew in current circumstances that could change quickly. He was mentally prepared if he had no other choice, despite the horrific images of cramped overflowing Philippine prisons he'd seen on TV; the potential consequences of taking someone's life made him shiver.

Sophie walked up the beach towards him, looking refreshed.

Peter said, 'You slept well, I take it?'

'Like a log.'

'And Declan?'

'He was up at the crack of dawn, anxious to see if an overnight soaking's made any difference to the trophy.'

'I don't think it'll be that quick.' But he understood Declan's haste. 'Well, we may as well go and take a look.'

They walked over to the salvage hut where Rocky's man sat expressionless outside the entrance. However, when Sophie smiled at him, he smiled back. *Typical*, thought Peter as they headed up the steps and entered the temporary laboratory.

Declan was hunched over the bench, sitting on a stool with his back to them. The smell of chemicals was overpowering. 'Didn't think you'd be long,' he said mockingly.

A small transistor radio was playing calypso music from a local station.

'Anything shown up?' Sophie asked.

Declan didn't answer immediately, but rotated the wooden stool to face them, a small magnifying glass wedged into one eye, like a jeweller. 'Just so happens it did.' He held a coin which he tossed to Sophie, who caught it one-handed.

Holding it up to the light, she saw one side was impressed with the image of a Hindu God, while across the other was stamped ONE ANA. Around its circumference was stamped EAST INDIA COMPANY, 1762.

'Then there's this.' Declan gave a smirk, flipping another coin to Peter. 'Different coinage, same year.'

Peter caught it cleanly, recognising it as a Piece of Eight, the primary global currency back in the day. Made of silver, it was stamped 1760.

'So, we've got our year, or thereabouts,' said Declan, 'and the coins suggest it was an Indiaman, but we still need provenance to stake a claim on a specific ship.'

Sophie looked at the workbench behind him. 'What about the trophy?'

Declan swivelled, picked it up, and turned to face them, unable to suppress a smile, enjoying his theatrics. 'There's an inscription. But it's faint. The chemicals haven't had time to work their magic yet, but ...'

They walked over with a sense of excitement. A shaft of light from the window above illuminated the damaged cup, where a portion of the encrustation had been removed at the front.

Peter realised Declan must have been there for hours.

'Gentle,' Declan said, handing the cup to Sophie. 'It's fragile.'

She held it up in the shaft of sunlight so Peter could also read the faint but legible letters:

CAP. AI . T. N. HAR. I ...

Sophie looked at Declan. 'Captain Harrison was commander of the Earl of Suffolk, wasn't he?'

Declan couldn't suppress a grin. 'Yes, he was.'

The top third of the cup was crushed by almost 45 degrees, with part of the inscription illegible, still encrusted in the indentation. They would have a better chance of cleaning and being able to read it if it could be straightened, although they knew they'd need to be careful not to damage it further. The bottom was comprised of a hollow inverted bowl for it to stand on. One looped arm was broken, but the other was still in amazingly good shape. There would likely have been a sizeable lid at some point, but that was long gone.

'It's a good start,' Declan said. 'A really good start. If we didn't have bloody Bekker and Johansson to contend, with it'd be so much easier.'

'Well, that's not going to change, is it?' Peter challenged. 'We can't run a salvage operation with criminal gangs trying to kill us.'

'You know as well as I do, staking a claim in a place like this is risky, full stop.'

Peter made to interject, but Declan held up his hand. 'Hear me out, please. I agree with you – we can't initiate a salvage operation with open warfare.'

'So, what do you suggest?'

'We need to set a trap.' Declan's smile had gone, his face now deadly serious.

'How do you propose to do that?' Sophie clearly didn't like the direction this was heading.

'What are we all after, huh? What's this all about?'

'The diamond,' Sophie said.

'Exactly. But I'm betting only Karl knows that. Bekker, like Rocky, probably thinks it's generic treasure.'

'What difference does it make?' said Peter.

Declan's eyes were hard. 'Karl wants the diamond beyond anything else. He can't let me take both that and Ingrid. I know how his mind works.'

'And Bekker?' Sophie said.

'He'll want to fuck Karl over and get his hands on the treasure. But Karl will use him till he's served his purpose.'

Picking up his train of thought, Peter said, 'You think they'll be desperate to know what we've discovered, given Franz radioed Bekker or Johansson telling them we'd found something when he told him the location of the island.'

'The bottom line is they don't know what we know, or what you found. We have the boxes, the map and your findings. That gives us leverage.'

'Johansson wouldn't risk coming here.' Sophie evidently didn't buy it.

'No. He'll get Bekker to do his dirty work,' Declan concurred.

'So what do we do?' said Sophie. 'We've a full complement of guests. We don't want a repeat of the Ramón episode.'

'I need to speak to Rocky. Let me make a few calls. Put the trophy and the other things back in solution. They'll clean up better the longer they're in there.'

Sophie and Peter obliged and then they all went outside. Declan locked the hut and gave instructions in Tagalog to Rocky's hood, which made the man laugh coarsely.

When they reached the clubhouse, Gabe intercepted Peter looking anxious. 'Urgent message for you, sir,' he said, handing him a piece of paper.

When he read the message, Peter's face turned white. He stopped dead in his tracks. 'I need a phone,' he said, panicked, ducking behind reception into the office.

After what seemed an age, Sam answered the phone

'Jesus, Sam, what's going on? Are you all right?'

It was a terrible line. He could just about make out what she was saying.

'Henry?' he repeated with one hand covering his ear, listening intently as she told him what'd happened. 'You need to pack some things and go and stay with friends immediately,' he said. He wasn't asking. 'I promise I'll be back as soon as I can, but you need to go somewhere safe. Trust me. Buy a pre-paid burner phone with a random number and call me when you're safe. Don't use your normal mobile or landlines.'

Sam listened carefully, clearly frightened but staying sensible. After what had happened in Manila, and now to Henry, she knew she was in serious danger.

Peter felt shaken when he rang off. If anything happened to Samantha, he'd never live with himself. He cursed himself for not having been in contact and looking after her better.

He went and sat on one of the rattan sofas, and put his head in his hands, racked with guilt. Things were spiralling out of control. He needed to get some perspective. His father was dead. Henry was dead. Samantha was alive but in serious danger. As were they all.

Sophie came and sat next to him, and massaged his neck tenderly. 'What happened?' she asked softly.

He looked up, his eyes red and tired.

'I don't know the details, but apparently Henry went out of his office window from thirty stories.'

'Suicide?'

Peter shook his head. 'I don't think so.'

He felt conflicting emotions. He'd known Henry all his life. He'd been his father's best friend. And he'd suspected him. Which made him feel guilty. Somewhere, deep down, he knew Johansson was behind this. Who else could it be?

Declan reappeared, looking elegant in chinos and a blue polo shirt, quickly realising something was amiss. Sophie got up and explained, whispering to him. Declan nodded in understanding, then made his way over to Peter who looked at him and said, 'We've got to end this, Declan. One way or another. And soon.'

Declan gently nodded. 'I agree. And we will.' He sat down next to Peter with a serious expression.

There was fire in Peter's eyes. 'Tell me one thing, Declan. How the hell can you have that photo up there, reminding you every day of what happened so long ago?'

A calm serenity descended upon Declan as he leant on his cane. He looked at Peter and said gently, 'I'm glad you asked, son.'

It was clear Sophie was just as keen to hear his answer. She'd often wondered but never asked the question. The photo had always just been there.

Looking soulful and wise, Declan said, 'Well, there's the past, the present and the future, and we're comprised of all three. But it's the emphasis you place on each that determines who you are and what you become.'

Peter hadn't expected a long-winded, philosophical answer.

Declan appeared transported back to the time of the photograph, his gaze far away, not focused on anything except some mirage in the middle distance.

'We were friends once.' He smiled weakly. 'They were happy times. We were young and carefree. Pioneers in one of the most beautiful archipelagos on earth. I sometimes wonder myself, but I think I leave it there because one can't erase history. And we were friends. I can't explain it but for some reason I can't remove it.'

His eyes welled up. 'I guess that's why in my stupidity I let Karl go after he kidnapped Sophie. I wanted to believe, deep down, that he wasn't capable of killing my wife and daughter. In some subliminal way I felt sorry for him because I took his fiancée, the woman he loved.'

Sophie put an arm around her father. But he gently prized her away and shakily got to his feet.

'Rocky's sending reinforcements to secure the island. They'll arrive later today,' he said gruffly. 'I'm going to have another go at cleaning the trophy. Then, later this afternoon, I'd like us to convene on *La Señora* in the channel if you'll humour me?'

Sophie nodded.

'Peter?'

He nodded too.

'I'll see you both at the salvage hut at 5pm, then,' he said, and headed off.

'I suggest you take it easy,' Sophie said gently to Peter. 'You need to digest what's happened. It's a big shock. I've some admin to sort out, but come and find me when you're ready, okay?'

Peter smiled wanly. 'Thanks. I'll be okay. I'll do that.'

Needing time to process things, he decided to check his emails, which he'd neglected with everything that had happened over the past few days. In the small office behind reception, he logged into Gmail and scanned a stack of unread emails, his eyes settling on a recent one from Henry, which he clicked into.

*Dear Peter,*

*If you're reading this, I'm dead, killed by Karl Johansson and his long reach.*

*I want you to know two things: firstly, that I loved your father as only a best friend and confidant could, and secondly, I wanted to honour his last will and testament and what he confided in me. My position and integrity were compromised shortly after he died when a certain parcel was tracked from the UK to Australia, containing a writing box sold by Sotheby's at auction.*

*I had no knowledge of the box until I was asked to locate it after you set out for the Philippines. I was shown photographs of my two grown-up nephews with known criminals behind them, and was told if I didn't help them find it, they would kill them. I had no choice but to tell them where you had gone. I hope you understand.*

*This email will automatically be sent in the event of my death by my lawyer, who is fully briefed as to how to carry out all Harry's instructions given to me before his death.*

*I sincerely hope you can forgive me and get out of this mess alive. After all, you're a Blake! Who knows, perhaps you'll even find the treasure, whatever it is.*

*Yours,*
*Henry*

Peter logged out. Staring into space, he thought about Henry, his father, his stepmother and half-sisters, and everything that had happened since Harry's death, and he knew deep down that Henry was a good man, and he forgave him for what he'd done.

He scanned through an email from his boss who had another

marine project lined up, wanting to know if Peter could commit. The honest-to-God truth was he didn't know what he wanted, except to resolve their situation and ensure Sam and Sophie were safe. That much was clear.

He decided to go for a swim to clear his head and give some serious thought as to what to do next, knowing he needed to fly back to Perth.

# CHAPTER 33

## *La Señora, the Channel*

L
ater that afternoon, a banca beached on the island and six men disembarked. Declan had stressed to Rocky they should look like a diving party but despite their best efforts, they didn't look like anything other than gangsters. As they lugged their kit up the beach, Declan, with Gabe's help, ushered them quickly behind the clubhouse, out of sight of the pool area, asking them to keep their weaponry hidden so as not to scare the guests.

Their leader, a swarthy-looking Filipino called Isko, was older than the rest, with a battle-hardened appearance and a certain intelligence to his dark eyes. He listened carefully to Declan's instructions, then barked orders at the men. Gabe led them hastily to two adjacent cabins, well out of sight of the resort and guests. There were now ten of Rocky's men on the island to protect them.

At 5pm, Peter and Sophie met Declan at the salvage hut where he'd been working diligently on the trophy. He put it carefully in a protective canvas bag and they walked down to the jetty where they took a rib over to *La Señora* which was moored in the hidden lagoon halfway down the channel, out of sight of the entrance.

They tied the rib to her stern and climbed aboard. As they made their way into the saloon, Peter thought it a fitting place to discuss their plan of action, given it was where Declan had first recounted the story to him and Sophie and, perhaps more significantly, the same location where he'd first recounted the story to Harry and Karl all those years ago.

Spread out on the teak table was Jean Sutton's *Lords of the East*, one of the most comprehensive books ever written about East Indiamen, open at a cross-section of an Indiaman called the *Falmouth*.

'That's as near as damn it of similar construction and design to the *Earl of Suffolk*,' Declan said, closing it and setting it aside. 'A magnificent feat of engineering,' he added as he carefully extracted the silver trophy from the canvas bag and placed it proudly on the small table.

Several more hours of soaking and hard cleaning had made a large difference and the full name of the Captain was now clearly legible: CAPTAIN T. N. HARRISON

However, the rest of the engraving had unfortunately corroded beyond repair.

Sophie looked at Declan expectantly. 'That's fantastic, Dad, but does it give us provenance without the ship's name?'

Declan didn't reply, but took his iPad from the canvas bag, tapped in the four digit password, and then laid it on the table in front of them, smiling.

A portrait of a ruddy-faced man with curly blond hair and blue eyes filled the screen, his gaze authoritative, his expression kind. Looking resplendent in a tailored blue jacket with gold epaulettes, white breeches and black leather boots, with a sword hanging dashingly by his side, it was a flattering portrait of a naval officer.

'Ladies and gentlemen, I give you Thomas Nathaniel Harrison,' Declan announced theatrically, with a flourish of his arm.

Peter and Sophie leant in for a closer look. A plaque at the bottom of the portrait read:

Captain Thomas Nathaniel Harrison
The Earl of Suffolk 1760
East India House

'Bloody, hell, Dad! Where did you find this?'

'In the National Maritime Museum, in Greenwich.' Declan cocked an eyebrow. 'Notice anything else?'

Sophie and Peter scrutinised the portrait. 'Holy shit,' said Sophie, noticing the trophy on the sideboard behind Harrison.

Grinning like a shark, Declan said, 'Well, thanks to serendipity, we have our provenance.' He lent back with his hands behind his head. 'But, as always, the question is what do we do now?'

As the sloop undulated in the current, Peter could see the small cove where he and Sophie had first been intimate through one of the small portholes.

'What do you think the trophy was for?' asked Sophie.

'I'm guessing it was a present from the East India Company in commemoration of Harrison's first command,' replied Declan, 'after being elected by his predecessor and paying him for the honour. Because, unless you messed up – which arguably he did, though not by his own hand – it was your ticket to riches, social elevation and a comfortable retirement, command of an East Indiaman being like gold dust.'

Whatever it had been in honour of, they revelled in the fact that it gave them their provenance, proving beyond doubt that the wreck items they'd found were from the *Earl of Suffolk.*

'So, what happens next?' Peter asked. 'Rocky's protecting the wreck site. Some of his men are here. And Bekker and Johansson can't be far away.'

Declan told them Rocky's team were spread out in strategic positions around the island in case Bekker tried anything, but they needed to come up with a plan to lure him in, so they could not only take him out but get to Johansson too. He thought the best way to do this was to circulate rumours through appropriate channels that they'd found something priceless.

Sophie wasn't happy. 'I don't like this. We're just making ourselves targets, putting the guests in danger.'

Declan had to use all his charm to calm her down and talk her round to his point of view. In reality, they were caught between a rock and a hard place. Their priority was to disable Bekker and Johansson, and have a clear unhindered run at a full-blown search to locate the wreckage of the Indiaman if they were to have any chance of finding the diamond.

It was early evening. The water was calm, and the air cooler: one of the pleasantest times of day. As they debated the merits of Declan's plan, they heard the sound of reggae music. Peter stuck his head through the hatch and saw a Dufour 460 cruising towards them from the channel entrance, its sails reefed: it was the yacht owned by the French couple.

He ducked back into the saloon to inform Declan and Sophie.

'Who the hell said they could come in here?' said Declan, clearly pissed off. It was an unwritten rule other yachts weren't allowed in the channel unless there was rough weather.

He got up, his leg giving way slightly, and Sophie tried to help him but he shook her off irritably.

Bob Marley's *Lively Up Yourself* blared loudly, which Peter thought suited their surroundings; after all, these guys were on holiday.

Peter and Sophie went up on deck and saw a man at the helm, wearing a white polo shirt and pink-patterned Vilebrequin swim shorts, shades propped on his head. He shouted over, 'What a place, huh? How far down does she go?'

Next to him stood a woman wearing a black, one-piece swimsuit, stylish straw hat and large dark glasses, looking chic in the way only Mediterranean women seem able to.

Although the man spoke good English, his accent was hard to place. *Definitely not French*, thought Peter.

'Mind if I come aboard?' Sophie shouted over, thinking it would be better to explain in person about the channel being off limits.

'Sure,' the man shouted back, sizing her up as the music was turned down. 'I'll come alongside.'

The yacht veered close to *La Señora*, and Sophie stepped easily across onto it.

As she walked towards the helm, Peter clocked movement

through one of the portholes, and the hairs on the back of his neck rose. The yacht suddenly veered away, the gap now too wide to jump, and Bekker's huge frame and ginger head appeared from the hatchway. Within seconds, he had one arm firmly around Sophie's neck, making her scream, a sound which reverberated around the natural amphitheatre.

Declan flew up the wooden stairs, defying the pain in his leg, clutching wildly at the handrail.

Now about 20 feet away, the Dufour had its stern parallel with *La Señora*'s. The channel had an eerie calm to it despite being just around the corner from the bustle of the dive resort.

'That's twice now!' shouted Bekker. 'You really should take better care of your daughter, O'Connor.'

Declan clenched his fists and gritted his teeth. 'I assume you're working for Johansson?' he shouted, a steeliness to his voice.

'Wouldn't you like to know?' A smoker's chuckle and a coughing fit.

'I'm betting you've no idea what this is all about.' Declan's voice resounded across the channel. 'Perhaps you'd like to get your own back on Johansson. After all, he cut you loose in Manila.'

The sun had begun its slow descent and part of the channel was now in shadow, the water a darker hue as Peter wondered whether Declan had any weapons on board and where Rocky's men were positioned around the island, knowing they'd assumed an attack would come at night. He cursed the fact Declan had given Gabe strict instructions for no one to disturb them.

'Do anything stupid, O'Connor, and she's shark fodder,' shouted Bekker, his ugly turtle-face grinning. 'No walkie-talkie. No radio. No nothing. Got it?'

'Loud and clear,' Declan shouted back.

Bekker pushed Sophie towards another figure they couldn't see clearly, who roughly pulled her down into the cabin, followed by the woman.

Pointing a silenced semi-automatic at Peter, Bekker said, 'Jump in and swim over, Blake. Fuck about, I'll put a bullet in you and your girlfriend.'

'Do it,' Declan said out of the side of his mouth. 'We don't have a choice.'

Peter didn't hesitate. He jumped over the side, seconds later hauling himself onto the retractable transom of the Dufour. Bekker shoved him towards the skipper, who tied him up in a sitting position next to the helm.

A figure unfolded from the cabin, turning to face Declan, his tall frame and strong physique immediately recognisable. Declan looked as though he'd been punched, the air sucked out of him, his legs about to give way.

Karl Johansson stood erect, facing him as they eyeballed one another. Neither spoke until Johansson broke the silence: 'So we're back where it all started,' he shouted. His distinctive Nordic English and the familiar smirk on his face transporting Declan back in time. 'It's a shame Harry's not here to join us.'

Bekker kept his pistol aimed at Declan as the skipper edged the Dufour so it kissed *La Señora*, enabling Johansson to deftly step across where he towered a good three inches over his former friend.

'You look tired,' he said. 'But then you've been busy, haven't you?'

He kept a distance between them so Bekker could keep his pistol trained on Declan. 'You know, it pains me to say it but I think congratulations are in order.'

Declan just stared at him, coiled in anger, his hatred of the man straining every muscle within him. 'Let Sophie go,' he said. 'You can have whatever you want, Karl. I mean anything. I'll tell and give you everything. It's all yours.'

The Swede laughed, mockingly. 'You always were a good negotiator and bluffer, Declan. But no more. It's mine now, anyway. I should have killed her the first time so she could join her mama.'

Declan lunged, surprisingly fast. But Johansson, quicker and fitter, dropped him to the deck with a single punch. Winded, clutching his stomach, kneeling on the deck, Declan looked up at Johansson. 'I should have fucking killed you when I had the chance, you piece of shit!' he snarled.

Johansson nodded congenially as though this was just another business discussion, two differing points of view being debated. 'Yes, you really should have.' He looked down at his nemesis in disgust, his voice calm and clinical. 'I'd say that's your biggest weakness. You always try to look for the good in people.'

Declan tried to stand but Johansson swivelled and kicked his bad leg out from under him, knocking him onto the deck again. He smiled cruelly, clearly enjoying himself. 'I made you a promise a long time ago, Declan, and being a man of my word, I intend to keep it.'

He reached behind him and drew out a .38 Colt semi-automatic. 'Let's go inside. You can show me what you've found.'

In pain and exhausted, Declan struggled to his feet. Someone had to win. It looked like it was going to be Karl. He had one priority now: keep Sophie alive at all costs. How in God's name he was going to manage that, he had absolutely no idea. As he turned to go down to the saloon, he clocked slight movement out of the corner of his eye in the jungled undergrowth near the waterline beyond the Dufour.

Johansson glanced around, then turned and stooped to follow him, smiling at his own ingenuity. 'Never expected a Trojan horse, did you?' he said.

'Cut the shit, Karl.'

Johansson motioned Declan into the rear of the cabin, looking at what was lying on the table. He picked up the trophy, then looked at the iPad, which had timed out.

'Fire her up and put the password in,' he said, brandishing the gun.

Declan obliged and Captain Harrison's portrait filled the screen.

Johansson waved Declan into a chair, then read the inscription on the trophy and the plaque on the portrait, shaking his head in disbelief and whistling as he noticed the trophy in the painting.

*

Isko made his way deftly down the steep and overgrown bank to the foreshore. He'd been scoping the island, looking where to place sentries, when he'd seen the yachts and what was happening. Experienced, unlike some of the younger gang members, his gut told him he needed to act fast. He'd seen Sophie taken into the cabin. Bekker, whom he'd met at Rocky's, was easy to identify, aiming the pistol at O'Connor, and then the tall foreigner boarding *La Señora*. His assessment was that this was an end game, not a holding strategy.

He veered off the narrow path, pushing his way through jungled vegetation, and came out near the waterline close to where the yachts were. He found an opening to the water where the bottom shelved slightly, then dropped silently in, staying close against the rock, his face partially covered by overhanging yucca fronds.

Estimating Bekker's yacht was 25 metres in a diagonal, he took several shallow breaths in quick succession then one very large one, and dived as deep as he could. He swam with strong confident strokes, skimming deftly over the coral towards the Dufour, praying no one looked over the side through the crystal-clear water and grateful that much of the channel was now in shadow.

*

'So, it *is* the *Earl of Suffolk*,' Johansson said smugly, looking at Declan with cold eyes. 'I was pretty sure. And you've even found the provenance to prove it. Impressive.'

'You know as well as I do that the chances of finding the diamond, if it's not some bullshit story from a delirious, fever-ridden captain or a dreamy Condesa, are ten million to one,' said Declan.

Johansson nodded. 'They're long odds, I agree, but I've done my research too. Everything fits. The diamond existed and went missing after Plassey. Sinclair existed, as did the Condesa. And now we have the wreck site of the *Earl of Suffolk*.'

The crazed obsession in his eyes confirmed he'd lived and breathed the story ever since Declan had first recounted it all those years ago in this very place. And having his fiancée stolen from him by the man standing before him had eaten away at him, fuelling his desire for revenge.

'I want everything,' Johansson said. 'And I mean everything.'

'It's all here,' said Declan. 'On the iPad, and the little else we found in a makeshift lab behind the resort.'

'Where are the writing boxes and diary?'

'In Manila. I'll get them for you if you don't hurt Sophie. But all documents and photos of everything relating to the boxes and the diary are on the iPad.' He looked up at Johansson, leaning on a stool to take the pressure off his leg. 'I swear to you that's everything.'

Johansson stared coldly at him until Declan said, 'So, what happens now?'

Johansson grinned. 'You say goodbye and go join that bitch wife of yours!'

A three-round burst of semi-automatic gunfire shattered the silence.

Declan took his chance and catapulted into Johansson.

*

As the two old men confronted one another in the saloon of *La Señora*, Isko surfaced silently next to the Dufour, stealthily holding on to one side of the wide collapsible transom, keeping his body low. Peter caught the movement out of the corner of his eye, recognising him at once. The Filipino gave him an imperceptible nod, indicating one, two, three with his fingers then, in one swift movement, levered himself up and sprang forwards, firing off shots at Bekker.

Peter simultaneously bulldozed the skipper against one of the large steering wheels; the man's semi-automatic let off a round as it slid from his hands onto the deck. Bekker, who'd been hit, shot back at Isko, who weaved, firing several shots in quick succession. This time the impact hurled Bekker backwards and, lunging at the rail, he lost his balance and fell with a large splash into the deep water between the yachts.

Isko spun low, firing two rounds into the skipper as he stretched for his weapon, and the man sprawled with two holes in his chest.

Isko quickly untied Peter, who grabbed the skipper's pistol and rushed towards the entrance to the cabin only to come face to face with Sophie being shoved up the steps towards him, a knife at her throat. The man holding the knife had his other arm wrapped tightly around her waist. From the prominent scar on the left side of his face, Peter knew it was Ramón, the bogus diving instructor who'd kidnapped Sophie from Manta Reef.

'Drop the guns!' the man ordered, drawing blood from Sophie's neck with the razor-sharp knife.

Peter dropped his weapon and raised his hands.

'You too,' said the hood to Isko just as Sophie unexpectedly slammed her elbow into Ramon's face as hard as she could. Deftly stepping to one side and grabbing the wrist holding the knife, she flipped the man onto the deck. *Probably a Kali move*, thought Peter, remembering Declan had told him Sophie had studied the martial art from an early age.

Isko dived onto Ramón and as they grappled on the deck, Peter stepped over them, waiting until he had a clear shot before firing repeatedly at the hood, who collapsed, gurgled, then went still. Isko pushed off him and ran into the cabin to deal with the woman.

Meanwhile, Bekker was floundering in the water. It was his worst nightmare: he couldn't swim. Somehow he managed to kick and lunge for *La Señora* but her stern was too high to reach up to. Bleeding and in serious pain, for once he was really panicked.

After overpowering Declan, Johansson had run out onto *La Señora*'s stern, clutching the trophy and iPad. Frantically looking around him, he'd taken in the change of events and saw Bekker desperately floundering at the back of the yacht.

Seeing Johansson tower above him, Bekker desperately reached up one arm, yelling, 'Help me!' through clenched teeth. Johansson, however, just gave a thin smile and fired his revolver twice point blank into the turtle-like face, watching Bekker collapse into the channel, his large frame drifting between the yachts before disappearing below the surface of the dark water.

'So, what are you going to do now, Karl?' yelled Declan in his thick Irish brogue. 'I'd say you're the one who's fucked.'

The Swede turned, visibly panicked, aiming his gun at Declan who was propped awkwardly at the top of the steps from the saloon.

'You can kill me but there's no escape,' Declan said confidently, knowing Sophie was now safe as she stood on the other yacht next to Peter.

Johansson kept his arm outstretched, the .38 aimed at Declan. With a taunting smile, he said, 'Don't you want to ask me something?'

Declan said nothing, his heart pounding, suddenly swamped with fear.

Johansson fired a shot that splintered the hatch near the Irishman's head. 'Well?' he persisted.

Declan just stared at him, his eyes filled with hatred and dread.

'You need to know,' Johansson said slowly, his eyes glacial, with a cruel smile, 'that there was nothing wrong with that pony. At least not before we tampered with it.'

The pain the Swede inflicted on the Irishman with his words was more than anything he could inflict with a bullet. Declan's legs gave way, and he dropped to his knees, putting his head in his hands, preparing to die, closing his eyes to the image of Ingrid floating against the wheelhouse, screaming like a wounded animal.

As Johansson's finger closed on the trigger of the .38, one of Isko's sharpshooters, way above on the main island, took him out with a single shot to the head. The flat-headed bullet removed half his jaw and he crumpled, dropping the iPad, which smashed on the hard teak deck, while the trophy bounced off the gunwale into the channel.

Looking on in disbelief, Declan watched Peter dive over the side of the Dufour, much to the surprise of Sophie and Isko.

Although the water was clear, the sun was now partially obscured by the towering limestone cliffs, leaving most of the channel in shadow. Peter swam as though his life depended on it, trying to spot the trophy in the strong current, knowing it would sink quickly. He was driven by the motivation that if they lost it, they'd lose their provenance and everything would have been for nothing.

He swam with strong strokes, spotting it several metres below and ahead of him as it span like a gyroscope, sinking, gathering momentum, propelled by the current. A blacktip flicked past him as he pushed faster and deeper with limited air, given that diving after the trophy had been a reflex action.

A large reef shark appeared from the depths and shot towards the sinking trophy, flicking its tail before accelerating away. There was little light. For a nanosecond Peter remembered the first time he'd swam in the channel, thinking how deep and strong the current had seemed as if somehow preparing him for this moment.

He swam frantically, momentarily losing sight of the trophy, then spotted it again, its looped arm having snagged on a coral outcrop. Above it, a frenetic group of reef sharks were ripping into something in a feeding frenzy. As Peter got closer, he recoiled as Bekker's battered body emerged like a rag doll torn by a pit bull, huge chunks of it missing. His head hung grotesquely at ninety degrees. One eye was missing. A large shark charged the others, breaking the piece of coral on which the trophy had snagged, causing it to spiral back into the current where it sank fast, sucked towards the narrow exit at the end of the channel.

Knowing he had just one chance, Peter lunged with every ounce of what he had left, snatching the trophy by its waist, then kicking hard, propelling himself as fast as he could towards the surface, his lungs screaming until he exploded into the fresh air, gulping huge lungfuls of it, realising he was almost at the narrow outlet which funnelled into the open ocean beyond.

As he savoured the fresh air, *La Señora* made its way over to him, and minutes later strong hands pulled him aboard. He slumped against the gunwale, trying to get his breath back, clutching the trophy tightly as Declan and Sophie looked down at him.

'Looks like a rag's caught in it,' Sophie said.

Declan reached down. 'Let me take a look.'

Peter handed it up and between deep breaths said, 'Be careful. It's damaged.'

As Declan examined it, his face broke into a broad grin and he slumped on the deck next to Peter. 'Well, I'll be damned!' Gripping the trophy tightly, he then slammed it repeatedly against the hull like a madman.

'What the fuck are you doing?' Sophie yelled as the bottom sheared off and the Blue Moghul ricocheted across the deck, spinning to a standstill in front of them.

Sophie and Peter stared at it, stunned, while Declan looked up to the sky and, crossing himself, began to laugh uncontrollably. 'Sometimes you've just gotta have a little faith!' he shouted as somewhere, high above, the Condesa, Robert Sinclair, Ingrid and Harry smiled down on them.

## THE END

# ABOUT THE AUTHOR

A UK-based Chartered Surveyor, the author spent many years as an expatriate in Hong Kong and developed a deep love for the Philippines during numerous visits. With a passion for adventure, geography, history, travel, and the natural world—especially the marine environment—the author draws inspiration from the adventure novels of Wilbur Smith, Desmond Bagley, and Hammond Innes. These influences have fueled a desire to create the kind of escapist novels that transport readers, much like the ones they'd eagerly pick up from an airport bookshop before embarking on a holiday. Good, honest escapism.

Printed in Dunstable, United Kingdom

72134349R00188